GAME ON

"Am I correct in understanding that you dislike me, Ms. Donovan?" he asked coyly, circling around her in amusement.

Taylor followed him with her eyes, her voice even. "I won't let my feelings about you compromise my career, Mr. Andrews. You got me in a lot of trouble at work, you know."

Jason stopped, surprised to find himself uncomfortable at the thought. "I'll tell you what," he said magnanimously. "Let me buy you a drink. We can start over—get to know one another properly." He flashed her the smile that made hearts flutter worldwide. Five and a half billion dollars in lifetime box office gross for his "little projects." Take that.

Taylor cocked her head, appearing to consider his offer. Then, with her arms folded across her chest, she took a few steps toward him. When she was close enough that they were practically touching, she stared up at him, her green eyes boring deep into his. Jason could feel the warmth of her body, and he wondered if she knew what he was thinking right then.

Apparently, she did.

"Let's get something straight, Mr. Andrews," she said steadily. "This is business. Nothing else."

Before Jason could get in one word edgewise on the matter, Taylor backed away and turned to leave. "And I'll expect you to be at my office first thing tomorrow morning. Do try not to be late."

Just the Sexiest Man Alive

JULIE JAMES

BERKLEY SENSATION, NEW YORK

THE BERKLEY PUBLISHING GROUP
Published by the Penguin Group
Penguin Group (USA) Inc.
375 Hudson Street, New York, New York 10014, USA
Penguin Group (Canada), 90 Eglinton Avenue East, Suite 700, Toronto, Ontario M4P 2Y3, Canada
(a division of Pearson Penguin Canada Inc.)
Penguin Books Ltd., 80 Strand, London WC2R 0RL, England
Penguin Group Ireland, 25 St. Stephen's Green, Dublin 2, Ireland (a division of Penguin Books Ltd.)
Penguin Group (Australia), 250 Camberwell Road, Camberwell, Victoria 3124, Australia
(a division of Pearson Australia Group Pty. Ltd.)
Penguin Books India Pvt. Ltd., 11 Community Centre, Panchsheel Park, New Delhi—110 017, India
Penguin Group (NZ), 67 Apollo Drive, Rosedale, North Shore 0632, New Zealand
(a division of Pearson New Zealand Ltd.)
Penguin Books (South Africa) (Pty.) Ltd., 24 Sturdee Avenue, Rosebank, Johannesburg 2196,
South Africa

Penguin Books Ltd., Registered Offices: 80 Strand, London WC2R 0RL, England

This is a work of fiction. Names, characters, places, and incidents either are the product of the author's imagination or are used fictitiously, and any resemblance to actual persons, living or dead, business establishments, events, or locales is entirely coincidental. The publisher does not have any control over and does not assume any responsibility for author or third-party websites or their content.

JUST THE SEXIEST MAN ALIVE

A Berkley Sensation Book / published by arrangement with the author

PRINTING HISTORY
Berkley Sensation mass-market edition / October 2008

Copyright © 2008 by Julie Koca.
Excerpt from *Practice Makes Perfect* copyright © 2008 by Julie Koca.
Cover photo by Corlis.
Cover design by Rita Frangie.
Interior text design by Laura K. Corless.

ISBN: 978-0-425-22420-5

BERKLEY® SENSATION
Berkley Sensation Books are published by The Berkley Publishing Group,
a division of Penguin Group (USA) Inc.,
375 Hudson Street, New York, New York 10014.
BERKLEY SENSATION and the "B" design are trademarks belonging to Penguin Group (USA) Inc.

PRINTED IN THE UNITED STATES OF AMERICA

10 9 8 7 6 5 4 3 2 1

*To my grandfather
for inspiring me to start the journey,*

*and to my husband
for being my partner along the way.*

Acknowledgments

First and foremost, I would like to thank my film agent, Dick Shepherd, who believed in this story, and me, from the very beginning, and without whom none of this would have happened.

I would also like to express my deepest appreciation to all my family and friends for their love and continuing encouragement.

I am forever grateful to my earliest readers who took the time to read this story back when it was called *The Andrews Project*, and especially to Ami Wynne, Brian Guarraci, Brendan Carroll, and Karen Schmidt for their thoughtful input, and to Mason Novick for his advice on the value of conflict in romantic comedies.

A special thanks to my literary agent, Susan Crawford, whose passion and enthusiasm are truly inspiring, and also to my wonderfully supportive editor, Wendy McCurdy; her assistant, Allison Brandau; and everyone at Berkley.

Finally, and most importantly, I want to thank my husband, Brian, for tirelessly reading every draft, being my toughest critic, and making it all possible.

One

TAYLOR DONOVAN MAY have been new to Los Angeles, but she certainly recognized a line of bullshit when she heard one.

It was 8:15 on a Monday morning—frankly, a bit early, in Taylor's mind anyway, to be dealing with this latest round of nonsense coming from her opposing counsel, Frank Siedlecki of the Equal Employment Opportunity Commission. But hey, it was a gorgeous sunny morning in Southern California and her Starbucks had already begun to kick in, so she was willing to play nice.

Frank's call had come in just as Taylor had pulled into the parking garage of her downtown L.A. office building. After answering, she had let her opposing counsel go on for several minutes—without interruption, she might add—about the righteousness of his clients' position and how Taylor and her utterly nonrighteous client should consider themselves lucky to be given the chance to make the whole lawsuit go away for a paltry $30 million. But at a certain point, one could only take so much nonsense in one Monday-morning phone call. Luscious Starbucks or not.

So Taylor had no choice but to cut Frank off mid-rant, praying she didn't lose the signal to her cell phone as she stepped into the lobby elevator.

"Frank, Frank," she said in a firm but professional tone, "there's no way we're going to settle at those numbers. You want all that money, just because your clients heard a few four-letter words in the workplace?"

She noticed then that an elderly couple had gotten into the elevator with her. She smiled politely at them as she continued her phone conversation.

"You know, if the EEOC's going to ask for thirty million dollars in a sexual harassment case," she told Frank, "at least tell me somebody was called a 'slut' or a 'whore.'"

Out of the corner of her eye, Taylor saw the elderly woman—seventy-five years old if she was a day—send her husband a disapproving look. But then Frank began rattling on further about the so-called merits of the plaintiffs' position.

"I have to be honest, I'm not exactly impressed with your case," she said, cutting him off. "All you've got is a sporadic string of some very minor incidents. It's not as if anyone slapped an ass or grabbed a boob."

Taylor noticed that the elderly couple was now subtly but quickly moving away from her, to the opposite end of the elevator.

"Of course I'm not taking you seriously," she said in response to her opposing counsel's question. "We're talking about thirty million dollars here!" Instead of shouting, her voice had a laughing tone, which experience had proven to be far more infuriating to her opponents.

Not seeing any reason to waste another minute, she summarized her position with a few simple parting thoughts.

"Frank, this case is a publicity stunt and a shakedown. My clients did nothing illegal, and you and I both know I'll have no problem proving that to a jury. So there's no reason to discuss your ridiculous settlement offer any further. Call me when somebody sees a penis."

Taylor slammed her cell phone shut for emphasis. She slipped the phone into her briefcase and smiled apologetically at the elderly couple. They had their backs pressed against the elevator wall and were staring at her, mouths agape.

"Sorry about the whole 'penis' thing," she said, trying to make amends. "I guess I get desensitized to it." She shrugged innocently as the elevator announced its arrival at the twenty-third floor with a high-pitched ding. She glanced over at her grandparently co-riders one last time.

"It's an occupational hazard."

Taylor winked.

And with that, the elevator doors opened and she stepped out onto the busy office floor that awaited her.

TAYLOR LOVED THE sounds of a bustling law office. The phones ringing off the hook, the furiously righteous conversations that spilled out behind closed doors, the printers busily shooting out fifty-page briefs, the mail carts wheeling by as they dropped off court orders—this was all music to her ears. They were the sounds of people working hard.

And no associate—or so Taylor hoped the senior partners agreed—worked harder than she did. From the moment, now seven years ago, she had first set foot in the Chicago office of Gray & Dallas, she had done her best to make sure everyone knew she was an associate who was going places. And now the firm had sent her to Los Angeles to litigate a highly publicized class-action sexual harassment case involving one of the nation's most upscale department stores. She was fully aware it was a test to see exactly what she was capable of.

And she was more than ready.

That morning, Taylor strolled through the hallway to her office, gliding by her secretary's desk just as she had done every morning for the past two weeks since coming to Los Angeles.

"Good morning, Linda. Any messages?"

Linda sprung to attention at her desk. There was something about Taylor that apparently made others around her feel as though they needed to look busy.

"Good morning, Ms. Donovan," Linda replied efficiently.

"You do have one message—Mr. Blakely would like to see you in his office as soon as you're available."

Taylor paused briefly. That was odd—she hadn't planned to meet with Sam that morning.

"Did he say what it's about?"

"Sorry, no, Ms. Donovan."

Taylor headed into her office as she called back a message to Linda. "Call Sam's secretary and let him know I'll be there in five minutes."

Then she poked her head back out the door and smiled at her new assistant.

"And Linda, remember—it's *Taylor*."

TAYLOR COULDN'T HELP but pause in the doorway to admire Sam's office before knocking to announce herself. It was a gorgeous corner office with a massive cherrywood desk and matching bookcases, plush cream carpet, and floor-to-ceiling windows covering two walls.

To her, the richly decorated partner's office constituted far more than a mere status symbol designed to impress clients and other lawyers. It was an indication of true success. And one day, in the hopefully not-too-distant future, she would have such an office of her own—the sign that she had accomplished the one primary goal of her adult life.

Years ago, Taylor's parents had made sacrifices in order for her to get where she was standing on that Monday morning. Growing up in Chicago in a decidedly blue-collar neighborhood, her three rambunctious and not particularly academically oriented older brothers had gone to the local boys' Catholic high school. Taylor, it was first assumed, would similarly go to the local girls' school. But after seeing their only daughter's remarkably high grade-school aptitude test scores, Taylor's parents decided that she deserved the best education money could buy, even if that meant spending money they didn't have. So, in order to make the annual eighteen-thousand-dollar University of Chicago Lab School tuition payments (while still supporting four kids), her parents took out a second mortgage on their house and her father sold the 1965 Corvette Stingray convertible he had been restoring in the garage.

Deeply appreciative of these sacrifices, Taylor promised her parents that they would never regret the investment they had made in her education. This was a promise that guided her all through high school and college, and eventually on to Northwestern Law. It was a promise that still motivated her to this day. After law school graduation, Taylor had chosen to work at Gray & Dallas for the simple reason that it was the top-ranked law firm in Chicago and one of the best worldwide. It gave her a sense of pride to be part of such a machine.

And she would do whatever it took to succeed there.

Fortunately for Taylor, unlike so many of her law school classmates who had turned to the practice of law because med school was too hard and took too long to make any money, or out of family pressure, or because they simply couldn't think of anything better to do, she genuinely loved being a lawyer. From the moment she'd conducted her first mock cross-examination in her law school trial advocacy class, everything felt like it clicked into place.

And so, as she stood in the doorway of Sam's plush partner's office, she couldn't help but smile not only in admiration but also in anticipation of what she hoped was soon to come.

One day, Taylor vowed silently to herself. One day.

She straightened her suit and knocked on Sam's door. He looked up from his computer and smiled warmly in greeting.

"Taylor! Come on in."

She took a seat at one of the chairs in front of Sam's desk. In the style of all shrewd attorneys, the guest chairs were positioned six inches lower than Sam's own, giving him the advantage of looking down on his visitors.

"Settled in yet?" Sam inquired.

Taylor grinned guiltily at the question, thinking of the unpacked boxes scattered along the hallway outside the living room of the two-bedroom apartment the firm had rented for her. "Almost."

"Moving's a pain in the ass, isn't it?"

"It keeps me busy when I'm not here."

Sam studied her. "Yes, I've seen you burning the midnight oil already. You should take some time to settle in before your case gets going full throttle."

Taylor shrugged determinedly. For her, there was no speed other than full throttle. And Sam Blakely—the head of the litigation group in Los Angeles—was a man she very much wanted to impress.

"I just want to hit the ground running, that's all."

Sam had sharp, fox-like facial features that became even more pronounced as he grinned approvingly at Taylor's all-business style.

"Then tell me how the case is going."

Taylor eased back in her chair as she gave Sam her summary. "It's going very well. We have the call for our motions in limine this week—I think we'll be able to keep out nearly half of the EEOC's evidence. And one of their lawyers called me this morning to discuss a settlement."

"What did you say?"

Taylor tilted her head coyly. "Let's just say they understand we're not interested."

Sam chuckled. "Good. Keep me posted, and don't hesitate to stop by if you need any guidance."

Taylor nodded agreeably, appreciating Sam's hands-off approach to their case. So far since she'd come to L.A., he had been more than happy to let her take the ball and run with it—a management style she thrived under.

She assumed that would be the end of their meeting. But instead of dismissing her, Sam shifted in his chair as if he had more to say.

"Something else on your mind, Sam?"

His body language right then seemed a little . . . odd. She didn't know Sam all that well yet, so she couldn't read him like she could the partners back home in Chicago. She waited as Sam eased back in his chair and stared at her with a poignant pause, creating the dramatic buildup for whatever he was about to say. Like so many trial attorneys Taylor had come across, Sam appeared to believe in acting out his entire life as if in front of a jury.

"Actually, there is another matter on which I was hoping to get your assistance," Sam began carefully. "I know we only have you on loan from Chicago for the harassment case, but this wouldn't be a full-time assignment."

Taylor was intrigued by this lead-in. She was already working nights and weekends, so she figured this mystery assignment had to be a great opportunity if Sam thought she should squeeze it into her schedule.

"Is it a pro bono matter?" she asked.

Sam leaned back in his chair as he considered this question carefully, like a trapped witness at a deposition. "Well . . . not exactly. I'd call it more of a favor."

Taylor's bullshit radar instantly went into high alert. So-called "favors" for partners generally meant wasted non-billable hours preparing a bar association speech or researching the DUI laws of Natchitoches, Louisiana, to help out a wayward-but-good-hearted nephew.

"What kind of favor?" Taylor asked, although she already knew exactly what Sam's response would be. "It's a very interesting situation . . ." he'd begin. All partners described the criminal activities of their ne'er-do-well relations as "interesting situations."

Sam leaned forward in his chair. "It's a very interesting situation . . ." he began.

Bingo.

Taylor tried to appear enthusiastic as he continued.

"It's a favor to one of the partners here, Bill Mitchells," Sam said. "I'm sure you're familiar with him—he's head of the tax group. One of his clients asked him for a favor."

Taylor could barely keep from rolling her eyes. Great—*client* criminal relations. The only thing worse than the spoiled prep-school offspring of rich partners was the spoiled prep-school offspring of *insanely* rich CEOs. She steeled herself for the rest of Sam's pitch.

But what he said next surprised her.

"As you likely are aware, Bill does tax work for most of the big names in Hollywood. One of his clients, an actor, is about to start filming a legal thriller. He's asked to work with one of our litigators to get a feel for how real lawyers act in the courtroom. You know, demeanor, where to stand, those kinds of things."

Sam paused once again for dramatic effect. This provided Taylor an opportunity to digest what he was saying.

Babysit an actor when she was just three weeks from trial?

Preposterous.

It had to be a practical joke. Ha ha, yank the chain of the new associate from the Midwest who thinks everyone in Los Angeles is obsessed with celebrities.

Taylor smiled and shook her finger at Sam to let him know she was in on the gag.

"I'm guessing you're joking."

But Sam's face turned serious, and he gave her that "what's the problem?" look partners give associates when assigning a three-month document review.

He wasn't joking.

Balls.

"Let's be honest, Taylor," Sam said in his best we're-all-buddies-here tone. "I'm not going to put a partner on this. I've got better uses for those of us that bill out at eight hundred dollars an hour." He winked at her. In public and around clients, partners loved to put on a big show of feigning embarrassment over their ridiculous billing rates. But behind closed doors, they were a source of great pride.

"However, it's an excellent client development opportunity," he went on, "so I need an associate who will make a good impression. You."

Taylor folded her hands in her lap and thought quickly of the best way to graciously decline Sam's offer. She knew he meant the opportunity as a compliment, but working with some prima donna actor on his overly melodramatic "You can't handle the truth!" courtroom scenes was hardly her idea of *serious* lawyering.

So she flashed Sam her best soft-rejection smile.

"Sam, I'm flattered. But don't you think one of the associates from this office would be better suited for this kind of project? I'd hate to waltz in here as the new girl and steal their opportunity to work with a Hollywood actor."

That didn't sound half bad, she mused. Apparently, she had a bit of a flair for acting herself.

But then Sam topped her with his trump card.

"Well, Taylor, Chicago assures me that you're the best litigation associate this firm has. If that's true, then don't you think it should be you representing us?"

A direct challenge to her skills as a lawyer. Taylor's kryptonite.

She sighed, having only one answer to that.

"When would you need me?"

Sam grinned victoriously, looking ever fox-like once again. "Thursday."

For a brief moment, Taylor saw a possible way out of this situation. "Oh . . . that's too bad," she said. "I have to argue those motions to compel on Thursday." She snapped her fingers. Damn.

But Sam was not about to let her off so easily.

"And as much as I know it will kill you to miss a chance to be in court, I'm sure you can get someone else to cover it." Then he folded his hands politely, indicating that the discussion was over.

And so Taylor stood up to leave. She gave Sam her best team-player, I-couldn't-be-more-thrilled-to-squeeze-this-shit-into-my-schedule grin.

"No problem, Sam, I'll work it all out."

She turned to leave and had made it all the way to the door before she realized something. She glanced back over her shoulder.

"I didn't even think to ask—who's the actor?"

Sam peered up distractedly from his computer, having already turned his attention back to $800-per-hour work.

"Um . . . Jason Andrews."

And with those words, Taylor's hand slipped just the slightest bit on the doorknob.

She turned back toward Sam, trying to appear nonchalant. "Really. I see."

But unfortunately, her initial reaction had not gone unnoticed. Sam's face turned serious as he rose from his desk and crossed the room to her.

"You know, Taylor, I told his manager that your reputation in this firm is that you can go head-to-head with any man. And win." Sam paused meaningfully and stared down at her like an army drill sergeant.

"Do *not* get starry-eyed on this," he lectured firmly.

Taylor's eyes narrowed at the mere insinuation. After Daniel, her days of being starry-eyed, dreamy-eyed, or any other-eyed over any man, celebrity or not, were finished.

Sam was right; she was more than capable of going head-to-head with any man. She had, essentially, been raised that way. Growing up, her father, a police sergeant, worked double shifts and her mom, a nurse, often worked overtime, so Taylor had frequently found herself being watched by her three older brothers. And in their minds, the only way to handle being stuck after school and on weekends with a girl was to pretend that she was, in fact, a boy. (Albeit one who had pigtails.)

One of Taylor's favorite movies was *A League of Their Own*, and in that movie Tom Hanks's character had a line that had always resonated with her: one of his girl ballplayers was crying after he had chewed her out for missing a play, and Tom Hanks told her, "There's no crying in baseball." That could have been the mantra for Taylor's youth, except in her world apparently, not only was there no crying in baseball, there was also no crying in kickball, hide-and-seek (even when her brothers forgot about her and left her in the neighbor's shed for two hours), climbing trees, falling two stories out of said trees and breaking her arm, and even fishing when her brothers used her pet caterpillar collection as bait.

Yes, Taylor learned at a very young age that the only way to get boys to shut up and play fairly was to show them that you took crap from *no one*. It was a lesson that served her well working at a large law firm, where women comprised roughly 15 percent of partners despite the fact that they generally constituted, year after year, more than half of every entering first-year associate class. Somewhere along the way, these women were getting lost, ignored, weeded out, or were choosing a different path.

Taylor, however, was determined not to fall victim to what

these law firms accepted as inevitable reality. Even if it meant she had to eat nails for breakfast.

So in response to Sam's directive that she not get "starry-eyed" on this particular assignment, she folded her arms definitively across her chest, having only one thing to say.

"Not a chance."

Sam smiled. He nodded, satisfied.

Then something occurred to her. She cautiously asked Sam one last question.

"But I have to wonder, Sam, given the . . . reputation . . . of this particular client, did the fact that I'm a woman have anything to do with choosing me for this project?"

Ever the litigator, Sam paced grandly in front of his desk, ready to show off the interrogation skills he had honed over the past twenty years.

"Taylor, in your sexual harassment practice, who do you tell your clients they should have leading their defense team, a man or a woman?"

"A woman," she replied without hesitation.

"And why is that?"

"Because it makes the client seem more credible if they have a female lawyer saying they treat women fairly."

Sam paused meaningfully before his imaginary jury. "So then you agree, don't you, that there are times when—in addition to being the best litigator—your gender can be an advantage to this firm?"

Taylor got the message. Shut up and play the game.

She smiled at her boss.

"Thursday it is."

Two

JASON ANDREWS.

He would be at their offices on Thursday. The biggest actor in Hollywood.

Jason Andrews.

The movie star. In every paparazzi-following-your-every-move, crazed-fans-showing-up-naked-in-your-bedroom sense of the term.

Later, when Taylor's secretary did her "research," she would stumble across *Rolling Stone* magazine's June cover interview, which summed up Jason Andrews as: "devilishly good-looking, and a true legend of his day. Like Clark Gable or Cary Grant, he exudes effortless charm and confidence. Thinks he's smarter than most and frankly, probably is. A lethal combination that seemingly has left him with respect for very few."

Devilishly good-looking. Effortless charm and confidence.

Jason Andrews.

And she was going to be working with him.

As Taylor left Sam's office, she suddenly found herself wondering where she was in her bikini wax cycle. Hmm . . . she may have been due . . .

Then she immediately shook off the ridiculous thought. Please. She was a *professional*.

And so Ms. Professional straightened her suit and calmly shut Sam's door behind her. She made her way through the office with what she assumed was a casually dismissive air, as if she acted as legal counsel to fabulously famous sex gods all the time. She had never, ever, let anyone at work see her rattled—not even during the worst point in her breakup with her ex-fiancé a few months ago. She'd be damned if she now was about to let some actor unnerve her in front of others.

"Linda, I need to clear my schedule for Thursday," Taylor said as she approached her secretary's desk. She was peering at her calendar, trying to figure out how best to move things around to accommodate her new "assignment."

"There's been a change of plans—a new matter has come up."

She had barely gotten the words out when Linda flew out of her chair. It fell backward to the ground with a loud thunk, which Linda didn't seem to notice.

"Oh my god! So it's true then? You're really going to be working with Jason Andrews?"

How the hell did that get out so fast? Taylor glanced around the office and saw that the other secretaries all had paused in what they were doing. They were staring at her, wide-eyed, and holding their breath as if their very lives depended on her reply. Looking over, she saw that most of the lawyers, too, lingered in their office doorways. For that moment, all business at Gray & Dallas had utterly, completely stopped.

With the one hundred sets of hopeful eyes on her, Taylor cleared her throat and addressed the waiting office, like the town crier announcing that the king was on his way.

"Yes, it's true. Jason—uh, Andrews—will be here. On Thursday." Taylor began to fan herself, suddenly feeling a little flushed. Strange how warm it had become in the office right then. Probably a poor ventilation spot, she mused. She'd have to speak to Linda about calling the maintenance people.

All around her, the secretaries and lawyers had erupted in a frenzy of frantic conversations at her exciting news.

"What should I wear?"

"What do you think *he* will wear?"

"Didn't you just love it when he [insert favorite Jason Andrews movie/scene/line here]?"

"Do you think"—gasp—"he could ever possibly be as gorgeous in person?"

Taylor stood in the middle of all the chaos. As always, she felt the need to maintain control over the situation, so she gestured calmingly to the secretaries that hopped about her like over-caffeinated jackrabbits.

"You all need to pull yourselves together," she said firmly, over the racket. "We need to treat this like any other project."

At this, the secretaries simmered down and stopped dancing. Linda stared at her incredulously. "Any other project? It's *Jason Andrews*."

Taylor felt herself getting all flushed again. Damn ventilation. Someone really needed to see to that soon.

Linda's expression was one of utter disbelief. "Are you seriously trying to tell us that you're not the least bit excited about this?"

Taylor sighed loudly in exasperation. "Oh, Linda, come on . . ." With that said, she turned and coolly headed toward her office. But when she reached the door, she looked back at her secretary and winked.

"Hey—I didn't say it wouldn't be a *fun* project."

With a sly grin, she disappeared into her office.

IT WAS AFTER eleven that evening when Taylor finally pulled into the driveway of her apartment building. For the remainder of the day, she had tried to put all thoughts of the "Andrews Project" (as it had widely come to be known throughout the office) out of her mind. But fate, of course, had been conspiring against her.

Shortly after her meeting with Sam, she had received a phone call from one of "Mr. Andrews's" assistants, who had informed her in clipped, brisk terms that "Mr. Andrews" (the assistant's repeated use of the surname conjured up visions in Taylor's mind of a stuffy eighteenth-century British servant) would arrive at her office on Thursday morning at nine o'clock.

It was expected, said the servant-assistant, that Ms. Donovan would not be late, as Mr. Andrews kept a very busy schedule.

The whole tone of the conversation had irked her.

Let's get something straight, Taylor had been tempted to say. I *am doing* him *a favor.*

She hadn't been in Los Angeles long enough to adjust to the fact that catering to celebrities with overinflated senses of self-importance was simply part of the city's framework, never to be questioned. She may have been living—temporarily—in the city of dreams, but her life was quite grounded in reality. And that life, whether in L.A. or Chicago, was in The Law.

Moreover, since her work schedule generally permitted her to see only about four movies per year, she simply didn't have enough interest in "the industry" to give a crap about stroking Jason Andrews's ego. Besides, she was quite certain that—given his infamous reputation—he'd already had enough things stroked to last a lifetime.

But despite the strong opinions she had on the matter, Taylor thought she had been highly diplomatic in her response to the servant-assistant's instructions.

"Now, is it customary that I curtsy *before* or *after* I'm presented to His Highness?" she had innocently inquired.

The servant-assistant had not been amused.

After ending the call on that note, Taylor had set off to find a way to miraculously fit three days of work into the two days remaining before His Royal Wonderfulness arrived. Her first priority had been to meet with Derek, the second-year associate assigned to work with her on the sexual harassment case.

Poor Derek, always a bit of a nervous type, appeared ready to break out in hives when Taylor told him he'd be arguing the motions on Thursday. For a moment, she thought about sneakily whispering a trade—seven motions in limine for seven hours with you-know-who—but she knew Sam expected that she personally handle the actor.

Even to the likely detriment of their motions.

And the possible harm that would then befall their client.

Not to mention what she personally wanted.

Not that she had any opinions on the matter. Really.

But for the rest of the afternoon, Taylor had other, far more important things to worry about. And so, between the seventeen class member deposition transcripts she needed to review, and the eleven telephone arguments with opposing counsel over jury instructions, it was not until late that night, as she exhaustedly made her way to her front door, that she remembered the envelope Linda had handed her before leaving for the day.

Research, her secretary had called it. She had smiled in amusement, thoroughly enjoying the new project.

Given Linda's mischievous grin, it was with dread that Taylor pulled the envelope out of her briefcase as she walked up the bricked path to her apartment. She slid out the envelope's contents, and found herself staring at that week's edition of *People* magazine.

Taylor rolled her eyes. Oh, for heaven's sake—like she had time to read this.

But tabloids have a sneaky way of grabbing the attention of even the most resolute of scoffers, and Taylor was not immune. It was the cover story that caught her eye.

"The Women of Jason Andrews!"

The image below the headline consisted of three side-by-side photos of the film star with a different starlet/model/bimbo hanging all over him.

Taylor shook her head disdainfully at the pictures. Typical. There was something about the sight of this particular man, the way he so deliberately flaunted his parade of conquests, that rubbed her feminist sensibilities the wrong way.

Or maybe it was something more personal.

Right, like she would ever admit that.

She opened the magazine, and a multiple-page foldout of Jason Andrews and his various dalliances fell out.

And spilled all the way to the ground.

For a moment, Taylor could only stare at the pages and pages and pages of "The Women of Jason Andrews!"

With a scornful snort, she bent over to pick up the foldout. The last photo in the series happened to catch her eye: the actor with a classically beautiful blonde in her midtwenties, who Taylor immediately recognized. She may not have been particularly interested in "the industry," but even the four times a year she crawled out from under her rock to see a movie was enough to know who Naomi Cross was. She saw that written in big, bold letters above the waiflike actress was the urgent question, "Jason's Next Conquest?"

Deciding that she could somehow manage to go on living without getting an answer to that question, Taylor tucked the Jason-plus-starlet/model/bimbo pages back into the magazine and headed up the walkway to her front door. It was then that she stumbled upon something sitting on her front stoop.

A large bouquet of flowers.

As all women do when first receiving flowers, Taylor silently scrolled through the list of potential senders. Coming up with no pleasant suspects, she eyed the flowers with suspicion. She scooped them up and sifted through the bouquet until she found the card. She instantly regretted bothering to look.

I'm sorry. And I love you. Daniel.

DANIEL LAWRY.

The biggest mistake of Taylor's life.

Ridiculously big. Gargantuan.

They had met in law school, when she was a third-year student and Daniel had just joined the Northwestern faculty as their new evidence professor. He was young for a professor, only twenty-nine, but his Harvard Law degree and four-year stint at the New York U.S. Attorney's Office had been too attractive for the law school to ignore.

"Too attractive to ignore" was also the general consensus among the law school's female student body. With icy blue eyes and streaks of golden blond in his light brown hair, he looked more like a Ralph Lauren model than a law school professor.

The first time Daniel had asked Taylor out was at her law school graduation. She, of course, had said no, having heard rumors from a classmate of hers who lived in the downtown high-rise across the street from Daniel that he frequently was seen around the area with women but much less frequently seen with the *same* woman.

Six months went by before he asked her out again. The second time was a Saturday morning, when Taylor found him waiting on the steps of her three-flat condo on her walk home from the gym.

He came bearing Starbucks, he said to her with an easy smile, and he had her order exactly right: a grande skim latte with two Splendas. Apparently, he had called her secretary earlier in the week for the info.

It took five Saturday mornings of waiting, and five grande skim lattes with two Splendas, until Taylor finally agreed to meet Daniel for coffee somewhere other than her front steps. Coffee led to drinks, which led to dinner and then dating, which eventually led to Daniel saying all the right things about Taylor being "the one." She finally agreed to move in with him and a year after that, they were engaged.

It by no means had been a whirlwind affair. She had been cautious and careful throughout the first couple of years of their relationship, but eventually, Daniel's charm and constant affection had brought down her guard.

She believed he had changed his womanizing ways.

But now here she was in Los Angeles, living alone. And without the two-and-a-half-carat Tiffany ring that used to sit on the fourth finger of her left hand.

Taylor stepped into her apartment. With that now-ringless left hand, she tossed her keys onto the console table by the front door and headed into the kitchen.

She had gotten lucky in terms of the apartment the firm had found for her. Since her case easily would last at least four months (after the inevitable posttrial motions were taken into account), putting her up in a hotel for the duration had not been either her or the firm's first choice. So one of the legal assistants for the Chicago litigation group had been assigned the task of searching for apartments Taylor could rent. The paralegal was only a few days into her quest when one of her counterparts in the Los Angeles office contacted her with a suggestion: the daughter of one of the partners would be studying abroad in Rome for the fall semester. She wanted to backpack through Europe and Asia for the summer before her classes began, and they were looking for someone to sublet her furnished Santa Monica apartment.

The deal was done as soon as Taylor saw the photographs

the L.A. office emailed over. Just minutes from the beach, with a quaint little garden off the living room and cozy cream-and-brown Pottery Barn decor, the apartment was far better than anything else the legal assistant had shown her and easily worth the ten extra miles it would add to her daily downtown commute.

Unfortunately on this night, however, the apartment's charm was lost on Taylor as she stepped into the kitchen and set the copy of *People* magazine down on the black-speckled granite countertop. She threw the bouquet of flowers next to the magazine, not noticing as Daniel's card slipped into its pages.

She leaned against the far side of the counter and stared at the two dozen red roses with the same enthusiasm as if she were looking at a dead skunk.

How ironic that in the five years they had been together, Daniel had never figured out that she didn't even really like flowers. They're not practical, she had tried hinting on several occasions. Well, at least now she no longer had to humor him.

She opened up one of the kitchen drawers, searching for a pair of scissors, when she saw her blinking answering machine. It sat atop the wine chiller, one of the "top of the line kitchen appliances" the legal assistant had eagerly included in her description of the apartment. What the legal assistant hadn't realized was that the far stronger selling point in Taylor's mind was the Chinese restaurant down the street that delivered until 2 a.m.

Taylor reached across the counter and hit the play button on her answering machine. After the beep, she was relieved to hear Kate's voice cheerfully greeting her.

"Hey, girl! It's me, just calling to see how L.A.'s treating you. Val and I are already planning a visit. Miss you."

Taylor couldn't help but grin—in truth, Val and Kate had been planning their visit pretty much from the moment she had first announced that she'd be moving to L.A. for the summer. And starting about two weeks ago, Val had stepped it up a notch by emailing her with "suggested places to visit"—a list Taylor suspected was comprised primarily, if not entirely, of the restaurants and bars mentioned in that week's Page Six columns or *Us Weekly* "VIP Scene" section.

Taylor glanced down when her answering machine beeped again, indicating that there was a second message. She held her breath, tensing in anticipation.

A familiar husky voice cut through the quiet of her kitchen.

"Taylor, it's Daniel. I hope you got my flowers . . . I'd really like to talk. Please call me."

She reached over and instantly deleted the message. How the hell Daniel had gotten her phone number and address in Los Angeles, she had no clue. Five years together meant too many mutual friends, she supposed. She leaned back against the counter and replayed his words in her head.

I'd really like to talk.

Really? Why? She couldn't possibly think of one thing they had to say to each other.

With this in mind, Taylor walked over to the sink and began to run the water. She pulled a vase out of the cabinet below the sink—feeling obligated to at least put the flowers somewhere—and tested the water for its temperature. As she removed the paper wrapping from the bouquet, her mind drifted back to his card.

I'm sorry. And I love you.

How sweet. Daniel always had been such a charmer.

That is, until the day she walked into his office to discuss their wedding guest list and found him fucking his twenty-two-year-old teaching assistant on top of his desk.

Doggie-style, by the way.

With their backs to her, not noticing, so they just kept right on going. Evidently, they had not been expecting anyone to show up for what was supposed to be Daniel's "office hour."

Even now, whenever Taylor actually allowed herself to think of her ex-fiancé, the visual that always came to mind was that of him standing in front of his desk with his pants around his ankles, his hands feverishly holding on to the girl's hips in ecstasy. Naked ass checks thrusting back and forth in all their glory.

Lovely.

"It's how every girl *dreams* of seeing her fiancé," she had said in sarcastic bitterness to Val and Kate as they sat on her living-room couch later that night, consoling her. They had a bottle of Grey Goose vodka standing by on ice. But with Taylor, there hadn't been the expected breakdown and hysterics, nor even a single cry of "why me?" And there certainly had been no tears.

Because there's no crying in baseball.

Taylor vowed that she would at least hold on to that last shred of dignity. She would get over Daniel and move on with her life. And she vowed to never, ever again go against her instincts when it came to a man.

Standing there that night in her temporary Santa Monica kitchen, having finished unwrapping the flowers, she realized with a good deal of satisfaction that she'd barely thought of Daniel in the couple of weeks since she had moved to Los Angeles. That was a large part of the reason his flowers and card had come as such a surprise.

I'm sorry. And I love you.

What a nice sentiment. Daniel, apparently, was not finding it quite as easy to stop thinking about her.

With that thought in mind, Taylor reached over and flicked a switch just above her kitchen sink. The garbage disposal roared to life with a loud garbled crank.

She had found just the perfect spot for his flowers.

THE NEXT AFTERNOON at work, when she came out of her office for a much-needed coffee break, Taylor discovered a large crowd of what had to be virtually every one of the firm's secretaries huddled around the credenza behind Linda's desk.

Without diverting their gaze, the secretaries parted so that Taylor could get a look at whatever it was that had so captivated them.

A television.

Taylor could barely hide her disdain. Oh, come on—he wasn't worth this much fuss. Whether it was the patronizing tone of his assistant during their conversation the day before or the brazenly sexist bravado of "The Women of Jason

Andrews!" article, she had recently found herself developing several preconceived notions about the actor she soon was going to be working with. And none of them could exactly be considered positive.

She glanced over at the television, just in time to catch a quick montage of images of Jason Andrews flashing across the screen.

"Where did you guys get this?" she whispered to Linda, not wanting to divert the larger group's attention from such obviously important matters.

Linda responded to Taylor without tearing her eyes away from the TV screen. "They aired an interview with him last night on E!, so I recorded it."

Seeing the slightly dazed look on her secretary's face, Taylor had to bite her lip to keep from laughing. She couldn't help it—a vision flashed into her head: Jason Andrews walking through the office corridor the following morning, as the administrative staff swooned and fainted one by one to the floor as he passed by.

With that image in mind, Taylor turned her attention back to the television, where Jason was being interviewed in some posh hotel room. She couldn't help but notice, as he leaned against the couch, how natural and relaxed he appeared—undoubtedly due to the many, many times he had been interviewed before.

Of course, she also couldn't help but notice how good he looked on camera. She'd hazard a guess that his face was one of the most recognized in the world: the rakish dark hair, the perpetual glint of confidence in his brilliant blue eyes, and that trademark devilish smile. He pretty much was the standard against which male attractiveness had been defined for the past ten years.

Taylor recalled being at a party a few years ago where, as a game, Kate had asked each male attendee the same question: Who would they choose if—for whatever reason (gunpoint, to save the world, etc.)—they *had* to have sex with another man? Without exception, every man at the party had picked Jason Andrews.

"Is there really any other answer?" Chris, Kate's boyfriend at the time, had laughed. He refreshingly had been the only guy not to utter the token "I'd rather die" protests before finally answering. The other men at the party had nodded in universal agreement: if (upon pain of death) the deed had to be done, Jason Andrews was the only way to go.

Taylor turned her attention back to the on-screen Jason as he stretched his long legs out in front of him. There was something different about seeing him on television that morning. It was kind of strange, but up until that point she somehow had never viewed "Jason Andrews" as a *real* person. He was so larger than life that he seemed more like some Hollywood creation than an actual flesh-and-blood man. So in many senses, she felt as though she was watching the man himself for the first time.

Taylor glanced at her watch. She supposed she could spare a few minutes checking out the interview before getting back to her dep transcripts. For research purposes, of course.

The reporter who sat across from Jason was a man in his mid-thirties who Taylor vaguely recognized from last year's Academy Awards red carpet preshow. He launched eagerly into his first question.

"So let's see, Jason, you've earned three Golden Globe nominations—one of those a win, and two Academy Award nominations, again with a win for your dramatic performance as an undercover narcotics police officer in *Overload*. Tell me: Is there anywhere you can go from here?"

Jason flashed that famous smile at the reporter's question.

"Of course. I'm always looking for something that will challenge me."

The reporter shifted in his seat, ready to move into tougher territory. "There are rumors you were interested in the lead role in *Outback Nights*, but that your salary—which currently is the top in the industry—was simply too high for the film's budget. Care to make any comment on that?"

"Only that I wish everyone involved in that project the best of luck."

Jason's relaxed gaze gave away no hint of animosity. Taylor

wondered if he was acting. Actually, she wondered if he ever *wasn't* acting.

The reporter pressed on. "Do your best wishes extend to Scott Casey, who landed the role instead of you?"

Jason continued to smile as he nonchalantly adjusted his watch, turning it around his wrist. He seemed very indifferent to the whole affair.

"It's a big town, and there are plenty of roles for all of us. Besides, I'm very excited about my next project—a legal thriller with Paramount."

The secretaries surrounding the television erupted into cheers and pointed at Taylor. She waved off the attention with some embarrassment.

On screen, the reporter appeared resigned to the fact that he wasn't getting any gossip out of the actor, at least not on that subject.

"So with all the roles available to you, how do you know which one to choose?"

Jason crossed one leg over the other and stretched an arm casually along the back of the couch. The fitted V-neck sweater he wore emphasized the broad shoulders and lean muscular physique Taylor knew was underneath. As infrequently as she went to the movies, even she had seen *Overload*, and she recalled with a fair amount of detail the scene in the shower where Jason's character leaned emotionally against the wall, letting the water wash the blood of his slain wife off his naked body. Not since *Psycho* had a shower scene more affected the female moviegoing public.

"You know, Billy, you just have to go with your instincts," Jason explained in response to the reporter's question. "Something clicks, something comes alive inside you—feelings you maybe didn't even realize you had—and you suddenly know you've found the right fit."

The reporter shifted eagerly in his chair at the opening Jason had just provided him. "Speaking of finding the right fit . . . you've led into my next topic. Women."

Jason laughed and folded his arms behind his head. "You guys are all the same. You always ask me about this."

"Can you blame us?" the reporter inquired with an innocent grin. "You've dated supermodels, a pop star, and many of the most beautiful actresses in Hollywood."

Jason nodded along with the list, obviously quite proud of his accomplishments.

"And I think the only thing that gets more media coverage than the names of the women you date is the speed at which you go through them. Let's see, you are . . ." The reporter trailed off as he shifted through his notes, appearing puzzled. "Oh, I see that for 'age,' your publicist tells us only that you are in your 'thirties.' "

The reporter glanced up questioningly at Jason.

Who clearly had nothing further to add on that particular subject.

After a semi-awkward moment, the reporter pressed on. "I guess my question is this: when it comes to women, what are you looking for?"

The camera zoomed in on Jason. And Taylor watched as he answered as only a man in his position could.

"My philosophy is that relationships should be treated the same as a new script. If it doesn't hold my interest after an hour, I'm not going to waste any more time on it."

Taylor's mouth fell open at the pure, unadulterated arrogance of his words.

Linda, who was standing next to her, leaned over and mumbled under her breath. "Wow—actress, supermodel, whoever—I feel sorry for any woman who has to get over him."

Taylor turned to Linda, scoffing vehemently at this.

"Please—after hearing what he just said, any woman dumb enough to go out with *him* can't complain when she inevitably gets hurt."

"That's a little harsh, don't you think?"

"Maybe. But I'll tell you this—smart women don't date Jason Andrews."

Linda nodded as she turned back to the television. "I suppose that's true."

But then she peered over at Taylor with a sly grin. "Except . . . let's see how much that resistance holds up once you're alone with him." Listening in, the other secretaries all laughed in implicit agreement.

Taylor defiantly flung her long hair over her shoulders. Jason Andrews had hardly made much of an impression on her thus far.

"Please—I'm sure in real life the man can barely hold an intelligent conversation."

Linda considered this. "Well then, I guess you better find a way to keep him from doing a lot of talking." She threw Taylor a wicked grin. "How big is your shower?"

The secretaries burst into tittering giggles.

Taylor found herself oddly flustered by Linda's words. It had to be the temperature in the office, she thought with annoyance, which had suddenly become ridiculously hot again. All that money, and the firm couldn't even afford damn decent air-conditioning.

Realizing she had been fanning herself—and that everyone was watching—Taylor stopped and pretended to be waving off the group's giggles.

"Don't you people have any work to do?"

The secretaries exchanged amused looks at her tone. With a dismissive flick of her hand—figuring she'd wasted more than enough time on nonsense that morning—Taylor abruptly turned back toward her office.

And stumbled most ungracefully over a file box sitting in the hallway.

After an ungainly balancing act, Taylor managed to right herself. She looked down in annoyance. Stupid stinking box. She kicked it with her heel.

Behind her, the secretaries giggled even louder.

Taylor straightened her suit and pulled herself together, then hurried off to the sanctity of her office. On her way, she gestured to the object of everyone's fascination.

"And why do we have a television in here, anyway?" she demanded in an attempt to at least get the last word in. "This is a law office!"

Linda shrugged this off nonchalantly.

"This is L.A."

Three

TAYLOR CHECKED THE clock on her desk for what had to be the tenth time that morning. 11:07. She tapped her pen impatiently.

He was late.

She should have been in court that very moment, arguing her motions to compel. As it turned out, Derek had nothing to worry about—if they lost on one single issue, she would hold Jason Andrews entirely responsible.

She glanced up hopefully when Linda stopped in the doorway.

"Any word?"

Linda sadly shook her head. A deep depression had begun to creep over the office at the actor's failure to appear thus far. "None."

They went through this routine for the rest of the morning, and then the afternoon, too. Assuming Jason Andrews would eventually show up at some point, and having cleared her schedule for the entire day, Taylor found it difficult to concentrate on any meaningful task. So when six o'clock rolled around, she began the futile task of filling in her daily time sheet with a whole lot of nothing.

Great, she thought—say hello to another Saturday in the office.

But then she was interrupted by a frantic knock at her office door. She looked up to see Linda, flushed with excitement and out of breath, as if she had run to Taylor's office the moment she had received whatever news she was about to convey.

"His assistant just called. She said there was a mix-up, but that Mr. Andrews will be here first thing tomorrow morning."

"Tomorrow?" Taylor repeated. Then she frowned. "Perfect," she muttered in annoyance. Say hello to Sunday in the office, too.

"Did his assistant at least apologize?" she asked.

Linda put a finger to her chin and paused, as if trying to remember. "Hmmm . . . now that would be a 'no.'"

Taylor rolled her eyes. Now there's a fucking surprise.

BUT BY THE next day, Taylor could definitively say that she had gotten over the issue of Jason Andrews's lateness.

Because being late was no longer the problem.

The jerk had completely blown her off. No phone calls, no apologies, and no explanations.

So by late Friday afternoon, after a second day spent mumbling obscenities, pacing through the hallways, and generally huffing about, Taylor decided she was not going to waste one more minute of her life on Jason Andrews.

She shoved a stack of files into her briefcase, grabbed her suit coat off the back of her chair, and resolutely strode out into the hallway, past Linda's desk.

"I'm going home. And I will be unavailable for the rest of the afternoon if, by some miracle, a certain person should happen to show up." The haughty way she said this left Linda no doubt as to who the "certain person" might be. "For anyone else, I can of course be reached on my cell phone or at home."

Linda panicked. She leaned over her desk and shouted frantically to Taylor, who was already halfway down the hall by that point. "But what am I supposed to say if Jason Andrews shows up?"

Ten responses inappropriate for the workplace came to Taylor's mind.

Not bothering to stop, she called back a simple message for Linda to relay.

"Tell him I hope his movie bombs."

SATURDAY AND SUNDAY thankfully passed by without further needless (and highly inconsiderate) delays. Taylor used the weekend hours to get back on track in terms of her pretrial schedule. Derek had informed her that the judge had continued one of their motions—the one most critical to their case—until Monday morning. Although neither mentioned it, both of them were quietly relieved that she would be able to cover the motion after all. Derek, a little on the shy side, had always been slightly uncomfortable with the subject matter.

Come Sunday afternoon, having billed almost fifteen hours over the weekend, Taylor decided to reward herself with some shopping at Fred Segal. As she left the mall a mere hour after getting there, she tried to figure out why she felt *good* about dropping almost $500 on one pair of jeans and a small black velvet clutch. Then it hit her: she had just had her first "L.A." experience.

As Taylor cut across the parking lot, she reached into her purse for her cell phone. She knew Valerie would be proud of this moment.

"Guess where I am right now," she said as soon as Val answered on the other end of the line. She didn't bother with an introduction, as Val had carefully selected a different ring tone for each of her friends. For Taylor, she had chosen the Darth Vader theme music.

Val quickly threw out a few guesses. "Lying on the beach. Hiking in the mountains. Matt Damon's bedroom."

Taylor juggled her phone as she took her Chanel sunglasses out of her purse and slid them on. It had been warm and sunny every day since she'd come to Los Angeles. She'd have to concede the fact that the city certainly had the advantage of weather over Chicago, which could be a miserable fifty degrees and rainy even in June.

"If I was in Matt Damon's bedroom, I'd hardly be taking a telephone break," Taylor joked.

"I thought you said you liked him for his intellect."

"I caught a few minutes of *The Bourne Ultimatum* on cable the other night. My feelings for Matt now extend far beyond his Harvard education. Like how he looks in a fitted T-shirt."

"Good. Because I used to think your attraction was pretty shallow."

They both laughed. Their conversation quickly turned to Val and Kate's visit, which was only a few weeks away. As Taylor listened to Val rattle on about hanging poolside at Chateau Marmont and dinners at Les Deux, she kept silent about the whole Jason Andrews debacle. She had decided, for now at least, not to mention it to anyone back home. At this point, she figured, it was a nonstarter of a story. What could she say, really? I was *supposed* to work with Jason Andrews, but he never showed up? Wow, that was exciting. Plus, she didn't particularly feel the need to share with everyone the fact that she'd been blown off by the man.

He may have been Jason Andrews, but she still had her pride.

ON MONDAY MORNING, Taylor rushed around her apartment getting ready for work. She had the television on in her living room, hoping to catch the traffic report. Although from what she had observed in the past couple of weeks, this was a meaningless exercise. Like the weather, the traffic in L.A. was always the same. Everywhere took twenty minutes.

Having traveled fairly extensively across the country for depositions and trials, she'd had the opportunity to observe that local morning shows kept to certain schedules. L.A.'s version—appropriately named *L.A. Mornings*—was no exception. National news followed by local news, with weather and traffic on the "sixes." And at precisely 7:20, Sarah Stevens, the show's exuberant entertainment correspondent, treated Los Angeles viewers to the day's "Hollywood Minute."

And so it was on that particular Monday morning, as the clock struck 7:20, that Taylor happened to be in the kitchen pouring coffee into her portable mug when she heard the anchorwoman's telltale introduction coming from the television.

"And now, Los Angeles, it's time for Sarah Stevens and the day's Hollywood Minute."

Taylor had a view of the television from the kitchen, so she peered over with mild interest. She would generally watch "Hollywood Minute" if she happened to be in range when the segment came on, but it was hardly something she ran out of the bathroom with a mouth full of toothpaste for.

She watched as the television cut to Sarah Stevens greeting her public with excitement.

"Good morning, everyone! Today I have a treat for all you viewers—at least the female ones, that is." The reporter lowered her voice conspiratorially. "This weekend, Hollywood Minute caught up with someone special as he enjoyed a four-day gambling spree in Las Vegas—none other than our favorite leading man, Jason Andrews!"

The coffee mug fell from Taylor's hand and tumbled loudly into the sink.

She stood there and watched in disbelief as the television cut to footage of Sarah Stevens holding a microphone outside the Bellagio hotel. Just then, Jason Andrews exited through the revolving door, with some grungy-looking guy who appeared wholly uninterested in the mob of fans and paparazzi that immediately swarmed them.

The reporter pushed her way through the crowd and called out eagerly.

"Jason! Hi! Sarah Stevens with *L.A. Mornings*." She barreled over to him, cameraman in tow. "Do you have a minute to say hello to our viewers?" She immediately shoved the microphone in his face.

For the quickest second, Jason appeared annoyed. But then he flashed Sarah Stevens one of his perfect-teeth smiles.

"Of course. I always have time for fans."

"Have you been enjoying Las Vegas?" The reporter asked breathlessly.

"I always enjoy Las Vegas."

Taylor noticed how the reporter glowed, positively basking in Jason's presence. Or maybe it was just the blinding white light of his teeth.

"You know I have to ask," Sarah continued coyly. "Who are you here with?"

Jason gestured to the grungy guy, who stood somewhat uncomfortably on the outskirts of the crowd.

"Sorry, no gossip to report this time. We decided to come out here on Thursday, sort of a last-minute guy's trip. You know how it is—sometimes, the tables just call you."

Taylor's mouth fell open as she glared incredulously at the twenty-seven-inch prick in her living room.

A last-minute guy's trip? *That* was the reason she had to work all weekend?

But that wasn't enough. Oh no, far from it.

"I hear you're about to start production on a new film—a legal thriller," Sarah Stevens said. "That must be keeping you awfully busy."

Jason shrugged this off with a breezy smile and delivered the final blow.

"Obviously not busy with anything important enough to tempt *me* to miss a weekend in Vegas." He and Sarah Stevens shared a hearty laugh over this.

But back in her kitchen, Taylor Donovan was not laughing.

Jason Andrews had just insulted her in front of the entire world.

Well, fine—maybe only the people who were watching "Hollywood Minute" on that particular morning. And really only those people who actually knew he had been scheduled to meet with her last week.

Jason Andrews had just insulted her in front of at least fourteen people.

And suddenly, Taylor's feelings toward the actor were no longer very cordial.

She grabbed the remote control and with a satisfactory push of the button, made Jason Andrews disappear.

"Asshole!"

It was the only word she could manage.

Four

GIVEN HER FOUL mood, when Taylor walked into Judge Fowler's courtroom that morning to argue her motion in limine, she was ready to kick some serious ass.

She and Derek took their seats at the defendant's table. Her opposing counsel, Frank, was already waiting at the table opposite them. Seeing that all parties were present, the clerk of court called the room to order as the judge entered.

"All rise! This court is now in session, the Honorable Arlander Fowler presiding." The clerk, judge, and court reporter all sat. Taylor and Frank approached the podium as the judge sifted through his papers.

"Frank Siedlecki, representing the EEOC, Your Honor."

"Good morning, Your Honor. Taylor Donovan, for the defendant."

And then the most extraordinary thing happened in that courtroom that morning, at the very moment when Taylor stated her name for the record.

Jason Andrews walked in.

Hearing Taylor introduce herself, Jason looked over curiously. Without being noticed, he took a seat in the empty back row of the galley as the judge, Taylor, and Frank continued on with their business.

The judge pulled Taylor's motion out from the stack of papers in front of him. "All right, we are here today on a continuance of defendant's final motion in limine." He peered down from the bench at Taylor. "Counselor, why don't you tell me what this is all about?"

Taylor addressed the judge from the podium, fully aware that this motion was crucial to the success of their case.

"Your Honor, the EEOC intends to have several witnesses testify about non-gender-based profanity they allegedly heard in the workplace. We're moving to prohibit all such testimony."

Frank jumped in. "Your Honor, this is a sexual harassment case—"

And Taylor promptly cut him off. "That's right. This is a *sexual* harassment case, and we are moving to prohibit testimony about language that, while profane, certainly is not *sex*-based. I apologize for my language, Your Honor, but I just don't see what the word 'shit' has to do with sexual harassment."

Over in the gallery, Jason smiled at this.

Up at the podium, Frank tried to regain control over the argument. "But these plaintiffs are women, Your Honor, and the EEOC can establish that they often heard that particular word and others like it in the workplace, and that they found such language to be harassing."

Taylor quickly responded. "The EEOC's problem is that *everyone* in the workplace heard this kind of profanity—both men and women."

"Your Honor, our position is that the defendant should have been aware that women as a whole, as a gender, would be more . . . sensitive to these types of words," Frank said in his most self-righteous tone.

At that, Taylor held up a hand with disdain.

"I'm sorry, Judge. But that kind of paternalistic view is more offensive than anything my client is accused of. The purpose of the Civil Rights Act is not to turn our workplaces into Sunday school; it's meant to prevent *discrimination*. The

EEOC might not like the word 'shit,' but too bad. It's not discriminatory."

Considering the argument finished, Taylor folded her arms over her chest and waited for the ruling.

Up at his bench, the judge peered down at the parties as he debated the merits of each position. After a moment, he spoke.

"I have to agree with Ms. Donovan on this one. There are a lot of things that all of us have to put up with at work, things we don't particularly like, but that doesn't make those things discriminatory. Defendant's motion in limine is granted."

The judge banged his gavel as the clerk of court stamped the motion. "I think that wraps us up for today, counselors. Submit your joint pretrial order to me by Friday. This court stands in recess."

As the judge stood to leave, everyone in the courtroom rose. Satisfied with the ruling, Taylor turned pleasantly to Frank.

"So, should we plan to talk tomorrow about the pretrial order?" Arguing was like a sport to Taylor and like all professionals, she left the game on the field.

Frank, however, did not appear to be of a similar mind-set. Ignoring her, he grabbed his briefcase and stormed off without saying one word.

Taylor shrugged this off. Oh well. He probably was just pissed he didn't get to swear in court, too.

She returned to the defendant's table and began packing files into her briefcase. Suddenly, she felt Derek nudge her hip.

"Isn't that Jason Andrews?" he asked in a low, excited whisper.

Taylor glanced up and saw a man heading over from the galley, walking up the aisle toward her.

It was indeed Jason Andrews.

The twenty-five-million-dollar-per-picture star paused for a brief moment when she first looked up. Then he flashed her that famous smile.

"You must be Taylor."

Taylor maintained her even stare. Well, well, well. His Exalted High-and-Mightiness had finally decided to drop in after all.

As Jason Andrews strolled over in his black button-down shirt and charcoal-gray pin-striped pants (both of which fit so perfectly they appeared to have been hand-tailored just for him), two thoughts crossed Taylor's mind.

One—he wasn't wearing a suit and tie in court.

Two—he was unbelievably gorgeous in person.

She quickly obliterated this second, wholly irrelevant, thought from her mind. She managed to keep her face a mask of steady indifference as the actor sauntered up to her.

"Your office said you would be here," he said easily, explaining his presence. "Looks like I got here just in time for the fireworks." He winked as if they were in on some joke together.

Taylor glared at him. So deadly was her look, a lesser man would've been out the courtroom door in two seconds flat.

But Jason was undaunted. He smiled amiably. "You're right—where are my manners? I haven't properly introduced myself." He held out his hand in introduction. "I'm Jason—"

Taylor cut off the whole charm routine ASAP. She had seen smiles like that before and was now decidedly immune from them.

"I obviously know who you are, *Mr. Andrews.* I also know that you were supposed to be at my office on two different days last week."

Jason pulled back his hand, as if surprised by her curt tone.

Off to the side, Derek had been wholly forgotten in the fray. The junior associate stepped forward and cleared his throat to remind Taylor and Jason of his presence.

"Um, Taylor, I'm going to head back. Should I stop by your office tomorrow to talk about the pretrial order?" He glanced between the two of them.

Taylor eyed Jason coolly as she answered. "You can come by later today, Derek. I won't be long with this."

With one final glance between the two, Derek gathered the

case files and hurried out of the courtroom. Leaving Taylor and Jason alone.

She folded her arms across her chest. "What exactly can I do for you, Mr. Andrews?"

She noticed that the corners of his mouth twitched almost into a grin, as if he found her formal use of his last name to be amusing. This only annoyed her even more.

"I see you're a little upset about the appointments I missed last week," he said in a teasing tone. A tone, Taylor noted, that was very similar to the one she herself used when deliberately attempting to infuriate her opponents.

How dare he.

"Unfortunately, I got tied up at the last minute," Jason continued, with no attempt to conceal his air of condescension. "Surely you understand . . . I'm a very a busy man, *Ms. Donovan.*" He emphasized the last two words, letting her know that two could play the last-name game.

Then he brushed their differences aside with a wave. "But I'm here now, so let's get down to business." He clapped his hands together as if this settled the matter.

"But see, now *I'm* busy, Mr. Andrews."

Jason smiled patiently at her reply, like a teacher to a wayward child. He took a step closer, and Taylor noticed that he towered over her. She thought all actors were supposed to be short in person. Of course, *he* would have to be the exception.

Because Taylor refused to budge an inch, they now stood quite close. Jason peered down at her, his eyes boring straight into hers.

"Ms. Donovan," he said in a matter-of-fact tone. "*No one* is too busy for me."

He paused to let his words sink in. Taylor's eyes narrowed, but she said nothing. Jason apparently took this as a sign of acknowledgment.

"Good, now that that's settled . . ." He stepped away and gestured grandly to the courtroom as if issuing a command. "Why don't you show me something . . . lawyerly?"

He looked around as if trying to get familiar with the environment. "The script has several scenes where I have to cross-examine witnesses. Start by showing me an example of that. But not the crap you see on TV—I want to look real."

Taylor bit her lip and peered down at the floor to keep from laughing out loud. He was so ridiculously arrogant, it was almost amusing. Unable to conceal her smirk, she looked back up at him and folded her arms across her chest. "I'm afraid I can't do that."

Jason turned around. "Why not?"

"For starters, I don't have a witness."

He pointed to himself. "What about me?"

And in that moment, Taylor was struck with sudden devious inspiration. She cocked her head in contemplation, then nodded agreeably for the first time since Jason had shown up.

"Okay, sure." she gestured across the courtroom. "Why don't you take a seat in the witness stand?"

Jason threw her an approving look—apparently glad to see she was back with the program—and did as she asked. She waited for him to get comfortable, then positioned herself directly in front of the witness stand.

Taylor launched into the first question of her "mock" cross-examination.

"Mr. Andrews—you are aware, are you not, that your assistant made arrangements for you to be at my office last Thursday?"

Jason smiled as if he found her challenge to be amusing. He eased back in the witness stand, getting comfortable. "Yes, I am aware of that, Ms. Donovan."

"You did not show up for that appointment, did you?"

"That is correct."

"And you are aware that after failing to show up for that first appointment, your assistant made subsequent arrangements for you to be at my office on Friday morning; is that correct?"

Jason stretched out and crossed one leg over the other, seemingly unconcerned with such a trifling line of questioning.

"That is also correct. As I indicated earlier, I got tied up unexpectedly with other matters. A film emergency." As he said this, he casually turned his watch around his wrist.

Taylor raised an eyebrow incredulously. "A film emergency?"

"That's right."

She let this sit for a moment, and then walked over to the lawyer's table and pulled her cell phone out of her briefcase. "Let me show you what has been marked as Exhibit A." She crossed back to Jason and held up the cell phone.

"Do you recognize Exhibit A, Mr. Andrews?"

Jason leaned forward and peered at the phone with mock uncertainty. "Well, now, I can't be sure . . . but it appears to be a cell phone."

"Do you own a cell phone, Mr. Andrews?"

"Three of them, actually."

"And do you know how to operate your three cell phones?"

Jason humored her with a smile. "Of course."

At this, Taylor eased back, sitting on the edge of the lawyer's table.

It was time, she decided, to kick things up a notch.

JASON WATCHED AS Taylor casually crossed one high-heeled leg over the other. Unable to resist, his eyes flickered down to her legs for just the briefest second. Then he quickly glanced back up.

When his gaze met Taylor's, he detected the faintest trace of a smug smile in her eyes. It was then he realized something.

She was toying with him.

She was toying with *him*.

Taylor paused until she appeared satisfied that Jason's eyes were focused back on hers, then continued with her questions.

"By any chance, did you have any of your three cell phones with you last week in Las Vegas, Mr. Andrews?"

"Of course."

"So you could've called my office to say you couldn't make our meetings?"

Jason laughed as if this was the funniest thing he'd ever heard. "Like I make any of those calls myself."

Taylor eased off the table and strolled casually toward the witness stand.

"Well then, couldn't you have asked one of your numerous assistants to call me? Or were things at the Bellagio hotel—oh, sorry—your 'film emergency'"—she made mocking finger quotes—"so crazy that you couldn't get around to it?"

She waited expectantly for Jason's answer.

He deflected the question easily. He certainly hoped she had something better than that.

"So you got me, Ms. Donovan. I was in Las Vegas. That's some impressive lawyering, considering I was only *caught on television*."

"And the reason you didn't have someone call my office?"

"It didn't seem like a big deal," he replied breezily. "I didn't think I needed an excuse."

"Well if that's true," Taylor asked pointedly, "then why did you first try to make up the story about a film emergency?"

Jason paused at this.

Oops.

He shifted uncomfortably in his seat, suddenly a bit tangled up in his "testimony."

Taylor approached the witness stand, her eyes sparkling triumphantly. "What exactly was your plan here, Mr. Andrews? To just walk in and flash your little smile, no questions asked?"

Actually, that pretty much had been his plan.

Jason folded his arms across his chest and merely shrugged dismissively at her question.

Taylor seized upon his gesture, her voice dripping with sarcasm. "Oh, I'm sorry, Mr. Andrews, but your answers have to be audible for the court reporter. Was that a 'yes'?"

Jason gazed at her evenly, annoyed by her tone. She returned the look.

"*Yes*, Ms. Donovan," he finally replied. "That may have been my plan. To flash my little smile, no questions asked."

She leaned against the witness stand. "How's that plan working out for you, Mr. Andrews?"

His eyes locked with hers.

"Not so well."

Taylor smiled confidently, as if to say her work there was finished.

"Good. I have no further questions."

And with that, she strutted over to the lawyer's table and threw her briefcase over her shoulder. Without so much as a second glance, she walked out of the courtroom with her head held high. The door swung, then shut firmly behind her.

Leaving Jason alone.

Sitting stupidly in the witness stand.

He looked around, waiting for the cameras and people to come pouring out, letting him in on the practical joke. Clooney loved to pull stunts like this.

So Jason waited. And waited some more.

But . . . nothing.

And it then began to occur to Jason that this was not a joke, that indeed Taylor Donovan had actually *meant* to insult him. Which then raised one very serious question.

What the hell kind of shit was *that*?

Jason quickly flashed back through every detail of his encounter with her. Each and every sassy, sarcastic word. He hadn't been spoken to like that in years.

Jason glanced over at the door that Taylor had just stormed out of. And slowly, his face changed into a smile.

Interesting.

Very interesting.

Five

"**SO HOW DID** the meeting with the lawyer go?"

Jason glanced over at the passenger seat, surprised that Jeremy remembered. He had mentioned the meeting in passing to his friend last Friday in Vegas, around four in the morning as they devoured burritos from some sketchy dive seven blocks off the Strip. (Jeremy had used the old "at least no one will recognize you here" trick.)

Of course, Jason hadn't mentioned then that the meeting with the lawyer was supposed to have occurred earlier that very same day, right about the same moment when he and Jeremy had sidled up to the craps table in the Bellagio's VIP room. If Jeremy had known that particular detail, he undoubtedly would've made some sarcastic remark that Jason—by Friday night being over $100,000 down from said craps table—was in no mood to hear.

It wasn't the money, Jason repeatedly told Jeremy (who had quite unsympathetically pointed out that he made about ten times that amount in one day of filming)—it was the principle of the matter. He simply hated losing.

Jason turned his eyes back to the road as he considered

how to answer his friend's question. Driving like Mario Andretti on crack cocaine—he had learned a long time ago that it was the only way to avoid being followed by the paparazzi—he skillfully sped his black Aston Martin Vanquish to the off-ramp that would lead them to the Staples Center. He and Jeremy had tickets that evening to the Lakers/Knicks game. Courtside seats, of course. It was one of the few perks of Jason's fame that Jeremy actually lowered himself to take advantage of.

Jason tried to think of the best way to describe his meeting with the illustrious Ms. Taylor Donovan, Esquire.

"The meeting with the lawyer was . . . enlightening," he finally settled on.

Jeremy stopped gripping the black leather armrests of the passenger seat, relaxing now that Jason was pulling off the highway. "Was he any good?"

"*She* does one hell of a cross-examination, I can tell you that," Jason said, smiling to himself.

Jeremy glanced over and studied him carefully. "What aren't you telling me here?"

Somehow, Jeremy was the one guy who always seemed to know when he was hiding something. The two of them had come to Los Angeles almost sixteen years ago, with big dreams of making it in the film industry. When Jason's acting career took off like a rocket, virtually every aspect of his life had changed. Their friendship was one of the few things that had not. Jeremy was the last remaining bridge to normality in Jason's world—a fact Jeremy never missed a chance to remind him of.

"What makes you think I'm not telling you something?" Jason asked innocently.

"The last time you made that face was two months ago at the Four Seasons bar, after your interview with the reporter from *Vanity Fair*. When you asked me to come up in one hour and scream 'Fire!' outside your room."

Jason laughed. Good times. "Hey—that *worked*. In the scramble to evacuate the building, I didn't even have to promise to call her."

"I'm sure the forty other people who had to run down twenty flights of stairs at one a.m. would be happy to know they saved you from another awkward postcoital moment."

"Come on—it was the thrill of their lives. They all thought it was very magnanimous of me to offer to hold the fire door open for everyone."

"Of course, you were the only one who knew there was actually no fire."

Jason brushed this aside. "Details, details."

Jeremy rolled his eyes. "Just tell me about the lawyer."

So many possible responses, Jason mused to himself. He could tell Jeremy how it really pissed him off that "Ms. Donovan" wasted a day of his time, when he had so few of them left to prepare before filming began; how it irked him beyond all measure that she was too stubborn to get off her high horse and let bygones be bygones (so he had missed a few appointments—that was hardly a crime); or, worst of all, how angry he was that she managed to get the better of him in her little cross-examination exercise.

Or maybe he could talk about the fact that he had literally stopped in his tracks when she first turned around and looked at him.

Because Taylor Donovan was stunning.

And he certainly hadn't been expecting that.

Long, dark hair—a deep chestnut brown—that swept across one eye and tumbled well past her shoulders in wavy layers. Fair skin that blushed a little when she was angry (as he had definitely seen firsthand) and deep, expressive green eyes.

It was her eyes that made him stop. They had a lively sparkle—a little gleam—that said she was five steps ahead of you at all times and knew it.

Of course, it also could've been the legs, Jason conceded. She had smugly caught him checking those out and *that* pissed him off, too. But he couldn't resist: in her pencil-thin knee-length skirt and Mary Jane high heels, she looked both classic and sexy at the same time, like the women in the black-and-white movies they used to watch in his film classes.

But no matter what Taylor Donovan looked like, Jason

firmly concluded, the thought of her insulting *him* and storming out of the courtroom was absolutely ludicrous.

Or highly amusing. He still couldn't decide.

Jason glanced over and saw that Jeremy was waiting for an answer.

"She was *angry* with me," he finally said with a smile, thinking that was the best way to sum up their experience.

"Angry with you?" Jeremy paused, mulling this over. "And you haven't even had sex with this one yet." Then he considered the source. "Have you?"

Jason threw him a look. "This wasn't angry like 'But didn't those three nights in London mean anything to you?' angry." He imitated a clingy woman's voice.

"More problems with the supermodel?"

"Marty's on it."

Jason cocked his head in careful contemplation. "It was different with this lawyer. She was . . ." He trailed off, searching for the right word. It was somewhat of a surprise when it came to him. "Condescending."

He glanced over at Jeremy for support. Just in time to catch his friend's grin.

"Condescending?" Jeremy repeated, as if appalled. "To Jason Andrews? Do I dare ask why?"

Jason shrugged as he pulled the Aston Martin in front of the VIP entrance of the Staples Center. "I may have blown off one or two meetings with her last week."

He shut off the car and threw Jeremy an innocent look. "I didn't think it would make a difference when I showed up this morning."

Jeremy clutched his heart in feigned shock. "You mean she didn't immediately fall on her knees in gratitude when you walked through the door?"

Jason grinned as he stepped out of the car.

"It's fair to say that's not exactly how she reacted."

"AND MAKE SURE she gets the message immediately."

Jason and Jeremy sat courtside at the Lakers game. They had just barely gotten to their seats when Jason whipped out his cell phone two minutes into the first quarter. He had made a decision during the car ride over.

This morning had not been the last he would see of Taylor Donovan.

Upon arriving at this conclusion, Jason had called his manager and asked him to personally convey the following message to her, word for word: "Mr. Andrews very much enjoyed the lesson he learned from Ms. Donovan and respectfully requests the opportunity of another meeting."

He knew she'd be amused by the subtext. He grinned as he thought about her reaction: she'd smile coyly—perhaps even toy with a lock of that fabulous long, dark hair—as she contemplated an appropriately flirtatious reply.

After hanging up with his manager, Jason happily turned his attention to the game, his mind wandering only once or twice to speculate what Taylor Donovan would be wearing during their next meeting. He liked the whole smart, sexy lawyer thing she had going on that morning. Now if she would merely undo one or two more buttons of her shirt, one might even call her a *naughty* lawyer. Perhaps she had a pair of serious librarian-like glasses to finish the look. She could pull her hair up in some sort of no-nonsense, I'm-all-about-business twist, which of course would come tumbling down in a most unbusinesslike manner right as they—

Jason's cell phone suddenly rang, interrupting his internal debate over the most comfortable position to have sex in a jury box. He liked the possibilities that little half wall presented.

He frowned when he saw that the caller was his publicist, Marty. He had expected it to be his manager, with Ms. Donovan's feigned reluctant (but secretly delighted) acceptance of his proposal. And he frowned because he was fully aware of the belief shared by his agent, manager, and lawyer that only Marty knew how to "handle" him when bearing bad news.

Jason answered his phone on the second ring.

"Yeah, Marty. What's up?"

SITTING NEXT TO Jason, Jeremy glanced over and watched as his friend's publicist delivered what apparently was some unexpected news. Jeremy could've laughed out loud when he heard Jason's reply.

"What do you mean, she 'regretfully declines' my invitation?" he said, stunned. "Well—did she say anything else?"

Although Jeremy typically had little interest in Jason's various escapades, he listened with curiosity to this particular exchange. He had overheard the message Jason had sent this Taylor Donovan person, and noted—with quite a bit of surprise—that it had bordered on being an apology. And as far as Jeremy knew, Jason Andrews hadn't apologized to a woman other than his mother in fifteen years.

Jeremy watched as Jason's expression turned to one of amusement as Marty conveyed whatever was the rest of Taylor Donovan's message.

"That's what she said?" Jason leaned back in his seat and chuckled. "Well, tell her that I *saw* her ass as she stormed out of the courtroom, and I might be tempted to do just that."

Jason listened to his publicist talk for another moment, then pointed at the phone with emphasis. "Listen to me, Marty, I don't *want* to work with anyone else. I want her. The one who thinks she can walk out on *me*. Make sure her firm understands that. And then I need you to focus on the London thing."

He waved his hand impatiently at his publicist's next words. "I told you, the whole thing was a misunderstanding. I only asked her to go *to* London. I never said she'd be coming back with me. Tell her manager that I don't want to see her name next to mine in one more gossip rag. The publicity ride is over."

With that, he firmly slammed his phone shut.

Jeremy glanced over. "The supermodel again?"

Jason frowned. "Trust me, if you had to listen to that inane babble for three days, you'd have left her in London, too. I don't care how she looks in a swimsuit—or out of it."

Hearing Jason's terse tone, Jeremy said nothing and decided to let the game distract them for a while. He knew full well how much it annoyed Jason when the women he got involved with courted the media's attention. Actresses, singers, models—it never failed: one phone call from Jason Andrews and they had a table booked at the Ivy and Ted Casablanca on their speed dial.

Jeremy glanced over as two guys in their midtwenties took the empty seats in the row behind them. He vaguely recognized one of the guys as Rob Something-or-Other, an actor on one of those CW shows, who Jeremy had met at a party being thrown by the director attached to his latest script. If he remembered correctly, Rob had been hanging around as part of Scott Casey's entourage.

As Jeremy nodded in greeting at Rob Whoever, he noticed one of the Laker girls on the sidelines, jumping up and waving frantically at them.

"I think someone's trying to get your attention." Jeremy pointed the cheerleader out to Jason. She waved giddily when Jason glanced over. He flashed her a polite half smile, then turned away disinterestedly. He rolled his eyes at Jeremy.

"Been there. Done that." Then he grinned slyly, unable to resist, and proudly pointed out several other Lakers girls. "And that. Oh, and that and that, too." He winked deviously. "Together."

"And amazingly, combined they total one brain." Jeremy replied dryly.

Jason shook his head regretfully at this.

"Unfortunately, not quite."

LATER THAT THURSDAY afternoon, when Taylor was well into her second grande skim latte of the day, she finally managed to finagle a few free moments to sit in her office and review Derek's third draft of their proposed jury instructions.

Time, she realized, had not been on her side in the three days since her encounter with Jason Andrews. Ever since Frank of the EEOC had gone on the warpath and begun viciously bashing her client, in the media, that is.

She had immediately recognized the tactic for what it was: a blatant attempt to prejudice the defendant in the eyes of potential jurors. So in return, she had personally served Frank with an emergency motion for sanctions. And after her impassioned oral argument, the judge issued a gag order in the case and severely admonished that any lawyer seen or heard speaking to the media "better bring his or her toothbrush to court" (a colloquial way to threaten lawyers with being jailed for contempt). It had been the second time that week that Frank had stormed out of the courtroom refusing to speak to her.

Now, having been sidelined for the last three days with the emergency motion, Taylor was feeling behind the ball in her trial preparations. She had just barely sat down at her desk and started her review of Derek's draft when her phone rang.

As soon as she saw the familiar 312 area code on the caller ID, Taylor picked up the handset and copped an immediate guilty plea.

"I know, I know. I'm a horrible friend."

On the other end of the line, Kate laughed. She too worked at one of Chicago's top law firms and knew full well how crazy things could get.

"You get a free pass since you're preparing for trial. They made you partner yet?"

Taylor sighed blissfully at the thought of her goal, the one thing she wanted more than anything in life. "Two years, one month and three weeks away. Give or take."

"I find it truly scary that you know that. I suppose I shouldn't even bother to ask if you're having any fun out there?"

"Before you start lecturing me, just know that some of this busyness wasn't my fault. I was temporarily sidetracked by—"

Taylor stopped, realizing that telling Kate she had met Jason Andrews would result in hours of conversation, retelling every moment in excruciating detail. Not to mention, out of fairness, she would then have to call Valerie, too. And that was a discussion that could go on for *days*.

"Never mind," Taylor said instead, covering. "I'll tell you about it some other time, over a drink." Or maybe two, or three, she thought. It would take her that long to forget how brilliantly blue Jason's eyes were when they'd fixed on her.

Whoa.

Where the hell that particular thought had come from,

popping all uninvited into her head like that, she just didn't know.

Not that she denied the fact that Jason Andrews was handsome. Tall, lean but built, with the aforementioned cobalt-blue eyes and chiseled features—she knew full well that this was the stuff that women dreamed of. But *come on*.

The man was a total penis.

Taylor forced her attention back to Kate, who was asking whether she possibly would have any free evenings in the near future.

"I don't know. Why—what's up?" she replied distractedly.

Kate hesitated. "There's someone in L.A. that I want to set you up with."

"No."

Her tone couldn't have been more definitive.

"It doesn't have to be a date, just someone to hang out with once in a while," Kate pressed. "They're not all assholes like Daniel, you know." She suddenly fell silent, presumably not having meant for that last part to slip out.

Taylor turned quiet, her expression softening at her friend's words.

"I know, Kate, but . . ." Her voice trailed off as her mind momentarily drifted back to Chicago.

But then she pulled herself together. This simply was not something she was going to think about at work.

"I appreciate the offer," she told Kate, striving for a light tone. "But I'm swamped right now, you know? It's just not a good time. Speaking of which, unfortunately, I've got to run—we're filing something tomorrow and I'm running way behind." She mumbled a quick good-bye and hung up.

After hanging up the phone, Taylor leaned back in her chair, suddenly feeling very tired. But right then, out of the corner of her eye, she saw Linda hesitating in the doorway.

Seeming to sense she had caught Taylor at a bad time, Linda smiled awkwardly. "Sorry. But Mr. Blakely wants to see you. Immediately."

A slight pit formed in Taylor's stomach. "Immediately" never boded well for an associate at a large law firm. It generally meant you had either royally screwed something up or were about to be assigned an emergency TRO.

With that in mind, Taylor nodded. She put her game face back on and quieted the butterflies in her stomach. She stood up and gracefully smoothed out her skirt.

Then she headed down the hallway to the head partner's office.

Six

SHE COULDN'T DO it.

It was late that evening, and Taylor sat in her car, the silver Chrysler PT Cruiser she had rented for her stay in Los Angeles, outside some bar called Reilly's Tavern. She tried to figure out if there was any chance she could finesse her way out of her current situation. Thinking back to the stern look Sam had given her, she seriously doubted it.

From the moment she had walked into Sam's office earlier that afternoon, she could tell they weren't there to discuss an emergency TRO. Partners doled those out as merrily as Santa's elves with candy canes, while Sam on the other hand, appeared far from happy when Taylor took a seat in front of his desk.

"I got a call today," he began in a serious tone. "Would you mind telling me what the problem is with the Andrews Project?" Sam peered down at her from the perch of his desk chair.

Oh, for crying out loud, Taylor had wanted to shout. He's *just* an actor.

But seeing the look on Sam's face, she instead attempted to

smooth things over. "Sam, I just don't think I'm well suited for this type of project. I'm sure whoever you assign next will be far—"

Sam cut her off abruptly. "Jason Andrews doesn't want anyone else. His people told me that he specifically said he wants to work with you."

Taylor found herself growing even more annoyed by this. His "people"? Oh, far be it that the mighty movie star actually pick up a phone himself. Lazy, she thought to herself. Arrogant. Self-centered, condescending, patronizing—

She noticed Sam staring at her, and suddenly wondered whether she'd been speaking out loud.

Taylor regrouped. Surely she could make Sam understand the merits of her position. "Look—it's just some stupid pride thing with him. Trust me, Jason Andrews will get over it. Plus, I'm in the middle of preparing for a trial. I know I don't need to remind you of the stakes in this case against the EEOC. Now simply isn't a good time for me—"

Sam cut her off again. "Taylor, I respect you completely. I think you're the most talented young lawyer this firm has seen, so please don't take it the wrong way when I say that I frankly don't give a *damn* what your issue is."

He held up a hand when he saw Taylor about to speak. "Jason Andrews is a very important client of this firm. We do his taxes, and we've been trying to get his litigation business for years. The guy sues anyone and everyone who prints bullshit about him."

Taylor looked up at the ceiling, trying to remain quiet. From what she had seen so far, she doubted much of it was bullshit.

Then Sam leaned forward in his chair. He peered down at her with a firm expression and said words that sent chills running down her spine.

"You go back to Jason Andrews. And you fix this."

AND SO HERE she was five hours later, sitting in her car parked on some random street in West Hollywood. Taylor peered through her windshield to get a better look at the bar, and wondered what kind of name Reilly's Tavern was for a hot celebrity hangout. She rechecked the address on the Post-it note Linda had handed her to make sure she was at the right place.

Taylor tapped her fingers nervously on the steering wheel. The thought of crawling back to Jason Andrews was just *so* humiliating. It infuriated her that, due to his "status" (which she doubted was the product of little more than sheer looks and being in the right place at the right time), people automatically gave him such deference—that with one snap of his fingers, *she* was expected to smile politely and apologize to *him*.

Hopefully Jason Andrews knows the Heimlich, Taylor thought to herself. Because she most definitely was going to choke on her words.

Realizing she couldn't sit in front of the bar all night, she got out of her car and strode briskly in her heels to the front door of Reilly's Tavern. A quick peek in the window told her that she'd been very wrong—the bar by no means was any sort of hot celebrity hangout.

As Taylor opened the door and stepped in, she felt as though she'd been transported back to the south side of Chicago, back to one of her father's off-duty cop hangouts. Decked out in aging mahogany wood, Reilly's Tavern was part sports bar, part Irish pub—complete with dartboards, pool tables, and two small televisions (both showing the same basketball game) mounted over the bar. The after-work crowd consisted almost entirely of middle-aged men, many still in their service or government uniforms.

Definitely the type of crowd who wouldn't notice a celebrity in their bar, Taylor thought, and probably wouldn't care even if they did. Maybe that was the point.

She stood hesitantly in the doorway, scanning the faces of the men seated at the bar, who in turn stared right back at her. Clearly, womenfolk didn't often frequent this particular establishment.

And just when Taylor thought she couldn't possibly have felt more self-conscious, she heard a feigned loud gasp and a voice call out her name with delight.

"Ms. Donovan!"

She turned and saw Jason Andrews near a pool table in the back. He walked over to her, pretending to be shocked.

"Why, imagine seeing you here!"

At the sight of his smug, victorious look, Taylor staggered back a few steps and fell against the door. Oh god, she couldn't do it.

Feeling a little woozy at the thought of continuing, she closed her eyes and silently said a few oms from her yoga class for serenity.

WITH HIS ARMS folded expectantly across his chest—he did indeed know what was coming—Jason's grin grew wider as he watched Taylor's reaction to his greeting. This girl seriously cracked him up. At the nauseated look on her face, he half expected her to turn around and walk right out the door without one further word.

But instead, she took a deep breath. Jason watched as she pulled herself up to what he guessed had to be no more than her full five-feet-five height and strode efficiently over.

"Don't be coy, Mr. Andrews," she said in that all-business tone of hers. "I know your assistant told you I was coming."

Jason's eyes widened innocently. At the way she'd walked over all snappy-heels, he couldn't resist hamming it up.

"*You* were looking for *me*? Whatever can I do for you, Ms. Donovan?"

Taylor stood there, staring evilly at Jason as if she wanted nothing more right then than to grab him by his cashmere zip pullover and zip it right up to his eyebrows.

But then she took another deep breath.

"It seems I may have been a bit . . . hasty when I walked out of the courtroom the other day," she told him. "My firm would very much like to work with you on your . . . little project."

He ignored her not-so-subtle dig at his film. "And you?"

She responded matter-of-factly to this. "I'm willing to put my personal preferences on the matter aside."

Jason gazed down at her. She really wasn't affected by him at all.

He found this fascinating.

"Am I correct in understanding that you dislike me, Ms. Donovan?" he asked coyly, circling around her in amusement.

Taylor followed him with her eyes, her voice even. "I won't let my feelings about you compromise my career, Mr. Andrews. You got me in a lot of trouble at work, you know."

Jason stopped, surprised to find himself uncomfortable at the thought. "I'll tell you what," he said magnanimously. "Let me buy you a drink. We can start over—get to know one another properly." He flashed her the smile that made hearts flutter worldwide. Five and a half billion dollars in lifetime box office gross for his "little projects." Take that.

Taylor cocked her head, appearing to consider his offer. Then, with her arms folded across her chest, she took a few steps toward him. When she was close enough that they were practically touching, she stared up at him, her green eyes boring deep into his. Jason could feel the warmth of her body, and he wondered if she knew what he was thinking right then.

Apparently, she did.

"Let's get something straight, Mr. Andrews," she said steadily. "This is business. Nothing else."

Before Jason could get in one word edgewise on the matter, Taylor backed away and turned to leave. "And I'll expect you to be at my office first thing tomorrow morning. Do try not to be late."

Then she flipped her hair over her shoulders and, in what was admittedly not a half-bad impersonation, threw the very words Jason had said earlier right back at him.

"Surely you understand, Mr. Andrews . . ." she drawled mockingly, "I am a *very* busy woman."

And with that, she turned on her heels and strode out of the bar.

Jason stood there, staring after her once again. How the hell the woman kept getting the last word in, he just didn't know.

As he watched Taylor pass by the windows outside, Jeremy pulled up next to him. For a moment, even he seemed uncertain what to say.

"Well," Jeremy finally managed, "she seems *very* nice." He appeared to have enjoyed Jason and Taylor's little exchange. "Very spirited."

"You're right about that." Jason shot Jeremy a devilish look. "Now I just need to channel that spirit into a more . . . enjoyable outlet."

Jeremy shook his head doubtfully. "I don't know. I think you've met your match."

Jason scoffed at the very idea. "There's no such thing."

"Well, from what I've seen and heard so far, the lawyer is up by *two*."

Jason considered this. He may not have liked losing, but he loved the thrill of the game.

"We'll see how long that lasts . . ." he mused out loud. Then he followed Jeremy back to the pool table and confirmed that the next shot was his. He studied the pool table, suddenly feeling lighter, more alive than he had in a long time. In fact, he couldn't remember the last time something had piqued his interest as much as this lawyer had.

Jason leaned over the pool table and aimed. He shot and expertly fired the cue ball off the corner of his own striped nine ball, which spun and rolled neatly into the left side pocket. He straightened up and smiled confidently at Jeremy.

Game on.

THE NEXT MORNING, Taylor could feel the buzz the minute she stepped off the elevator. Perhaps it was the fact that everyone stopped and stared as she walked through the corridor on the way to her office. Or perhaps it was the gaggle of secretaries who huddled around Linda's desk, passing a mirror between them as they reapplied lipstick and fluffed their hair. It could mean only one thing.

Jason Andrews was in her office.

Taylor headed over to Linda's desk. When she got there, her secretary pointed to her office, then raised a finger to her lips to indicate they should be quiet.

"He's here!" she said in an excited whisper.

"I guessed that, yes."

Linda looked ready to burst into a million happy pieces as she babbled on. "I showed him straight to your office—I can't remember anything I said after 'hello'—oh my god, he's even hotter in person—and then I shut the door because people were staring." Then she quickly added for Taylor's benefit, "Not that I would do anything like that."

Taylor nodded. She realized then that she hadn't thought he would actually show up. If anything, she had expected an angry phone call from Sam that morning, asking her what the hell kind of apology involved imitating Jason Andrews to his face.

She turned toward the closed door of her office. Time to face the enemy. She glanced back at Linda, trying to buy another minute or two. "Uh, Linda, could you reserve us one of the mock trial rooms? Maybe—"

"It's already taken care of. You're in conference room A."

"Oh. Good. Lovely."

Taylor still found herself stalling. By now the entire office was watching.

Linda gestured to the door. "Well, go on. He's all yours," she said with a wink. The other secretaries giggled.

Not wanting to draw any further attention to the situation, Taylor grabbed the handle to her door and strode resolutely into her office.

"Mr. And—"

Her words trailed off because Jason, who had been standing in front of her office window checking out the view, turned around when she entered. Like a shot from a movie, the morning sun shone brilliantly around him like a god—his dark hair glinted warmly in the light, and his eyes gleamed bluer than the south Pacific Ocean.

Taylor's mind went blank. And suddenly, she couldn't remember why the hell she ever had been angry with Jason Andrews.

But then he spoke.

"Sleeping in this morning, Ms. Donovan?" he drawled.

Moment over.

"How lovely to see you again, Mr. Andrews," Taylor replied sarcastically. At least he wore a suit this time, she noted. No comment on how he looked in it.

From behind his back, Jason pulled out a medium-sized box with a blue ribbon wrapped around it.

"I brought you a peace offering."

He held the box out to her.

Taylor looked over, caught off guard by this. After hesitating for a moment, she took the box from him and sat down at her desk. Jason took a seat in one of the chairs across from her.

"I guessed you're not the flowers type," he said. Taylor glanced sharply at him, wondering how he knew that from their short interactions.

"This seemed more appropriate for you. I thought you could wear it the next time you're in court."

She raised a suspicious eyebrow at this. Oh really? But Jason's face gave nothing away.

Curiosity got the better of her, so Taylor opened the box. She rifled through the tissue paper until she found a T-shirt. When she pulled it out, she saw two words printed on the shirt in perfect reference to her infamous court argument: SHIT HAPPENS.

Taylor laughed out loud.

She looked over at Jason, reluctantly amused by the joke, and smiled.

"Okay, Mr. Andrews," she conceded. "Let's get started."

Seven

"I DON'T CARE what the script says. That's not how it works."

Taylor stood in front of the lawyer's table peering stubbornly down at Jason. They were in their tenth hour of work. She had been shocked when she checked her watch a few minutes ago and saw how late it had gotten. She supposed things would go faster if he didn't insist on fighting her over virtually every change she suggested to the script. See, for example, their current debate.

"And *I* don't see what difference it makes," Jason replied defensively. He held his script in his hand, waving it at her.

"It makes a big difference," she argued back. "While you might think you look 'pensive' and 'unimpressed' "—she finger-quoted the words he had used just moments before—"by remaining seated during your opposing counsel's argument, that's not the way it works in a real courtroom. You have to stand *every time* you argue before the judge."

Then she gestured at the script and said for the umpteenth time that day, "Didn't anyone talk to a *real* lawyer before writing this?"

My, my, Jason observed. Apparently he wasn't the only one who was a little cocky.

He watched as Taylor positioned herself at the corner of the jury box farthest from the witness stand. Earlier, she had gone and ruined their lovely "Shit Happens" moment by turning all serious the minute they stepped into her firm's mock trial room. But Jason figured there had to come a point when her armor would crack again—even if just for the slightest moment. Not that he particularly minded watching her strut sassily around the courtroom for ten hours.

"Now, we were talking about the differences between direct and cross-examination," Taylor called over from the far end of the jury box, back in teacher mode. "Unlike cross, when doing a direct examination you want to stand by the jury, so that you force the witness to look at the jurors when answering questions. That way you draw in their attention, almost as if the witness is talking directly to them."

Jason frowned at this, peering down at one of the pages in his script.

"But if I'm all the way across the courtroom, how am I supposed to throw a book at the witness?"

Taylor whirled around, appalled at such a mocking insult to the practice of law.

"The script says you're supposed to *throw a book* at a witness?" She stormed across the room and grabbed the script from him. She skimmed furiously, turning the pages back and forth as she searched for the offensive passage.

After a few moments, she looked up at Jason, confused. "That's not what it says."

He smiled. Gotcha.

Taylor folded her arms across her chest. "Very funny."

"It's just too easy." He laughed. Then he braced himself for the expected stinging retort.

But instead Taylor was silent, having already turned her attention back to the script. She flipped through several pages.

"This dialogue . . ." She trailed off, as if troubled. She sat down at the table next to Jason.

He looked over and saw the particular section of the script she was focused on: the midpoint of the screenplay, where his character destroyed a key witness for the opposition with a brutal cross-examination. The scene was one of his favorites, so he was surprised she seemed bothered by it.

"What's wrong with the dialogue?" he asked, peering over her shoulder. "I didn't think it was bad."

"It's not that it's bad," she replied. She glanced up at him and blushed slightly, hesitating.

"Never mind. I'm being too much of a lawyer here."

Jason gazed firmly at her. He never compromised with acting, no matter how small the details. And for whatever reason, he found he valued Taylor Donovan's opinion quite a bit.

"No, seriously. I want to know what you think."

Taylor took in his earnest expression. She frankly had been surprised by his attitude during their ten hours together. Blowing off their meetings for a weekend in Las Vegas certainly had, in her mind, been a good indication of his work ethic. But, quite to the contrary, she would have to admit that Vason seemed truly interested in the various trial techniques she had demonstrated and had asked her many questions throughout the day. Some of them were even good ones.

So Taylor slid the problematic script over so that they both could read from it.

"Well, for starters, this scene is supposed to be a cross-examination, right?" She pointed to the troublesome sequence.

Jason frowned. "Yes. Why?" He moved in closer to get a better look at the script.

"See—your problem is that none of these questions are leading questions." She saw his head tilt in confusion, so she explained further. "All of these questions are open-ended. You would never ask them on cross, because cross-examination is all about controlling the witness. You force the witness to say the things *you* want, and only those things. And you certainly don't give the witness any opportunity to explain himself."

Taylor picked up the script to demonstrate. "Like here— your character asks: 'So what, exactly, was your intention that evening, Mr. Robbins?' and a few lines further down you say, 'Then tell us exactly what you were thinking when you realized your wife was dead.' The problem is, those questions give your witness all sorts of wiggle room. You should say something more like this—"

She faced Jason to demonstrate and began to reinvent his lines.

"And your intention that evening was to tell your wife about the affair you were having, wasn't it?" She slipped easily into the part. "Weren't you, in fact, *relieved* when you saw your wife's lifeless body floating in the swimming pool, Mr. Robbins?"

As she proceeded to demonstrate—off the top of her head, no less—a modified cross-examination, there was no doubt in Jason's mind that she had just made the scene about five times stronger. He watched, impressed, and it struck him how much he liked looking at her while she worked.

In fact, he realized, he just liked looking at her.

At that moment, Taylor seemed to notice that he was staring at her. She stopped and smiled in embarrassment.

"Sorry. I'm completely boring you with all this, aren't I?"

That smile did the craziest things to him. Jason tried to brush this off, clearing his throat. "No, not at all," he told her. "Please—continue."

Taylor cocked her head, curious.

"You're awfully serious about this, aren't you? I mean, playing a lawyer can't exactly be your most challenging role."

Jason studied Taylor for a long moment, considering her question. Then he leaned in—close enough so that his arm brushed lightly against hers.

"How long have you been practicing law?" he asked, seemingly out of nowhere.

Taylor blinked, a bit surprised by the transition. "Six years. Why?"

"How many cases have you won?"

She smiled matter-of-factly. "All of them."

"Do you prepare any less now, just because you're more familiar with what you're doing?"

"No, of course not."

"Why not?"

"Because I always want to do the best possible job."

Jason looked at her pointedly. "Ditto."

Taylor tilted her head in concession. "Fair enough."

Jason smiled with her, and for a moment they were just two people being themselves, without anything else mattering.

Until the ring of his cell phone shrilly interrupted the mood, that is.

With a good deal of reluctance, Jason turned his attention away from Taylor and pulled his phone out of his jacket. He checked to see who was calling, then glanced over in explanation. "Sorry—it's my publicist, Marty. He has a fit if he can't reach me." He rolled his eyes in exaggeration.

Taylor smiled. Kind of like partners, she thought.

"Marty! How are you?" Jason answered his phone with affection, knowing full well that he drove the man crazy. As Jeremy liked to joke, Jason's publicist was the busiest man in show business.

Taylor watched as he listened to whatever news his publicist conveyed. She saw that his expression turned strangely serious.

"I understand," Jason said, sounding very disappointed. Taylor wondered if he had just lost out on some part. "I guess it was to be expected." With a terse good-bye, he hung up the phone.

Taylor noticed that Jason stared at his cell phone for a moment longer. When his eyes looked up and found hers, she could've sworn he seemed angry.

"Well, Ms. Donovan. It seems we have a problem."

TAYLOR STARED OUT the lobby windows of her office building, at the enormous mob of paparazzi that had gathered outside. Hovering like vultures and perched with their cameras, they waited in anticipation for their five-hundred-thousand-dollar shot to emerge. She saw that a few photographers had even gone so far as to climb the trees that flanked the building's courtyard.

"It's a madhouse out there," she murmured in amazement, taking in the scene. "I don't think I've ever seen so many cameras in one place."

Jason stood behind her, not amazed in the slightest.

"Any idea how they found out I'm here?"

Mesmerized by the media circus, Taylor didn't notice the sharp edge to his voice.

"Probably one of the secretaries, if I had to guess."

She looked away from the windows and noticed that the office building was deserted. She had worked late many evenings since coming to Los Angeles, so she was familiar with the routine.

"They lock the other doors after seven," Taylor said. "This is the only way out."

"How convenient."

Jason didn't bother to hide his bitterness. For some reason, he felt like he'd been punched in the gut since the moment Marty had called to let him know that someone had tipped off the media to his whereabouts. Of course, he should've known that Taylor Donovan would inevitably use his name to make one for herself. How typical. He just couldn't figure out why it bothered him so much this time.

She suddenly turned away from the windows and faced him. This is the part, Jason thought, where she feigns annoyance, then asks how she looks as she primps for the cameras. Ready for my close-up, Mr. DeMille.

And so Taylor shrugged, as if accepting the fate of their situation. "Well, I guess this is where you do your thing," she said, gesturing to the door that was their only way out. "Have fun." And with that, she did the unthinkable.

She walked away.

She had gone only a few steps when she glanced back at Jason, apparently with one final thought. "It's been . . . interesting, Mr. Andrews," she said. Then she hurried off toward the elevator bank.

Jason stood there, speechless. Funny how he seemed to be like that quite a bit whenever he was around her.

He watched for a few moments, thoroughly confused, as

Taylor walked away. Then he finally managed to find his voice.

"Wait!"

She stopped abruptly when he shouted and turned around. He gestured questioningly to the door.

"Aren't you coming, too?"

Taylor stared at him incredulously. "Are you crazy? There must be a hundred cameras out there. I'll leave later, when everyone's gone."

Jason's jaw almost hit the floor. "Let me get this straight," he said slowly. "You *don't* want to be seen with me?"

He then looked at Taylor with such disbelief she couldn't help but smile. He was quite cute when utterly clueless.

"I have a trial in one week," she told him. "I can't risk being accused of trying to bias the jury pool by being seen in the media with a celebrity. The judge could throw me off the case for that."

Then she looked at Jason pointedly. "Besides, my client is trying to beat sexual harassment charges. They need to look as morally upright as possible. It would border on malpractice for me to link them to you."

Jason blinked and almost laughed. No offense taken.

And it was in that moment, at her refreshing disinterest in the publicity that constantly surrounded his life, that Jason felt the strangest sensation—a slightly panicky, breathless feeling, like riding on a roller coaster.

It was an odd feeling for him—something he couldn't quite identify—but he knew one thing.

He didn't want her to leave.

"But what about the film?" he blurted out, trying to think of something, anything, to keep her from walking away. "You said it yourself, there are problems with the script." He looked at her pointedly as his words tumbled out in a rush. "And how about me? We didn't cover all of my courtroom scenes—I need to be sure I look like I know what I'm doing."

Taylor turned all the way around to face him. She took him in for a moment, then smiled.

"You will make a great attorney. Jason."

It was the first time she said his name.

Then, just like that, she turned and sprinted off to the elevator bank. And before Jason could say anything further, she was gone.

He stood alone in the lobby, staring after her. Oblivious to the fact that the paparazzi were on the move, that they had caught sight of him and were beginning to descend with their cameras. They lined the windows and surrounded him, moving in as a pack. But Jason didn't notice the bright, burning flashes that exploded all around him, because he had only one thought on his mind.

There was no way this was over.

Eight

JEREMY WAS ABSOLUTELY correct in calling Jason's publicist the busiest man in show business. Marty Shepherd, cofounder of the Shepherd/Grillstein Company—the top publicity firm in Los Angeles—could not recall the last time he had slept more than four hours in a row.

Being the eyes, ears, and voice of most of the film industry's top acting talent was no easy feat. Not that he had any problem representing directors or writers, but no one ever cared what they did. Ron Howard or M. Night Shyamalan could snort cocaine off the ass of the script girl in the middle of an on-set orgy, and that still would be less gossip-worthy than whether Jennifer Lopez wore her wedding band while eating lunch at the Polo Lounge.

For a de minimis 5 percent of all gross earnings, Marty's responsibilities could be boiled down to one pithy mantra that every associate in his firm was expected to eat, sleep, and die by: make sure your client is someone whose fuckups are newsworthy, and fuck anyone that makes up news about your client.

It was the second half of Marty's mantra that kept him in

the office so late on this particular Friday evening. Rebecca, an associate whose only assignment was to assist Marty in the various issues that arose with one particularly challenging client, had just stopped by his office.

"We've gotten calls from *Us Weekly*, *In Touch*, and *Star*. They want to know what Jason Andrews was doing in an office building downtown," Rebecca reported. "They claim he was with a woman, although she apparently slipped off before anyone snapped her picture."

For a brief moment, Marty wondered how the woman—who he assumed was this Taylor Donovan person Jason insisted on working with—managed to get out of the building without being photographed. Not an easy feat when traveling with Jason Andrews.

"Tell them he was getting cash from the ATM"—Marty almost laughed at the idea himself—"and that the woman was a building employee who stopped him for an autograph." With those instructions, Rebecca nodded and left.

And then for the next half hour, Marty sat alone in his office and contemplated just how big of a problem Taylor Donovan was going to be.

It went without saying that Jason Andrews was his top client. In fact, Jason Andrews was the top, period. The biggest name in Hollywood—a status he had held for a long, long time.

Which was precisely what worried Marty, who got paid to worry when no one else did.

God knows it wasn't easy to get to the top. But staying there was even tougher. Jason had that rare kind of star quality that came around only once a generation: women loved him, and men wanted to be him. *Rolling Stone* magazine had hit the proverbial nail on the head: his quick wit and easy charm did indeed call to mind Cary Grant or Clark Gable. But there was something about Jason that was just that little bit more down to earth than the icons of the classic films. Marty had never been able to figure out exactly what that "something" was, although he secretly suspected it had something to do with the fact that Jason was from Missouri.

Unfortunately, Hollywood—like many of its inhabitants—had a wandering eye. There was nothing the town liked more than the "new face," or discovering the next person who everyone would hail as "up-and-coming."

And after sixteen years in the business, being an undisclosed "thirtysomething" years old, Jason Andrews was neither of those things.

Luckily, the end was nowhere in sight. Jason's next movie, *Inferno*, would be released in just a few weeks and had been predicted to be the blockbuster of the summer. He would follow that tent-pole pic with the legal thriller he was about to begin filming for Paramount, a film for which Marty had high hopes of a third Oscar nomination.

In Marty's mind, therefore, the only thing Jason needed to do was to keep doing everything *exactly* as he had for the past sixteen years. Which—from a publicity standpoint—meant wining and dining only the most famous of actresses, supermodels, pop stars, and the occasional billionaire heiress.

Taylor Donovan, however, was none of those things. As far as Marty was concerned, in terms of media exposure, the only thing worse than dating nobody was dating *a* nobody.

With *Inferno* about to be released, the public was ready for another full-fledged Jason Andrews romance. And Marty Shepherd—publicist to the stars and eighth most powerful person in Hollywood (once talent and studio heads were excluded)—was determined to give them one.

With these thoughts in mind, Marty picked up the copy of *People* magazine that Rebecca had handed him earlier that week. He flipped through "The Women of Jason Andrews!" article until he came to the last picture of Jason and the actress who'd been cast as the female lead in the legal thriller—Naomi Cross.

Marty smiled, thinking how nice Naomi looked standing next to Jason. She was an ingénue and a media darling. Even better, she was British, which meant double the UK and European exposure.

Yes, Marty mused to himself, Naomi Cross was just the answer he'd been looking for.

WAY ACROSS TOWN, in a recently purchased five-bedroom home nestled in the heart of the Hollywood Hills, someone else was looking at that very same picture of Jason Andrews and Naomi Cross.

But unlike Marty, Scott Casey was not smiling.

In fact, he was pretty damn pissed off.

His publicist had promised that *he* was going to be on the cover of that very issue of *People*, not Jason Andrews. Again.

The story—or so his publicist had said—was supposed to focus on Scott's move from Sydney, Australia, to Los Angeles. How he had made the decision, given his recent film success, to live full time in the States.

Scott doubted there were few people in America who didn't already know his story (not that he minded it being told over and over again in *GQ*, *Vanity Fair*, *Esquire*, and *Movieline*). The interviews all focused on the same basic facts: he had shot to fame little more than thirteen months ago after costarring in the epic fantasy-adventure, *A Viking's Quest*. Women had gone absolutely mad for the character he played in the film. In fact, during the five months the movie ran worldwide in theaters, his name was Googled more than any other search term.

It was nothing that Scott, nor any of the people working with him during the production of *A Viking's Quest*, had foreseen. In fact, Scott had had to fight just to audition for the role. His look was too "pretty boy" to play a Viking, the director had originally said. But his agent cajoled, pleaded, pulled strings, and got Scott the audition, which eventually led to a screen test. After much deliberation, the director and producers decided that Scott's picture-perfect handsome face was an interesting contrast to the lead actor's rugged, unkempt look. And to match his lean appearance, they gave Scott's character a kick-ass bow and arrow to fight with instead of a clunky sword.

It worked. Boy, did it ever work. On screen, he was fierce

and feral—yet somehow graceful at the same time. And when the camera zoomed in and held longingly on his soulful hazel eyes—his blond hair ruffling in the wind—no woman in the audience could help but be breathlessly glued to every frame.

A star was born.

After the release of the film, Scott was immediately labeled Hollywood's "It Guy" and offered a wealth of the best parts in town. Seizing the day, he went after a role he had dreamed of playing since his high school Contemporary Lit class: the lead in the film adaptation of the novel *Outback Nights*.

Although it was one of the most sought-after parts in Hollywood, Scott believed himself to be a shoo-in. Notwithstanding the fact that he had launched onto the industry's A-list virtually overnight, he had the added benefit of actually being Australian. So he went to lunch with the producers and even sacrificed an entire Saturday night of clubbing with his friends to have dinner with the film's director at his ranch in Santa Barbara. Two days later, his agent called with the big news.

They had offered him the fucking *supporting* role.

The part of the sidekick, the friend who dies violently on page eighty-eight of the script, whose death spurs the protagonist—the *lead* actor—to face his adversaries and demons, save the town, and get the girl in the climatic third act.

A lead role that had been offered to Jason Andrews.

The studio had apparently gotten a copy of the script to him last minute, and Jason was interested. It was an unbelievable coup, the producers said, certain that Scott would understand. They simply couldn't pass on a chance to land Jason Andrews. No one did.

Amidst a string of Aussie-flavored profanities, Scott told his agent in no uncertain terms that he was *done* playing supporting parts (unless of the indie, Oscar-garnering type, of course). And he certainly was no sidekick to Jason Andrews. Then he angrily took off to Cabo San Lucas to fume in a twenty-five-hundred-dollar-a-night bungalow.

It was on the second day of his trip, as he was halfway through his fourth Corona of the afternoon and getting a poolside blowjob from Chandra, a reality television "actress" who happened to be staying at the same resort, when his agent called again.

The studio's negotiations with Jason Andrews had come to a halt over a salary dispute. They wanted Scott for the lead role.

Scott accepted, but not until after the producers, the director, his agent, and the studio had all sufficiently pacified his ego. He resented being second choice for a role that should have been his from the start. And so he resolved that he would prove something to the producers, the director, his agent, the studio, and anyone else who doubted him.

Jason Andrews was nothing special.

The time had come for the king's reign to end.

It was a vow that Scott repeated that very Friday evening, as he flipped through the pages of *People* magazine. He sat poolside again, but this time by his own swimming pool in the new house he had purchased with the money he had earned from *A Viking's Quest*. After finishing the 500 laps his personal trainer ordered, Scott had turned to the weekly gossip magazines his assistant dropped off every Friday morning.

Feeling a cool evening breeze cutting across the Hollywood Hills, Scott pulled on the Von Dutch T-shirt he'd left on the lounge chair. His pool overlooked an amazing view of downtown Los Angeles that should have captured his attention. But the picture of Jason Andrews sitting on the chair next to him sullied the sight on that particular evening.

Scott ripped the picture of Jason out of the magazine and crumpled it into a ball. Then he pitched it into the garbage can sitting on the edge of the deck.

This cover story would be the last thing he lost to Jason Andrews, Scott vowed. Next time, it would be *Jason* who wanted something. Something important.

And he would be there to make sure Jason didn't get it.

Nine

"HOW WILL THE alleged harassers do in court?"

Taylor confidently met Sam's gaze from across the gray marble conference table. They were now only two days from the start of trial, and he had called her earlier that morning wanting to meet for a last-minute "strategy talk." This was partner-speak for making sure Taylor knew what the hell she was doing.

"They are prepped and ready," she replied without hesitation. "They'll do great."

Derek sat to Taylor's right, taking notes on his laptop as Sam continued his questions. He had been firing them at Taylor all morning.

"And your cross-examination of the named plaintiffs?"

"By the time I'm done, the jury will want to sue *them* for wasting their time on this ridiculous lawsuit." Sam, Taylor, and Derek all got a good chuckle out of this. A little lawyer humor.

Taylor subtly checked her watch and saw that it was almost noon. She hoped they were nearing the end of their meeting, since she and Derek had over twenty exhibits to compile and she still had an opening statement to write. It was time to move things along to the standard pretrial partner wrap-up: a brief lecture on the subject of managing client expectations, followed by closing remarks of the pep-talk variety.

As if reading Taylor's mind, Sam ceased his interrogation and eased back in his chair.

"Well, it looks as though you and Derek have all the bases covered," he told her. "One last thing we should briefly discuss is making sure our client fully understands the risks—"

Just then, Sam was cut off as the door to the conference room slammed opened, rattling the walls as if a tornado had just hit the building.

And a very angry-looking Jason Andrews stormed into the room.

Linda followed closely on his heels, looking highly apologetic. "I'm so sorry, Taylor—I tried to stop him," she said, out of breath.

Wholly oblivious to (or simply uninterested in) anyone else in the room, Jason stopped before Taylor and pointed furiously at her.

"Why haven't you returned my calls?"

The shock of his entrance and his demanding tone rendered her temporarily speechless.

"I called you three times today," Jason continued his rant. *"Myself,"* he added pointedly.

Taylor quickly pulled herself together and nodded reassuringly to her secretary. "It's okay, Linda. I can handle things from here."

Then she turned to face Jason.

"Mr. Andrews . . ." she said in a coolly professional tone. "Isn't this a pleasant surprise, you dropping in unexpectedly like this?" She glared at him frostily. How *dare* he interrupt her in the middle of an important business meeting with what appeared to be some sort of ridiculous celebrity tantrum. For about ten minutes when they'd been working together last Friday, she'd actually begun to believe that maybe there was some semblance of a normal guy hidden beneath the self-centered, arrogant, movie-star façade.

Apparently, she'd been mistaken.

"I wasn't aware you had called today," she told him. "I've been away from my office, in this conference room all morning."

Jason appeared to have a retort ready on his lips, but then he paused when he heard her explanation. It apparently had not been the response he had expected.

"Oh."

But his next words were far more eloquent.

"I see."

Jason looked around the room, took in Sam and Derek (who sat frozen at the table, wide-eyed), then turned to Taylor with his most charming smile.

"So how are you this morning, Ms. Donovan?"

TWENTY MINUTES AGO, when Jason had jumped into the Aston Martin and sped down to Taylor's office, his actions had seemed perfectly rational. There wasn't a person in Hollywood who didn't immediately drop everything to take his call. So when Taylor hadn't returned the three—count them, *three*—messages he had left with her secretary, he had assumed she was blowing him off. And he'd been furious thinking this—especially after the progress he thought they had made last Friday.

Unfortunately, they now appeared to have reverted back to the whole "Mr. Andrews" routine. But before Jason could say anything to clear up what obviously was just a simple miscommunication on the part of someone other than him, the gray-haired guy at the head of the conference table stood up.

"What the hell is going on here, Taylor? You told me you and Mr. Andrews had completed your project."

Quick to make amends, the gray-haired guy headed over to Jason with his hand outstretched. "Mr. Andrews . . . I'm Sam Blakely, head of the litigation group here at Gray and Dallas. I've spoken on the phone with your manager a few times."

Jason shook his hand. "Of course."

"I was under the impression you and Ms. Donovan had

finished your work together," Sam said quickly. "I want to sincerely apologize for any problems or inconvenience she has caused you."

Being taller, Jason could see over Sam's head to Taylor, and his eyes met hers at the partner's unctuous words. If looks could kill right then, Jason had no doubt he would've been lying flat on the ground with an expression of wide-eyed shock on his face and a twelve-inch hatchet lodged deep in his forehead.

Taylor came around the table to defend herself. "I'm not sure what the problem is either, Sam. It was my understanding that Mr. Andrews was very satisfied with the assistance I provided him last Friday."

"Clearly, that's not the case," Sam snapped at her. "Otherwise, why would he be here?"

Jason saw how surprised Taylor was by the angry tone of the man who presumably was her boss.

"I . . . I don't know why he's here," she faltered, turning to Jason in confusion. And in that brief moment, she suddenly looked utterly and completely lost.

It got to him. When Jason saw Taylor like that, he felt something odd . . . something he hadn't felt in a long, long time . . . an unfamiliar emotion that took him a few seconds to place.

Guilt.

Jason saw that he needed to remedy the situation. If for no other reason than to avoid future hatchet-in-forehead death glares from Taylor.

So he turned to her boss. Of course he could fix this—he had won an Oscar for chrissakes.

"I think I may have created some confusion here," Jason said. "Taylor and I did indeed finish our work last Friday. Today, I was calling her about a separate issue—a new matter on which I hoped she could share her immeasurably learned legal expertise."

He winked at Taylor, proud of this last detail. Now this Sam character would think she had brought in new business for the firm.

He was a hero.

But the Sam character apparently wasn't buying it.

"A new matter on which you need the advice of a *sexual harassment* attorney?" he asked skeptically.

Jason paused to think about this—damn lawyers with their pesky questions—when Taylor jumped in.

"That's right," she said, picking up Jason's lead. "Mr. Andrews mentioned this to me during our last meeting. He owns a production company, and was looking for advice on some employment issues that have recently arisen at his office."

Jason nodded along—hey, it worked for him. "Yes, yes, that's right—employment issues that have arisen at my production company offices. Of course."

Sam eyed them both suspiciously. "What kind of issues?"

Taylor didn't bat an eye.

"Well . . . it appears that Mr. Andrews has some problems determining what is and is not appropriate behavior in the workplace."

Jason—who had been nodding along—stopped and glanced over sharply. "Excuse me?"

Ignoring him, Taylor shook her head in grave disapproval. It was quite a performance.

"Unfortunately, it seems that Mr. Andrews has a fondness for telling dirty jokes around the office." She leaned in toward Sam, whispering. "And not even good ones—juvenile stuff. Fifth-grade humor, really."

Seeing Sam's eyes dart over toward him, Jason shifted uncomfortably. Normally he was all for ad-libbing, but this was going a little far off script.

"Umm . . . Ms. Donovan, perhaps we should discuss this in—"

"And another thing," she immediately cut him off, "he apparently demands that the women in his office address him only as 'Your Hotness.' And when speaking about him in the third person, he wants them to refer to him only as '*The* Hotness.'"

The Derek guy, who still sat over at the conference table, snorted loudly at this.

Jason threw Taylor a look of warning. "I really don't think—"

"—And of course there was the incident last week," she said, cutting him off once again.

"The incident?" Sam asked, looking slightly uncomfortable.

With a coy glance clearly thrown in for Jason's benefit, Taylor turned to Sam to explain.

"Last week, Mr. Andrews thought it would be amusing to sound the fire alarm and yell over the intercom that it was—quote—'Time for all the cute girls to run around naked.'"

Jason broke into a loud coughing fit—at this point he was ready to try anything to shut her up.

He felt Taylor patting him on the back.

"There, there, now, Mr. Andrews, that's okay," she said reassuringly. "You don't have to say a word. As your attorneys, we'll do all the talking." She turned to her boss with a wink. "Isn't that right, Sam?"

Sam took a moment, then nodded. "Yes, of course," he said politely. "Our firm would be more than happy to help Mr. Andrews with his . . . uh . . . issues. You carry on with that, Taylor."

Standing by Jason's side, Taylor smiled proudly.

"Thanks, Sam. And don't you worry—I'm quite certain that Mr. Andrews is quickly learning that there are just some things you don't do in somebody else's workplace."

She looked up at Jason with a smile that was as sweet as pie. "Isn't that right, Mr. Andrews?"

He glared at her.

It didn't take a genius to catch her real meaning.

THE MINUTE HE and Taylor stepped out into the hallway, Jason could control himself no longer.

"Are you crazy?"

Taylor furiously shushed him, and before he could say anything further, she pulled him into a corner alcove. She looked around to be certain they were alone, then whirled on him.

"Who do you think you are, storming into my office like that?" She pointed angrily in his face. "Do you realize how much trouble you almost got me into?"

"Wait—you're angry with *me*?" Jason stared at Taylor incredulously. "Do you realize the mess you've made?" Realizing that time was of the essence, he whipped out his cell phone and pushed the speed dial.

"Marty—we've got a problem," he barked into the phone as soon as his publicist answered. "Listen, in about fifteen minutes, there's going to be real shit storm—"

He was cut off as Taylor suddenly reached over and grabbed the phone out of his hand. She slammed it shut.

Jason stared at her in disbelief. "What the hell do you think you're doing?"

Furious now, he stalked toward Taylor, backing her up against the wall. Under other circumstances, his mind would have wandered nefariously at their close physical proximity, but by then he was angry even beyond the point of Naughty Lawyer fantasies.

"You know, I tolerated your little charade in there because I felt bad for getting you in trouble," Jason hissed at her. "But if you don't hand over that phone right this second, I swear I'm going to—"

"Calm down," Taylor interrupted smoothly. "There's nothing to worry about."

"Nothing to—" Jason managed to refrain from shouting the rest. He looked up at the ceiling and counted to ten to keep from throttling her.

"You just told those people that I'm a sexual deviant," he said through clenched teeth. "And apparently, one with the intelligence of a ten-year-old. Those stories will be on the Internet by this afternoon."

"Those men won't talk."

Jason glared at Taylor and grabbed his cell phone out of her hands. "You obviously need a lesson on how my life works, missy." He hit the redial button. *"Everyone* talks."

"They think I was telling the truth in there."

"No shit."

"So, if they think the things I said in there were true, then they also think that information is protected by the attorney-client privilege. Those men are legally bound *not* to repeat what I said."

His eyes meeting hers, Jason paused as this information sunk in. After a moment, he hung up his phone.

She winked. Gotcha.

"I'm not completely heartless, Mr. Andrews," she said with a grin. She turned and headed down the hallway.

Jason watched her walk away. There was something about that confidence she always had. He liked it very much.

He hurried and caught up with Taylor in the middle of the buzzing hallway. "Wait—there's something I need to talk to you about. You haven't even asked the real reason I was calling."

People stopped to stare all along the office corridor as Taylor and Jason breezed past them. "I'm very busy today, Mr. Andrews," she said efficiently. "Perhaps you could make an appointment with my secretary for us to talk another time?"

Jason laughed out loud at this—surely she must be joking. But when Taylor said nothing further, he decided it was best to just ignore her.

"Anyway, as it turns out," he explained, "the screenwriter did *not* consult a lawyer when writing his script. And now the director and I have realized there are several problems with the film."

"I'm sorry to hear that," Taylor said distractedly. She stopped in front of her secretary's desk to pick up her messages. "Can you call Tom Jacobs and see if he has a few minutes to discuss his trial testimony?" After her secretary nodded, she stepped into her office.

Jason stood awkwardly in the hallway, unaccustomed to being left unattended to. After a few moments, when Taylor didn't return, he followed into her office.

Inside she was already seated at her desk, riffling through some files. Jason decided it was best to cut to the chase.

"I want you to work with me on the script."

Now *that* got her attention.

Taylor paused her work and peered up. She looked him directly in his eyes.

"No."

"Why not?"

She gestured at the stacks of files in front of her. "Because I have a *trial* starting in two days."

Jason waved his hand dismissively at her files. He was unconcerned with such things.

"We'll work in the evenings."

Taylor looked over at the wall, muttering "why me" under her breath.

"Because you're good," Jason said matter-of-factly.

Taylor paused, and Jason noticed she didn't try to argue with *that*.

"I'll tell you what," she said, appearing to soften slightly, "I know some attorneys at this firm who would be perfect for this kind of thing. I'll make a few calls—"

"No. It has to be you."

Taylor peered across her office at him, crossing her arms over her chest.

"Well, I'm sorry, but I'm afraid I'm not available."

"We both know I can make this happen in one phone call," Jason said matter-of-factly.

Her green eyes flashed at the threat. She got up from her desk and walked over, stopping just a few inches from him. Jason did a quick check for any sharp objects hidden in her hands.

But instead, she surprised him by speaking in a soft voice.

"Why me? Really, Jason. Why me?"

Hmm . . . his first name again. This was indeed progress. Moving in, Jason gazed down at her with a devilish smile.

"What can I say, Ms. Donovan? . . . You intrigue me."

It did the trick.

Jason watched as Taylor gave in with the slightest of smiles. He knew she couldn't help it.

She inched closer to him. "I intrigue you?"

"You know you do," he replied boldly, his eyes burning into hers. Wow—things were suddenly heating up *fast*. He wondered if they would have sex right there on her desk. Somebody better move that stapler.

With a coy look, Taylor stood up to whisper in Jason's ear.

"Then I think you're going to find this next part *really* intriguing," she said breathlessly.

He gazed down at her—he liked the sound of that—and raised one eyebrow expectantly as Taylor grinned wickedly and—

Slammed the office door right in his face.

For a moment, Jason could only stand there in the hallway with his nose pressed up against the cold wood of her door. After a few seconds, he knocked politely.

Taylor whipped open the door, unamused.

Jason grinned at her. "I just gotta ask: Where did you get the whole 'all the cute girls run around naked' thing?"

"I defend sexual harassment cases, Mr. Andrews," she replied coolly. "I've seen and heard things even you haven't thought of."

"Care to test out that theory?"

She slammed the door in his face again.

This time, Jason rolled away and saw the entire law office staring at him. He gestured nonchalantly to the door.

"It's a little drafty in here." With a wink, he straightened up and headed through the hallway with a spring in his step. So . . . she wanted to play hard to get, huh? That was just fine—it was his favorite game.

Jason grinned as he pulled his cell phone out of his pocket, more than ready to match Taylor Donovan's move.

"Marty—it's me. Call Sam Blakely. Yes, again."

Ten

"I CAN'T DO it. There's no way."

Taylor stopped and stood resolutely before Sam.

"I *cannot* work with that man."

Sam sat quietly at his desk, watching as Taylor resumed her pacing. This had been going on for the past six and a half minutes. They were making progress—at least she was speaking now. On her first three attempts, she had made it only two steps into his office before turning right back around without a word.

Taylor listed her grievances at punctuated intervals between the furious high-heeled turns she made on the carpet in front of Sam's desk.

"He's impossible.

"He's ridiculous.

"Selfish. Conceited.

"*Beyond* arrogant.

"Condescending, too—you should've see the way he waved off the mountain of work on my desk with his little 'Oh, pooh-pooh, but I'm a movie star.'"

Sam tried to keep from smiling at her imitation.

"As if *I* have any interest in working on his silly little script." Taylor argued to the air before her as she paced. "As if *I* don't have enough *real* things to do with my life."

She glanced over at Sam. "I mean—have you ever seen anyone so filled with his own self-importance?"

Sam raised an eyebrow. Maybe he had.

Taylor finally took a seat at his desk.

"All right—let's get serious, Sam. My trial starts in two days. I can't be trying to squeeze this shit in right now. I realize that this is Los Angeles, but come on—what's more important: a thirty-million-dollar lawsuit, or babysitting Hollywood's number one prick?"

Taylor paused as she waited for his answer.

Sam leaned in with an understanding smile.

THE DOOR TO Reilly's Tavern flew open with a bang as Taylor stormed in. Jason stood there, waiting expectantly with his cue stick in hand.

"Ms. Donovan! Back so soo—"

He was silenced by a hand as Taylor sailed by him and headed straight to the bar. She took a seat at one of the stools and nodded at the bartender. "Grey Goose, rocks," she growled, like a hard-nosed detective in some 1940s film noir.

Jason slid into the stool next to her. As he opened his mouth to speak, Taylor warningly held up her hand. Not yet.

The bartender set the drink in front of her, and she polished it off in two swallows. Then she sat the glass down gently, and finally turned and looked over at Jason.

He smiled.

"I was told I should expect an apology."

Taylor held her glass up to the bartender.

"I'm gonna need another."

Jason laughed—he couldn't help it. He had never met anyone so utterly, charmingly stubborn. He was about to compliment her choice in vodka when they both heard someone shout her name.

"Taylor!"

They looked over and saw Jeremy heading over, with his

arms outstretched as if greeting a long-lost friend. Taylor glanced at Jason in confusion.

"Do I know him?"

"Oh, that's just Jeremy," he explained. "Don't mind him—he's a screenwriter. He thinks he owns the place because they let him work here during the day. He gets inspired while playing pool."

"That's a little odd."

Jason shrugged. "He's been that way since college."

"College?"

"Columbia. We were roommates."

Jason took in her look of surprise. "Oh, you didn't think lawyers were the only people in this town with degrees, did you?"

Before Taylor could respond to his teasing, Jeremy approached and stopped formally.

"Counselor. At last, we meet." He held out his hand. "Jeremy Shelby."

She smiled at the introduction. "Call me Taylor."

Jason rolled his eyes. Oh, sure. *Jeremy* got to call her Taylor.

"I hear you've had the pleasure of working with Jason," Jeremy said. "How did he look in the courtroom?"

"Be honest, Ms. Donovan," Jason interjected confidently.

In response, Taylor looked him up and down. "I suppose it's the one area where I can't fault you," she said archly. "You might actually make something of yourself one day with this whole acting bit."

"Still with the sarcasm?"

"I have an audience now—I'm recharged," she said sweetly, gesturing to Jeremy.

Jeremy feigned shock. "Surely you're not implying that there are areas in which one can find fault with him?" He pointed. "You do realize that this is *Jason Andrews* we're talking about, don't you?"

"You two do realize that I'm standing right here, don't you?"

They ignored him.

"Well, in that case," Taylor said to Jeremy, "then I better

not say anything else. Since we're talking about *the* Jason Andrews."

Jeremy thought about this, then held up his hand. "No, wait—I changed my mind. I think I should hear everything." He threw his arm around Taylor's shoulders. "Let's adjourn to my office," he said, gesturing to a table in back that was covered with empty beer bottles. "I need to hear this story in proper detail, to assess its potential damage. And you should walk very slowly through all the parts where Jason looks like a total ass."

Left alone, Jason hung back at the bar, watching the two of them go. Nice talking to ya. But after giving his order to the bartender, he turned back and watched Jeremy laughing with Taylor.

He smiled to himself, strangely relieved by his friend's approval.

ACROSS THE BAR, Taylor and Jeremy watched as Jason was distracted by something the bartender asked him. Jeremy leaned across the table as soon as Jason's eyes were no longer on them.

"Quick—this is the part where I should get all crafty and try to squeeze information out of you."

Taylor laughed. She liked this Jeremy guy, despite his apparent choice in friends. "I'll save you the trouble. I'm just a lawyer from Chicago—I don't have any information anyone out here would find very interesting."

"You know Jason Andrews," Jeremy told her. "That means people will have lots of questions for you, if they get the chance."

Taylor considered this. "All right," she said gamely. "Show me your craftiness. I'll give you one question."

Jeremy thought for a moment.

"I'm a big believer in first impressions," he finally said. "Tell me what your first thought was when Jason walked into the courtroom."

Taylor took a sip of her drink and grinned. This one was easy. "I vowed to hate him forever."

Jeremy's brown eyes twinkled at this. "That's exactly what I said nineteen years ago, five minutes after he first walked into our dorm room."

Jeremy's words hung in the air as Jason arrived at the table with his drink. As he took a seat, Taylor studied him, intrigued.

Jason caught her look. "Did I miss something?"

Taylor mentally chewed on the information she had just acquired from Jeremy. She looked him over slyly.

"You're a bit older than I thought, Jason Andrews."

Jason glanced quickly at Jeremy, who held up his hands innocently.

"I swear, she forced it out of me."

LATER THAT EVENING, as Jason walked Taylor to her car, she had what she could only describe as a momentary "realization"—a moment where it struck her who Jason actually was. It had happened when he cautiously looked side to side as he stepped out the tavern door, presumably checking for paparazzi or fans. Oddly, for the entire evening, she had somehow forgotten he was famous.

Frankly, those other moments—when it struck Taylor that Jason was pretty much the most famous film star alive—made her uncomfortable. Because those were the moments that made her feel as though they somehow weren't equals. She much preferred thinking of Jason merely as some random jerk who annoyed the crap out of her.

But truth be told, there was a second reason she disliked these momentary realizations: they inevitably seemed to be paired with the "realization" that Jason was, in fact, divinely gorgeous. And that was a dangerous line of thought, particularly for someone who hadn't had sex since the previous financial quarter. *Early* in the previous financial quarter.

"So we'll meet Friday evening then?"

Jason's question broke through Taylor's reverie. She cleared her throat.

"Yes, fine—Friday evening. I should be out of court by five."

"I was thinking we could grab dinner somewhere." Jason saw her suspicious look. "But if you have an aversion to restaurants, we could always meet at my place." He winked.

"A restaurant will be fine," she said quickly. They arrived at her car.

"Good—I'll set it up," Jason said. "Where haven't you been yet?"

Taylor laughed at this. "You'd be much better off asking me where I *have* been."

"Okay, where *have* you been?"

"My office cafeteria."

When Jason fell silent, Taylor looked over and saw his stunned expression. She straightened up defensively.

"I've been busy with work, you know. And I don't exactly know a lot of people—"

Jason cut her off with a wave. It was something else that had shocked him.

"Is *this* your car?" He pointed in disbelief at the PT Cruiser.

Taylor waved this off. "Oh no—tonight I figured I'd just take whichever vehicle was closest."

Jason ignored her sarcasm, unable to tear his horrified eyes away.

"It's just a car, Jason," she said, annoyed.

At that, he glanced over at her and grinned.

"You *definitely* are not from Los Angeles, Taylor Donovan."

The whole drive home, she tried to figure out whether that was supposed to be a compliment or an insult.

Eleven

THE NEXT TWO days flew by quickly with the trial and before Taylor knew it, she was standing in front of her closet on Friday evening. The night was not off to a good start—court had gone on longer than expected, so she was running late for dinner. And now she had the most pressing concern to deal with: what to wear.

Her suits were stylish enough—for suits. But this was Mr. Chow's in Beverly Hills, and her first official dinner out in Los Angeles. She didn't want to look like some jackass from out of town.

On the other hand, she also didn't want to look like she thought she was on a date. And most important, she didn't want *Jason* to think she looked like she thought she was on a date.

Taylor finally settled on jeans, heels, and a white button-down shirt. But even that had its issues: two buttons open, or three? Two or three? She went back and forth in the bathroom mirror at least ten times.

Twenty minutes later, Taylor pulled in front of the restaurant and handed over the keys to the PT Cruiser. The valet gave her the same appalled look that Jason had two nights ago.

Taylor smiled charmingly at him. "You're going to leave this baby out front, right?"

As the valet stammered some horrified response, Taylor stepped inside the restaurant, where she was greeted by a hostess with an aloof smile.

"Yes, can I help you, miss?"

"I'm meeting someone here," Taylor said. She paused, suddenly stuck in one of her "realizations." The whole thing was just so ridiculous. "I'm . . . um . . . meeting a Mr. Andrews here," she continued, attempting a casual tone. Then she wondered if he used a fake name when making reservations. She'd once heard that Brad Pitt checked into hotels under the pseudonym "Bryce Pilaf." Cute.

But from the look on the hostess's face, no secret password or code name was required. The woman straightened up immediately, and her entire demeanor changed.

"Of course," the hostess said in an awed voice. "You must be Ms. Donovan. It would be my pleasure to show you to your table." She led Taylor through the restaurant, to a private staircase in back. Upstairs, there were only a few tables. Jason sat at one of them, waiting.

"Sorry I'm late," Taylor told him when she got to the table. "Court ran longer than I had expected."

"It's fine," Jason said with an easy smile. "I'm just glad you could make it."

Taylor watched as his eyes skimmed over her shirt with an appreciative look.

Dammit. She knew she shouldn't have gone with the three buttons.

TAYLOR SCRUTINIZED THE script that was open on the table in front of her. Now immersed in the project (albeit *very* reluctantly) she took the job as seriously as any other.

"Then we just need to take out this line here, where you yell at opposing counsel in court . . ." She gave Jason a look, letting him know this was a big lawyer no-no.

The waiter refilled their wineglasses as she continued her lecture. "Remember—you have triangle conversations in court.

You speak to the judge, they speak to the judge, but you never speak to each other."

She turned back to the script and finished reviewing the scene they were working on. After a moment, she pushed the script away, satisfied. "Yep—I think that scene is finished."

"Do you think it's good?" Jason asked.

Taylor considered her answer, sensing he wanted more than a meaningless stamp of approval. "I think some of the legal aspects still need to be refined, but it has a good story that should connect with the audience."

Jason grinned. "You just sounded so Hollywood."

Taylor smiled guiltily. "I did, didn't I? See—one evening with you and I'm already corrupted." She gestured casually to her half-empty glass. "Or maybe the wine's affecting me."

"So you approve of my selection?"

"I doubt there's anyone who wouldn't," Taylor quipped. She was hardly about to give him the satisfaction of knowing that he'd somehow managed to pick the one label she'd been wanting to try since getting her first issue of *Wine Spectator*.

"But your approval is harder to earn and therefore worth more than the others," Jason returned.

Taylor couldn't help but smile at that. "Yes, I approve," she said. "At seven hundred dollars a bottle, I'd better." She was about to say something else, but decided to bite her tongue.

"Go ahead." Jason laughed. "I can tell there's more."

Taylor grinned. He thought he knew her so well. "I was just thinking that you really do lead a charmed life."

"Ahhh . . . good, we get it out in the open. My fame and fortune." Jason leaned in toward her. "Look—I'll save you the bullshit speech about how I don't like it, about the lack of privacy, all that. But there *are* some trade-offs." He shrugged. "I guess I've just accepted those things as part of the package."

"Trade-offs beyond the lack of privacy?"

Jason waved this off. "That doesn't bother me as much as it used to."

"Then what?"

He thought about this. When he finally answered, Taylor thought she heard something in his voice. Something . . . genuine.

"People think they know you because the magazines portray you a certain way, or because you've played a particular part in a movie. And most of the people who supposedly are close to you don't care about who you really are anyway, because to them you're just a product, a commodity to sell. So it's not real. None of it's real."

He glanced over at Taylor cautiously, as if expecting her to laugh. She didn't.

"Jeremy seems real," she said in a gentler voice than usual.

This made Jason smile. "Jeremy and I have been friends a long time. He is as real as they get. Also cocky, condescending, and sarcastic—"

"How do you two ever get along?"

Jason grinned at her sarcasm. He eased back, swirling his wineglass. "You can throw all the little barbs you want, Taylor Donovan. It doesn't bother me one bit. Because secretly, I think you like spending time with me." He winked at her. "It's okay, you can admit it—I already know."

Taylor rolled her eyes disdainfully. "You're way too confident."

"Do you know that the average American woman between the ages of eighteen and thirty-five has seen each of my movies six times?"

Taylor scoffed at this. "Who told you that bullshit statistic?"

"Okay then, how many times have you thrown down ten dollars to see me on the big screen?"

"Not six."

"How many times?"

She shrugged nonchalantly, trying to think of a way to lawyer herself out of the question.

Jason's eyes widened at her gesture. "Oh, I'm sorry, Ms. Donovan, but your answers need to be audible for the court reporter."

Taylor glared at him. "Do you have a point somewhere in this?"

"The point is," Jason said, "that you say I'm too confident. But *I* say the odds are heavily in my favor that you're attracted to me."

There it was, all the cards laid out on the table.

"But you said it yourself," Taylor told him, "that's just the part you play. Your image. But what about the women who see behind the curtain to the real you? Are they just as infatuated?"

Something about her question seemed to strike a nerve, and Jason fell oddly silent. Realizing she was onto something, Taylor's eyes probed his from across the low glow of the table's candlelight.

"Maybe they never have a chance to see behind the curtain," she said. "Maybe you're always gone too quickly for that."

Jason's eyes met hers, and for a moment neither of them said anything. Without all the ridiculous bravado, Taylor thought, he actually seemed kind of human.

Then he tossed his napkin onto the table.

"That's it—you're paying for dinner tonight," he declared.

Jason gestured to the waiter hovering attentively off to the side. "Bring us another bottle of the Screaming Eagle." He lowered his voice to a whisper and pointed at Taylor. "The lady's paying."

"Of course, sir," the waiter replied. With a flash, he was off to the restaurant's private cellar.

Satisfied, Jason turned back to Taylor, his arms folded across his chest. "Seven hundred dollars per bottle, counselor. Let's see how sassy you are when you're back in the kitchen, washing dishes." He paused, giving her a second look. "Not that your feminist ass knows what to do in there."

At this, Taylor couldn't help but smile. There was something about that sarcastic sense of humor of his. Sometimes, she liked it very much.

LATER THAT EVENING, Jason turned to Taylor as they were leaving the restaurant, eager to hear her verdict.

"So? What did you think of your first official Los Angeles dining experience?"

She grinned in acknowledgment. "This by far takes the award for the best place I've gone on a business dinner."

Jason stopped abruptly.

"Wait—are you *billing* your time for this dinner?

Taylor stopped, too, seemingly surprised that he was surprised by this. "Well, yes. At least the part we spent talking about the script."

Her answer bothered Jason. Quite a bit, actually.

Taylor shifted uncomfortably. "I'm sorry—is there a problem with that?"

What could he say in response? Jason tried to keep his words from sounding terse. "No, of course not—this was a work dinner for you. I'm sorry I kept you so long."

He held the door open for Taylor, hoping to get them out of the restaurant and off this topic as quickly as possible.

She looked at him, confused. "Jason, I hope you didn't—"

She suddenly was cut off by the blinding flash of a hundred cameras. She jumped in surprise, as Jason turned and saw an enormous mob of paparazzi gathered on the sidewalk outside the restaurant. At the sight of him, the photographers screamed his name and clamored to get closer.

Instinctively, Jason pushed Taylor back into the restaurant and slammed the door behind them. He took a peek through the window at the circus that had gathered outside. To him, it was a pretty typical sight.

Taylor, on the other hand, appeared to be seriously freaking out. While she paced, she stayed as far from the windows as possible, as if they were dealing with sniper rifles outside instead of cameras.

"This is . . . not good," she said worriedly. "Really, really not good." She turned to Jason with a hopeful look. "We were only outside for a second. Maybe they didn't get a picture of us?"

Glancing out at the multitude of perfectly aimed cameras held by men with hair-trigger reflexes, Jason shook his head.

"At this point, I think the best you can hope for is that they didn't get one like this . . . " He made a shocked, oh-my-god-who-the-fuck-are-all-these-people face, trying to make her laugh.

It didn't work.

Taylor sank miserably into a nearby chair. "I am so going to get kicked off my case." She despondently rested her chin in her hands. "I'm under a court order," she explained. "I can't be seen in the media."

As he walked over to her, Jason couldn't help but notice again how much she wanted *not* to be seen with him. "I'm sure the judge wasn't referring to this type of publicity."

Taylor shook her head. "No, he was very clear on the issue—no press attention. Period." She looked down at the ground.

Seeing her upset, Jason felt that strange feeling tugging at him again. He knelt before her and started to reach out to take her hands in his. But then, something instinctively stopped him from touching her. He rested his arms on his knees instead.

"I can fix this," he said gently.

Taylor peered up at him hopefully. "Really?"

"But I want something in return."

Her green eyes narrowed. She folded her arms over her chest. "What might that be?"

Jason's gaze was unwavering.

"One night."

Taylor's eyes widened.

Jason smiled and spoke quickly, before she slapped him. "I meant one evening that's not work-related. You let me take you somewhere fun."

She shook her head definitively. "No."

Jason stood up reluctantly. "Okay—have it your way." He pointed to the front of the restaurant. "There's the door. Don't let the paparazzi hit you on the ass on your way out."

Taylor peeked at the mob outside. Apparently finding this option unappealing, she turned back to Jason.

"If I agree to this, there would have to be certain parameters."

Jason shook his head. "This isn't a negotiation, Ms. Donovan. You have my offer—take it or leave it."

Taylor glanced outside one last time, then sighed dramatically. Jason bit back a smile. All women should have such problems.

"Does anyone ever say 'no' to you?" she asked him resignedly.

"No. But if it makes you feel any better, you try a *lot* harder than anyone else. So we have a deal?"

"Fine. Whatever. Just fix this."

With that, Jason whipped out his cell phone. He hit the speed dial, slipping into crisis mode.

"Marty!" he exclaimed affectionately into the phone. Never mind that it was almost midnight on a Friday. "Listen—I need you to do something for me. I'm at Mr. Chow's with a bunch of paparazzi outside. They just got some photographs that I would appreciate they not publish. I don't care about me, but tell these guys that if anyone prints the name of the woman I'm with, or a picture of her face, they won't get one word from me ever again."

Jason waved off all his publicist's protests. "It's your job to make sure they understand," he said firmly. "Tell the editors, the publishers, whoever you need to talk to, that this comes directly from me."

He paused at Marty's next question.

"Do I at least have a comment on the mystery woman?" Jason's eyes darted over to Taylor as he summed her up succinctly.

"Yes. Difficult."

Twelve

IT WAS ALL over the front page the following Monday.

"Jason's Mystery Woman!"

Of course, Taylor—apparently the only person in Los Angeles who did not have a subscription to *Us Weekly*—had no knowledge of this until she got to work and found Linda and the secretarial cohorts camped outside her office. Because of Taylor's connection to one Mr. Jason Andrews, her secretary had become the queen bee of the administrative staff.

Linda was agog. In her whole life, that word had never come to Taylor's mind, but it really was the only way to describe her secretary on that particular morning.

"Have you seen it?" she asked as soon as Taylor walked in.

Taylor thought perhaps the judge had sua sponte granted summary judgment in her case. "Seen what?" she asked excitedly.

Linda held up a copy of *Us Weekly*. Taylor stared at it, confused. Strangely, she recognized the white shirt and jeans before she realized that the woman in the picture was her.

But there it was.

Beneath the screaming headline—"Jason's Mystery Woman!"—was a photograph of the two of them stepping out the front door of Mr. Chow's. Per Jason's instructions, the photo showed Taylor only from the back, hiding her identity.

"It's you, isn't it?" Linda asked breathlessly.

It was indeed her. Right there on the cover of a national gossip magazine with the biggest star in Hollywood. For Taylor, the moment went beyond surreal.

She peered up from the magazine and saw Linda and ten other pairs of eyes staring at her.

"It's not what you think," she said quickly.

"You had dinner with Jason Andrews," Linda replied in awe.

Taylor shook a finger at her. "No, no. I had a *meeting* with Jason Andrews that happened to take place over dinner. There's a big difference." She braced herself for more interrogation.

But instead, Linda surprised her.

"Okay," she said, shrugging her shoulders. "If that's what you say, then that's all it was."

Taylor stood by and watched as Linda shooed the other secretaries back to work. That was far easier than she had expected.

"Oh. Okay—great." Taylor couldn't help but be a bit surprised by Linda's sudden indifference. "I'm glad that's settled, then." She waited for another moment. When no one said anything further, she turned and headed into her office. Once inside, Taylor took a seat at her desk.

Wow. That was the fastest fifteen minutes of fame she'd ever seen.

Not that she cared about such things, of course.

A FEW DAYS later, Taylor returned early to the office. Court had unexpectedly finished ahead of schedule when one of the plaintiffs' witnesses had failed to show up to testify.

Linda called out from her desk as Taylor walked by. "How was court?"

Taylor grinned proudly. The trial was going even better

than expected. If she wasn't such a modest person, she would have to say she was utterly destroying the plaintiffs' witnesses on cross-examination. She doubted it was coincidence that one of them hadn't shown up today.

Taylor was fully aware that she had flaws—lots of them, in fact. But the one thing she knew beyond any doubt was that she was a damn good lawyer.

"The plaintiffs are struggling," she told Linda, thinking that was a more than generous description of her opponent's position. "But we still have a long way to go—you never know what a jury's going to do."

Linda nodded in agreement. "True, true. Oh—by the way," she added casually, "Mr. Andrews called. He said to tell you that he'll pick you up tomorrow after work. He said he's keeping it a surprise where he's taking you, except that I should warn you that he'll be the one teaching *you* something for a change."

After relaying the message, Linda waited expectantly for any instructions. Taylor shifted uneasily. Somebody had some 'splaining to do.

"Linda, it's not—"

Her secretary held up her hand. "No need to say anything. I got it, this is purely business. Just like you said—we will handle the Andrews Project with the highest degree of professionalism."

Linda moved on to other matters. "Also, a Ms. Foster called for you. She said you could reach her at her work number." She turned back to her typing.

The office was quiet, unconcerned, as everyone went about their normal course of business. This gave Taylor an opportunity to ponder Jason's cryptic message. She spun around toward her office, wondering what he meant by—

She gasped in shock at the sight before her eyes.

A solid wall of Jasons grinned out at her.

Her entire office door had been wallpapered with the latest cover of *People* magazine. It was the "Sexiest Man Alive" edition and apparently, the votes were in.

The smiling Jasons all stared at her, mocking her with

their smug little the-odds-are-heavily-in-my-favor-that-you're attracted-to-me grins.

"This will do wonders for his ego," Taylor muttered dryly under her breath.

The cover photo had captured him perfectly. He looked amused, and devilishly so. He wore his usual confident look—the look that said he knew something you didn't and wasn't quite ready to tell. And those damn blue eyes . . . despite the fact that it was merely a photograph, they seemed to bore straight through her.

As she took in the photo, she heard giggling behind her. "Very funny, guys," she called over her shoulder, to the secretaries she knew were watching. "Very cute."

Linda appeared at Taylor's side. "You mean 'sexy,' don't you?" she asked innocently, gesturing to the pictures. Then she couldn't resist any longer—she burst into laughter.

As the other secretaries joined in, Taylor stood there, trying to hold back her smile. Finally, she gave in and laughed along with them.

Okay, fine. She probably deserved that.

DUE TO HER unexpected afternoon off from trial, Taylor had a few free minutes to return Valerie's call. She answered the phone just as Taylor was taking a seat at her desk.

"Hey, it's me," Taylor said. "I got your message—what the hell—"

Apparently, Linda and the cohorts had stuck an extra copy of *People* magazine on her chair—just in case she had somehow missed the fifty plastered on her door.

"Something wrong?" Valerie asked, amused by this intro.

Taylor pulled the magazine out from under her. "Nothing—I just realized I was sitting on Jason Andrews's face."

"Yum. Call me back in an hour and let me know if it's every bit as fantastic as I imagined."

Taylor laughed. "My secretary left *People* magazine on my chair," she explained.

"I just bought a copy this morning on my way to work," Val said breathlessly. "You know this is the third time they've named him the Sexiest Man Alive? That's more than anyone else."

"You're a music professor at an Ivy League university. How do you have time to keep up with all this stuff?"

"Are you kidding? We're talking about Jason Andrews. I've seen all of his movies. Like six times."

Taylor's smile quickly changed into a frown. That stupid statistic.

She glared at the picture of Jason for being right. It was then that a second photograph in the lower right corner of the magazine cover caught her eye.

"Hey—I like the picture of Scott Casey," she said appreciatively. Under the caption "Other Contenders" was a photo of the actor in his *A Viking's Quest* costume.

"He's so beautiful, isn't he?" Valerie sighed wistfully. "I mean, I know you don't usually say that to describe a man, but Scott Casey really is just the very definition of the word."

"Do you think he's almost too pretty?" Taylor examined the picture. She sighed, adopting a melodramatic air. "I suppose I could deal with it if I had to," she said. She laughed at the very thought. As if.

"Speaking of dealing with things . . ." Valerie treaded lightly at first, then came right out with it. "Kate tells me you've been wasting your days away, hiding out in that office of yours."

The comment instantly put Taylor on the defensive. "Doesn't anybody understand that I'm on trial?"

"I don't know who else you're referring to, but Kate and I are your *friends*. We wouldn't be doing our jobs during this posttraumatic period if we weren't encouraging you to get on with your life."

Taylor scoffed at this. "I'm not going through any 'posttraumatic period.' I promise you, I've moved on with my life." And as she said the words, she realized just how true they were. She hadn't thought once about Daniel since the day she had received his flowers. She'd been preoccupied with other things . . .

"And if it makes you feel better," she continued, "I'm even going out tomorrow night. But don't get too excited," she added quickly. "It's just a business"—she searched for the right word—"related event."

Val sounded somewhat appeased by this. "Is there at least a man involved?"

Taylor considered how to answer this question. She was tempted to tell Val all about Jason. But she had decided it was better to do it in person, when she and Kate came to visit. She needed to exercise some spin control, particularly where Valerie was concerned. Taylor loved the girl to death, but keeping information on the down low was not one of her strong points.

"A man is sponsoring this event, yes." Taylor figured at least that answer was true. Sort of.

"And by any chance is this a good-looking man?" Valerie asked hopefully.

Taylor glanced down at the picture of Jason on the cover of *People*. Oh, not really, she thought. Just the Sexiest Man Alive.

"I suppose some 'people' might say he's attractive." She giggled at her own joke.

Then immediately covered her mouth.

Oh god.

Valerie echoed this exact sentiment. "Holy shit." She paused. "Did you just *giggle*?"

Taylor shook her head. "No," she mumbled innocently from behind the palm of her hand. "Definitely not."

"Because you *never* giggle," Val continued. "That's not the Taylor Donovan way."

Taylor nodded resolutely. "That's right. I don't. I was just, um . . . coughing."

Lame.

Valerie was highly suspicious. "I'm going to get to the bottom of whatever's going on with you as soon as I get out there, you know."

Taylor smiled. "Two weeks, Val. I promise—I'll tell you everything."

SCOTT CASEY GLANCED again at the copy of *People* that his now ex-publicist, Leslie, had just dropped off.

"Other Contenders."

To say he was not pleased with this distinction would be an understatement.

It was the second time in less than two weeks that he had been promised the cover, only to see it go up in smoke on account of Jason fucking Andrews. It was enough to make a movie star—Hollywood's It Guy, no less—want to fire his publicist.

Which is precisely what he had done, three minutes after arriving at Chateau Marmont and seeing the magazine Leslie had brought to their lunch meeting. What else was an It Guy supposed to do?

He certainly didn't have time to bother with her tired excuses that she'd only promised he would be "on the cover" not "be the cover." Whatever. He had waved her and her tired excuses off with a flick of his hand.

Scott knew that his time was now—he was hotter than hot coming off the success of *A Viking's Quest* and landing the coveted lead role in *Outback Nights*. He needed someone who could deliver the best publicity 5 percent of all gross earnings could buy.

So now, sitting at one of the hotel's poolside tables, Scott needed to come up with a strategy. He looked over at Rob, who had joined him for lunch once Leslie's chair had opened up.

"I need Marty Shepherd," Scott declared resolutely.

Rob nodded his agreement as he took another bite of his cheeseburger. "You should have Adam set it up," he said while he chewed, referring to Scott's manager. "Tell Shepherd that next year, you'll settle for nothing less than Sexiest Man Alive *and* Most Beautiful Person of the Year."

Scott glared at him. "That's not what this is about."

Rob eyed him skeptically, mumbling with a mouth full of food. "No? What's it about, then?"

"Making sure I don't end up a paunchy actor on some CW show whose biggest film break is Guy Whose Ass Gets Eaten in *Anaconda 4*."

Rob looked hurt. "Hey—I'm on *hiatus*. So I've gained a few pounds . . . I'll lose it by fall." He pointed his burger at Scott. "And don't take your Jason Andrews angst out on me."

"I don't have any angst," Scott retorted. He held up the other magazine Leslie had dropped off, the most recent issue of *Us Weekly*. Jason's so-called Mystery Woman.

"I'm just sick of hearing about the guy all the time. And I'm sure everyone else is, too."

"Angst," Rob whispered under his breath.

Scott rolled his eyes. "Never mind."

Seeing Scott's frustration, Rob adopted a more sympathetic air. Scott was higher then he on the celebrity food chain, so this meant that occasional ass-kissing, placating, and general ego-stroking was required.

"Look—you're gonna call Marty Shepherd. The guy's the master of publicity." Rob grinned. "Even slightly round but cuddly character actors on CW shows whose biggest film break is a small but pivotal part in the newest *Ocean's* sequel know that." He proudly grabbed a french fry off his plate and bit down with relish.

Scott was surprised. "You got the part?"

"I'll be filming in Vegas this Friday."

"One day? That is a small part."

Rob chose to ignore this. "Anyway, with Marty Shepherd, in a few weeks, that"—he pointed to the *Us Weekly* cover—"will be you."

Scott set the magazine on the table in front of them. "So you think this whole thing with the Mystery Woman is just a publicity stunt?"

Rob shrugged nonchalantly, taking in the two bikini-clad pretty young things that passed by their table. It was the fourth lap of their not-so-subtle attempt to get Scott's attention. He gave them one more walk-by before they finally gave up and said something.

"Isn't everything these days?" Rob answered, eying the ass of the larger girl, who he guessed was pushing a size 6. If things went down with these two, this was the ass he'd be getting. "Jason Andrews has a movie coming out soon, doesn't he?"

Scott nodded. "*Inferno*. Next month."

"This sure would be a convenient way to get everyone in a frenzy over him before the film's release."

Scott saw the truth in this. He studied the photograph of Jason coming out of Mr. Chow's with the so-called Mystery Woman. The woman, a brunette, had her face turned away from the cameras.

"Who do you think she is?" he asked.

Rob tore his eyes away from the pretty young things—who now were halfway around the pool—and leaned in for a better look. "I don't know . . . she kind of looks like Kate Beckinsale. No wait—Eva Green." He whistled his appreciation. "Definitely the best Bond girl yet. No doubt."

Scott agreed with Rob's guesses. The long, dark hair and body, from what he could see, definitively resembled either actress's features. "Maybe it's one of them . . . I can't tell," he mused. "She sure looks pretty fucking hot though."

"She wouldn't be with Jason Andrews if she wasn't."

When Scott glanced up sharply, Rob shrugged. "Sorry. But it's true."

"Who said she's 'with' Jason Andrews?" Scott pointed to the photograph. "All I see are two people coming out of a restaurant."

Rob humored this with a look. "I don't think Jason Andrews does a lot of platonic entertaining."

Before Scott could respond, the two pretty young things stopped in front of their table.

"Oh my god," the size 2 exclaimed gleefully to Scott. "I was right—I told her it was you." She gestured to the size 6, who also stared all dreamy-eyed. "We're totally your biggest fans."

Scott checked the women out, looking them up and down. Feeling a little generous that afternoon, he grinned and glanced over at Rob and his nearly finished cheeseburger.

"Well, my friend, did you save any room for dessert?"

Thirteen

WHEN THE CAR first stopped, having arrived at its destination, Taylor assumed there had been some sort of mistake. But then the driver got out and opened the door, quashing all her hopes of a mix-up.

"Mr. Andrews is waiting for you inside," the driver said with an efficient nod. As Taylor got out of the car and took in the sight that ominously greeted her, all of her preplanned early exit strategies fell to pieces.

Looming before her was a jet.

A private jet, from the looks of things, not that Taylor had ever ridden in one before.

Having seen the car pull up, Jason stepped out onto the jetway and welcomed her with a smile. "Hello, Ms. Donovan. Ready for this?"

Not at all sure that she was, Taylor eyed the jet warily as she crossed the tarmac and climbed the metal steps leading up to the passenger hold. When she got to the top, she stopped before Jason, going for an unimpressed look.

"How original. Didn't I see this in *Pretty Woman*?"

Jason smiled pleasantly. "Let's hope the evening ends as well for me as it did for Richard Gere." He winked.

That shut her up right quick.

Taylor coolly passed by him and stepped into the plane. She took in the rich cream leather captain's chairs—eight of them—the matching double couches that flanked both walls, and the tawny marble wet bar near the back. Not a bad setup.

"You rented this?"

Jason gave her a look. Hardly.

"I bought it three years ago. Commercial travel got to be too much of a hassle."

Taylor's eyes darted nervously to the cockpit. "Please tell me you're not *flying* it."

Jason laughed at the horrified look on her face. "You're safe. I'll be back here with you."

Taylor glanced around the small seating area. Great. How cozy.

She took a seat near the back, in the chair closest to the bar, thinking a Grey Goose on the rocks might soon be in order. Jason eased into the chair next to her.

"*Now* can you tell me where we're going?" she asked as she fumbled with her seat belt.

He shook his head. "Not yet. Although I'll give you a clue: from what I've seen so far, it's a place that suits you well."

Taylor considered this hint. Then an excited look crossed her face.

"Napa Valley?"

Jason shook his head. "It's not Napa. And no more guessing."

"I hope I'm at least dressed appropriately," she said, gesturing to her outfit. "Someplace 'where you'll be teaching me something' didn't give me a lot to go on."

Jason deliberately took in the black V-neck tailored shirt and fitted gray skirt she wore. Taylor self-consciously crossed her legs at his gaze, inadvertently drawing his attention to the slit in her skirt that parted mid-thigh.

"I think you'll do just fine, Ms. Donovan," he said.

Taylor was just thinking that perhaps this was a good time

to restate her "this is only business" speech, when the plane's engines suddenly roared to life. At the sound, she turned in her chair and peeked out the window. Without thinking, her leg began to bounce nervously.

After a few seconds of checking out the runway, she glanced back and saw Jason looking curiously at her bouncing leg. Never one to show any weakness, Taylor steadied herself and feigned a casual smile.

"So . . . I guess we're off now. Good. Great."

The jet taxied to the runway, completed its turn, then shot forward with a thunderous firing of the engines. Taylor self-consciously began to tap her fingers on the arms of her seat.

Okay, fine. Yes, it was true.

She hated flying.

Feeling Jason's eyes on her, she made an attempt to cover her nervousness with casual conversation. "So what kind of maintenance goes into a jet like this? I assume you have it serviced regularly?"

Jason shrugged unconcernedly. "I have no idea. I pay other people to worry about those things."

Taylor's eyes widened at this. Good god, they were toast. She spun back around to peer out the window.

The plane ascended, and they rose smoothly for a few moments. But then they hit a patch of turbulence, and Taylor's hands tightly gripped the armrests of her seat. She closed her eyes, trying to push all thoughts of screaming death-plummets from her mind. Surely fate was on her side in this flight, she thought. Jason was her insurance policy, after all. The world would probably stop spinning on its axis if something were to happen to its Sexiest Man Alive.

"So I've been reading about your trial in the papers," she heard Jason say.

She opened her eyes. "You have?"

The plane dropped with the turbulence, and Taylor's heart nearly jumped out of her chest. She glanced out the window, uneasily studying the ground below as the plane began a turn.

Meanwhile, Jason reclined unworriedly in his chair. "And I have a question for you."

"Hmmm." Taylor looked up. "Wait." She had *definitely* just

heard a sound she had never heard on a plane before. She quickly looked over at Jason.

"Does the engine sound normal to you? I think we're losing altitude."

He ignored this. "Anyway, I've been thinking about your trial—"

"—Seriously, is this pilot certified? How long has he been working for you? And what kind of training do you need to fly private planes, anyway?"

"—and here's the question I've been meaning to ask, Taylor: as a woman who defends companies from sexual harassment claims, don't you feel like a traitor to your gender?"

Whoa.

Suddenly refocused, Taylor turned away from the window and stared at Jason.

Her look was death.

"A *traitor* to my gender?" she whispered in disbelief.

The hand came up.

"Let me tell you something, mister . . ."

They had leveled off at 40,000 feet before she paused to take her first breath.

". . . AND WHILE I don't disagree that there are legitimate instances of sexual harassment out there . . .

". . . Frivolous cases do more to undermine feminist causes by clogging up the courts and creating bad precedent . . .

". . . Clients I represent do everything they can to prevent such behavior, and in those rare cases where I do find a problem, I'm the first person . . .

". . . Hardly deserves millions of dollars just because some low-level jerk-off with a manager's badge doesn't get laid enough and looks at porn on the office computer . . ."

Jason sat there, listening to the entire tirade. When Taylor had finally finished, she folded her arms over her chest.

"So? Does that satisfy your concerns over my being a *traitor* to my gender?"

She waited expectantly for his retort. But instead, Jason surprised her by nodding agreeably.

"All very good points. I hadn't thought about things that way." He got up from his seat and headed over to the wet bar. "Would you like a drink?" he asked politely.

Taylor blinked. Wait—that was it? He was just going to . . . agree with her?

Jason raised an eyebrow questioningly, still standing at the bar. Taylor tried to think through her surprise.

"Um, red wine, I guess. If you have it.

She watched as Jason opened a bottle, poured her a glass, and fixed himself a vodka martini. When he handed Taylor her drink, she looked at him knowingly.

"You were trying to distract me with the whole traitor-to-my-gender thing, weren't you?"

Jason grinned guiltily. "I had a feeling that might do the trick. Have you always been a nervous flier?"

Taylor debated whether to answer that. Then, realizing the jig was up, she leaned back in her seat and got comfortable for the first time in the flight.

"Since I was a summer associate at my firm," she admitted. "They asked a bunch of us to be test jurors for this big class action they were working on, an airplane crash case. As part of the evidence, they made us listen to the black box recordings so that the lawyers could get a sense of how a jury might handle that kind of evidence." She paused. "Needless to say, *that* was the summer I developed a fear of flying."

"That bad, huh?"

Taylor cocked her head, considering this. "It made me realize that things would be completely out of my control, if anything ever were to happen on a plane."

Jason studied her. "I sense this control thing is a big deal with you."

"Says the man who stormed into my office when I didn't return his phone calls within the hour."

Jason grinned. "Fair enough." Then he looked at her interestedly. "I feel like I should know more about you."

"Such as?"

"Do you date a lot?"

"Don't be a jackass."

Jason laughed, then held up his hands innocently. "What?

Is there something about my question that makes you uncomfortable, Ms. Donovan?"

From his teasing look, Taylor sensed that refusing to answer would only invite more probing into the subject.

"I'm sure that by the standards of the Sexiest Man Alive, no—I don't date a lot."

Jason was delighted. "You saw it."

Taylor thought of the fifty magazine covers plastered to her door. "My secretary brought in a few copies for the office," she said vaguely.

"And what do you think?"

"About what?"

"Would you say you agree with the magazine's characterization?"

Taylor waved this off. "You already have enough people complimenting you."

"That's not a denial," Jason noted.

Taylor saw his eyes sparkling with amusement. "You really need me to tell you what I think?"

"Of course. Your good opinion is always welcome, Ms. Donovan."

She looked Jason over. Truth be told, as he sat there with the sleeves of his button-down shirt rolled up casually around his forearms and his long legs stretched out in front of him, she wasn't sure there was much room to debate the magazine's claim.

"I suppose you're attractive," she told him. "Physically speaking."

"Stop—you're making me blush."

"Your personality, on the other hand, appears to have several defects."

"I see. Such as?"

"How long did you say we have left on this flight?"

Jason laughed. And Taylor couldn't help it; she smiled, too. Just then, the pilot's voice came over the intercom, with the announcement that they were expected to have a smooth ride for the rest of the flight.

Taylor exhaled in relief. Taking advantage of the interruption, she steered the conversation to safer topics. The time flew by as she and Jason chatted amiably about nothing, anything, and she was surprised when the pilot's voice interrupted them again, indicating that they soon would be landing.

Taylor immediately set about trying to find her seat belt, when she caught a glimpse out the window. She leaned over in her chair to get a better look at the dazzling spectacle outside. Before her blazed the brilliant glow of millions of sparkling lights. The sight was unmistakable—only one place on earth could illuminate the night sky that way.

Taylor turned back to Jason in surprise.

He grinned. "Ever been to Las Vegas, Ms. Donovan?"

Fourteen

THINGS HAPPENED SO quickly the moment she and Jason landed, Taylor barely had a chance to catch her breath. A car met them at the jet, where a driver and two security guards whisked them off to the Strip. Jason still refused to give her any clue as to their plans for the evening.

They pulled up at what appeared to be the back entrance of a hotel—a large hotel, but that was all Taylor could gather. The two guards escorted them through an elaborate maze of hallways and corridors, until they somehow popped out into the casino and were quickly shuffled over to the VIP room.

When Jason and Taylor were safely ensconced behind the red-velvet ropes of the private VIP area, Jason gave the security guards a nod of dismissal. As Taylor watched them walk away, trying to process everything that had just happened, the casino's director approached to shake Jason's hand. It was then that she finally learned where they were.

"Welcome back to the Bellagio, Mr. Andrews," the director welcomed them with a warm smile. As he led the two of them to a table, Taylor pulled Jason closer.

"You're taking me gambling?" she asked in a low whisper.

She'd never been gambling before. Frankly, she didn't see what all the fuss was about.

"Not just gambling," Jason said with an excited catch in his voice. They came to an energetic high-rollers table and he gestured grandly.

"Craps," he said reverently.

Taylor checked out the game. From what she could tell, something happened when somebody rolled the dice and everybody started yelling. The guy holding the stick at the center of the table suddenly screamed "Yo!" and chips began flying everywhere.

She nodded. "Oh, craps, sure."

After watching for another moment, she leaned over toward Jason.

"Um . . . where are the cards?"

With a smile, he grabbed her hand and pulled them up to the table.

"OKAY, LET'S REVIEW what you've learned."

Clearly enjoying his position of authority far too much, Jason ran through their lessons. Things had been improving since her first debacle, when it was her turn to roll and she'd unknowingly switched hands before throwing the dice. From the way everyone screamed, Taylor had thought someone had been shot. When she realized they were yelling at her, she had gotten so nervous that she dropped the dice on the floor. And that's when everyone *really* started fussing.

But now, under Jason's alleged tutelage, Taylor knew a thing or two about this game called craps. Raring to go, she nodded along impatiently as he rolled through his lecture.

"First, you've got your pass line—always take full odds on your pass line bet," he said. "Then, if you want to step it up a notch, make a come bet, and take odds on that as well. After that, you have your place bets—the six and eight will be your most common payoffs there. And, if you're feeling really lucky, you could always try for the yo, the hardways, or the any crap."

Taylor took a sip of her vodka tonic. The waitress kept bringing drinks around, and by now she and Jason had each had a few.

"And then there's the field," she said, pointing to the middle section of the table with the big "2, 3, 4, 9, 10, 11, 12" written across the green felt.

"I told you, you don't want to bet the field," Jason lectured her. "That's a rookie's bet."

Taylor waved this off. "But I like the field. You get seven chances to win."

"Do you want to look like you know what you're doing, or do you want to look like a girl?"

Taylor rolled her eyes. "I can't believe you just said that."

"It pretty much slipped out before I could think about it."

Taylor smiled. Perhaps the warm glow of vodka was beginning to set in. "Not as smooth when you're not working off a script, are you?" she teased.

Jason cocked his head. "Oh, I don't know, I seem to do all right."

Taylor suddenly realized how close they were standing. She hadn't meant to sound so . . . flirtatious. It had just kind of come out like that. Stupid vodka. She was cutting off the gravy train of free drinks right then and there.

"Excuse me, miss?" she heard a voice say.

Tearing her gaze away from Jason, she looked over and saw the stickman tapping the dice on the table in front of her.

"Are you in?" he asked. "Because you're up."

Taylor could still feel Jason's eyes on her. With a nod, she took a long sip of her drink, needing a moment to clear her head. Then she picked up the dice.

"All right, boys . . ." she said confidently. "Let me show you how this game is played."

At this, Jason pointed to the small bank of chips in front of her.

"Easy there, hotshot—don't get all crazy with those five-dollar chips." He nodded appreciatively to the pit boss for waiving their usual five-hundred-dollar minimum. "Thanks again for that."

"No problem, Mr. Andrews," said the pit boss.

Taylor turned back to Jason, annoyed.

"Will you *please* stop pointing that out to everyone?"

AT THE NEXT table over, Rob couldn't believe what he was seeing. Jason Andrews and the Mystery Woman stood just a few feet away, right before his very eyes.

Scott had indeed been correct about one thing—the girl was *hot*.

Earlier that evening, he had finished filming his small but pivotal *Ocean's* scene and (thanks to a call from Soderberg) had headed down to the casino's VIP room. More than anything, Rob had come just to make an appearance. Someone on set had mentioned that there were tons of paparazzi outside, and it was a great opportunity for him to be seen. Of course, if the tables turned cold, he'd have to make a quick exit—cuddly character actors on CW shows couldn't exactly hang long on $500 minimum tables.

He hadn't noticed them when he had first walked in, but now Rob thoroughly scrutinized Jason and the Mystery Woman's every interaction, like a spy who had snuck behind enemy lines. From what he could tell so far, it appeared Scott may have been right about one other thing: while it bordered on ludicrous to think that the biggest movie star of the twenty-first century wasn't fucking a girl who looked like that senseless, Rob got the distinct impression that they were not, in fact, together. Not yet, at least.

But the one thing he was certain of, beyond any doubt, was that Jason Andrews liked this Mystery Woman. A lot. Whether it was the way he looked at her with all his attention, or the way she made him laugh, or the way he was clearly trying to make *her* laugh, Rob couldn't quite say. But as someone whose cuddly and chubby stature went back to his high school class-clown days, he could tell when a guy was pulling out all the stops to make a good impression on a girl. Even if that guy was Jason Andrews.

The woman, on the other hand, was harder to read. A "mystery" indeed. She wasn't hanging all over Jason like most girls would; in fact, she seemed to avoid getting too close to him. Rob wished he could hear what they were saying, but that was impossible from across the room. Still, what he could see was enough for him get his cell phone out for a surreptitious call. He lowered his voice when his friend answered, relying on the raucous noise of the casino to drown out his words.

"Scott—dude, you are not going to believe who I'm looking at right now."

LATER THAT EVENING, after Jason watched as Taylor proudly cashed in her little stack of three-hundred-dollars worth of chips—how cute—he took her outside to a private terrace on the second floor. From there, they would have a view of the hotel's spectacular lake and fountains.

As they pulled up to the balcony railing, Jason noticed that the evening air had turned cool. Seeing Taylor hug her arms to her chest, he offered her the corduroy blazer he wore. She surprised him by actually accepting it.

Jason had a plan for the remainder of the night, and that plan had one key element: that he absolutely *not* kiss Taylor. He suspected she suspected he would try just that, and he wanted to keep her guessing. Besides, they would have plenty of time for such things later. Of that, he was quite confident.

He watched as Taylor stood against the railing, admiring the fountain show. *Clair de Lune* played through the terrace speakers as the water danced before them. The desert breeze swept through her hair, and she had never looked more beautiful to Jason than she did right then. He realized why.

"You're smiling," he said, unused to seeing her so relaxed and content.

Taylor turned to him. "I was just thinking about what my family would say, if they could see me right now. My brothers would never let me live down this evening if they knew about it."

Jason realized then that she hadn't told her family about him. He doubted there were many people in the world who would keep such a connection secret.

"How many brothers do you have?" he asked, seizing on the rare opportunity to learn more about her.

"Three. All older."

"Are they lawyers, too?"

She shook her head. "No. Police officers, like my dad. Except for Michael, the youngest, who rebelled and became a fireman."

Jason moved next to her at the railing. "And then came you," he said teasingly.

Taylor smiled. "And then came me."

"Do they have any idea what to do with you?"

She laughed at the truth of this. "Not really, no."

"What would they think of me?"

At first, she seemed surprised that he would ask such a thing. "They would think you're a little . . . fancy," she said.

"Thanks," he said dryly, offended.

Taylor paused and looked him over. Then she gave him an answer with more substance.

"They would think you're everything they expected, and yet not anything they expected, all at the same time."

Jason liked the sound of that much better. He moved closer to Taylor. "I think that's what *you* think."

She looked away and changed the subject. "So how's the movie coming?"

"We began filming last week."

Jason saw her look of surprise. "We shoot out of order," he explained, "so we'll work around the scenes you and I still have to fix."

Looking her over, he casually added, "You should come visit the set sometime."

The words had slipped out before he even thought about them. He had never, ever before invited a woman to watch him during filming.

But Taylor shook her head. "Unfortunately, my days are taken for the foreseeable future with this trial."

Jason stared at her in amazement. He didn't know anyone who would turn down such an offer.

"You're the perfect model, you know," he said.

"Excuse me?"

Seeing her confusion, he explained. "The character I'm playing in the film is this driven, workaholic lawyer who has never lost a case. When I'm playing him . . ." He paused, his voice softening. Somehow they were now standing just inches apart. "I think of you."

When their eyes met, Jason grinned and added, "With a penis."

"Is that what this is all about?"

"Penises?"

Taylor laughed. "I meant, you needing a model for your character. Is that why you . . ." She trailed off, as if uncertain how to finish her sentence.

"Is that why I . . . what?"

Jason realized then that despite the fact that Taylor was trapped between him and the railing, she seemed to be making no attempt to move away.

Her eyes searched his. "Why you keep . . . pestering me," she said softly.

"Is that what I'm doing?" Jason murmured, stepping closer.

Drawn in, Taylor's eyes lowered seductively as she raised her face to his. "Yes," she whispered, "you're definitely very pesty."

And suddenly, Jason couldn't help himself.

Despite all his best-laid plans, he was lost . . . his hand reached up to the nape of her neck and he gently pulled her in to him . . . she wasn't stopping him, in fact her hand slid up his chest and her lips parted invitingly as she pulled him closer and his lips came down to hers and—

"Oh my god, it's Jason Andrews!"

The scream came from the terrace below.

Jason watched as it happened—the dreamy fog dissolved from Taylor's eyes, like a method actor who'd been deeply into character when the director suddenly yelled "Cut!" Reality set in.

She immediately stepped away from him as if caught. He looked down and saw that a crowd had formed on the terrace below them. Several women shouted frantically, pointing, crying out his name. Paparazzi appeared out of nowhere. Cameras began to flash as everyone scrambled to get photographs. Suddenly, it was pure bedlam. Jason took a step back from the balcony and reached for Taylor—

But she was gone. Inside.

With a look of disappointment, Jason waved to the crowd, then turned and headed to the terrace doors.

The screams of his fans were upon his back all the way inside.

AS JASON WALKED Taylor up the brick path to her apartment, she was quietly relieved that the evening was coming to an end. She'd been internally berating herself over the Terrace Snafu (as she'd come to think of it) and externally had been doing her best to let Jason know that whatever he thought was about to happen back in Vegas was not, in fact, what had been about to happen.

Of course, she knew full well what had been about to happen.

God only knows what she'd been thinking, but she had, in fact, been about to kiss Jason. Such a move would have been unprofessional and unethical, not to mention overwhelmingly stupid. She blamed the vodka and the heat for getting to her. Never mind the fact that it had been only sixty-five degrees on the terrace and she'd gone instantly sober the minute the crowd had begun screaming.

"Did you have a good time tonight?" It was the fourth time Jason had asked her that since they'd landed.

She nodded. "Yes."

For once, conversation seemed to elude them. Luckily, they arrived at her front door. Taylor was careful to keep a good distance between her and Jason as they said good-bye.

"So, thank you, again, for the gambling lesson and, you know, everything else," she said lamely.

Jason, too, seemed to be struggling for something to say.

"So . . . okay, then." He shifted uneasily.

When another awkward moment passed, Taylor nodded efficiently. "Good-bye, Jason." She turned and unlocked her door and was just about to step inside her apartment when—

"I'm having a party next Saturday."

Taylor glanced back over her shoulder. Jason stood there, on her doorstep, wearing the same lost-but-adorable expression he'd had that first evening when she'd left him alone with the paparazzi outside her office building.

"You should come," he said, shrugging with a boyish grin. "If you don't have other plans, that is."

"Next Saturday?" Taylor quickly tried to think of an excuse.

Jason nodded. "June twenty-first. Mark it in that little Black-Berry you carry everywhere."

The words hit Taylor with a shock, like a bucket of icy water that had been dumped over her head.

"June twenty-first?" she repeated.

Her wedding day.

Or rather, her *former* wedding day, before she called it off after finding Daniel in flagrante doggie-stylo with his assistant. With everything going on, the date had completely slipped her mind.

Jason saw the expression on her face. "Do you have other plans that day?"

Taylor shook her head slowly. "No. Um, not anymore."

Jason smiled, the matter having been settled in his mind. "Great. Then I'll see you there."

HE HAD MADE up the whole thing about the party, of course.

Jason had been struggling, trying to think of anything to say to get a second nonwork date/meeting/whatever with Taylor, and he'd just blurted the words out. He hadn't hosted a party in years (he hated having people in his house), but it had been the first thing that had come to mind that wouldn't so obviously convey to her exactly what he was trying to do.

"A party?" Marty was surprised the next morning when Jason stopped by his office on the way to the set to pass along the news.

Jason nodded. "I'll let you handle the list." He relaxed on the couch that fronted the wall of windows in Marty's office.

"Is there anyone special I'm supposed to put on this list?" Marty asked.

"Whoever. The usual people." Jason's tone was casual. "And Taylor Donovan."

Marty paused at this. Then he nodded. "Sure, sure, Ms. Donovan—of course. But I also think we should invite some of the other actors from *In the Dark*," he said, referring to the legal thriller Jason was shooting. "Like Naomi Cross."

Jason shot Marty a knowing look. His publicist had been pushing Naomi Cross on him since the day she'd been cast. It would create great buzz for the film, Marty had urged repeatedly. One of the favorite strategies of any Hollywood publicist was to leak a web of hints, suggestions, innuendos, and whispers that two costars were hooking up on set. All of which, of course, would then in turn be vehemently denied by said publicist when asked.

"I've talked to Naomi's publicist, and we agree it would be great for the two of you to be seen together," Marty continued. "Her publicist is probably having the same conversation with her right at this very moment."

Jason sighed. Normally, he didn't mind this part of the business. In fact, typically he didn't have to be asked by his publicist to be "seen" with his costars because he was already sleeping with them anyway. But something didn't feel right this time. He didn't like the thought of Taylor reading about him and another woman in the press. He already needed to handle things delicately with her. He didn't see any reason to add more obstacles to the mix.

"Feel free to put Naomi or anyone else you want on the list," Jason told Marty. "But for now, this party is the only thing you should focus on."

TRUTH BE TOLD, Marty had been a bit perturbed by Jason's flat-out refusal to discuss the Naomi issue any further. They were costars, they both were single—*of course* there had to be rumors spread about them. It was the Hollywood way of things. He didn't understand why Jason was being so damn stubborn about the whole thing.

Luckily, within twenty-four hours, Marty's annoyance with his number one client dissipated as word spread around town that Jason Andrews was having a party that weekend. All of Los Angeles seemed to be talking about it. Funny, even

Scott Casey mentioned it to Marty when the two of them met for lunch at Ago a few days later to discuss the possibility of Marty becoming his new publicist. Over their steak salads, Scott casually mentioned that he had always been curious to see Jason Andrews's famous mansion.

Of course, since Scott was now a potential client, Marty was more than happy to put his name on the invite list.

Fifteen

WHEN SATURDAY EVENING rolled around, as many of Hollywood's biggest names and most beautiful faces were presumably being primped and dressed, and as frantic publicists undoubtedly raced around coordinating the all-important last-minute details of who would arrive exactly when and with whom, Taylor sat quietly alone in her apartment.

She wasn't going.

She took the Terrace Snafu as a warning sign that Jason Andrews plus alcohol (she still blamed the vodka) was not a good mix, and that things between them should remain on a purely professional level from here on out.

Yes, true, not going would mean spending another Saturday night by herself while the one person she knew in Los Angeles threw what appeared to be the biggest party of the year. And yes, not going would mean pathetically sitting home alone on what was previously supposed to be the night of her wedding, while being forced to listen to the long and pitiful messages Daniel kept leaving on her machine (he had called three times that day already).

And not going also meant not seeing Jason.

This was a good thing, Taylor reminded herself. After their night in Las Vegas, she had a pretty good idea what Jason was after and—judging from her completely unthinking reaction to him on the terrace—she worried that she couldn't keep him at bay forever. Or rather, that she wouldn't want to.

And she worried that this seemed to be worrying her less and less.

Taylor had replayed that moment on the Bellagio balcony a thousand times in her head. Actually, it wasn't just in her head—the shots the paparazzi had gotten of her and Jason, right before they had almost kissed, had made the covers of all the tabloid magazines. "Jason and the Mystery Woman: It's On!"; "Hot Desert Nights: Jason with Mystery Woman in Vegas!"; "Romance at the Bellagio!" Every morning, Linda left a different tabloid on Taylor's chair. And every morning, she promptly tossed them in her garbage can.

Possibly after taking a quick peek or two.

She had paused the first time she'd seen one of the photographs of them on the terrace. Her back had been to the cameras, but Jason's face could be seen as clear as day. Something about his expression had struck her, something about the way he had been looking at her right then. Like nothing existed except for her and him, in that moment.

But that was a ridiculous thought. A ridiculous and *dangerous* thought, and one that could get her into a whole mess of trouble.

And *that* was why she wasn't going to the party.

SHE WASN'T COMING.

Jason stood on the balcony outside the living room of his Beverly Hills home. The party was crowded and wild, with people everywhere—around the pool, by his guesthouse, even spilling onto his basketball court. At least the security staff had done a good job of keeping everyone outdoors. So far.

He had stopped having interest in his party guests well over an hour ago, about the time when the degree of Taylor's lateness had gone beyond being fashionable. He glanced at the front gate, the entrance to the party, once again.

"I don't think she's coming."

Jason glared at Jeremy, who stood next to him on the balcony. To think this was one thing, but for Jeremy to actually vocalize the sentiment was pure treachery.

"She's coming," Jason assured him, sounding far more confident than he felt.

"I don't know . . . it's getting late," Jeremy said, shaking his head skeptically.

Jason checked his watch. Four minutes since the last time he had looked, and still no sign of Taylor.

"You actually look anxious." Jeremy sounded both surprised and amused by this.

Jason threw him another cautionary look—he was not in the mood to be trifled with that night—when he spotted something at the front gate. Or rather, someone.

Seeing the expression on Jason's face, Jeremy turned and followed his gaze. Both men watched as Taylor walked into the party.

For a moment, Jason was speechless.

She wore a dress that would have no place inside a courtroom—a black strapless dress with a slit up to *there* that molded perfectly to her every curve. Her hair was long and wild and wavy, and her eyes were smoky. He had never seen this side of Taylor before, so overtly . . . hot. He vaguely heard Jeremy's voice in the distance, telling him to pick his jaw up off the floor before someone tripped over it.

Jason swallowed, then turned to his friend. "I told you she was coming," he said confidently. Then he quickly headed down the steps that led from the balcony and worked his way through the crowd. As he approached Taylor, her eyes met his and did not break away. He slowed as he drew near and stopped before her.

"You're here."

"I am."

Jason boldly took in the way she looked.

"I take it you don't often wear that dress in court."

"Probably not a good idea."

He grinned. "Yes, I can imagine it would be somewhat awkward standing before a judge who has a huge hard-on."

"Is that the effect this dress has?"

Taylor's eyes traveled downward, to the zipper of Jason's pants, and he was momentarily caught off guard by her bluntness.

Her eyes sparkled, amused.

"You're blushing, Jason. That's cute."

He smiled at her sassiness, then grabbed her hand. "Come on. I'll show you around."

He led Taylor through the crowd, past all the people who stared, and the two of them headed inside the house.

AS JASON GAVE her the grand tour, Taylor couldn't help but be impressed by his passion for and sizable knowledge of architecture, which appeared to be mostly self-taught. As he pointed out one detail after the next—everything from the teak floors up to the intricate crown molding—she learned that he had personally overseen the design of the 12,000-square-foot French Normandy–style mansion when he had built it five years ago.

Jason led her through the six guest bedrooms, master suite with two separate sitting rooms, vaulted glass foyer, screening room, private wine cellar, spa, steam room, and two-story reading studio/library. At several points along the way, Taylor couldn't help but think how she had never before seen wealth like this. She was not someone who was particularly impressed by money—her firm paid her over a quarter million dollars per year and that constituted a far greater income than any other Chicago Donovan had ever seen—but being in that house with Jason was so far out of her league it was downright dizzying.

After the tour, Jason took her outside to one of the bars that had been set up on the first-floor terrace. As he handed her the French martini she had ordered (getting into the spirit of the Normandy style of the house), he gave her a coy look.

"So . . . is there any reason you waited until after midnight to finally show up?"

"Sorry. I had to stop at a party at Jack Nicholson's along the way."

"Actually, Jack is sitting about ten feet behind you, smoking a cigar in that lounge chair."

As Taylor turned to look, Jason pressed on. "Seriously, I know you debated whether to come tonight. What made you decide?"

She shrugged nonchalantly. "It sounded like fun."

"But I know how busy you are. So I'm touched by the gesture."

Dismissing this with a wave, Taylor moved away from the bar. Jason followed her. Slowly they weaved through the crowd, going back and forth.

"You're reading too much into this. I just thought I needed to get out for a few hours."

"And you chose to spend those few hours with me."

"I *chose* to go to a party. You just happened to be the host."

"You *chose* to wear that dress."

"Surely you're not suggesting that a woman's attire is an indication of her intentions?"

"No, but when this woman spends the little free time she has with *me*, I start to get curious."

Taylor came to a stop in an alcove that was set off from the rest of the party. She leaned against the wall, holding her martini with one hand.

"Going to Las Vegas with you was part of the deal we made," she said casually.

Jason moved in close and rested one hand on the wall next to her. He stared down into her eyes.

"But coming here tonight wasn't—you did that on your own. Why?"

Taylor avoided the question. The truth was, she wasn't exactly sure what she was doing there. On an impulse, she had hopped in the PT Cruiser and driven over—a totally last-minute, spur-of-the-moment decision.

After twenty minutes spent doing her makeup.

And thirty doing her hair.

And four dress changes.

Totally spur-of-the-moment.

Avoiding Jason's gaze, Taylor gestured to the party. "You probably should get back out there. You're ignoring your other guests."

"Screw them."

"I'm sure that many of them, you already have."

She regretted the words the instant they came out.

Jason cocked his head with a knowing grin. "Hmmm . . . now that sounds a little bit like jealousy. How intriguing."

Taylor could have smacked herself for making the comment, for giving him any ammunition. He was standing too close to her, that was the problem, she realized. It was . . . distracting. She needed to quickly extricate herself from the situation.

She stared him in the eyes defiantly. "Whatever you're trying to get me to admit, Jason, it's not going to happen."

And, having gotten in the last word, Taylor slipped under his arm and walked away.

JEREMY HADN'T MOVED from his position on the balcony. It was the only place in the crowded party where he could safely drink his beer without being jostled by some drunken early twenties asshole threatening to throw his scantily clad date into the pool, or accosted by a hopeful starlet who believed that flirting with him would get her that much closer to Jason.

Frankly, Jeremy disliked the whole Hollywood scene, but he tolerated it not only as a sometimes-necessary part of his life as a screenwriter but also as an always-necessary part of Jason's life. It was one of those things that anyone close to Jason inevitably had to accept, for better or worse, like the constant presence of the paparazzi.

He was not particularly surprised when Jason rejoined him on the balcony that evening, in a huff and alone. He personally thought Jason was approaching this thing with Taylor in entirely the wrong way. But once his friend set his mind to something, it was nearly impossible to steer him in a different direction.

"Any luck?" Jeremy asked as Jason pulled up alongside him at the balcony's ledge, where they had a good view of the party below.

"Maybe . . ." Jason mused. He looked over with annoyance when he saw that Jeremy was smoking so close to the house. But he said nothing, as smoking was a necessary part of Jeremy's life and something that anyone close to *him* inevitably had to accept.

"Maybe how?" Jeremy exhaled smoke out of the corner of his mouth.

Jason considered this. "I think I'm starting to get to her."

"I bet that's what she's telling Hayden Stone right now."

Jeremy nodded to the party below, where Taylor was engaged in what appeared to be a friendly conversation with the good-looking director.

With a look of disbelief, Jason pulled back from the ledge.

"I don't get it," he said, frustrated. "She should be coming up here right now to tell me she changed her mind. Or waiting in my bedroom, naked, to surprise me. Or giving you a secret message that I should meet her in the gazebo, where she'll be waiting, naked. Or in the bathtub, with bubbles, champagne, and—"

"Naked. I get the point."

"The *point*, Jeremiah, is that this is not how things were supposed to go tonight."

Jeremy reached out and solemnly put his hand on the Sexiest Man Alive's shoulder.

"I'm sorry, Jason. But maybe she's just not that into you."

It was a joke, but Jason's face suddenly filled with worry. "Do you really think that could be it?"

Despite the fact that he generally enjoyed any fun that could be had at Jason's expense, Jeremy felt a little bad seeing the look of concern on his friend's face.

"No, I actually don't think that's it," he said. "But I also don't think she's going to admit how she feels."

The words seemed to reinvigorate Jason. "Well, too bad for her." He ignored the look Jeremy gave him. "Hey—don't get me wrong, I'm enjoying this game of hard to get she's playing. It's been like three weeks of foreplay."

Jeremy rolled his eyes. The comment wasn't even worth responding to.

"But it's time for things to start moving along, to where she and I both know this is headed," Jason continued.

"And I suppose, Evil Genius, that you have just the plan to accomplish this?" Jeremy paused when he saw the sly smile on Jason's face. "You actually do have a plan, don't you?"

"I do," Jason said proudly.

"Do I even dare to ask what this plan might be?"

"Every woman's weakness," Jason told him. "Jealousy." He folded his arms and leaned back against the balcony ledge. "Let her see me with someone else, and then we'll see how stubborn she is."

Jeremy waved this off. "Taylor's hardly the type to get into some catfight for you."

"That's not what I'm looking for," Jason said. Then he paused, as if suddenly getting the visual. "As hot as that might be . . ."

Jason shook this off. "Look—all I need is to see her reaction. Trust me, I know how a woman looks when she's upset with me. And if she's upset, that means she's jealous, and that tells me everything I need to know."

Jeremy shook his head. "This is not a good plan. I'll tell you what—I've got a better idea for you."

Curious, Jason leaned in as Jeremy lowered his voice conspiratorially.

"Now I know it's a bit radical, but in desperate times—" Jeremy paused dramatically.

"Give her . . . time to trust you."

He glanced around furtively to make sure no one had overheard his devious plot.

Jason glared, unamused by Jeremy's antics. "I don't want to give her time to trust me. That'll take too long."

"So what if it does?" Jeremy asked. "Are you going somewhere? Dying? I better get the Aston Martin."

"I'm just tired of waiting," Jason said. "I want to know how she feels. I need to know how she feels."

Jeremy glanced over, intrigued by this choice of words.

But seemingly not wanting to discuss the matter further, Jason turned away and headed back inside the house.

UNDERNEATH THE BALCONY, Scott and Rob huddled in a corner of the patio, out of view. They had just overheard everything Jason had said.

Scott grinned victoriously. "I told you they weren't together."

Rob nodded. "It's the same thing I saw in Vegas—he has seriously got a thing for that girl." He peeked around the corner, trying to get a better look at Taylor. "I wonder what her deal is? I mean, the guy could get anyone he wants."

Scott yanked Rob back into the alcove. Perhaps a little rougher than necessary.

"Hey," Rob complained, fixing his shirt. "I just meant, what's so special about her?"

Scott thought about this for a moment. "You know, I think we should find out." He moved Rob aside in order to have an unobstructed view of Taylor. "I think it's about time that Jason Andrews's Mystery Woman became a little less of a mystery." With a purposeful grin, he headed back into the party.

Rob watched him go, calling after him. "Great! Sounds like a plan." He pointed to the buffet table. "I'm just gonna grab a few snacks first."

Sixteen

JASON FOUND NAOMI Cross out by the koi pond, chatting intimately with a group of women. He approached her with a warm smile.

"Hello, Naomi. Are you enjoying yourself?"

The actress turned when she heard Jason's voice. She was long and blonde and tan, appearing every inch the California girl until she spoke.

"Darling, you know I always enjoy myself at your parties. I'd never miss one." Her smooth British accent was the only indication that she was London born and bred.

"Got a second?" Jason gestured to a table off to the side. When Naomi nodded, he led her away from her girlfriends.

As Jason was about to sit down at the table, he spotted Taylor across the pool, still talking to Hayden Stone. Deciding it was high time to put an end to that, he grabbed a bouncer who was walking by.

"Got a cell phone?"

The bouncer nodded affirmatively.

"Good." Jason pointed. "Hayden Stone is over there, talking

to a dark-haired woman. Walk up to him with the cell phone and say that his wife wants to speak with him."

Satisfied when he saw the bouncer take off in Taylor's direction—that should take care of that—Jason joined Naomi at the table.

"So Cindy told me that she and Marty have been talking," Naomi said, referring to her publicist.

"The two of them seem to be quite the matchmakers these days. Marty suggested that you and I have drinks at the Peninsula." Jason rolled his eyes at the unoriginality of the idea. "It was the same place he sent Jen and Vince before the release of *The Break-Up*."

The two actors shared a grin. Although this was the first time they'd worked together, they had known each other for years and got along well.

"Drinks at the Peninsula?" Naomi laughed. "I give it three weeks before the tabloids say we're engaged."

"And five before you're pregnant."

Naomi groaned. "Another bump watch. Cindy would love it."

Jason leaned in, peering at her across the table. It was time to get down to business. "Naomi—I need to ask you for a favor. There's something I'd like you to help me out with tonight."

Always one for a good intrigue, Naomi met Jason halfway across the table, tilting her head in toward his. She lowered her voice to a secretive whisper.

"What exactly did you have in mind, darling?"

TAYLOR NODDED ALONG politely as Hayden Stone rattled on about his newest project, a romantic "dramedy" about a self-centered man at a crisis point in his life who becomes a better person through the love of a quirky-but-cute woman, all set to an eclectic classic rock soundtrack. Given that Hayden was the only person at the party who had bothered to talk to her other than Jason, she resisted the urge to point out that this sounded strikingly similar to the plot of his last three films.

While Taylor was talking to the director, she couldn't help

but see Jason out of the corner of her eye, sitting at a table near the pool with Naomi Cross. She recalled the *People* magazine article Linda had given her a few weeks ago that suggested Naomi was Jason's "next conquest."

A few weeks ago, Taylor could have cared less about such gossip. But now, for some reason, seeing them together made her stomach feel as though it was tied up in knots.

She forced herself to look away from Jason and the actress, just as Hayden wrapped up his ten-minute diatribe on the protagonist's "character arc."

"So that's the point where we see that the character has really come full circle," he said. "What do you think?"

Taylor blushed at the question. This *really* was not her field of expertise.

"Oh, I'm not the right person to ask," she said lightly. "I don't see that many romantic comedies."

"Dramedies," Hayden corrected her. "And why is that? You don't believe in love?"

Taylor was momentarily put off by his bluntness. But she grinned, trying to play nice. "Of course I believe in *love*." She deliberately put just a tinge of mocking emphasis on the word. "Although I'm not sure I believe in love like you see in movies."

Hayden appeared to like this challenge. In the Hollywood food chain, as Taylor quickly was about to learn, the only person more arrogant and self-assured than an Oscar-winning actor was an Oscar-winning director.

"Oh? What is it you don't believe in?"

Under his probing gaze, Taylor suddenly felt like she was back in law school, being grilled by her torts professor over the court's holding in *Hadley v. Baxendale.*

"I don't know . . ." she said, shifting her drink to the other hand. She saw that the director was not going to let her off that easily. "I suppose it's the idea that there's one person out there for you. The so-called perfect match. It's not a logical concept."

Taylor quickly glanced around the party, looking for a way out. This whole conversation had turned a little flighty for her taste.

Hayden rocked back and forth on his heels, smug in his obvious superior knowledge on the subject.

"You know, just because love like that hasn't happened to *you* doesn't mean it doesn't exist."

At this, Taylor tried to recall what her torts professor had said about justification being a legal defense to smacking someone upside the head. But she managed to resist the urge to find out.

"I'm sure you're right," she said to Hayden with a polite smile. "I suppose I'm not your target audience, that's all."

Hayden leaned in closer. "Let me give you a bit of friendly advice, Taylor. Life isn't always about logic and reason—sometimes you just have to close your eyes and jump. Particularly when it comes to relationships."

Taylor tried to keep from rolling her eyes. It now was most definitely time to make her escape.

But Hayden, apparently (and quite mistakenly) believing his conversation skills were charming, moved closer to her.

"But perhaps we could continue this discussion further. Maybe sometime over dinner?"

Taylor shook her head regretfully. "Sorry, I'm afraid I can't. I'm really too busy with work these days."

Hayden appeared quite offended—and surprised—by the rejection. "Is there a problem here? I own a restaurant with Bruckheimer, you know."

Taylor tried not to smile. Ahh . . . Hollywood. Just when you might think all the stereotypes and clichés aren't true, you realize, yep—they are.

She gave Hayden a look. "Aren't you married?" Everyone knew his wife was an actress who had been in two of his movies.

"Separated," he said insistently. "I haven't spoken to my wife in *months.*"

Just then, a bouncer walked up to Hayden and Taylor, holding a cell phone.

"Excuse me, Mr. Stone—but your wife is on the phone for you."

Taylor watched in amusement as the director's face turned red with embarrassment.

"And on that note . . . I think I'll go," she said.

She headed off to find a bathroom, the one place she hoped Hayden Stone wouldn't try to follow her.

THE GUEST BATHROOM of the pool house had been richly designed in beige-and-black marble and dark mahogany wood, with a separate lounge area. With an appreciative glance, the lawyer in Taylor couldn't help but think that if Jason ever did get married, he better have one hell of a prenup.

She had just shut the bathroom door when she heard the loud, gossipy voices of two women entering the lounge.

"It has to be her," the first voice was saying. "She looks just like the woman in that photograph on the balcony at the Bellagio. And didn't you see the way he stared when she first walked into the party?"

"But I thought he and Naomi Cross were supposedly hooking up on set," the second voice said. "You know Amanda, who works in the mail room at Marty Shepherd's firm? She told me that."

It took her a moment, but Taylor realized that the women were talking about her and Jason. Such petty gossip. Thankfully, she was above that kind of nonsense.

She pressed her ear tightly against the door to hear better.

"That thing about Naomi is just a rumor," the first woman said knowingly. "You know Max, the waiter at Mr. Chow? He told *me* that he was there when Jason had dinner with the Mystery Woman, and that he couldn't take his eyes off her."

Without meaning to, Taylor smiled at this.

"And supposedly," the woman continued, "she made him smile. A lot."

Taylor quickly thought back to their dinner. Yes . . . she had been particularly charming that evening.

"Do you think she's a model?" the second woman asked.

A model? Wow. Behind the door, Taylor proudly tossed her hair back over her shoulders.

"I bet she has extensions."

Taylor stopped, mid hair-toss. Her mouth opened defensively. Hold on there.

"And I think she's got lip implants." The second woman raised her voice in a mocking imitation. "Excuse me, doctor, I'd like the Angelina Jolie."

Taylor's hand self-consciously flew to her mouth.

"And what about her boobs?"

Taylor peered down at her chest. Okay—wait just a second there—

She heard the other woman scoff.

"Are you kidding? Who actually has *real* boobs anymore?"

"I don't know—maybe that's why Jason was smiling so much during their dinner."

The two women shared a laugh at this.

Taylor heard their voices fade as they left the bathroom. She cautiously opened the door, stepped out into the lounge, and headed over to the mirror.

Of all the things the little trixies had said, two comments stuck with her most.

Jason had dinner with the Mystery Woman, and he couldn't take his eyes off her.

And supposedly, she made him smile. A lot.

Taylor couldn't help it—she felt a rush of excitement hearing this. She stared at her reflection in the mirror.

What had gotten into her these past few weeks?

First, she'd almost kissed Jason in Vegas. Then she'd made the decision to come to his party despite the fact that there was a pile of work waiting for her at home. Despite the fact that she definitely knew better.

Standing there, her mind wandered back to the way Jason had greeted her when she'd first walked into the party. He'd looked really happy to see her.

Maybe that look was genuine.

Maybe it wouldn't kill her to be a little less cynical.

Maybe she should . . . well, she didn't know exactly how to finish that thought, but maybe just thinking "maybe" was enough for now.

So Taylor gave herself a long, hard look in the mirror.

Then she smiled.

She turned and headed out of the bathroom, ready to rejoin

the party. But she stopped just before she reached the door and glanced back in the mirror. She paused, then most discretely adjusted her dress to show a tad more cleavage.

Fake, huh?

Taylor grinned knowingly.

Like hell they were.

TAYLOR HAD JUST stopped off at the bar to refresh her drink when she heard a familiar drawl behind her.

"There you are, Ms. Donovan . . ."

A smile crossed her face. Just the man she was looking for. With a coy toss of her hair, she turned around and—

Found herself staring right at Naomi Cross.

Jason graciously made the introductions. "Taylor, I thought you might like to meet Naomi. She's one of my costars in the film you're helping me out with."

He turned to the actress to explain. "Taylor's the attorney I've been consulting on the script."

Naomi shook Taylor's hand. "Oh, so you're the one who's responsible for all the last-minute page changes they keep sliding under my trailer door."

Recovering from her fluster at encountering the actress, Taylor smiled. "Sorry—I'm sure I'm being way too picky with all the legal issues."

Naomi dismissed this. "It's not your fault. The whole shoot has been a challenge, particularly with the schedule the director is trying to keep." She glanced back at Jason and, after a slight pause, wrapped her arms around his neck.

"That's why this weekend will be so great, darling." With a grin, she turned back to Taylor. "Did Jason tell you? We're sneaking off to Napa Valley—just the two of us."

And despite herself, Taylor couldn't help it.

Her face fell in disappointment.

"No," she said quietly. "He didn't mention it."

She looked away, trying to hide her surprise. When she glanced back up, she noticed that Jason was watching her intently.

Naomi ran her fingers along Jason's arm as she peered

adoringly at him. "How could you forget it? I know how much
we're both looking forward to this trip. Aren't we?"

"I can't think of anything I'd rather do." Jason smiled
wickedly as he casually turned his watch around his wrist.

Naomi returned his look with one of her own. "Anything
you'd rather do . . . or anyone?"

Alrighty, then—Taylor had heard quite enough. "Listen—I
really should get going," she interrupted. "It's getting kind of
late. Naomi, it was nice meeting you." As she left, she brushed
by Jason with a curt nod in good-bye.

"Jason."

She had made it only a few steps from the bar when she
heard him calling after her.

"Taylor, hold on a second—"

She stopped and turned around.

Jason stood there, staring at her innocently, with Naomi at
his side.

"We're still on for Thursday, right?" he asked. "There are
those changes the writer made to Act Two that I want you to
take a look at."

Taylor paused, but somehow managed to keep her cool.
"Sure. Thursday," she said evenly. "I'll see you then."

Without further ado, she turned and walked away.

NAOMI AND JASON watched Taylor leave, waiting until
she was safely out of hearing range. Then the actress glanced
over.

"So? Did you get what you wanted?"

"Definitely," Jason said. Did he ever.

"I did all right then?"

"You were perfect, Naomi, as always. I owe you."

She threw him a coy wink. "You know how you can make
it up to me, darling." Then she sashayed off to rejoin her girlfriends.

More than pleased with the way things had turned out, Jason stepped up to the bar to order himself a victory cocktail.
He thought back to the crushed look Taylor had been unable
to hide when she heard he would be spending the weekend

with another woman. In Napa Valley, no less. Throwing in that detail last minute had been a stroke of pure genius.

Yes indeed, Taylor Donovan had put up quite a fight for a while. But now, well . . . Jason smiled at the thought of what was soon to come. As they say, to the victor goes the spoils.

The bartender set a drink down on the bar. Jason picked up the highball glass and tipped it with a self-satisfied grin.

"Cheers."

Seventeen

TAYLOR HURRIED OUT the front gate, eager to put as much distance between her and the wall that surrounded Jason's estate as fast as possible. When she got to the end of the cobblestone driveway, she looked up and down the street, trying to remember where the hell she had parked her car. The stupid Beverly Hills side streets all looked the same: walls and fences and ten-foot hedges, created for the single purpose of keeping the riffraff from sneaking peeks at the fabulous houses and people inside.

"Shit, shit, shit," she swore under her breath.

The real problem, of course, was not that she couldn't find her car.

The real problem was that she had been an utter and complete fool.

What had she been thinking, convincing herself that maybe Jason had—

She stopped herself mid-thought. The idea was so ridiculous she couldn't even finish it.

She had felt like such an idiot, just standing there as Naomi draped herself all over Jason. And as for him, Mr. I'm-So-Hot with that—what was up with that smug grin, anyway? When he had called her name as she left, there had been about a thousand things she'd been tempted to say. But when she turned and saw Jason standing with Naomi, and then glanced around at the rest of the party, it had occurred to her that she really didn't belong there anyway. She may have put on the dress and looked the part, but at the end of the day, she was still just a lawyer from Chicago.

The worst part of the situation was that Taylor had no one to blame but herself. She had set herself up to be disappointed by a man who was infamously known worldwide for disappointing women. Despite what she might have wanted to believe for a few brief seconds after overhearing the little bathroom trixies, she was no different from any other woman Jason Andrews had ever met.

But knowing this still did not make things hurt any less.

For a brief moment, Taylor's thoughts drifted back to Jason. There was something about him—his eyes, his smile, the way his voice sounded when he said her name, the things he said that made her laugh, the way he could look at her as if there was no one else in the room . . .

She resolutely shoved this line of thinking out of her mind.

"Shit!" she muttered again as she paced the driveway. So bothered was she, even her profanity lacked its usual flair.

Suddenly, a voice came out of the darkness.

"Well, it can't be that bad."

Taylor whirled around and saw—whoa, nelly—Scott Casey standing just a few feet away. How long he had been hanging out by the driveway, she had no idea.

Scott smiled at the surprised look on her face.

"Is something wrong?"

Taylor had noticed a lot of famous faces at Jason's party, but certainly didn't recall seeing Scott Casey there. And he would be *very* hard to miss. Val was right—he was absolutely beautiful in person, with his blond hair, lean build, and model-perfect features. A walking Calvin Klein ad. And apparently, talking, too.

To her.

Right then.

"Sorry." Taylor regrouped, managing to find her voice. "I can't remember where I parked my car, that's all."

"I'd be happy to give you a ride if you need one."

Taylor gave him a look. He may have been Scott Casey, but she was no fool. At least not twice in one night, anyway.

"I'll be fine," she told him. "It's around here somewhere."

"You're leaving the party so soon. I hope nothing's wrong?"

For some reason, Taylor found herself warming a little to him. Perhaps it was the look of concern in his light hazel eyes. Or possibly the killer Australian accent.

"Nothing's wrong," she said lightly. "I just need to get an early start tomorrow, for work."

"Work on a Sunday?" Scott made a face. "What do you do?"

"I'm a lawyer." Taylor saw that this registered with him.

"I should've guessed," he mused. "You were wearing a suit in that one photograph, and no one in this town wears suits except lawyers and agents."

"Photograph?" Taylor tried to imagine where on earth Scott Casey would've seen *her* photograph. Then it hit her. "Oh, the magazines."

He stepped a little closer. "You're on all the covers again this week. You are the Mystery Woman, aren't you?" he asked in a coyly curious tone.

"Would it surprise you if I was?"

"Not at all." His eyes took her in appreciatively. "I'm only surprised they didn't photograph you from the front. Your face belongs on a magazine cover."

Taylor paused. That was actually kind of smooth.

Admittedly, she had a secret weakness for compliments like that. Growing up with three older brothers, she hadn't paid much attention to fashion trends, makeup, hairstyles, or other things of the type that the typical teenage girl devoted hours to studying. The one time she had actually dared to sneak home a copy of *Seventeen* magazine had yielded disastrous results: her brothers had mocked her incessantly for *days*. So instead, Taylor had gone through high school as the "smart girl," and she'd been just fine with that. Although, admittedly, "smart girls" were not exactly what teenage *boys* were interested in.

Eventually, when Taylor got to college and teamed up with Valerie and Kate, her friends convinced her to get rid of the out-of-date glasses and tomboy ponytail. One rainy Saturday morning, Val even managed to talk her into a makeover. The results had surprised not only Kate and Val, but Taylor herself. The three of them, using their fake IDs, had gone out to the campus bars that night, and it had taken Taylor all of about fifteen seconds of obvious male appreciation to decide that her new look was one she could live with.

Nevertheless, as is often the case despite a person's latter achievements, Taylor's high school "smart girl" label stuck with her into adulthood, and she still blushed whenever a good-looking guy told her she was attractive.

Which was exactly what she did right then, hearing Scott's compliment.

"Thank you," she smiled modestly. "It's sort of an arrangement Jason made with the tabloids. They can't publish any pictures that identify me."

"Hence the 'mystery' part," Scott said cutely.

Taylor studied him curiously. He didn't exactly seem like the kind of guy who often used the word "hence." Was it possible that he—Scott Casey—was actually trying to impress *her*?

She decided to throw out a little test.

"But now the mystery is out. Unless . . . I can trust you to keep my secret safe?" she asked in a deliberately flirtatious tone.

Scott instantly took the bait. "Absolutely." He grinned at her, all boyish charm. "On one condition: that you tell me all about yourself."

"What do you want to know?" Taylor shrugged innocently. Damn, it felt good to be flirting. The hell with cheating fiancés and ex-wedding nights and brilliant blue-eyed Sexiest Men Alive going on sex romps to wine country with their gorgeous blonde toothpick costars.

"Well, for starters, how long have you and Jason been seeing each other?"

Taylor scoffed at this. Perhaps a little too vehemently.

"We're not dating," she said definitively. "Jason and I are just . . . business associates."

Scott looked deep into her eyes, taking another step closer. "Are you sure about that?"

Taylor nodded. "I'm positive."

He grinned.

"Then maybe, Mystery Woman, you should start by telling me your name."

LATER THAT NIGHT, after the last of the party guests had straggled out, Jason fell asleep thinking about how perfectly the evening had gone. He pushed aside all of Jeremy's annoying negativity: So what if he had to trick Taylor into admitting her feelings? In the long run, none of that would matter.

After letting Taylor stew for a day or two, he would put into effect the second half of his plan: he would sweep in, assure her that Naomi meant nothing to him, that *she* was the only woman he thought about. And Taylor, in turn, having already implicitly admitted her feelings with the jealous look, would have to concede her loss and have no reason not to explicitly admit her feelings as well.

But despite the fact that everything was smoothly falling into place, Jason had a terrible dream that night.

He dreamt that he was back at the party. He knew Taylor was there, but he couldn't find her anywhere. Finally he spotted her at a secluded table in the garden, drinking a glass of wine that he knew came from Napa Valley. But Taylor wasn't alone. Sitting next to her—too close to her—and wearing some sort of weird painter's beret was Brad Pitt. For some reason, Taylor kept calling him Jason.

Jason called her name, but Taylor ignored him. He tried walking over to her, but a stone wall suddenly popped out of the ground like a medieval fortress. Then Brad grinned and held out his hand and led Taylor into the house. Jason watched the two of them through the windows; he saw them head up to his bedroom, and he shouted for Taylor to stop. But nobody could hear him except for Jeremy, who popped out of nowhere dangling upside down from a tree while wearing a court jester's costume and giggling something about the party being over. Then Jeremy's laugh turned maniacal and he flung his cigarette into some nearby bushes. Walls sprung up all around Jason, closing him in, and he had no choice but to watch helplessly as his beautiful twelve-thousand-square-foot French Normandy–style house burst into flames and burned to the ground.

Jason woke up with a start.

Gasping for breath, he shook the nightmare off and tried to clear his head. Parched with thirst, he got up and gulped down a glass of water in the kitchen. He peeked through his windows and briefly opened the back door just to make sure he didn't smell any smoke.

But by the time he got back into bed, Jason was once again convinced that all was right with the world. As his head hit the pillow, he smiled at the sheer ridiculousness of his dream.

Brad Pitt. Jason almost laughed out loud at the thought.

He *wished* he was Jason Andrews.

Eighteen

THREE DAYS LATER, satisfied that he had given Taylor sufficient time to see the error of her ways, Jason headed up the walkway of her apartment building with a spring in his step.

Whistling merrily, he knocked on the front door. He grinned, thinking how Taylor's dreams were about to come true. And his, too, finally—he'd certainly waited long enough.

Jason heard footsteps, and the front door flew open. Taylor greeted him in the doorway, wearing jeans and a fitted gray T-shirt. Her face broke into a wide smile when she saw him. He had been expecting this very reaction, of course.

"Hey! Come on in," Taylor beamed enthusiastically.

"Wow—you almost seem happy to see me, Ms. Donovan," Jason teased as he stepped inside, willing to prolong the game a moment or two longer.

"I am. There's something I wanted to talk to you about."

Jason smiled. Of course there was.

"Really? What's that?" he asked innocently.

"I hope you don't mind, I was just making dinner," she said over her shoulder. "Feel free to pour yourself a glass of wine. You're welcome to stay."

Of course he was.

Jason followed her into the kitchen. When he got there, he saw that "making dinner" in Taylor's mind meant mixing the dressing into a premade salad she had presumably picked up from the grocery store on the way home from work.

The woman truly was helpless in the kitchen. But he was willing to overlook this.

Jason spotted the open bottle of wine on the counter. Taylor pointed to the cabinet that contained her wineglasses, and he took out one for each of them. They certainly were about to have plenty to celebrate.

"Actually, there's something I want to talk to you about as well," he said as he poured each of them a glass.

"Okay." Taylor shrugged agreeably. "You go first."

Jason paused, wanting to appear contemplative, as if he needed a moment to begin. In reality, he had run through this monologue three times in the Aston Martin on the way over. Always a perfectionist, he wanted to be certain he nailed his lines just right.

"Well . . ." he began carefully, "I've been doing some thinking. About Naomi." He quickly glanced over to catch Taylor's reaction. She appeared nonchalant, concentrating on the salad. He gave her props for her acting skills.

"And I've decided that things aren't going to work out with her after all."

Taylor looked up. "Oh? Why's that?"

"Because there's someone else I'm more interested in," Jason said. With that, he moved closer to her and brushed a lock of hair off her shoulder. He handed her one of the wineglasses and gazed down at her seductively.

"Why don't we go away this weekend instead? I'd love to take you to Napa, Taylor." His voice was husky and intimate. "Just the two of us."

She peered up at him, and Jason recognized the telltale devilish sparkle in her eyes. He wondered whether they would have sex right there on the counter. He moved the salad bowl out of the way.

Taylor's eyes held his.

"No."

Jason cocked his head, confused. What was this word, "no"? She was always saying it around him.

"Excuse me?"

"Sorry, but *no*," Taylor repeated. "As in, *no*, I can't go away with you this weekend." She casually took a sip of her wine and set her glass down. She turned away, slid the salad bowl that he had just moved back into place, and resumed her dinner preparations. Jason's visions of crazy counter sex and flying arugula began to fade.

"What do you mean, you *can't*?"

"Well, for starters, I have other plans this Saturday."

Jason scoffed at this. "Plans? What plans?"

Taylor shrugged innocently, keeping her eyes on the salad she was making. "Oh, just, you know, other plans."

Ahh . . . *now* Jason understood what was going on here. A last-ditch effort to play hard to get. But really, he felt that it was time for them to cut through all the crap. A man like him could only wait so long.

He spotted something on the kitchen counter: *People* magazine, with his picture on the cover. Sexiest Man Alive. Aha! Evidence. Deciding to call Taylor's bluff, Jason grabbed the magazine and held it up to her.

"Really, Taylor, you don't have to keep up the charade. I mean, who wouldn't want to go away for the weekend with *this* guy?"

She cocked her head, considering this. Then she pointed to something on the magazine's cover. "Somebody who has a date, on Saturday, with *that* guy."

Come again?

Jason turned the magazine around to see what she was pointing to. He saw a picture of Scott Casey in the corner, under a caption that read "Other Contenders."

He glanced back at her.

"Scott Casey?"

Taylor raised an eyebrow proudly. "Yes. Kind of funny, huh? We're going out this Saturday."

Jason's face fell.

No.

This could not be.

"Scott Casey?" he repeated dumbly.

Taylor cocked her head. "Why do you keep saying it like that? Yes, *Scott Casey.*" She reached around him to grab a fork out of one of the drawers.

Jason needed to sit for a moment. He suddenly felt a little . . . fragile. He sunk onto one of the counter stools, in a daze. "I don't understand," he managed to mumble, disoriented. "When did this happen? How did this happen?"

Taylor dished some salad onto her plate, tilting the bowl to ask Jason if he wanted any. He waved this off, impatient for her to continue.

"I met him at your party," she said. "It's a funny coincidence—we must have been leaving at the same time. Anyway, we hung out for a while, and you know what?—he was actually kind of fun to talk to. And *whew*—well, let's just say that he is not exactly tough on the eyes.".

Taylor looked him over, then pointed with her fork. "He could even give you a run for your money." With a wink, she took a bite of her salad.

Jason sat at the counter, speechless. By now, the two of them were supposed to be deep in the throes of I'm-so-glad-you-chose-me-Jason makeup sex.

He cleared his throat. "So where's he taking you on Saturday?"

Taylor waved this off as she took another bite of her salad. "I don't know, we didn't talk about that." She smiled slyly. "Besides, as you've pointed out several times, it's *Scott Casey.* Does it really matter where we go?"

Jason stood up so quickly the stool banged against the counter. He could not *believe* the shit she was saying.

"Seriously, Taylor—do you *know* who I am?" he demanded.

She smiled at this. "You celebrities actually say that? That's cute."

Jason raked his fingers through his hair in exasperation. "I don't believe this," he muttered, more to himself than anyone. Thoroughly worked up, he glanced around the kitchen.

"I need something to drink—why is it so fucking hot in here?"

He went over to the sink, dumped his wine, and hurriedly filled his glass with water. He gulped the whole thing down, then finally turned back to Taylor.

She studied him for a long moment, then cocked her head. "Is something wrong, Jason?"

He was quite certain he detected the faintest trace of a smile on her lips.

JEREMY WAS DEEP in thought, typing on his computer at a table in the back of Reilly's Tavern. The bar was quiet and empty, except for the manager, who occasionally wandered out of his office to accept deliveries from beer trucks in the alley.

The studio that had bought Jeremy's latest screenplay wanted a "stronger midpoint." According to the know-it-all development execs assigned to the project, things were proceeding too easily for the hero halfway through the story, and they wanted to shake things up a bit.

"Maybe there's some villain who's been quietly lurking in the shadows, and suddenly he makes a play for the heroine," one of the studio execs had said. The rest of the suits in the room nodded excitedly in agreement as Jeremy rolled his eyes.

Fucking Hollywood.

Jeremy quickly reminded them that this was a *serious* film about vampire/alien hybrids waging a battle for world domination against an evil zombie/warlock hybrid empire, not some lame-o chick flick.

But, since nobody was listening to him—which apparently was the theme of the week—Jeremy plodded along, typing in the requested changes to the script.

When suddenly the door to the bar slammed violently open.

Startled, Jeremy peered up from his computer and saw Jason standing in the doorway, looking all dark and stormy.

"You."

He pointed accusingly at Jeremy.

"Did you set this up?"

Jason furiously walked over to Jeremy's table. "Fess up, funny boy. Did you set this up?"

Jeremy stared blankly at him. "Did I set what up?"

"This thing with Scott Casey."

"What thing with Scott Casey?"

Deciding this could go on all day, Jason changed tactics.

"Okay, you got me." He grinned sheepishly. "Ha ha, very funny. When did you and Taylor come up with this . . . what? This little trick to put me in my place?" Ready to be a good sport, Jason wagged a finger at him. "Very clever."

Jeremy folded his hands politely on the table.

"Jason. I have no fucking clue what you're talking about."

Jason's face fell. "Really?"

"Yes, really," Jeremy said. "I haven't seen Taylor since the night of your party."

With this news, Jason slumped into the empty chair at Jeremy's table. He fell silent for a moment, then peered over at his friend in shock. "Then she really does have a date with Scott Casey."

Jeremy blinked at this. "Taylor's dating *Scott Casey*?" He began to laugh. He held up one hand, clutching his side with the other. "Wait, wait." He gasped for breath. "This really is too good. I gotta write this down to use one day."

Jeremy turned to his computer, reading out loud as he typed. " 'And then the evil, arrogant movie star learned that lying does not pay.' "

Jason glared silently as Jeremy leaned back in his chair, still chuckling.

"Ahhh . . . Scott Casey . . . now that's classic."

"Are you finished?"

Jeremy peered over innocently. "They say he's the It Guy, you know."

Jason's eyes narrowed warningly.

"All right, all right, I'm done," Jeremy finally acquiesced. "Tell me how this happened."

Jason leapt out of his chair. "The hell if I know! Last night, I went over to Taylor's apartment to tell her about Naomi, but the next thing I know, she's talking about Scott Casey and how they have some date on Saturday." Jason pointed. "He picked her up at *my* party." Then he punched the air. "I *knew* I should've thrown that little punk out the minute I saw him."

"Wow. That's not exactly how you saw this playing out, is it?"

"No, it isn't," Jason retorted. He paced angrily. "What can she seriously see in that guy? He's as dull as a lamppost."

"A slightly younger lamppost," Jeremy quipped.

Jason looked over, stung. That hit below the belt.

Jeremy immediately held up his hands in contrition. "Okay, okay. I'm sorry." He got up and followed Jason over to the pool table. "So what's your game plan now?" he asked as Jason picked up a cue stick.

Jason shook his head. "I don't know. I can't think straight. Something's off."

"Did you sleep last night?"

"Barely."

"Are you mad at Taylor?"

"Yes. Definitely."

Jeremy leaned against the pool table and lit up a cigarette as Jason racked the balls for a game. "Do you have any right to be?"

Jason glared at Jeremy for this. But after a moment, his expression softened.

"Probably not," he acknowledged.

Jeremy nodded, rubbing his four-day stubble like a detective on the case.

"Yep, I've seen these symptoms before . . ." he mused. "I believe it's called 'jealousy.' Something common men unlike yourself experience from time to time."

"Yeah, well, it sucks," Jason replied pissily. He aimed his stick at the cue ball and took a shot. He whiffed, missed the ball entirely, and hit the pool table face-first.

Jeremy barely stifled his smile. Ahhh . . . if only the paparazzi could capture moments like this.

"So I guess this means you and Taylor are friends now," he said.

Jason scoffed emphatically while rubbing his nose. "Please—I'm never just 'the friend.'"

"Scott Casey might beg to differ with you on that."

Jason pointed at him. "You say his name again, and I swear I'll get you fired off that vampire flick of yours."

Jeremy was highly offended by this.

"Hey—let's get something straight. It's a vampire/alien/zombie/warlock *hybrid* flick."

Nineteen

AND JUST LIKE that, everything had changed.

On an impulse after losing three straight games of pool at Reilly's Tavern, Jason had declared to Jeremy that they were going out for the evening. But now, as he sat in one of the booths at Hyde, he found that his heart just wasn't into the whole West Hollywood nightclub scene that night.

Because everything had changed.

The bar was packed. Underneath the candles that hung from the club's copper ceiling, Jeremy and the other guys they had come with—friends from Around—argued over which Ben Affleck/Michael Bay collaboration ranked higher in the biggest cinematic disasters of all time, *Pearl Harbor* or *Armageddon*.

Jason heard Jeremy's irate shout over the music, obviously voting for the latter.

"Come on—that scene with the animal crackers? Are you kidding me with that shit? I almost gagged up my Jujyfruits."

Now normally, Jason would have been tempted to enter this fray, especially since he not only enjoyed any opportunity to contradict Jeremy, but also because he personally thought that *Pearl Harbor* should be placed on the American Medical Association's list of potential causes of eye cancer.

But tonight, he found he couldn't quite muster up the enthusiasm. Tonight, there was no fight left in him.

She was going out with someone else.

Scott Casey.

Jason couldn't imagine how the situation could possibly get any worse.

As he took a long sip of his drink, finishing off his fifth Stolichnaya Elit on the rocks that evening, he wondered how, exactly, things had gone so far awry. For the first time in over ten years, he didn't know what to do.

Yes, call *Us Weekly.* Call Page Six, the *Enquirer,* and everyone else.

Jason Andrews had woman problems.

"Should I order us another drink?"

The question came from Jason's right, from the ravishing blonde with fantastically long legs that sat next to him.

Hey—he was in a bar and he was Jason Andrews. *Of course* there was a ravishing blonde with fantastically long legs sitting next to him.

Jason turned his attention to the girl. He was a wee bit buzzed from the vodka and more than a wee bit melancholy.

"Do you have goals, Shyla?" He sighed. "Tell me what a woman like you wants to do with her life."

"Shay-na," the blonde corrected him.

Jason leaned his head back against the booth and closed his eyes. Suddenly, this entire conversation made his head hurt.

He opened his eyes to find Shayna sitting in his lap, leaning over him. From what Jason could tell, the woman already had two pretty nice assets working for her in life, and the push-up bra she wore shoved them straight into his face.

She whispered seductively in his ear.

"My goal is to blow you in your car tonight when you drive me home to fuck me."

Jason sighed tiredly. It was always the same thing. *Jason, I want to blow you. Jason, let's go back to my trailer and fuck like wild dogs. Jason, I'll bring my girlfriend next time, she's in Cirque du Soleil and can do things to her body you wouldn't believe.* Blah, blah, blah.

With Shayna's two ample assets presented right at eye level, Jason tried to muster some interest in her suggestion. But try as he might, it was a different pair of assets—a pair of lively green eyes to be exact—that he couldn't get out of his mind.

So he shook his head.

"Sorry—it's a guy's night out tonight." With that, he scooped the blonde off his lap, stood up, and turned to Jeremy. "Let's get out of here."

Jeremy glanced over at Jason and nodded. He disliked the L.A. club scene even more than the L.A. party scene, so it didn't take a whole heck of a lot to convince him to leave. Besides, the guys they had came with were total friggin' morons—one of them had just argued that *Armageddon* had strong "situational character development."

Shayna, on the other hand, was not quite ready to call it an evening. She reached for Jason's hand.

"Wait, what's the problem?" She smiled invitingly. "You're here with your boys; I'm here with my girls. Why don't we leave with you and all party together?" She pointed to an attractive redhead seated at a table nearby. "That's my friend, Eve. She and I *love* to party together."

Jason sighed again. Ho-hum, another threesome. It was all so passé.

With an apologetic smile, he leaned down to give Shayna a polite kiss on the cheek. "Thanks, darling, I appreciate the offer. But not tonight."

Suddenly, there was a voice from behind.

"Well, well, well . . . what do we have here?"

Jason closed his eyes. He *knew* he shouldn't have come to this fucking club. It was like one big frat party for celebrities, the place they all came together to be misunderstood and put-upon by the exhausting demands of the outside world.

With great annoyance, Jason turned around.

Scott Casey stood before him, looking smugly at Jason and the long-legged Shayna. Jason checked out Scott's entourage and immediately dismissed them all. The only one he even vaguely recognized was that Rob Who-Gives-a-Shit Jeremy had pointed out at the Lakers game several weeks ago.

"Hello, Scott. Funny seeing you here," Jason said, keeping his voice calm.

Scott smiled magnanimously. "I'd just thought I'd say hello—I didn't get a chance at your party. You may have heard, I was a little busy that night."

Jason knew he was being baited. But he was hardly about to let some pretty-boy wanker think he cared one bit about anything that had happened last Saturday or any other day. So his smile remained as smooth and cool as ice.

"Did I hear you're chasing after Marty Shepherd these days?" he asked, faux-politely.

Scott's smug expression faded just a bit. Then he recovered. "I don't chase anyone, my friend." He held his arms out wide. "I just wait for them to come to me. Speaking of which . . ."

Jason looked up at the ceiling, knowing what Scott was about to say before the words even came out.

". . . I'm going out with someone you know this weekend," he continued. "A lawyer. Taylor Donovan. She tells me you two are business associates."

Jeremy, who had been standing next to Jason during this exchange, whistled low under his breath.

"Business associates? Ouch. That's worse than friends."

Jason threw him a look. Perhaps they could do without the commentary for a few minutes.

Overhearing Jeremy, Scott leaned over to Rob and whispered something under his breath. Then he turned back to Jason, eying Shayna, who unfortunately had moved her hand to Jason's arm.

Scott smiled. "Well, I'll be sure to tell Taylor I ran into you and your little friend here. I'm sure she'll be very interested to hear all about it."

Jason's eyes narrowed at the threat. "Don't bother, I'll tell her myself. We're having dinner this Thursday; didn't she mention it?"

As the two men faced off, Jeremy apparently felt it was time to step in. He stood in front of Jason, blocking his view of Scott.

"Okay, okay," he said to Jason. "Now that we've established that you have the bigger penis, I think we should leave."

Since Jeremy had inserted himself into the fray, Scott's friend Rob now needed to chime in as well. It was part of the sacred celebrity entourage code.

"Hey—buddy," he jeered at Jeremy. "Who the hell are you? The comic sidekick?"

Jeremy turned around to face Rob and coolly looked him up and down.

"Sidekick? Fuck you, porky."

Scott's entourage gasped. For a sometimes-working Los Angeles actor, there was no greater insult.

Rob's face turned bright red. "How many times do I have to tell you people? I'm on *hiatus!*" he shouted, just before taking a swing at Jeremy.

And just like that, all hell broke loose.

"YOU GOT INTO a *fight* with *Scott Casey*?"

The next morning, Jason was in the car the studio provided, being driven to the set. The minute his cell phone had rung and he saw Marty's name, he knew what was coming.

"How do you know about that already?" Jason asked. "That only happened like"—he checked his watch—"six hours ago."

"How do I know?" Marty shouted across the line. "I know because I know *everyone*, Jason. For chrissakes, you were at Hyde. I've got half the staff there on my payroll. You do realize those little coke parties you celebs like to throw in the bathrooms don't actually go unnoticed, don't you?"

Jason leaned back against the seat of the limo and closed his eyes. He had a hangover and was not at all in the mood for a lecture.

"Then you should check your sources, Marty, because *I* didn't get into a fight with anyone last night. *I* was the one pulling my friend away from that portly D-lister with the serious stick up his ass."

Jason could hear Marty barking orders to his secretary on

the other end of the line. He could just picture his publicist, storming into the office while on his cell phone, all frantic and "Get me *Us Weekly*, *stat*!"–like.

"I've got four eyewitnesses who say that you and Scott Casey exchanged words, Jason."

"Yes, well, 'words' are still the way human beings communicate, Marty," Jason threw back at him.

"Just tell me this—did this alleged fight with Scott Casey have anything to do with Taylor Donovan?"

Jason bristled at the question. "No, you tell me—does the reason you're so pissed about this alleged fight have anything to do with the fact that you're allegedly trying to land Scott Casey as a client?" He paused for a moment to let this sit. "I know everyone, too, Marty."

Marty fell quiet for a moment. Jason wasn't sure if he had lost the connection or if his publicist was simply taking a moment to decide what spin to put on his answer.

Marty finally answered.

It had been the latter.

"Jason, Jason . . ." he oozed soothingly. "You know you are my number one priority. You always have been my number one priority, and you always will be—until the day you either run off to some private island in the Pacific, build a compound, and have fifteen babies with your native housekeeper, or kill me with a heart attack from all the shit you'll still be getting into when you're eighty fucking years old."

Hearing Jason's silence, Marty took a breath before continuing.

"And since you are my number one priority, I would be remiss in my obligations as your publicist if I didn't speak to you when I sense something at odds with your image. Tremors in the force that is Jason Andrews, if you will."

Jason repeated this to himself. Tremors in the force that is Jason Andrews. Classic.

"Dumping supermodels in London is *you*," Marty went on. "Getting into petty fights at some Hollywood nightclub? That is *not* you. Dating international actresses, like Naomi Cross for example—that is *you*. Dating some lawyer from Chicago? *Not* you. Do you see what I'm getting at?"

"We're not dating, Marty," Jason said. "For the record, Taylor and I aren't sleeping together, having an affair, or anything. We're . . . I don't know. Something else."

Marty snorted at this.

"No offense, Jason, but having been your publicist for the last thirteen years, I think I know. You don't *do* 'something else.' "

THAT EVENING, JASON knocked decisively on Taylor's front door. Marty's words had plagued him all day and he needed to do something about it. Now.

Taylor opened the door, surprised to see him.

"Hey—I thought we were meeting later this week," she said.

Standing on her doorstep, Jason knew the way he handled this next moment would determine everything.

"Come with me to the Pacific Design Center." Shit—he hadn't meant for that to come out sounding like a command.

Taylor looked at him strangely. "Why?"

Jason stared awkwardly at the ground. He definitely should've done a run-through of this in the Aston Martin on the way over.

"Because I need help picking out a new couch," he said, peering up at her uncertainly. "Isn't that what *friends* do?"

He watched, trying to gauge Taylor's reaction. Seemingly unsure at first, she studied him as if debating, looking him over with those bold green eyes of hers.

Finally, she nodded. "Okay."

Jason's face broke into a relieved smile. "Okay." He exhaled, glad that was over. "Should we go?"

Taylor went back inside her apartment and grabbed her keys. As she followed Jason out to his car, she tapped him on the shoulder. "Hey—can I drive the Aston Martin?"

"No."

"But isn't that what *friends* do?"

"No."

Jason opened the passenger door for her and walked around to the driver's side. As he got in the car, Taylor glanced over.

"My, my, you're awfully grumpy today . . . Is something wrong?"

Jason looked at her, sitting by his side. Actually, it was the best he had felt in the last two days.

True, it was not exactly the way he had envisioned things going with Taylor. But at least it was something.

So he grinned as he fired up the Aston Martin.

"Buckle up, sweetheart," he told her. "This ain't no PT Cruiser."

And with that, he gunned the car to life and they drove off into the sunset.

Twenty

TAYLOR WATCHED AS Scott expertly chopped up some asparagus and tossed it into the sauté pan simmering on the stove. He added a dash of olive oil.

"You know, when you invited me to dinner, I didn't know you were planning to cook it," she said. She sat across from Scott on the other side of the chef's counter, sipping the martini he had poured when she first arrived.

"Your rules about not being seen in public don't leave room for much else," he grinned teasingly. Taylor noticed that a stray lock of blond hair had fallen across his forehead, nearly into his eyes, as he worked. There was something inherently sexy about a man who knew his way around a kitchen.

"Thanks for being understanding about that," she told him. "I'm trying to keep a low profile for my trial."

Scott shrugged this off. "No problem. This isn't yet the best moment for me to be spotted with the famous Mystery Woman anyway."

Taylor straightened a little in her chair. That was kind of an odd thing to say. "What do you mean?"

Scott glanced up from his cooking and saw the expression

on her face. He smiled reassuringly. "Oh, I just meant you'd probably be hounded even more if the press saw us together."

Taylor's nodded, softening. "Oh. Of course."

Stop being so suspicious, she told herself. Trying to relax, she glanced around what she could see of his house. The kitchen, foyer, and living room suggested that Scott (or his decorator) had ultramodern taste. With stark white walls, metal staircases, slate countertops, and stainless steel cabinets, Taylor found the decor a little . . . cold. In her opinion, the best feature of the house was the deck outside that opened to a spectacular view of downtown Los Angeles.

Deciding to take a closer look, she grabbed her martini and headed over to the sliding glass doors.

"Do you mind?" She gestured outside.

Scott shook his head. "Not at all. Make yourself at home."

Taylor stepped out onto the deck and felt the cool breeze cutting across the Hollywood Hills. She leaned against the railing and gazed out at the twinkling lights of the city.

For what had to be the hundredth time that week, she wondered what the hell she was doing.

She had debated over and over whether she should cancel her date with Scott. She had a whole list of reasons ready: she was too busy with her trial, she barely knew him, she didn't want to get involved in a relationship in Los Angeles, et cetera. But none of those reasons had sounded particularly convincing, even to her.

Scott Casey had asked her out on a date.

Scott Casey.

Taylor knew that millions of women would die to be in her position that night. And that had been the clincher: she had realized that if she couldn't say yes to a date with Scott Casey, then she seriously needed to examine what was stopping her. Or rather, *who* was stopping her.

And that was something she did not want to think about.

Scott popped his head out onto the deck. "Dinner should be ready in about five minutes. Do you want another drink?"

Taylor glanced down at her empty martini glass. "Sure, that'd be great."

Determined to have the best night of her life—because

that's what a date with Scott Casey should be—Taylor followed him inside.

"SO WHERE DID you learn how to cook?"

Scott (or his assistant) had elaborately set the dining-room table with dozens of flickering candles. Music—what sounded suspiciously like the *Garden State* sound track—played throughout the house through unseen speakers.

Scott smiled in response to Taylor's question about him. "You don't know this?" He appeared surprised when she shook her head, no.

"Chef's school," he told her.

"Really? When did you do that?"

"Back in Sydney. That's how I got started in acting." Scott peered at her curiously. "You really don't know this?"

Taylor shook her head again. Okay, she got it. She lived in a hole.

So he gave her the rundown. "Well, one day this casting director walked into one of my classes, looking for culinary students for a daytime cooking show. I got the job, and I did the show for about a year. But I really got into the acting side of things, so I got an agent who sent me on a few auditions. My first real acting gig was on a prime-time show for that same network, and from there I moved into film, smaller roles at first, then bigger, until finally I got the call about *A Viking's Quest*. And then the rest, as they say, is history."

"That's a pretty interesting story," Taylor said, impressed.

Scott grinned. "Thanks." He reached across the table and laced his fingers through hers. "But enough about me. I want to know all about you, gorgeous."

Normally, Taylor hated questions like that. They were so interview-y. Good conversation should just flow organically, from the moment.

She quickly tried to think of a topic she and Scott had in common. "Well, I mentioned before that I'm from Chicago. Let me ask you something—was it hard when you first moved to Los Angeles? Did you miss home?"

But Scott waved this off, uninterested. "We can talk about that some other time. What I want to know is how I ever got lucky enough to get a beautiful girl like you to go out with me."

Taylor burst out laughing. Surely he had to be joking with a line like that. She stopped when she saw the confused look on his face.

"Wait—you're serious?"

Scott pulled back. "What's that supposed to mean?"

"Nothing, sorry." Taylor bit her lip and tried to disguise her misunderstanding by gesturing to the windows that ran along the dining-room wall. "So, that's really some view you have there."

Scott smiled. "Yes, it is." He turned back to Taylor with what was presumably a "seductive" look. "But not as good as the one I have right here."

Taylor laughed again. "All right, now I *know* you're joking."

Scott abruptly sat back in his chair. "I'm just trying to pay you a compliment, Taylor," he said defensively. "I didn't realize it was that funny."

Taylor shut up. Again.

Okay . . . so . . . awkward moment here . . .

It appeared pretty safe to say that Scott didn't go for the whole dry/sarcastic humor thing. She would just have to come up with some other material. Too bad she really didn't have any other material.

An uncomfortable silence followed, and Taylor was just thinking that perhaps she might compliment the salt and pepper shakers sitting on the table—they were the *loveliest* shade of pewter, when—

—thank god, her cell phone rang.

Taylor dove immediately for her purse, which sat on the chair next to her. "Sorry, I have to keep it on for work," she apologized to Scott. How terrible—she found herself almost hoping it was some kind of work emergency.

She checked the caller ID and instantly recognized the particular 310 area code number that showed up on the phone's display. A number that just happened to belong to one Mr. Jason Andrews.

Taylor defiantly flung her hair back. Oh, sure—like she was going to take *his* call right then. She was a little busy.

Seeing Scott's curious look, Taylor smiled. Suddenly, her date seemed ten times more interesting.

"It's no one," she told him. "I'll just turn it on vibrate."

She adjusted the phone and set it off to the side of the glass dining table. Then she leaned in toward Scott flirtatiously, peering deep into his light hazel eyes. "So . . . where were we?"

Liking her sudden interest, Scott smiled coyly and leaned in the rest of the way across the table. "I was just about to tell you—"

Right then, Taylor's phone began vibrating. Loudly.

Glancing over, she saw the same 310 number on the phone's display. The *nerve* of that man. Seriously.

When she didn't immediately pick up, the phone began rattling louder, sliding across the glass table toward her. Apparently, a certain someone refused to be ignored.

Taylor grabbed the phone, stuffed it into her purse, and resolutely zipped it shut. That should take care of that. She smiled apologetically at Scott. "Sorry. You were saying?"

"Are you sure you don't have to get that?" he asked skeptically.

Taylor waved this off. "Oh no, it's fine. Anyway, tell me about this movie you're filming, *Outback Nights*."

Scott seemed happy to oblige her. "Well, I play this sort of loner, rebel type . . ."

As Taylor listened while he went on about the film, her cell phone suddenly began to vibrate again, this time from inside her purse. Irate at the prospect of being ignored, the phone rattled around demandingly.

Buzz-*buzz*!

Buzz-*buzz*!

Despite herself, Taylor fought back a smile, trying very, very hard to pay attention to Scott's story.

Buzz-*buzz*!

Buzz-*buzz*!

". . . Of course, the director said he could think of no one other than me for the part from the first moment he read the script . . ."

Buzz-*buzz*!

Buzz-*buzz*!

Suddenly, it stopped. The phone in her purse lay quiet for a moment, then—

Buzz-*buzz*!

Buzz-*buzz*!

Taylor had to stifle her laugh. Ahh . . . if nothing else, the man was persistent. She had to give him that.

Right then, Scott's cell phone rang, too. She was saved by the proverbial bell.

Scott made a face. "Wow—crazy night, huh?" He pulled his own cell phone out of his pocket, then glanced up at Taylor. "Sorry—it's my agent. I really should take this." He stepped out of the room to take the call.

As he left the room, Taylor's phone vibrated once again. Buzz-*buzz*! Oh, for heaven's sake—she reached in, yanked the phone out of her purse, and flipped it open.

"What the hell are you doing??" she whispered furiously.

Jason's smooth voice came over the other end of the line.

"Well, hello, Ms. Donovan. Goodness, I was starting to get worried. Is everything all right?"

"Why are you calling, Jason?" Taylor hissed. She checked to make sure Scott was still in the other room.

"Hmm? Oh yes—see, I couldn't remember what time we're meeting tomorrow to go over the third act of the script. Is it seven or eight o'clock?"

"Jason—" Taylor began warningly.

"—And I also wanted to know whether I should bring dinner to your apartment. Or will you be providing the edibles?"

Part of her wanted to reach through the phone and strangle him. The other part of her couldn't help but smile.

"Stop being cute. You know this is a bad time for me."

"Why? Wait—is tonight the night of the big date? Oh . . . I had completely forgotten all about that. Oops."

"You're a better actor than that, Jason."

She heard him chuckled.

"So true. Fine—I just thought I'd see how everything's going."

Taylor deflected the question. "Where are you?" She could hear loud voices and music in the background.

"Reilly's Tavern. Playing darts." Jason paused for a moment. "But you didn't answer my question."

Now it was Taylor's turn to pause. "The date's going great," she said convincingly.

"How nice. And where has Junior taken you to eat?"

"Actually, I'm at his place. He's cooking for me."

There was a long silence on the other end of the line.

"Really," he finally said, through what sounded like clenched teeth.

Taylor smiled into the phone. "Why, Jason—that sounds a bit like jealousy, doesn't it?"

He snorted disdainfully. "Jealous of Scott Casey? Please." He got a good laugh out of this. "Hey—if you find him interesting, Taylor, more power to you. I also know a nice box of rocks you could cuddle up with, if that's your thing."

She glared into the phone. "Yeah, well, maybe I *do* happen to find him interesting."

"Really? Then why are you spending your date talking to me?"

"You know, that can easily be fixed."

She hung up the phone.

Taylor tossed the phone back into her purse, thoroughly annoyed. *First* he talked about going to Napa Valley with her when he obviously had been planning on going with Naomi Cross just a few days before. As if women were as interchangeable as the parts of a Mr. Potato Head. And now *this*? Deliberately interrupting her date? The boundaries of the man's self-centeredness were truly limitless.

Underscoring this point, Taylor's phone rang again. This time, she didn't even bother to look before answering.

"You know, if you're trying to mark your territory, you could've just peed on me before I came over here and saved us both a lot of time!"

On the other end, Jason burst out laughing. "I always suspected you were into kinky shit."

Despite herself, Taylor laughed, too. He somehow always managed to do that—completely infuriate her one moment, then make her smile the next. It was actually quite sneaky.

"Good-bye, Jason. I'll see you tomorrow," she said, amused. Then she hung up the phone and stared at it for a long moment, until she heard someone clear his throat behind her. Taylor glanced up and saw Scott watching her from the doorway.

Looking very displeased.

OVER AT REILLY'S Tavern, Jeremy watched as Jason tucked his cell phone into his pocket.

"Not jealous of Scott Casey, huh?" He glanced pointedly at the dartboard, where Jason had taped Scott Casey's "Other Contenders" photograph to the bull's eye. Three darts jutted out prominently from the young actor's forehead.

Jason ignored the question. He walked over and yanked his darts out of the board.

"He's *cooking* for her," he said disgustedly, as if this were a felony. "Like she's going to fall for *that*. It's so . . . amateur."

"*I* cook for my dates," Jeremy volunteered.

"You have to. You can't afford to take them anywhere."

"This is true," Jeremy conceded good-naturedly. "Although I have also discovered that women really seem to like the taste of macaroni and cheese."

Not even bothering with a token sarcastic response, Jason stared intensely at the picture of Scott Casey on the dartboard before him.

Suddenly, he vehemently rapid-fired all three darts.

He turned and took a swig of his beer as Jeremy nodded, impressed. Over at the board, a dart pierced right through each of Scott Casey's eyes. The third jutted out prominently from his throat.

"Not bad," Jeremy said. "But perhaps this is a good time to discuss your anger management issues."

Jason sat down at their bar table as Jeremy lined up for his turn at the board. "You don't think Taylor really likes this guy, do you?"

Jeremy shrugged, about to throw. "I don't know. I haven't met too many women who wouldn't be impressed by Scott Casey." He pointed the darts at Jason, thinking. "Then again, I haven't met *any* other woman who has been so wholly unimpressed by you, so maybe there's hope yet."

Jason didn't even crack a smile. In fact, he looked utterly miserable. Jeremy gave up his position at the dartboard and took a seat.

"Come on, Jason—what's going on with you and this girl? This isn't like you."

"So everyone keeps telling me."

"Then what is it?"

Jason sighed. "I don't know . . ." He looked over at Jeremy, suddenly serious. "All I know is that I can't stop thinking about her."

Now it was Jeremy's turn to sigh. "Ahh . . . the friend zone. Have I *been* there."

The two of them sat in dejected silence. Then Jeremy thought of something.

"Hey—you know what you need? You need a real guy's night out. None of this pansy-ass Hollywood nightclub shit. I heard about this poker game going on tonight. Just a few writers I know, nothing high stakes. We can smoke cigars, drink some Macallan, talk about—"

"Poker?" Jason's eyes lit up feverishly. "Why didn't you tell me about this before?"

"Well, I wasn't sure you'd be interested, given your track record."

"So I've been dealt a few bad hands," Jason said dismissively. "Who hasn't?"

Jeremy fought back his grin. The poor guy really had no idea. Any poker player worth his salt picked up on the whole watch thing in two hands or less. That was why he had subtly steered Jason toward craps a few years ago, when they had started going to Vegas and Jason had begun gambling serious money.

Of course, Jeremy supposed, a better man would've simply told his friend about his little tell. But as long as Jason never got into any serious trouble—hey, as long as he was still driving friggin' Aston Martins and living in twenty-five-million-dollar houses—Jeremy saw no harm in keeping quiet. Every once in a while, it came in quite handy to be able to tell when Jason was lying. Like that time, years ago, when he had insisted he'd lost *Speed* to Keanu because the director had said he was "too tall" for the shots on the bus.

So Jeremy remained quiet this time as well. "Yes, that's right, Jason," he said reassuringly. "You've been dealt some bad hands. That's all."

Jason eagerly rubbed his hands together. "And that means I'm due—I can feel the gods of luck smiling down on me." He pointed at Jeremy, highly confident. "You better be careful tonight. I'd hate for you to lose all your mac-and-cheese money."

To keep his mouth shut, Jeremy took a long swig of his beer. After polishing it off, he set the bottle down on the table and gestured to the door. "Should we go then?"

Jason nodded, and Jeremy followed him out the bar.

He had the funniest feeling steak dinners were about to be back on the week's menu.

LATER THAT NIGHT, Taylor let herself into her apartment. Not in the mood for a sudden flood of light, she turned on just one lamp in the living room. She kicked off her heels and sunk into the couch.

She wasn't exactly an expert—this having been her first, first date in several years—but she felt that an objective third party would have to say that the night had gone relatively well.

Her thoughts drifted back to what had been the turning point of the evening: the moment when she had hung up the phone with Jason and noticed Scott standing in the doorway. She could immediately tell by the look on his face that he knew who she'd been talking to.

"You should be careful around him," Scott said flatly.

Taylor tucked her phone into her purse. Yes, well, thanks for the news flash.

"We're just friends," she replied.

Scott took a seat next to her at the dining table. "So it's

friends now? I thought you said you and Jason were just business associates."

Taylor toyed with her wineglass. She wasn't sure she owed him any further explanation. They had known each other all of what—six days?

"We're just friends, Scott," she repeated simply.

Seeming to sense her wariness, Scott took his questioning down a notch. "I'm just worried about you, gorgeous, that's all. I know plenty of women who have had their hearts broken by Jason Andrews. It's not a pretty sight." He paused. "In fact, this friend of mine . . ." He trailed off, waving his hand. "Never mind, you don't need to hear this stuff."

Taylor thought about this. Did she? Perhaps whatever Scott had to say was exactly what she needed to hear. The lawyer in her decided it was best to have all the facts.

"No, go on," she told him. "I'd like to know whatever it was you were going to say."

Scott looked pained to have to tell the story. "Well . . . Jason once dated this girl I know. She's a supermodel—"

Of course she was a supermodel.

"—and apparently," Scott continued, "she and Jason took a trip to London together. For some photo shoot or something she had there. But on their third day together, he left the hotel after breakfast, telling her he was going to get fitted for suits on Savile Row."

Probably for the legal thriller he was filming, Taylor thought. So this was something that had happened fairly recently.

"But it must've been one hell of a long fitting," Scott marched on, "because your 'friend' Jason didn't come back to the hotel. *Ever.* He just left the poor girl alone in London, without even saying good-bye. She thought he was dead or had been kidnapped or something, until she saw his picture in the *Daily Mirror* the next morning. The British paparazzi had caught him at the airport, happily boarding a flight back to Los Angeles."

Taylor remained silent after Scott finished his story. Frankly, she didn't know what to say in response. Assuming the story was true, was she surprised to hear that Jason could be so callous? Was she disappointed? Angry?

She stared at her wineglass, feeling Scott's eyes on her. She knew she had to say something.

"Wow. I guess I don't know why Jason would do something like that."

"Because he can."

Scott took hold of Taylor's wineglass and set it off to the side, out of their way. He spoke cautiously as he peered at her from across the table.

"You know, Taylor, some people say he can get any woman he wants."

This struck a nerve with her.

Taylor thought about Scott's words. Really? Was that what people said? Right then, she knew what she had to do.

She reached over and pulled Scott toward her. And she kissed him—a long, deep kiss. When she pulled back, she stared directly into his eyes.

"You know what, Scott? I think you better start listening to different people."

SITTING ON HER living room couch, Taylor's mind drifted back to the present.

Okay, sure, it had been a good kiss. And in the interests of full disclosure, the kiss in the kitchen, when they were cleaning up after dinner, hadn't been too shabby, either. Nor the two in the foyer by the front door. Nor the really long good-night kiss against her car.

Yes, Taylor decided, all in all it had been a very nice first date. He had cooked for her, complimented her, even said all the right things about calling her the next day, and—for crying out loud, he was *Scott Casey*.

But.

Something was missing.

Taylor curled up and rested her head against the soft suede pillows of the couch.

She had just gone on a great first date with a handsome international movie star, and she thought something was *missing*. But she couldn't deny it, something had indeed been lacking in their date.

Because not a single kiss with Scott Casey had held a candle to her one almost-kiss with Jason.

Taylor closed her eyes in frustration. Hell, she supposed, it didn't matter that her night with Scott had ended with only a kiss. Because she was as good as fucked anyway.

She needed somebody to talk some sense into her.

She needed somebody to give her a swift smack upside the head and a good, strong kick in the ass.

She needed Val and Kate.

Quickly.

Twenty-one

THE WITNESS'S MONOTONE voice droned on end-
lessly.

Watching from the defense table, Taylor glanced over to
see how the jury was reacting to the woman's testimony,
which had been going on for hours with seemingly no end in
sight.

She saw that three of the jurors had already nodded off and
that the remaining six appeared ready to drop like flies any
moment. She watched as the juror in the far back corner began bobbing her head like a high school student in history
class. Wait . . . wait for it . . .

The juror's head dropped back against the seat, and her
mouth fell open.

Taylor grinned. Another one bites the dust.

Seemingly oblivious to these goings-on, Frank stood at the
podium asking one long, drawn-out question after the other.
Apparently, he was unaware of the torture he was inflicting
upon these jurors he would later ask for $30 million.

". . . And like I said earlier," the witness rambled on, "on many occasions, I would overhear my manager refer to women as 'chicks.' "

"How many times did you hear your manager use that word?" Frank asked.

The witness took a moment to answer, as if needing to compose herself. Taylor tried to keep from rolling her eyes at Derek, who sat next to her at the defense table.

"Oh, I couldn't even guess," the witness tearfully responded. "My manager used that derogatory term too many times to count."

Frank nodded sympathetically. "Then perhaps we should go through all the occasions you can remember your manager using the word 'chicks.' One incident at a time, in detail."

This was too much. Taylor rose from her table.

"I have to object to this line of questioning, Your Honor."

The judge peered over at her. "Grounds?"

"Well, for starters, it's entirely too boring for four o'clock on a Friday afternoon."

The jurors—the ones that were awake, anyway—laughed.

Frank pounded the podium furiously. "Your Honor—Ms. Donovan's objection is highly inappropriate! I ask that she be admonished for her conduct, and I move to strike her comment from the record!"

Taylor shrugged amiably. "Fine—I'll modify my objection to include the fact that nothing in this witness's testimony even remotely resembles sexual harassment."

The judge held up his hand before Frank could respond further.

"All right, counselors, that's enough. I agree that it's getting late. It might be a good time to take a break." He peered down from his bench at Frank. "Counselor, do you intend to continue this line of questioning on Monday?"

"Your Honor, if I may," Taylor interjected, "in order to keep the trial moving, the defendant will stipulate that this witness would testify that she heard the word 'chicks' in her workplace on several occasions."

"Not *several*, Your Honor, *numerous* occasions," Frank replied pissily.

Taylor held up her hands innocently. "Now counsel is just getting greedy, Your Honor."

More titters of laughter could be heard coming from the jury box. The judge rapped his gavel lightly.

"In order to keep this trial on schedule, I will accept the defendant's proposed stipulation. The record will reflect that this witness would testify that she heard the word 'chicks' in her workplace on *several* occasions." He gave Frank a stern look. "Mr. Siedlecki, you've already fallen two days behind on your witness list. I suggest you find ways to structure their testimonies more succinctly."

Then the judge turned to Taylor. "As for you, Ms. Donovan, in the future, please try to keep your objections within the confines of the Federal Rules of Evidence." His words were firm, but his expression held a trace of a smile.

"Yes, Your Honor," Taylor said demurely. She knew when she had pushed a judge just far enough.

"Good. Ladies and gentlemen, you are excused until Monday morning," the judge told the jury. "I remind you that you are not permitted to discuss this case with anyone, including each other, until it's time for your deliberations." He banged his gavel. "This court stands in recess."

"All rise! This honorable court is in recess," the clerk of court shouted.

The judge stood to leave, and the entire courtroom rose with him. As the bailiff escorted the jurors out, a few nodded and smiled as they passed by Taylor.

Derek leaned over. "They adore you," he whispered.

Taylor grinned proudly. God, she loved this stuff.

After the jurors left the courtroom, she quickly began throwing files into her briefcase.

"I'm late—I gotta run," she told Derek. "But we should plan to meet on Sunday evening to go over next week's cross-examinations."

Derek watched her with amusement. Taylor suspected that his knowing smile had something to do with the fact that she had received flowers on Monday from Scott Casey. The news had spread through the office faster than the clap.

"Big plans for tonight, Taylor?" he inquired. "Let me guess—happy hour at L'Ermitage with Johnny Depp, perhaps?"

Taylor looked up, surprised. "Well, well, well . . . so there's a smart-ass lurking inside you after all, Derek. I like it."

The junior associate grinned. "I think I'm turning into you. Another week and I'll be dropping F-bombs around the office."

Taylor patted his shoulder affectionately. "I think you're safe. I would never use the term 'F-bomb.'" With a teasing wink, she grabbed her briefcase, wished Derek a good weekend, and left the courtroom in a hurry.

DRIVING TO THE airport, feeling her excitement build, Taylor practiced various ways to tell Val and Kate about everything that had unfolded since she had moved to Los Angeles. Unfortunately, every scenario she had come up with so far made her sound totally, criminally insane.

"Hi, guys," she supposed she could always say, "guess what's happened to me? I've been working with Jason Andrews on his new film and he flew me in his private jet to Las Vegas where we almost kissed, and then I went to this glamorous party where Scott Casey asked me out, and oh—by the way, he and I *did* kiss, several times actually, after he cooked me dinner at his multimillion-dollar house up in the Hollywood Hills."

Now *there* was a surefire way to earn a straightjacket and a one-way ticket to Chicago's finest mental institution.

Taylor realized that this situation had to be finessed delicately, especially to avoid hurting Kate and Val's feelings for not telling them everything earlier. She decided she would wait until they got back to her apartment. They could settle in, and then she would slowly unravel the story for them, in a way that sounded at least somewhat plausible.

Driving along the highway that afternoon, Taylor felt for the first time since coming to L.A. as though she finally had a moment to catch her breath. Some time to herself, so she could really take stock of everything that had happened over the past month.

Jason Andrews.

Scott Casey.

Taylor suddenly began laughing. Really laughing, to the point where she needed to wipe the tears from her eyes in order to see the road in front of her.

Passing by her in a gray Mercedes, a tanned California couple looked at her oddly. True—she must have been quite a sight, alone in her car and laughing hysterically. For one crazy second, she was tempted to roll down her window and shout to them, "But don't you know who I am? I'm the Mystery Woman!"

But the Mercedes drove by, and the moment passed, and Taylor's laughter gradually subsided.

But her good mood lasted.

It was a gorgeous day in Los Angeles—not quite sunset—and she was about to see her two best friends for the first time in almost two months. She was excited to show them all the L.A. sights she'd been meaning to get to and looked forward to some quality girl time—something she definitely had been missing as of late.

Taylor wondered how her friends would react to her news.

She wondered what they would say about Jason. Oh yeah, and Scott Casey, too.

She wondered if straightjackets came in a size 2.

TAYLOR STOOD AT the secutity checkpoint, waiting for Kate and Valerie to appear. She saw Val first, who immediately broke into a run with her arms outstretched.

"Taylor Donovan!" she screamed excitedly. Val was like that—she wore every emotion on her sleeve. Every pant leg, sock, and shoe, too.

Kate followed, more sedate than Val, but no less happy to see her. "Look at you, California girl," she said to Taylor with a wink.

Within seconds, the three of them were jumbled up in their hellos and hugs, all talking excitedly until Taylor finally steered them away from the security gates.

"So how was the flight?" she asked. "Did you check any luggage?"

"Val had to," Kate informed her. "She brought fifteen outfits for two nights. And nine pairs of shoes."

"Ignore her crankiness," Val told Taylor. "She's just mad that I saw Josh Hartnett sitting in first class and she didn't."

"That wasn't Josh Hartnett; that kid was eighteen years old," Kate said.

"I told you, they age slower out here. It's all the fresh California air," Val replied.

"Yes, because that's *exactly* what Los Angeles is known for," Kate said dryly. "Clean air."

Taylor stopped and took in her friends. It was like being home again. "God, I missed you two," she said, taking them both in with a content smile. First Valerie, with her shoulder-length curly blonde hair and typical slightly eclectic attire of jeans, a flowy peasant top, and oversized hoop earrings. In stark contrast next to her stood Kate, with her stick-straight ebony hair pulled back in a serious bun and wearing a gray pinstripe pantsuit and no-nonsense Marc Jacobs one-inch heels.

The fact that these two women were finally in Los Angeles left Taylor feeling quite sentimental. "You guys look so great." She sighed happily.

At that, Kate leaned over and whispered loudly to Val. "Oh no—I think she's gone soft on us."

Val covered her mouth with one hand, "I *told* you about that giggle I heard," she said to Kate.

"That's right!" Kate pointed at Taylor, suddenly remembering. "You. Spill it. Giggling? Mysterious evenings out? What's been going on out here?"

Taylor gestured to their surroundings. "Can we at least get out of the airport? I think we're gonna need a few drinks for this."

Valerie shrugged amiably. "Fine, I want to get back to your place to freshen up, anyway."

Kate rolled her eyes. "Freshen up? You spent twenty minutes doing your makeup on the plane before we landed."

Valerie fixed Kate with an ultraserious stare. "Katherine. We are in *L.A.* One must look their best at all times out here. You never know who you might meet." Val looped her arm through Taylor's as the three of them headed in the direction of the baggage claim. "Tell her, Taylor."

Kate pulled her suitcase along, keeping up with them. "Yes, tell me, Taylor," she said teasingly. "Tell me how the celebrities are just falling off the trees around here, like oranges."

Taylor stared straight ahead as they walked, praying she didn't lose her shit right there in the airport.

"Um, well . . . let's get back to my place. Then I'll tell you everything you want to know."

BACK AT HER apartment, after getting Kate and Val set up in her guest bedroom, Taylor poured them a round of their usual mango martinis. She sipped her drink quickly, figuring the buzz would help loosen her tongue, which lately seemed to get stuck anytime she even thought the name Jason Andrews.

Oh yeah, and Scott Casey, too. Of course.

Realizing she couldn't delay any further, Taylor sat her drink down on the kitchen table. Determined to get this over with.

"Okay, look—I need to tell you guys something. Actually, now it's a couple of somethings." She took a deep breath. Slowly, ease into it slowly.

"So here's the deal: the firm put me on this project, and I had to keep things quiet to avoid any publicity conflicts with my trial." Taylor stopped. Damn—that had come out wrong. "Not that I thought either of you would purposely tell anyone," she backtracked, "but—"

"Oh my god . . ." Kate whispered. Her eyes widened in shock. "You're not coming back to Chicago."

Taylor shook her head. "Of course I am. That's not it." She regrouped. "Anyway, for this project, I had to work with a certain someone, and help him out with—"

Valerie gasped excitedly. "I knew it! You're dating some-body!"

Taylor pointed at her emphatically. "*No*. We are definitely *not* dating. Well, but then there's kind of this other guy, but I just met him last week and I don't really know where that's going . . ."

Seeing that her friends were totally lost, she pulled herself together. "Let me start over. About a month ago, I met—"

She was cut off by a loud knock at her front door.

Taylor held a finger up to Val and Kate. "Hold that thought for a second while I get this."

As she headed into the living room, she overheard Kate mumble to Val, "Hold *what* thought? I haven't understood a word she's said yet."

Taylor unlocked her front door and opened it. Before she could react, Jason barreled right in, all fired up.

"Where have you been?? I tried calling you—is your cell phone off? I need you to tell me who the hell I can sue. I just met with Marty—we got back the mock-ups for the new publicity posters the studio's going to use to promote *Inferno*."

Jason stormed into the kitchen, so engrossed in his rant he didn't notice Valerie and Kate. He opened Taylor's fridge and helped himself to a bottled water.

"And get this," he fumed angrily, "the dumbasses who de-signed the posters have me pictured in this scene where I'm putting out a fire with all these other firemen. But if you look at the poster from the side, the water from the hose of one of the other firefighters looks like it's shooting right out of my crotch. And the best part is, they want to put this poster over the theater entrance for the premiere. I can just see it—" He gestured grandly to the air. " 'Come see *Inferno*! Get pissed on by Jason Andrews!' "

With that, he threw Taylor a wink. "It should be right up your alley."

Finished with his rant, Jason took a sip of water. Then he finally noticed Kate and Val. He smiled charmingly.

"Oh. People. Hello."

Kate and Val sat in silence at the table. They stared at the sight of this god, this ideal man of modern time, standing before them in all his glory.

In their friend's kitchen.

Valerie began giggling nervously.

Kate held her martini glass aloft, still frozen in midair after Jason's grand entrance.

"Taylor Donovan," she whispered hoarsely. "What is this man doing in your kitchen?"

Jason tipped his Evian bottle. "Having a drink of water."

Taylor threw him a look—he wasn't exactly helping the situation. She turned to her friends to make the introductions. So much for easing slowly into the conversation.

"Kate, Val—I think you know Jason. Jason, this is Kate and Valerie, my friends from Chicago."

Valerie jumped out of her chair, finally finding her voice. "You little shit!" She wagged her finger in Taylor's face. "How could you not tell us this?"

Not waiting for an answer, Val rushed over to shake Jason's hand, gushing effusively. "It's so nice to meet you, Jason. I'm a big fan—I've seen every one of your movies. Like six times."

Hearing that, Jason proudly folded his arms across his chest and shot Taylor a satisfied grin. "Told you," he mouthed. Then he turned back to Valerie, who stared at him in a daze, still holding his hand.

"Thank you. That's always nice to hear," he said warmly. "So you two are friends of Taylor?"

Kate and Val managed mute nods.

"You're visiting from Chicago, then?"

More nodding. Chicago, yes, uh-huh, whatever. We saw you naked in *Overload.*

Jason turned to Kate, trying to draw her out. "So what do you ladies have planned for tonight?"

Val and Kate shrugged, silly grins still plastered on their faces.

Taylor intervened, gently extracting Val's hand from Jason's. "I tried to get us reservations at Koi, but they were booked this whole weekend. We'll come up with something else."

At this, Jason rolled his eyes. He whipped out his cell phone, unable to suppress his smile. "You never cease to amaze me, Taylor."

Despite herself, she felt her cheeks blushing.

Jason held Taylor's gaze as he spoke into his phone. "Yeah, Marty, it's me. Get me a table at Koi tonight. Party of . . ." He looked at her questioningly. "Is this a girls-only night, or are guys invited, too?"

"Oh my god, guys are so invited!" Valerie cried out, practically barreling Jason over in her excitement.

Over Val's head, he looked at Taylor teasingly. "I guess that means you're stuck with me again, Ms. Donovan." He grinned at Valerie, to explain. "She thinks she hates me."

He winked, as if to say they all knew the likelihood of *that* being true.

Twenty-two

THE GIRLS SCRAMBLED to get ready. As they rushed in and out of the bathroom, trying on various outfits (Val's fifteen now came in very handy), Taylor's friends demanded to know every detail of her relationship with Jason. So she told them.

How she couldn't stand him when they first met.

How he was arrogant and rude, and how he insulted her on national television.

How she fought and fought and fought to get off the Andrews Project, but nobody at her firm had listened.

"And now?" Kate asked, sitting cross-legged on Taylor's bed. They both were already dressed. Val, however, still fussed in front of the full-length mirror in the corner of the bedroom.

"And now, I don't know," Taylor said, shrugging. "I guess I find him, you know, tolerable."

"Tolerable." Val turned around from the mirror. "You find Jason Andrews *tolerable*."

"Well . . ." she hedged.

"Would you like to amend your answer, Taylor?" Kate asked in a sly lawyer's tone.

Then she told her friends about Vegas, and how in a moment of alcohol-induced weakness (that was still her story
and she was sticking to it), she and Jason had almost kissed.
Until they were interrupted by a horde of screaming fans.

"Man, I *hate* when that happens," Kate interjected.
"Screaming hordes of fans ruin everything."

Then Taylor also told them about the party, describing in
detail Jason's amazing house. But for whatever reason, she
didn't tell them about the run-in with Naomi. Pride, perhaps.

"So now what?" Val asked. She had finally settled on a red
sleeveless top and True Religion jeans. "What's going on with
you two?"

"Nothing is going on with us," Taylor said.

"Well, isn't that a crime . . ." Val mused. "You need to get
on that ASAP, Taylor. Like tonight. You're a fool if you
don't."

Before Taylor could respond, the doorbell rang. Val jumped
up and ran excitedly into the living room. Taylor and Kate followed and caught up with Val as she peeked out the front
window.

She turned around, gesturing outside. "This man you find
tolerable just sent a limo to pick us up. What do you have to
say about that?"

Curious, Taylor and Kate peered out the window.

"What on earth have you done to him?" Kate asked, taking
in the limo outside.

"Oh, you know, slammed a few doors in his face, hung up
on him a couple of times, tossed around a slew of insults."

Kate nodded. "Ah, the usual stuff."

She and Taylor shared a smile. Then they watched through
the window as Valerie hightailed it outside. She paused at the
limo and grandly blew air kisses to a few of Taylor's neigh-
bors before climbing inside.

EVERYWHERE THEY WENT that night, people stared.

At Koi, as the five of them (Jason had brought Jeremy
along) ate ridiculously expensive sushi and knocked back several drinks, people stared.

At Teddy's at the Roosevelt Hotel, as they laughed while at their poolside table, people stared.

When they left Teddy's and walked right past the line outside Privilege, people stared.

As they were ushered into the club, with its white walls and white floor, by a manager (dressed all in white), and seated at a private booth (white leather, natch), people stared.

And Kate and Val ate up every minute of it.

It had to be one of the best, if not *the* best, nights of their lives. And certainly the most glamorous. They were treated like royalty everywhere they went. All because of Jason.

After the waiter took the group's drink orders, Taylor found herself thinking about Jason's attitude that evening. Or rather, his complete lack thereof. He was being entirely gracious with her friends. Charming. Friendly. Downright nice, actually. Throughout the night, he had been eager to make sure her friends were having a good time. He talked at length to both Val and Kate, making an effort to get to know each of them. To the point, frankly, where Taylor felt as though she had spent almost the whole evening with Jeremy.

Which was perfectly fine. Her friends could have Jason Andrews—she'd spent enough time around him as it was.

Hadn't she?

They were on their second round of drinks when Taylor noticed that a thick crowd had grown around their table. When a sweaty drunk guy with overly gelled hair—some famous-for-being-famous oil heir who hung out with Paris Hilton (according to Val's knowing whisper)—knocked into Taylor and nearly spilled his drink on her, Jason appeared to reach his limit.

"Let's head to the back," he declared.

Taylor took advantage of their change in location by heading over to the bar to settle their tab. Jason had paid for everything else that evening, and she felt guilty continuing to take advantage of his generosity. He may have money, but she certainly could handle paying for a few rounds of drinks.

She got her credit card out of her purse and was trying to flag down their waiter when Jason pulled up next to her at the bar.

"What do you plan to do with that?" He pointed to her credit card with amusement.

"At least let me pay for the drinks," she insisted.

"Why? So you can turn around and expense them as part of my legal bills?" Jason grinned teasingly.

Recalling how awkward their earlier conversation on the subject of billing had been, Taylor blushed. "Don't worry—I'm not going to expense it," she told him. "I doubt I could get away with calling this work." She gestured to the bar and the crowd surrounding them.

Jason leaned against the bar. "No? Then what exactly would you call this?" He gestured to the bar and crowd, imitating her.

Right then, somebody bumped into Taylor, pushing her into Jason. He steadied her, putting one hand on her hip to protect her from the crowd. Pressed against him, Taylor glanced up and found his eyes staring straight into hers.

There were hundreds of people in the club that night.

But suddenly it felt like it was just the two of them.

AS THEY STOOD together amidst the low, seductive candlelight that illuminated the bar, Jason's mind raced in a million directions.

He watched as Taylor took a step back, putting some distance between them. She seemed a little flustered. Good, Jason thought. It was about time.

"What do you mean?" she asked, trying to continue on with a normal conversation. "What would I call *what*, exactly?"

He pointed between them. "I think you once described this as me 'pestering' you."

Taylor smiled. "Me? That doesn't sound like something I would say."

Jason could've sworn he heard a flirtatious tone there. "No, I distinctly remember the conversation," he said. "We were at the Bellagio, on the terrace . . ."

Taylor's cheeks flushed tellingly, and Jason knew then that she remembered not only the conversation but also what had happened, or almost happened, immediately afterward.

Just at that moment, the crowd surged again. To avoid crashing into Taylor, he braced himself against the bar, one arm on either side of her. Trapping her in.

He grinned down at Taylor, referring to their position. "Yes, I think this is exactly where we were last time."

She gazed up at him. "We should get back to our friends."

"We've already spent a lot of time with them tonight."

She cocked her head. "I thought you liked talking with Val and Kate."

"Because they're *your* friends." Jason paused. "It's all for you, you know."

He saw a flash in her eyes, but it wasn't anger this time. "Jason . . ." she said in a husky voice.

Man, that did it *every* time. Forgetting where they were, and everything around them, Jason leaned down and whispered in her ear. "Say it again, Taylor. I love the way you say my name."

He heard the quick intake of her breath at the intimacy of his words. He moved his head, so that their lips were just inches apart. Her eyes were dark and sultry. She turned her face up toward his and slowly began to lean in as if she, too, was being drawn in and couldn't help it—

"Jason."

But this time, the person saying his name wasn't Taylor.

It was Jeremy.

Jason glanced over and saw his friend standing next to him. His look said it all—*You have got to be fucking kidding me.*

Jeremy wore a sheepish expression. "Sorry, buddy—but we've got to get you in back. In case you hadn't noticed, these people are going crazy." He pointed to the crowd behind him. "I don't think the club's bouncers can keep everyone away from you for much longer."

Jason peered over Jeremy's head and saw that he was right. A throng of people, both women and men, surged forward, trying to slip past the three bouncers who had formed a perimeter to protect him.

Jason nodded in agreement. Normally, he was very cautious in public places, but he had completely forgotten himself in the past few moments with Taylor.

"Lead the way," he told Jeremy while eying the frenzied crowd. He glanced down at Taylor and put his arm around her waist. "Stay between me and Jeremy," he told her.

Right then, a woman in her midtwenties broke past one of the bouncers. She lunged for Jason, shoving both Jeremy and Taylor out of the way.

"Oh my god! Jason—I love you!" she screamed frantically.

One of the bouncers grabbed hold of the woman right before she got to Jason and pulled her away.

Jason reached for Taylor. "Are you okay?"

But she seemed not to hear him. Her gaze was fixed on the woman, who was making a scene, clawing frantically at the bouncer who pulled her away from Jason. "Wait—please!" the woman cried out desperately. "I only want to talk to him for a minute! I just want to talk to him!"

Taylor was mesmerized.

Jason took her by the arm. "Taylor, we have to move away from here."

Hearing his words, she snapped out of it and nodded. "Sorry. Of course."

Then she quietly followed Jason and Jeremy to a private room in back.

JASON BARELY GOT a chance to talk to Taylor again.

She spent the rest of the time with her friends, and he didn't want to intrude. He suspected she'd been unnerved by the incident with the woman and wanted to give her some space. People around him unfortunately had no choice but to get used to that kind of thing. Even if it was more than a little weird.

The group stayed until the club closed. As they were leaving, the bar manager told Jason that a mob of paparazzi had formed out front and suggested they exit out back. As the five of them headed toward the limo that waited in the alley, Jason could hear the girls chatting excitedly about their evening.

He watched as Taylor broke apart from her friends and headed over. Jeremy subtly walked ahead as she fell into stride alongside him.

After walking a moment or two, she stopped and reached out to him. "Jason—hold on."

She paused awkwardly, then looked up to meet his gaze. "Thank you. For tonight."

With a slight smile, Jason nodded.

"You're welcome."

The two of them stood there, and Jason noticed that for once, she didn't ruin the moment with a sarcastic comment.

Nope, instead the moment was decidedly ruined by Valerie, who yelled over to them.

"Hey! Slowpokes!"

Jason and Taylor looked and saw Val hanging out the roof of the limo. "Would you two mind stepping it up a bit?" she asked, clearly tipsy. "You can continue your secret little chit-chat at Taylor's—we're all going back there for after hours."

Jason glanced at Taylor, curious to see her reaction to this turn of events.

With a shrug, she grinned.

"Shall we?"

Twenty-three

SO THE GROUP adjourned to Taylor's, where there was much laughing and drinking. Merriment, Kate jokingly declared, that's how she would describe it when she told *Us Weekly* all about the night as soon as she got back to Chicago. Ballyhoo, Jeremy said, backing Kate. Taylor wondered if they were flirting.

Meanwhile, Valerie sprawled across the couch. In her inebriated state, she had just remembered something that now didn't seem to make much sense.

"Taylor, didn't you say something earlier about having a date?" She waved her glass around, mango martini sloshing precariously inside.

It was like a record had skipped to a stop in the room.

Somehow, Taylor had completely forgotten all about Scott Casey for the entire evening.

Reading the frozen look on Taylor's face, a more sober Kate quickly intervened. "Oh, who cares about *that* after everything we've done tonight? Taylor—you can fill us in tomorrow."

But then a voice spoke out from corner of the room.

"Actually, *I* would like to hear more about Taylor's big date."

Everyone turned and looked over at Jason, who sat in the armchair in the corner of the room.

"After all," he said, holding Taylor's gaze, "it's not every day that a woman is lucky enough to go on a date with Scott Casey."

This news was just too much for Valerie to bear.

"Scott Casey?" she gasped. She grabbed Taylor's hand, nearly cutting off the circulation. Sitting next to her, even the usually cool Kate appeared shocked at this unexpected development.

Taylor strove for nonchalance. "It was just one date. I planned to tell you about it in the morning."

And with that, mass hysteria erupted.

Val shrieked and leapt off the couch. Mango martini flew everywhere. Kate immediately began firing questions at Taylor. Who? What? Where?

"Oh my god, oh my god, oh my god," cried Val, her contribution to the interrogation. Kate continued firing away, full speed. How? When? And then what?

As Taylor tried to wave off their questions, she caught a glimpse of Jason out of the corner of her eye. To put it mildly, he looked pissed. His grip on the highball glass grew tighter and tighter with every question asked.

Suddenly, Taylor found herself a bit annoyed. First of all, *he* had brought up the subject of her date with Scott Casey, not her. Second (and far more important in Taylor's mind), *she hadn't done anything wrong*. In fact, it was just recently that Jason had been flaunting *his* date with Naomi in front of *her*. She didn't know exactly what kind of game Jason was playing, but she did know one thing for certain:

Two could play at it.

So she flung her hair back, happy to answer any and all questions her friends might have.

First they covered the basics. Including how Scott had cooked for her.

"Oh . . . how sweet." Valerie sighed romantically. This was about the point at which Jeremy excused himself to have a smoke in the courtyard outside. Jason, on the other hand, sat quietly in the corner, simply listening, and for a few minutes, the girls forgot he was there.

"So, what does this mean?" Kate asked, moving onto the more substantive questions. "Are you going to see Scott again?"

Taylor paused. "Yes. This Saturday."

Jason glanced over sharply. "You didn't tell me that."

Taylor shrugged. "You didn't ask."

Valerie turned toward Jason, leaning tipsily over the arm of the couch. "See, *women* know how to ask the right questions," she explained.

"I see that," Jason said. "Please continue. I'd like to know what else I've missed about this date."

Kate appeared uncertain. "Maybe we should finish this later."

Jason waved her on, encouraging. "No, really—keep going. Pretend I'm not here. What would you ladies normally cover next? What kind of shoes he was wearing? What type of dressing they had with their salads?" Scoffing, he took a macho sip of his drink, all haughty man–like.

Kate shrugged matter-of-factly. "Actually, I'd ask if he was good in bed."

Jason choked on his drink. He leapt out of his chair and pointed at Taylor.

"Well, I certainly hope you don't know the answer to *that*!"

She stared at him. "Why? How many first dates have you had sex on?"

Jason sat back down. Shutting up now.

"Exactly," Taylor sassed him. "So don't act so appalled. You men ask the same questions."

Jason snickered at this. "No, generally, men start with whether she has big . . ." He trailed off, considering his audience. ". . . whether she's well-endowed," he rephrased politely.

Kate shrugged, happy to play along. "Fine. Is Scott Casey well-endowed?"

Jason gasped and pointed at Taylor again.

"Not one word."

Taylor studied him carefully. This was an interesting development. If there was indeed some game being played between her and Jason—which of course there was not—then she would have to say that Team Donovan had just scored another point.

She got up from the couch and began picking up the group's empty glasses. "Is there a problem, Jason?" she asked casually. "I thought you said you weren't jealous of Scott Casey."

In response, Jason grabbed some glasses and followed her into the kitchen. "It's not jealousy," he said. "I'm just trying to rush us through the girl talk so we can move on to the pillow fight or whatever other activities you ladies have planned for your sleepover."

They passed by Jeremy, who was coming in from outside, having finished his cigarette.

"Because we don't have to talk about my date, if it bothers you." Taylor began stacking glasses in the dishwasher.

Jason laughed this off. "Go ahead, talk all you want. I don't care."

She looked at him, trying to decide if he was telling the truth.

Jason looked at her earnestly. "Really, keep going. I think maybe you were about to tell us whether you slept with Scott Casey."

Taylor was about to answer when, out of the corner of her eye, she caught a glimpse of—

Kate, Val, and Jeremy.

The three of them sat in a row, wide-eyed, staring over the back of the couch at her and Jason. Mesmerized by the scene. Val had gotten hold of some M&M's from the dish on the coffee table and was chewing them distractedly, as if watching a movie.

Taylor cleared her throat. *Ahem* . . .

Kate and Jeremy blinked and jumped off the couch, realizing they were busted.

"Oh, wow, look at the time," Jeremy said in a rush. "You know, Jason, I really think it's time for us to get going."

Kate grabbed Valerie by the wrist, thinking along the same

lines. "Come on, Val. It's time to crash—there's a lot we want to do tomorrow." She pulled her reluctant friend off the couch and led her down the hallway. Valerie dragged her feet the whole way. "But Katherine, this shit is better than *Grey's Anatomy* . . ." she whispered loudly.

And so the party came to an end.

Taylor walked the men to the door, where Jeremy held out his hand in good-bye. "Taylor, it was a pleasure, as always." With a wink, he left.

Leaving just her and Jason.

Jason leaned against the door with his arms folded across his chest. He didn't say anything, but Taylor knew what he was waiting for.

"Not that it's any of your business," she said, "but the answer to your question . . . is no." She braced herself, expecting his smug comment.

But instead, Jason's reaction surprised her. His entire demeanor changed. Softened.

"Okay . . ." He exhaled. Then he headed over and stood before her to say good-bye.

"Good night, Taylor," he said gently. He lightly kissed her cheek.

The kiss and the soft tone of his voice gave her butterflies. A moment later, he was gone.

Taylor shut the door behind him and leaned against it for support. Then she headed down the hallway to her room.

Val and Kate were sitting on the bed, waiting, just as she knew they would be. Kate pointed at her.

"Talk."

TAYLOR FLOPPED ON the bed next to them and sighed.

"I don't even know where to start anymore."

"Fine, I'll start then," Val said. She seemed to have sobered a little while waiting for Taylor. "I'll begin with the obvious: he's Jason Andrews."

She stared at Taylor pointedly, making sure they were on the same page with this. "He's *Jason Andrews*."

"I know that, Val."

"Do you?" she asked skeptically. "Because from what I've seen, I'm not so sure."

"Trust me, I know who he is."

"Good—then let's move on to the fact that he's gorgeous, smart, witty, and—I hate to say it—filthy rich."

Taylor stopped her there. "You know I don't care about that."

"That doesn't mean it can't go in the plus column."

"I'm already aware of all these things," Taylor told her. "Every woman in the world is aware of these things."

"But he doesn't look at every woman in the world the way he looks at you." Valerie smiled. "He's crazy about you, Taylor."

She considered this. "You know, Val, for one brief moment, I thought the same as you. But you're wrong."

Val held her hands out, frustrated. "How do you know that?"

Taylor was tempted to tell them about Jason's party and her encounter with Naomi Cross. But she knew that Naomi Cross was only a small part of a much bigger problem.

"He's *Jason Andrews*," she said. "I could name a hundred women—very famous ones at that—who would tell you that he once looked at them the same way you think he looks at me." She caught Val's skeptical look. "He's an actor. A very good actor." Taylor held up a finger warningly. "Don't ever tell him I said that."

Seeing that Val remained unconvinced, she continued. "Think about who he is. He's the guy who said on national television that women should be treated like film scripts: kicked to the curb after an hour if they don't hold his interest."

Valerie shook her head resolutely. "But that was before he met you." She turned to Kate, who had been strangely quiet thus far. "Help me out here. Talk some sense into her," she pleaded.

Kate paused. When she finally spoke, her words were cautious. "I don't know. I'm not sure what I think."

"Oh no, not you, too," Val said despairingly. "What am I missing here?" She glanced back and forth between Kate and Taylor.

Taylor saw Kate's hesitation. "Go ahead—you can say it."

"It's just that . . ." Kate proceeded carefully, knowing that she was about to enter very risky territory. "Well, you've been down this road before, Taylor."

Valerie snorted disdainfully at this. "Jason Andrews is *nothing* like Daniel."

"You're right—he's worse," Taylor said dryly. "He's the legend that men like Daniel only aspire to be. You guys should've seen it at the bar—this woman went crazy just trying to *talk* to Jason."

"All of us were so infatuated with Daniel in law school," Kate told Valerie. "And we all knew about his reputation. But the way he acted with Taylor . . . I thought he had changed."

She shook her head apologetically at Taylor. "Wow—was I ever wrong about that, huh?"

"We all were," Taylor said. "Most of all me. I should've trusted my instincts."

"And I think that's what you need to do this time." Kate squeezed Taylor's hand reassuringly. "As much as I might like Jason, as much I think it would be a dream come true to date a movie star like him, I can't be the one who tells you to go for it this time. You're not going to get any more bullshit from me about love changing people. They can save that stuff for fairy tales and movies."

Val was crushed by what she was hearing. "I think this is the single most depressing conversation I've ever heard." She turned to Taylor for assurance. "Tell her she's wrong, Taylor. You're living proof that these things can happen. Tell her you still believe that."

Taylor stared into Valerie's hopeful eyes. Her friend, the romantic, who idolized celebrities because to her, they lived the dream. The glamorous life. Beautiful people who had adventures and romance, who fell deeply in love with other beautiful people and lived happily ever after.

And in Valerie's mind, if it could happen to her—Taylor Donovan from the south side of Chicago, who didn't know a soul in Hollywood when she got there—then maybe, just maybe, it could happen to anyone.

But there was one small problem.

Taylor didn't believe it.

She believed in logic. She believed in studying the evidence and following it to its natural conclusion. She did *not* believe in fantasies and fairy tales. She had learned, all too well after finding Daniel and his assistant and the naked thrusting butt cheeks, that life is not a romantic comedy.

So she turned to Valerie with her answer.

"What I think, Val, is that the biggest mistake a woman can make is convincing herself that *she* is the one who will be different. I've made that mistake once—it's not going to happen again."

Taylor had nothing further to say on the subject of Jason Andrews.

The conversation was over.

Twenty-four

THE FOLLOWING WEEK flew by uneventfully. Business as usual with her trial, and before Taylor knew it, another Friday morning had rolled around.

Unfortunately, on this particular Friday morning, Taylor was stuck in some very nasty Los Angeles traffic. Possibly, she was lost. Most definitely, she was late.

Trial-wise, the past four days had proceeded smoothly. The plaintiffs were nearing the end of their case-in-chief and had begun presenting their final witnesses in support of their claims for emotional distress damages. From the skeptical looks she'd seen on the jurors' faces, Taylor suspected they had as much problem as she did awarding someone $30 million for alleged sexually harassing behavior that was about as sexual as a Hilary Duff movie. Nowadays, and nowhere more so than in Los Angeles, juries wanted to see trials like the ones they saw on television. They wanted drama. Scandal. In the era of HBO, they expected a little bada-bang for $30 million.

Taylor thought again about how much she wanted to win this trial. Actually, it was pretty fair to say that she *needed* to win this trial. Because lately, work was the only thing in her life that still made sense.

She had been hoping that Val and Kate's visit would provide her with some much-needed clarity. But all it did was leave her even more confused.

After their conversation late Friday night, in a silent agreement to keep the rest of the weekend stress-free, the three of them had avoided the subject of Jason. On Saturday morning, they woke up and treated themselves to the full California workup: shopping on Rodeo Drive, a ridiculously overpriced lunch at the Ivy, an afternoon at the beach, and dinner at a quaint outdoor bistro in Santa Monica. While the night hadn't been as glamorous as the previous one spent with Hollywood's Sexiest Man Alive, it was the perfect way for the girls to relax, talk, and leave all cares of men behind.

Sunday morning, after a late brunch at the Viceroy hotel, Taylor had dropped off Kate and Val at the airport, shocked by how fast the weekend had flown by. It was when they were saying good-bye that Val first dared to broach the topic of her love life.

"So call us next week and tell us how Saturday goes." She hugged Taylor tightly. "I can't wait to hear all about your second date with Scott Casey."

Taylor smiled tentatively at her friend. "It's okay, Val, I'll say it if you won't. I know you think I'm making a mistake."

Val shook her head. "I don't think you're making a mistake. I think the same thing as Kate—that you should follow your instincts. I just hope you're willing to listen to those instincts no matter what they tell you."

Val's final words on the subject had stuck with Taylor well after her friends waved good-bye and boarded their plane back to Chicago. The words were in the back of her mind later that evening, as she worked alongside Derek late into Sunday night. They had stuck with her all week, during her trial, as she cross-examined the plaintiffs' witnesses.

And they still echoed in her head that Friday morning, as she sat in that damn L.A. traffic.

Taylor tapped her fingers impatiently on the steering wheel.

She checked her watch again, growing more agitated by the minute. She had never once been late for court. But lucky her—this morning there had been a detour on Wilshire Boulevard that had led her to the freeway, where she had no clue where she was going.

Taylor peered out the windows, looking for any sort of sign or street name she recognized. By now, she had turned against the PT Cruiser. What, the stupid thing couldn't have a navigation system?

Traffic suddenly began to move. This turned out to be even more problematic for Taylor, who had no idea where she should be moving *to*. Figuring this was no time to be proud, she pulled out her cell phone and dialed up Derek for directions. He answered from his post at the courthouse, relieved to hear that yes, of course she was still coming and no, she had not run off to Lake Como, Italy, to do backflips with the boys off George Clooney's yacht.

As Taylor jotted down the directions Derek gave her on a valet sticker she found in the glove compartment, she went over the day's strategy. Never one to miss an opportunity to multitask.

"Just make sure the exhibits are ready to go, one on top of the next," she told him as she precariously balanced a phone, a pen, and the steering wheel all at once. "I don't want to give the witnesses any time to think between questions."

"Do you really think Frank's going to keep putting them on the stand?" Derek asked on the other end of the line. "They're all doing so horribly."

Glancing up at the road ahead, Taylor spotted the exit she was supposed to take. Thank god. She guided her car toward the off ramp, still holding her cell phone with one hand.

"You and I may see that," she answered Derek, "but Frank seems to be living in crazy—"

Suddenly, she was cut off as another car shot out of nowhere into her lane, trying to make the exit ramp. With barely any time to react, she yanked the steering wheel to the right, trying to get out of the car's way, swerving into the next lane and—

—felt the jolt of an impact as another car hit her.

Everything happened in a lightning-quick blur: the wheels of the PT Cruiser spun out as Taylor's head struck the driver's side window and everything spun around and around and around and then—

The car suddenly lurched to a stop in a ditch on the side of the road.

Taylor's airbag exploded.

Well, at least the stupid PT Cruiser had those.

WITH A GROAN, Taylor pulled her head away from the inflated airbag. She gingerly touched the side of her head where she had cracked it against the window. While it felt quite painful, she didn't feel anything warm, icky, or gushing, which she took as a positive sign. She then began mentally running through a checklist: fingers moving, toes moving, all teeth appeared to be intact.

After what felt like only seconds, Taylor heard a frantic knock to her left. In her daze, she turned in the direction of the sound and saw a middle-aged man wearing a light blue suit and a Mickey Mouse tie at the driver's side window. The man yanked open her car door.

Taylor's first thought was that she, Taylor Donovan, was about to be rescued by a man in a blue leisure suit and Mickey Mouse tie.

Her second thought was that she, Taylor Donovan, didn't need to be rescued by anyone.

Her third thought was that she was oddly thinking of herself in the third person, and that couldn't be a good sign.

The Mickey Mouse guy stuck his head into the car. "Miss! Are you okay? Are you all right?"

Taylor smiled reassuringly. No worries, man. After all, she was Taylor Donovan. Confident that, through her customary humor and wit, she could show just how unfazed and confident a person Taylor Donovan was, she held up her cell phone for the Mouse man to see.

"Could I be more of a cliché?" she asked jokingly.

And that was the last thing Taylor Donovan said before passing out cold.

"I'M TELLING YOU, I'm fine. There's *nothing* to worry about. I feel great."

The doctor scribbled something in his chart, ignoring Taylor's assurances. She sat on the edge of the examination table, thinking that the Los Angeles emergency room certainly must have had more important things to worry about than the little bump on her head. Wasn't there some Lindsay Lohan "heat exhaustion" crisis to tend to?

Taylor had already called the courthouse and, luckily, the judge had been very understanding. He had agreed to recess the trial until Monday and told her to take care of herself for the weekend. Now if she could just get out of this darn hospital.

The doctor finally finished his scribbling and snapped his file shut.

"Well, you have a concussion, Taylor. And that means I can't release you for the next twenty-four hours unless you're under the care of another adult."

"No, but look—I'm fine," Taylor insisted. "See?" She wiggled her fingers and toes for the doctor's benefit, although being fully dressed in her suit and high heels meant the toe part of the demonstration wasn't particularly impressive.

"I'm sorry, but that's hospital policy. Blame it on you lawyers for making us so careful." He grinned at the joke.

Taylor groaned, not because of the lame attack on her profession, and not even because her head felt worse than it did when she was seven years old and her brother Patrick had dropped her on the sidewalk in a chicken fight against the O'Malley brothers gone awry, but because she really, really hated hospitals—possibly even more than airplanes. They had a funny smell.

The doctor looked at Taylor sympathetically. "Isn't there anyone you can call to come pick you up?"

Taylor silently debated the ethics of asking one's secretary to babysit one's concussed self on a Friday night. Then her cell phone rang.

She sheepishly gestured to her ringing purse, which sat on the chair in the corner of the examination room. "Sorry," she apologized to the doctor. "I forgot to turn it off."

The doctor was wholly nonplussed. "This is L.A., Taylor. I've seen women deliver babies while on their cell phones."

Taylor jumped off the table and pulled the phone out of her purse. She saw it was Scott calling and answered with surprise.

"Hello?"

"Hey! Gorgeous!" Scott's voice rang out cheerfully. "I was just calling to see what time I should pick you up tomorrow."

Shit—she had forgotten all about their date. Again.

"Um . . . Scott, hi . . . there's a slight problem." Taylor moved to the corner of the room and lowered her voice, not wanting the doctor to overhear.

"I was kind of in a car accident," she whispered into the phone. "Nothing serious—but I guess I have a concussion or something. They say they won't release me today unless someone comes to pick me up. I guess it's hospital policy."

Taylor paused, debating whether to continue. She decided to go for broke, driven on by dreaded thoughts of staying in the hospital overnight.

"So I don't suppose you have any interest in changing our date to tonight, do you?" she asked Scott, laughing lightly to cover how stupid she felt. "You'd just have to make sure I don't vomit after eating or anything. Although I suppose in Los Angeles, that's more a sign of peer pressure than a concussion, right?"

Instead of a reciprocal (or even polite) laugh, there was a long, silent pause on the other end of the line.

Okay, so that hadn't been her finest one-liner, Taylor thought. She had a concussion, after all. Cut her a little friggin' slack.

Finally, Scott answered, sounding even more uncomfortable than her. "Shit, Taylor, you know . . . normally I would love to help you out, but see—we're in the middle of filming right now, and I can't leave the set. Plus I don't know how long the director wants to go tonight. You understand, don't you, gorgeous?"

Taylor nodded. What had she expected, anyway? She'd had

one date with the guy. "Sure, no problem," she said lightly, hoping to cover her supreme lameness. "Why don't I call you• later, when things settle down?" She hurriedly said good-bye and hung up.

Taylor turned around and saw the doctor watching her. Clearly, he had heard every word.

"It's not like jail," he said with a kind smile. "You can make more than one phone call. I know you're new in town, but you must know someone else."

Of course, Taylor's mind did indeed turn right then to the one "someone else" in Los Angeles she knew.

Oh sure, like *that* was a possibility.

Maybe, in Valerie's fantasy world, Taylor would call up Jason Andrews, the (alleged) Sexiest Man Alive, and he would ride up to the hospital like a knight in shining armor and whisk her off to his magnificent palace far, far away.

But this was the real world. And Taylor happened to know for a fact that Jason was tied up at that very moment, filming. She certainly wasn't about to ask another man for help, only to again be rejected. Especially this particular man.

So Taylor took her seat on the examination table. She shook her head definitively.

"No—I can't think of anyone else to call," she told the doctor. "At least, no one any less busy."

"Not even a colleague from work?" the doctor asked insistently. "I'd really hate to keep you overnight."

Taylor shrugged. "I guess I don't have any choice, do I?"

The doctor nodded reluctantly. He sighed and opened his mouth to say something when—

"She'll stay with me."

The voice came from the doorway. Taylor turned around to look—

And saw Jason standing there.

Ignoring the surprised look on the doctor's face, he stepped into the room.

"You'll stay with me, Taylor," he said firmly.

She stared at him in shock. "What are you doing here?"

Jason shrugged her question off with a grin. "I heard you were here," he said, looking a little embarrassed.

And when his eyes met hers, Taylor—who as a matter of pride never, ever, let people see her rattled—suddenly found that she had absolutely no idea what to say.

Jason waited for some kind of reaction from her. When she remained silent, he turned to the doctor worriedly.

"I thought they said she was fine. She's too quiet."

The doctor shrugged. "Ms. Donovan seemed perfectly fine until you showed up, Mr. Andrews."

"Oh. Yes, well, that's generally how it works with us." Jason rubbed his hands together. "So what do I have to do to spring her out of here?"

"If you agree to have Taylor released in your care, you'll need to watch her closely for the next twenty-four hours," the doctor said. "Most important, when she's sleeping, you need to wake her every four hours and ask her a few questions to make sure she's conscious."

The doctor peered over. "As for you, Taylor, I want you to promise to take it easy these next couple of days. If you do, you should be okay to go back to work on Monday."

But Taylor could not stop staring at Jason. "How did you know?"

"How did I know what?"

"That I was in the hospital."

"I called your office looking for you. Linda told me you were here."

The doctor interrupted, turning their attention back to the important matters at hand. "So, as I said, Mr. Andrews, you'll need to ask Taylor a few quick questions when you wake her up. Something like this." He turned to her to demonstrate. "Do you remember my name?"

Taylor gave the doctor a look. Of course she remembered his name, she was *fine*. Didn't he remember the wiggling fingers and toes? "Dr. Singer," she told him.

"What did you have for breakfast this morning?"

"I don't eat breakfast. Wait—does a grande skim latte with two Splendas count?"

The doctor gave her a look. No, indeed it did not.

"What's your mother's maiden name?" he asked.

"Jennings."

Bored with the interrogation—this was *really* basic stuff—
Taylor turned her attention back to Jason. "What were you
calling me about?"

Distracted, Jason had to think. "I had a question about the
courtroom scene we were filming."

"You were filming?" she asked incredulously. "And you
just . . . left? To come here? For me?"

At this, Jason turned back to the doctor and spoke to him
in a low whisper. "Are you sure she's really okay? Because it's
been at least three minutes and I haven't been insulted yet."

But for once, Taylor was not in a teasing mood. She put her
hand on Jason's arm. "I'm being serious, Jason. You left in the
middle of filming to come *here*?"

Jason looked down at her. Suddenly, he, too, turned serious.

"They said you were in the hospital, Taylor. Of course I
left."

It was the matter-of-fact way he said it. And the way he
looked at her right then. Taylor suddenly felt as though she
was back in the PT Cruiser, spinning and spinning and spinning.

Jason Andrews.

Her knight in shining armor.

Well, if she believed in such things.

She looked down at the floor so that Jason couldn't see her
smile. A moment later, she felt his hand on her chin, bringing
her gaze up to his. His eyes searched hers worriedly.

"Are you sure you're okay, Taylor? Say something . . . normal." He gently tucked a lock of hair behind her ear, being
careful to avoid the bump on her head.

Taylor stared up into Jason's amazing blue eyes. He really
was the most gorgeous man she had ever seen.

With great effort, she pulled herself out of the dreamy
depths of the Sexiest Eyes Alive and somehow managed a
casual smile. She knew she should at least thank him for coming for her.

But then she noticed something she had somehow missed
earlier. She peered more closely at Jason. "Wait a second—are
you wearing *makeup*?"

Oh yes, there it was—a little trace of powder dusted across his face. And was that a smudge of eyeliner along his bottom lid . . . ?

This was too precious.

Taylor raised an eyebrow teasingly. "Gee, Jason, it's just a hospital—you really didn't need to get all gussied up."

And with that, Jason smiled. He turned to the doctor, finally satisfied.

"Okay. She's fine."

Twenty-five

AT JASON'S INSISTENCE, being like-minded with the doctor in thinking that a grande skim latte definitely did *not* constitute an adequate breakfast, he and Taylor stopped for lunch after leaving the hospital. Given her weakened condition, Taylor decided it was only fair that she got to pick the restaurant. Back when she was younger, any time one of the Donovan children got hurt (which with three boys and Taylor was quite often), her father treated the whole family to McDonald's cheeseburgers, fries, and chocolate shakes. Feeling nostalgic, she told Jason she wanted to honor that tradition.

To which he promptly responded that Aston Martins did *not* do McDonald's drive-thrus.

But then he went anyway.

They brought the food back to Taylor's apartment so she could pack an overnight bag. While they were eating their cheeseburgers in her kitchen, Taylor jokingly pretended to pass out cold on the table while handing her pickle over to Jason.

Oh boy, did *that* little ruse cause quite a bit of panic and mayhem.

Come on, she laughingly apologized to Jason, she'd only been kidding around. She stood out on her driveway, where he had locked himself in his car refusing to speak to her until she swore to never do that again.

But a little while later, as the adrenaline rush of the car accident wore off, Taylor began to feel in earnest the effects of the concussion. She was already yawning as they pulled into Jason's driveway. As the metal security gates parted grandly before them, she stared in awe at the house that would be her home for the next twenty-four hours. She suddenly felt one of her "realizations" coming on, so she made a quick joke inquiring about the whereabouts of the servants. When Jason replied that he had given them the weekend off, Taylor realized that she had no clue whether he was being sarcastic or serious. What she did realize, however, was that she and Jason would be completely alone for the next twenty-four hours.

Thank god she had just gotten a bikini wax.

Hey—only in case she wanted to go swimming in Jason's pool.

Of course.

TAYLOR FOLLOWED JASON up the grand three-story staircase that led to the upstairs bedrooms. Halfway up, she stopped to rest on the landing. The doctor had warned her that, in the next twenty-four hours, she might experience drowsiness, confusion, fuzzy thoughts, and even potential changes in her personality. Taylor's symptoms could possibly be more extreme, he had said, considering that she had been so sleep-deprived prior to the accident.

"What, doesn't everybody get by on four hours of sleep nowadays?" she had innocently inquired. The doctor had given her another one of his looks. No, indeed they did not.

By now a few steps ahead of her on the staircase, Jason looked back when he realized Taylor had stopped.

"Why are there so many stairs in this place?" she pouted, leaning against the wall for support. She suddenly felt *so* tired. At least she wasn't experegiging any fuggy thofts.

In two bounds, Jason crossed the steps between them.

"Look at me." With a firm grip on her chin, he peered intently into Taylor's eyes.

"What are you doing?" She tried swatting his hand away.

Jason's gaze fixated first on her right eye, then her left. "Checking to make sure your pupils are even." He pulled back. "How do you feel?"

"I'm tired," she complained. "Can't you just get me to a bed?"

Damn. Even through her fuggy thofts, Taylor knew how *that* sounded.

Never one to miss an opportunity, Jason grinned. "Well, Ms. Donovan . . . all you had to do was ask."

Taylor rolled her eyes. She sure had set herself up for that one all right.

Stupic conprussion.

JASON OPENED THE door to the guest suite, carefully watching Taylor to make sure she didn't stumble or anything as she stepped in. He'd tried to help her up the stairs, but after several cranky "I got it, I *got* its," he figured it was best to simply leave her be. Not that he didn't find the whole thing pretty darn amusing, seeing her acting so un-Taylor-like.

Jason walked through the room, making sure everything had been properly set up for her arrival. He had designed his guest suite to have the feel of a luxury hotel. Lush cream damask silk bedding adorned the king-size four-poster bed. The adjoining sitting room boasted a chaise lounge that stretched before a crackling fireplace. He realized that the fireplace was a little unnecessary and flashy, but then again, so were a lot of things in Beverly Hills.

One look at the sitting room was apparently all Taylor needed.

"Ooh . . . a fire," she said, wide-eyed.

Jason carried her suitcase into the bedroom, keeping an eye out to make sure she didn't trip headfirst into said fire. Thankfully, she settled safely onto the chaise and leaned back against its pillows.

"Oh, excuse me? Mr. Andrews?"

She called out to him through sleepy eyes. Tired though she was, she still managed to have that devious little grin of hers.

"What time is the turndown service at this establishment?"

Jason headed into the sitting room to join her. "Anytime you'd like. Do you have any special requests for the turndown service this evening?"

Taylor curled up, tucking her feet under the cashmere throw blanket that rested at the foot of the chaise.

"I do," she said coyly.

Jason knelt down in front of the chaise lounge so that they were eye level. "And what might that request be?" he asked huskily.

With her head on the pillow, all snuggled in, Taylor smiled up at him.

"Warm cookies. Chocolate chip, preferably." Then she closed her eyes and fell peacefully asleep.

Jason sighed. He'd been hoping she might say something else . . . Oh well.

He pulled the blanket up, draping it over her shoulders. He stood up to leave and had just made it to the door when—

"Jason?"

He turned around to see Taylor peeking up at him, her eyes barely open. He wondered whether she was talking in her sleep.

"You know . . . if you like warm cookies, too, you could always join me later tonight." She winked coyly at him.

Then she conked out, fast asleep.

JASON PACED IN his bedroom.

Okay.

So.

This was an interesting predicament.

She wasn't herself this evening, he told himself. She didn't know what she was saying.

The doctor had warned them about fuzzy thoughts, confusion, and possible changes to her personality. This was all part of the concussion.

Or *was* it . . . Jason slyly mused this over.

All right, *all right*. He pulled himself together. He may have been a lot of things, but he was not the kind of guy who would seduce a helpless woman.

Well, at least *lately* he wasn't that kind of guy. Truth be told, until about a month ago, he didn't have much of what some people liked to call "scruples." And the sans-scruples Jason would've known exactly what to do in this situation.

As he continued to pace in front of his bed, Jason ran through several points of fact he believed to be highly relevant.

Fact one: Taylor Donovan was hardly any sort of "helpless" woman. In fact, she'd probably consider it an affront to her feminist sensibilities just to be thought of that way.

Fact two: Was it really seducing, per se, if the woman initiated things?

Fact three . . .

Jason drew a blank. Wait—there had to be a three. There was always a three.

But indeed, there was no three.

Because deep down, in his heart of hearts, Jason knew that letting anything happen with Taylor that night would be the wrong thing to do. He'd wanted her to stay with him because he'd felt things earlier that day that he'd never felt before about any woman—first when he heard she'd been in a car accident, and then the enormous relief he felt when he rushed into the emergency room and saw she was okay.

He had not invited Taylor over so that he could take advantage of fortuitous circumstances. Even if they were turning out to be some *really* fortuitous circumstances.

Jason sat down on his bed with a resigned sigh.

Fucking scruples.

A PHONE RANG somewhere in the distance.

Taylor came to on the chaise lounge. She realized the ringing was coming from inside her room. Her damn cell phone. She really needed to turn that thing off once in a while.

Taylor dragged herself over to her suitcase, where she'd packed the cell phone inside. She fell back on the bed and answered. It was Derek.

Yes, yes, she assured him, she was fine. Yes, she would be back in court on Monday. No, she was not playing hooky, smoking pot, and banging bongos naked with Matthew McConaughey. That was next weekend's plan.

After hanging up the phone, Taylor yawned and stretched out on the bed, trying to shake the sleep from her head. Funny—she didn't even remember lying down. The last thing she recalled was climbing that Mt. Everest of a staircase as she followed Jason to her room. And then . . . nothing. Although for some strange reason, she had a craving for chocolate chip cookies.

Even though she'd only been awake for a few minutes, Taylor felt as though she could lay on that bed forever. Maybe they had room service at Casa Andrews. She imagined herself picking up the phone on the end table to order. "Um . . . yes, hello. I'd like one Sexiest Man Alive, please. How would I like that prepared? Hmm . . . naked, if you have it."

Taylor covered her mouth and giggled sneakily. Now there was an idea . . .

Right then, there was a knock at her door.

Jason! He'd somehow read her mind! He knew the things she'd been thinking, the naughty things she'd been thinking! About the bed and the chaise and then the sunken tub in the bathroom and then that thing she'd briefly considered about the top of the dresser and—

Jason knocked again. More insistently this time.

"Taylor? Can I come in?"

Taylor ran over to the chaise lounge to make it look as though she'd just woken up. She quickly mussed her hair. Then smoothed it. Then straightened her clothes and casually positioned herself just so.

"Sure, come in," she called out calmly.

Jason poked his head inside the door. "Oh good, you're awake."

"Yes, just."

Jason cocked his head questioningly. "I thought maybe I should order us dinner."

"That would be nice, thank you."

He gave her a strange look. "Are you okay? You look a little flushed."

"It's the fire." Taylor pointed.

Jason nodded. He paused awkwardly.

"Pasta, then?"

"Yes, delicious."

"Good. I'll see right to it."

"Lovely. Excellent."

"Okay."

"Okay."

Jason left, shutting the door behind him. Taylor fell back on the chaise, exhausted.

Sometimes this witty repartee of theirs was so damn draining.

AS PROMISED, THEY had pasta for dinner. Wolfgang told Jason that he normally didn't make personal deliveries, but for him, he'd make an exception. As long as Jason would in turn be willing to drop by Spago sometime that week with a few dozen of his paparazzi friends.

Unfortunately, Jason wasn't sure Taylor even tasted the dinner he'd so lovingly and thoughtfully commanded be brought to them. About three forkfuls in, she'd abruptly stood up from the dining-room table and, tottering about like a drunk person, carried her plate into the living room while declaring couches to be far more comfortable places to eat. By the time Jason had followed her there, she had already abandoned her plate on the floor in front of his couch and appeared to be settling in for a long winter's nap.

Thinking he might as well get comfortable, too, Jason took a seat next to her. With the push of one remote control button, the 110-inch screen of his projector television smoothly dropped down from the ceiling. He quickly found the Lakers game and dug into his lobster diavolo, thinking Taylor hadn't exactly been wrong about the whole eating on the couch thing.

Somewhere during the second half of the game, Taylor shifted in her sleep and rested her head on Jason's thigh. He looked down at her, curled up next to him on the couch, and realized there was no other way he would've rather spent his Friday night. Despite the fact that she was essentially comatose, she somehow made his whole house feel different just by being there. Before it had been just a house—a very impressive house no doubt, but a house nonetheless. But for some reason, with Taylor there it felt more like a home.

The game ended and—as much as he didn't particularly mind having her head in his lap for hours on end—Jason figured he should probably get Taylor upstairs where she could sleep more comfortably. Since walking obviously wasn't an option, he scooped her up in his arms and carried her up the staircase to the guest bedroom. Taylor roused at this and, when she saw where they were going, giggled and mumbled something about *Gone with the Wind* and Scarlett O'Hara not getting any sex for two financial quarters. This apparently made a lot of sense at least to her because, with a lazy smile, she wrapped her arms around Jason's neck and slowly ran her fingers through the back of his hair.

And that was pretty much the point when he realized there was trouble on the horizon.

Jason carried Taylor into the guest room and to the bed, then stood her down beside it. He figured that was far enough and that, if he was serious about being a gentleman that night, he would make a fast getaway.

But instead of letting go, Taylor tightened her arms around his neck, pressing her body against his. She gazed up at him from beneath her long lashes as one of her hands drifted down from his neck. With a finger, she gently traced a path along his chest, then down his stomach . . . Jason sucked in his breath as his abdominal muscles tightened at her touch. This was certainly new territory for them.

"I've thought about this," she murmured in a breathless voice. "What it would be like . . ." She peered up at him. "Did you know that?"

Without waiting for an answer, she began to kiss his neck,

teasing him. Biting back a moan, Jason closed his eyes. It was too much—her hands suddenly were everywhere.

"Taylor . . ." His voice came out in a ragged intake of breath. "What are you doing?"

"Shhh . . ." she whispered in his ear. "I'm the lawyer—I'm the one who asks the questions, remember?" Then she pulled back, her lips hovering just before his.

"Do you want to kiss me?"

His eyes locked with hers.

"Yes."

She cocked her head. "Then what are you waiting for?"

With that, Jason took her by the back of her neck and kissed her. Her lips parted eagerly, and their tongues met as the kiss deepened. Jason didn't know how long that went on for, and he wasn't sure who led who, but at some point he realized that they had made their way to the bed and Taylor was lying beneath him. Her hands were at his waistband, pulling impatiently at his shirt, and her legs wrapped around him. Jason's mouth trailed teasingly along her collarbone, then dipped toward the V-neck of her shirt. Now it was her turn to moan.

"Jason . . ." she whispered urgently.

More than anything, he wanted this. Wanted her, wanted to do all the things he knew would have her moaning his name all night. But something made him pause.

He pulled back to look at her. He saw that Taylor's cheeks were flushed, her hair strewn wildly over her shoulders. She looked gorgeous and alluring and he was tempted as all hell but—there was one problem.

It was her eyes.

Like always, her eyes told him everything. They were dark and intense, but they were missing that knowing little gleam she always had. And without that gleam, Jason knew it wasn't really her—the Taylor he wanted—that he was kissing right then.

So he pulled back, unwrapping himself from her. "We're not going to do this. Not like this."

Surprised, Taylor looked up at him through half-lidded eyes as she stretched out across the bed. "Not like this?" She smiled. "Fine then, I can be on top. Unless you had something else in mind . . ."

With that, she giggled.

And if her eyes hadn't told Jason everything he needed to know, that giggle sure did. He pulled the blanket out from under her.

"You're going to sleep, Taylor."

She pouted at this. "Awww, come on . . . don't I get to see the Sexiest Man Alive's sexy bits?" She cracked up, thoroughly amusing herself.

Jason pulled the blanket over her. "I think it might be best if we save that show for another time."

Taylor reached for the blanket reluctantly, blinking up at him with one last disappointed look.

"No bits?"

He shook his head firmly.

"No bits."

She yawned, then with a dramatic sigh and a huffy "fine," she drifted off. Jason was just turning to leave when she opened her eyes halfway.

"But I just wanted one night where I didn't have to see the steps."

He had no idea what she was talking about, but the strange, almost sad expression on her face made Jason sit down on the bed. "What do you mean?"

Taylor gazed up at him as she explained, speaking in a soft voice.

"I bet other women don't have to think around you. But I do. Because I see the steps: if I do this, then this will happen, then this and this . . ." She trailed off, then sighed exhaustedly. "It's a lot of thinking sometimes," she confessed.

Jason tried to fight back his smile. He kind of liked Concussed-and-Nearly-Comatose Taylor. She gave him great insight into what the real Taylor had going on in that head of hers.

"I like that you're always thinking," he told her.

She frowned. "You said I'm difficult."

"Yes. But I like that about you, too."

Seeming at least somewhat mollified by this answer, Taylor

nodded solemnly and pulled the blanket over her shoulders. She quickly drifted off to sleep again. From her steady breathing, Jason could tell she was out for good this time. He checked the clock on the nightstand, making a mental note of the time he would have to wake her next. Then he got up and headed to the door.

With one last look over his shoulder, Jason turned off the light to Taylor's room and quietly shut the door behind him.

Tomorrow, he thought as he headed down the hallway to his bedroom. They would talk about all of this in the morning.

Twenty-six

SUNLIGHT STREAMED INTO the bedroom.

Taylor woke up slowly in her cozy silk cocoon, and it took her a moment to remember where she was. She glanced over at the alarm clock on the nightstand and saw it was well after ten in the morning. She sat up, unable to recall the last time she had slept in so late. Definitely not any time since she had started working at the firm.

Like a college girl waking up hungover in a strange dorm room, she slowly sifted through what she could remember of the night before. There wasn't much; the whole evening was just a blur of images, most of which seemed more like a hazy dream than reality. She'd certainly slept a lot, that she could recall.

Realizing she couldn't stay in bed forever, Taylor got up and headed into the bathroom. Her stomach growled, and she tried to recall whether she had eaten dinner last night. Pasta—good, she remembered something about pasta. Judging from the fact that she was wearing the clothes she had on the day before, she guessed she must've dragged herself upstairs after dinner and passed right out. Poor Jason—she supposed she hadn't exactly been the most stimulating of company.

Taylor showered quickly and headed downstairs. There, she discovered that Jason had set two places for them at the kitchen table. She was touched to see the extent of the effort he had made: he had carefully laid out orange juice, coffee, milk, cereal, and fresh fruit. And, sitting mysteriously in the center of the table was a large silver platter with a domed cover.

Curious, Taylor headed over to sneak a peak at whatever hid underneath. Touching the metal handle, she could tell there was something warm inside.

"You're awake."

Surprised by the voice, Taylor whirled around and saw Jason standing in the doorway of the kitchen. She grinned guiltily.

"Yes, finally. I'm feeling a lot better this morning. Did you have any problems waking me last night?"

Jason seemed surprised by this. "You don't remember?"

She shook her head. "I don't remember a lot about last night."

Now he seemed downright shocked. He peered at her cautiously. "What, exactly, *do* you remember?"

"Hmmm . . . I remember something about pasta."

Seeing the expression on Jason's face, Taylor began to feel a little uneasy. Oh shit—had she done something . . . bad?

"Is there something I should know about last night?" she asked with trepidation. When Jason hesitated, her stomach dropped.

Oh god.

"Oh god," she repeated aloud in a whisper. "Tell me. What happened?" Why wasn't he answering her? Why was he staring at her like that? "Did we, um . . . did something happen between us?"

She could see it in his eyes. Her mind rallied around her excuses.

She was concussed.

She'd been in a state; she was out of it.

She hadn't been thinking.

She was a ho.

Then Jason finally ended his silence with a chuckle. "Calm down, Taylor," he said reassuringly. "Nothing happened." He gave her a look. "Do you really think I would let something happen when you were that out of it?"

He held her gaze firmly with his question, staring her down, as if to say he was insulted at the mere accusation. Taylor instantly felt silly for being so worried.

She exhaled in relief. "Sorry." She smiled, making light of her crazy thoughts. "I didn't mean to sound so paranoid. I think it must be hunger delusions."

Oddly, for the briefest second, she could've sworn she saw a flicker of disappointment in Jason's eyes. But then she figured she was just imagining things. She pointed to the silver platter on the table.

"So? Can I peek? I'm starving."

Jason nodded. "It's nothing—I took a guess, I thought it might be something you'd like." He spoke quickly, as if nervous, and Taylor wondered what the hell he had stashed under there. She grabbed the handle, eager with anticipation. So hungry was she, she couldn't have been more excited if whatever lurked inside had been wrapped in a blue Tiffany box.

She lifted the cover.

For a moment, she could only stare in wonder at the glorious sight before her eyes.

"Do you like it?" Jason asked.

Taylor nodded mutely.

The platter was filled to the brim with rich, buttery silver-dollar pancakes. *Chocolate chip* silver-dollar pancakes. Just like a plate of warm cookies, all for her, at eleven o'clock in the morning.

Catching the scent of the warm baked goodness, Taylor sighed happily. "How did you know, Jason? It's *exactly* what I wanted."

ABOUT AN HOUR later, stuffed to the gills with about $10.79 worth of silver-dollar pancakes, Taylor rolled herself out to Jason's pool and languidly stretched out on one of the lounge chairs. She hadn't paid much attention to the pool during his party, but now she noted that it had been as carefully designed as the rest of the house. And it certainly was no less stunning: with a cascading waterfall and curved, flowing edges that ran along the surrounding lush foliage and rock landscaping, it looked like a hidden pool one might stumble upon while hiking on a tropical island.

"Now this is the life." She sighed to herself while taking a sip of her deliciously cold lemonade.

She pulled her sunglasses down from her forehead and eased back in her lounge chair. She glanced over at Jason, who sat on the chair next to her reading his copy of *Daily Variety*. He'd peeled off his T-shirt earlier and now wore only a pair of cargo shorts. And here Taylor had thought the chocolate chip pancakes were yummy . . .

"I'm sorry?" Jason looked over. Taylor started, having momentarily forgotten she'd said anything out loud. She quickly gestured to the pool.

"I was just saying that this is a pretty nice setup you have here."

Jason nodded, a bit distractedly. In fact, Taylor had noticed he'd seemed a little distracted the entire morning. Every time she'd snuck a peek at him—hey, he was Jason Andrews and he was shirtless, *of course* she'd snuck in a few peeks—he'd been staring off at nothing. As if something was troubling him.

They fell into a comfortable silence for a moment or two, when Jason turned back to her. "So you like being here, then?" He peered at Taylor through the dark lenses of his sunglasses.

His question caught her off guard. "At this house?"

It was probably just the sun, but she could have sworn she saw Jason's cheeks blush.

"I meant California," he said quickly. "You know *here*," he waved his hand, referring to their general locale. "Los Angeles."

Taylor smiled. It was eighty degrees and not a cloud in the sky. "What's not to like?"

Jason turned back to his paper. "Right, right." He nodded. A moment passed, then he glanced at Taylor once again.

"So you would consider this then, as a place you could live? You wouldn't miss Chicago?"

Taylor found his question a bit . . . strange. She could've sworn she heard a catch in his voice, as if their conversation had somehow turned into something more than idle chitchat. Too bad those damn sunglasses made it impossible for her to read his expression.

Then she shrugged these thoughts off. She was being too suspicious, she told herself. Too much of a lawyer. This wasn't a deposition; not every question had a secret purpose or trick behind it. Jason was just being polite. After all, she had been living in Los Angeles for a couple of months by now; it was a natural question for him to ask.

"I suppose I'd consider it, if there was some great opportunity for me in L.A.," she said. "But I guess I've always assumed that Chicago is where I'd live."

With that said, Taylor put her sunglasses back on top of her head, not wanting to get raccoon marks from the sun. She closed her eyes and eased back in her chair. "Luckily, I don't need to worry about that for a long time," she told Jason. "With this trial, it'll be a couple more months before I have to start thinking about leaving here."

Enough about Chicago already, she thought, basking in the warm California sun. That world was thousands of miles away for now.

But strangely, when she opened her eyes a few minutes later to take another sip of her lemonade, she noticed that Jason was staring off distractedly once again.

Twenty-seven

AT FIVE O'CLOCK Taylor's twenty-four hours were up. Her stay in paradise came to a reluctant end.

Jason pulled the Aston Martin up the driveway of her apartment building and shut off the engine. The two of them sat for a moment in his car.

"Back to reality." Taylor sighed. "Good old apartment living."

"You know, you could just ask the next time you want to sleep over. You don't need to crash your car."

Taylor laughed, relieved to see him joking again. He'd been so quiet all day, she had begun to worry that something was really wrong.

"I'll remember that," she told him. She was about to thank him for letting her stay over when it happened again—a shrill ring blared out from her purse. Cellphonus interruptus.

Despite the inconvenience of the moment, Taylor felt obligated to check and make sure it wasn't Derek with some trial-related crisis. She felt Jason watching her as she pulled the phone out and checked the caller ID. When she saw it was Scott who was calling, she said nothing and tucked the phone back into her purse.

"It's him, isn't it?" Jason asked.

"I'll let it go into voice mail."

But her phone was relentless. It began ringing again, immediately. Taylor smiled, thinking back to another person who had not so long ago similarly persisted in trying to reach her.

"I gotta say, you movie stars sure are tenacious," she said teasingly over the phone's ring.

Jason's face hardened. "I'm nothing like him."

She had meant the comment as a joke, but she saw that she'd insulted him instead. *You're right,* she suddenly felt the urge to say. *You are so much more than him.*

As her cell phone continued to ring, Jason turned away and stared straight ahead with a stony expression, his eyes fixed on the windshield of the car.

Say it, Taylor heard the voice in her head urging her. *At least tell him that. After everything he's done for you, he deserves to hear it.*

But she couldn't.

Because she knew that those words would lead to more words, and there were things going on between her and Jason that she wasn't ready to face. So much had happened in the last twenty-four hours; she needed time to pull her thoughts together.

So she hesitated. Seeing this, Jason set his jaw angrily and threw the car into drive.

"You should take your call, Taylor," he said, refusing to look at her.

Nodding, she grabbed her bag and stepped out of the car. She had barely shut the door when Jason threw the car into gear and took off. She stood in the driveway, watching as the Aston Martin sped around the corner of her street. It took her a moment to realize her cell phone was still ringing.

Shit—Scott. She had forgotten about him. Yes, again.

She answered her phone, having a pretty good idea what his first word would be.

"Gorgeous!" he exclaimed enthusiastically as Taylor mouthed along. She instantly felt horrible for doing that. After all, lots of women would be thrilled to have Scott Casey calling them.

"Hey, Scott," she said, trying to sound normal despite how flustered she was by Jason's angry departure. She headed up the walkway to her front door and let herself into her apartment.

"I've been thinking about you all day, gorgeous," Scott said.

Taylor suddenly wondered if perhaps he actually didn't remember her name. "Thanks, really, I'm fine," she told him. "I would have called, but I didn't want to bother you." Lies, lies, lies, she thought. But somehow, "I know we kissed five times but I can't seem to remember you exist" didn't have quite the same ring to it.

"You're not mad at me for not picking you up at the hospital, are you?"

"No, not at all," Taylor assured him. And this part was true—she of all people understood that work often had to take priority over personal matters.

Which is why she would never forget the moment she heard Jason's voice and saw him standing in the doorway of the hospital emergency room. In that moment, everything had changed.

Up until that moment, Taylor could've at least pretended she'd been doing a passable job of keeping her feelings toward Jason in check. And most of that success was due in large part to her firm belief that his attraction to her was little more than a passing fancy, merely a spoiled movie star's desire to have something he'd previously been told he couldn't.

But the emotions she'd seen on his face in the emergency room had been *real*. And seeing that was something she had not prepared herself for.

She could resist his charm and wit and devilish smile. She could try to ignore the fact that he was the most attractive man she had ever laid eyes on, both on film and in person. But she had no defense against the man Jason was when he wasn't busy trying to be Jason Andrews the movie star. *That* man was someone that somebody could really fall in love with.

And that thought was so very dangerous.

Falling in love with anyone was a gamble. Falling in love with a known womanizer—well, Taylor had been there, done that, and the results had been disastrous.

But falling in love with the most famous womanizer of all, a celebrity who proudly flaunted his bachelor ways on national television? The thought was sheer lunacy.

Still . . . that didn't mean the situation between her and Jason needed to end on such a sour note. There were things that needed to be said, she realized.

So distracted was Taylor with these thoughts, she barely paid attention to a word Scott said as he rambled on about his rough week of filming. She finally tuned back in when she heard him mention something about homemade chicken soup, realizing that he was asking if he could come over that evening.

"Oh, that's sweet," she said quickly. "But I really need to take it easy tonight and catch up on work."

The line went silent.

"But we have plans tonight."

From his sharp tone, Taylor sensed he was less concerned about not seeing her and more annoyed over the fact that he was being blown off. Or maybe that was just the unappreciative bitch in her talking.

"I know, I'm sorry, I'm just *so* exhausted," she said dramatically. Lies, lies, lies. "Can we do it some other time?"

Scott paused. "Well, I was planning on asking you about this in person, but since that's apparently not an option . . ." He paused grumpily before continuing. "Have you heard of the Black and Pink Ball?"

The Black & Pink Ball, he explained, was a black-tie (hence the black) charity benefit thrown every year at the house of Tony Bredstone, head of one of the major studios. The party was one of the most elegant and lavish thrown in Hollywood: a five-course dinner, followed by dancing and a silent raffle. All the proceeds were donated to a breast cancer research foundation (hence the pink).

Scott asked if she would like to go with him.

Taylor hesitated.

Being Scott Casey, he assumed there was only one reason any woman would ever hesitate to go anywhere with him.

"I saw that your friend Jason was on the invite list," he said pointedly. "Perhaps he already mentioned the party to you?"

Taylor couldn't help it—she felt a stab of disappointment. "No . . . no, he hadn't."

"Well then, gorgeous," Scott said, his confident tone restored. "How about going with me?"

And so she said yes.

In truth, her agreeing to go had almost nothing to do with Scott and pretty much everything to do with Jason. After the way he had sped off, Taylor wasn't sure when she would see him again and the Black & Pink Ball provided her with the perfect opportunity.

There were things she needed to say to Jason Andrews.

And next Saturday would be the night.

ACROSS TOWN, PERCHED high above the city in his Hollywood Hills home, Scott hung up the phone having the very same thought as Taylor.

Next Saturday would be the night, he told himself.

Jason Andrews's Mystery Woman had been the hottest story in every tabloid newspaper, gossip column, and entertainment news program for the past several weeks. It seemed as though the whole world was waiting with bated breath to discover the identity of the elusive dark-haired woman who had so obviously caught the eye of the Sexiest Man Alive.

Scott knew that Saturday night was the perfect time to introduce Taylor to her public. After Saturday, everyone would know who was merely the "Other Contender." Let the world see that Jason Andrews's Mystery Woman had moved on to bigger and brighter pastures.

Him.

Landing the lead role in *Outback Nights* had been one thing. But this was far better—Scott had a feeling that stealing Taylor from Jason would be a much bigger blow to the so-called King of Hollywood's ego.

True, he didn't exactly seem to have her eating out of the

palm of his hand. *Yet.* But this soon would change. Of that he was quite certain.

And it all would happen on Saturday night.

The thought put Scott into a great mood as he stepped out onto his deck. The scene hadn't changed much since he'd left to call Taylor: the three girls he'd picked up earlier at the Coffee Bean & Tea Leaf frolicked happily in the pool, splashing each other and drinking frozen margaritas. Off to the side, Rob reclined in a lounge chair, eating Cheetos and using his towel as a napkin.

Scott resumed his place in the lounge chair next to Rob.

"How did it go with what's-her-name?"

Ignoring Rob's question, Scott looked pointedly at the Cheetos bag that had started off full just twenty minutes ago and now appeared to be virtually empty.

Rob made a face in response. "They're *baked.*"

"Whatever. Just don't get into my pool with that orange shit all over your hands." Scott leaned back to watch the girls, who smiled at him in collective invitation. "As for your question, everything's fine with what's-her-name. I'm taking her to the Black and Pink Ball next Saturday."

"That should at least be worth a blow job."

"You would think so, right? But she needs to 'rest' tonight," Scott said with mocking finger quotes. Then with his arms folded casually behind his head, he eyed the girls in the pool. He wondered how much longer he should let them go on splashing each other before he jumped in and gave them something to really splash about.

"So I'm gonna have Marty make sure she and I are photographed together at the party," he told Rob. He had officially signed with Marty Shepherd three days ago and was eager to take his new publicist out for a spin. "Then he can leak her name to the press." He grinned, proud of this plan. "Taylor Donovan—the girl *formerly* known as the Mystery Woman."

Rob looked over as he scrunched up the Cheetos bag. "I thought you told me she had issues with the press—something to do with her trial or whatever."

"She does. But that's not my problem, is it?"

Scott glanced back at the girls in the pool, who were coyly gesturing for him to join them.

"Ladies . . . how's the water?"

In response, one of the girls took off her bikini top and smiled. The other two quickly followed suit.

"Looks like it might be a little chilly," Scott said, enjoying the view. He got up from his lounge chair, glancing at Rob as he walked by. "Now that you've finished your snack . . . I assume you know your way out?"

Rob looked at him in disbelief. "You've got to be kidding." He pointed an orange-tipped finger at the three girls in the water, whose bikini bottoms had now gone the way of their tops. "What about me?"

Scott shook his head with an oh-so-sorry grin. "Sorry, buddy—but this one's all mine. I told you, you need to lay off the desserts anyway."

And with that, Scott dove cleanly into the pool. When he surfaced in the midst of the three naked girls, Taylor Donovan was the last thing on his mind.

JASON HAD A meeting with Marty later that week to discuss his promo schedule for *Inferno*, which opened the following Friday. It was a whirlwind of a lineup that would have him jetting all across the country: press junkets, photo shoots, the *Today* show, *The Tonight Show*, *The Early Show*, *The Late Show*, Ellen, Oprah, and Barbara Walters on *The View*. All in the span of four days.

Since Jason would still be in Los Angeles the upcoming weekend, Marty asked if he planned to attend Tony Redstone's Black & Pink Ball. Jason was just about to caustically reply that indeed he was not so planning—Redstone was the head of the studio that had greenlit *Outback Nights* and supposedly (according to Jason's sources) the man who had balked at his salary and decided to go with the far less talented (again, according to Jason's sources) and less expensive Scott Casey.

But then Marty casually mentioned that if Jason was planning to attend, perhaps he could bring Naomi Cross. Given the fact that Taylor Donovan was already going with Scott Casey.

Hearing this, Jason felt a pit form in his stomach.

He hated the way he'd left things with her last weekend, but he'd been too mad and later, too embarrassed to call her. He had realized over the past couple days, however, that they really needed to talk. And not over the telephone.

So if Saturday night had to be the night, so be it. Fuck Scott Casey—he was a cocky little pissant and Jason could give a crap about the fact that he would be there, too. There were things he needed to say to Taylor. Important things.

So he told Marty to put him down as a yes.

Twenty-eight

TAYLOR PRIDED HERSELF in being a virtual expert in the area of labor and employment law. She had worked hard for this distinction: she subscribed to the various labor and employment trade publications, she kept on top of the case law and legislation and studied the trends and changes in her field, she attended conferences and seminars and was even the cochairwoman of the Young Lawyers Employment Law Committee of the Chicago Bar Association.

In short, when it came to labor and employment law, Taylor had skills.

On the other hand, when it came to the subject of black-tie Hollywood balls, Taylor's skills were, well . . . not so much. In this area, she needed reinforcements. She needed an expert in the subject of all things Hollywood, someone who worked hard to acquire *that* knowledge, someone who subscribed to the various trade publications and studied the trends and changes in that particular field.

So she called Valerie.

The woman was apoplectic.

"The Black and Pink Ball!"

Val screamed so loudly, Taylor had to hold the phone away from her ear.

"Taylor Donovan you are the luckiest goddamn woman in the world! I'd cut off my right arm to go to the Black and Pink Ball!"

"Then I'd recommend a strapless gown for you when the time comes."

"Taylor!" Valerie yelled warningly. "You are not taking this seriously enough! Your dress, your shoes, your hair and makeup—your very *existence*—needs to be planned down to the absolute last detail." Then Val began to fret, mumbling distractedly on her end of the line. "You call and give me three days' notice? It can't be done—there's no time. All right, fine then—yes, I will help you, you'll be gorgeous, and your fabulous movie star boyfriend will be unable to speak at the very sight of you." She paused pointedly. "Wait—who is it you're going out with this week?"

Taylor smirked. Ha ha. "Couldn't resist throwing in that last part, could you?"

"Without the snide comments, I might have to kill you, I'm that jealous." Then Val got down to business. "Okay—so for the Black and Pink Ball, we need to think classic Hollywood. Glamorous old-school Hollywood. Think Ava Gardner. Think Ingrid Bergman, Audrey Hepburn, Grace Kelly. You will wear black—"

"But I always wear black," Taylor interrupted. "I was thinking—"

"Taylor! Are you *trying* to kill me? We don't have time for you to run around looking for shoes that will match some peach nightmare you plucked off the clearance rack at Saks!"

Taylor was highly insulted by this. As if she would ever wear *peach*.

"Speaking of shoes," Val continued, "you will go to Christian Louboutin—write this down, Taylor . . ."

And so it went.

Thanks to the wonders of technology, Taylor felt as though Valerie was shopping right alongside her when she stopped off at Rodeo Drive Thursday evening after her trial. When the salesclerks weren't looking, she snapped photos with her cell phone of the various dress and shoe contenders and sent them to Val for immediate comment.

The two women exchanged several phone calls over the next two days. During their final conversation early Saturday evening, when Taylor was just about to start getting ready, Valerie heard the hesitation creeping into her voice and asked about it.

"I feel guilty about going to the party," Taylor admitted. "I think I might be leading Scott on."

"Think of it this way," Val told her, "by going with Scott Casey to the Black and Pink Ball, you saved our friendship. Because if I had ever heard you turned down such an invitation, I never would've spoken to you again."

Taylor smiled gratefully. "Thanks, Val, for that."

Valerie sighed wistfully. "Now go to your big fancy party, and call me tomorrow and tell me every detail. And Taylor—knock him dead."

Although it went unsaid, Taylor knew full well that the "him" Valerie had been referring to was not Scott Casey.

LATER THAT EVENING, when Taylor stepped out onto the veranda of Tony Bredstone's mansion, she instantly saw why the Black & Pink Ball was one of the hottest tickets in Hollywood. She tried to take in every detail of the grandness of the party, thinking how she would describe it to Val in the morning.

The studio head's home sat on a sprawling five-acre estate in Bel Air. The grounds behind the house had been elaborately transformed into an outdoor ballroom, complete with white linens and crystal-set dining tables. Low candlelight was sprinkled throughout, creating a warm glow. Twinkling lights were strung along the sculptured topiaries that surrounded the main dance floor. Waiters with bow ties carried silver platters of champagne, and a string quartet played classical music from the upstairs balcony.

To Taylor, it looked like a scene right out of a movie. Which was an appropriate thought, considering a good number of the guests mingling throughout were actors and actresses she had seen in those very movies. For a lawyer from

Chicago, it was like being at the Academy Awards. Only without the whole I'm-just-honored-to-have-been-nominated rigamarole.

Scott took Taylor by the hand and led her into the party. He looked great in his tux; there certainly was no disputing that. He headed straight for one of the bars, saying something about needing a drink. Taylor balked when she spotted some photographers hanging off to the side.

"What's wrong?" Scott asked her. Then he saw the source of her hesitation. "Oh that . . . don't worry, those are just industry photographers. They cover these charity events for the trade papers. Nothing your trial judge would ever see."

Taylor continued to hesitate. "I don't know . . . why don't you go ahead and get us drinks? I'll just wait here."

She could've sworn she saw a flicker of—disappointment? anger?—in Scott's eyes right then. But then he smiled.

"Don't be so paranoid, Mystery Woman." He held up his hand in a mock-solemn vow. "Your secret identity is safe with me. I promise."

But there was something about his smile that Taylor didn't quite trust . . . She was trying to figure out what that something was, when someone grabbed Scott from behind.

"You wouldn't be trying to sneak by without saying hello, would you, brother?" an Irish voice said.

Turning, Taylor saw two guys in their midtwenties who she recognized as Scott's costars from *A Viking's Quest*.

"Hey—who the hell let you scrubs in here!" Scott shouted at them. In his excitement, his Australian accent was more pronounced than ever.

Taylor had heard the tales—everyone had—about how close Scott and his *A Viking's Quest* costars had grown during their grueling thirteen-month shoot. There were even rumors that the cast had gone out one night after filming and gotten "AVQ" tattoos in "secret" places. Valerie had been highly disappointed to learn that Taylor had not gotten any confirmation of this.

Taylor watched as Scott's boys pulled him into a rough tumble of inebriated man-hugs.

"Scrubs? Ahh . . . look here at this guy, such a big shot," said the British actor. He, like Scott, had gotten his first big break with *A Viking's Quest*, and he too was doing well for himself, having landed a role as a recovering alcoholic on a new primetime television show that boasted the biggest ratings of the season.

"What the fuck is this shit?" demanded the Irish actor, the word coming out as "shite." As far as Taylor knew, he had done absolutely nothing since *A Viking's Quest*. "You got no drink—what's up with that?" he asked Scott in his thick brogue. "We need to address that situation immediately."

Before Taylor knew what was happening, the two actors dragged Scott off to the bar for a round of shots. Leaving her standing alone on the veranda.

Taylor looked around and recognized no one. Somehow, this kept happening to her at these Hollywood parties. Probably because *she* was the no one.

Not wanting to stand on the veranda forever, Taylor headed off in search of a washroom, thinking it was the only place for a girl to be alone at a party like this without looking pathetic.

WHAT TAYLOR DIDN'T realize, as she cut through the crowd, was that people at that party *were* paying attention to her. Very much so, in fact.

She never knew it, but the reason no one dared approach her was because they all assumed she was somebody they should know and were too embarrassed to admit they didn't. So instead, they turned to one another in low whispers. *Remind me—I know this, but the name escapes me right now—who is that woman?*

And with each person that couldn't quite place Taylor, the mystery surrounding her deepened.

She came with Scott Casey, someone said. *No, no—they just happened to walk in at the same time. See—there he is, over there, laughing with the other actors from that movie. If Scott Casey was here with her, wouldn't he at least get her a drink?*

And then something magical happened.

The voices dropped to a hushed awe.

Wait—look over there, isn't that Jason Andrews? Over by the other bar, sitting by himself. Look at how he's watching her.

A quiet frenzy swept across the party. *Do you think it could be—yes, yes, you can tell by the long, dark hair, it's the same as the photographs in the magazines, I think you might be right . . .*

It was the Mystery Woman.

In person, right there at their party. The crowd couldn't help but stare. It was generally agreed she had been expected to be a little taller.

The whispers quickly worked their way to the photographers who hovered along the edges of the party, snapping relatively unexciting shots of Alec Baldwin sneaking another cheese puff off a passing waiter's tray, or Salma Hayek spilling champagne on her Manolos while toasting Brad Grey.

Catching word of the whispers, paparazzi heads shot up in a state of ready alertness, like a herd of gazelle that had caught wind of a lioness lurking in the grass nearby. Their ears twitched and their eyes darted side to side as they scanned the vast Serengeti of the Bel Air mansion until they spotted her.

The Mystery Woman! Now *there* was the money shot—easily worth twenty times another photograph of one of them Gyllenhaal jokers. But not alone—she needed to be with *him*.

So now the paparazzi watched, along with the interested party guests, as the Mystery Woman made her way into the house. They stood by, ready, as Jason set down his drink and got up from the bar as if to follow her.

The crowd nudged one another. Such drama! Such excitement!

They couldn't wait to see what was about to happen next.

Twenty-nine

TAYLOR SEARCHED IN vain for Jason amongst the crowd that had gathered inside the Bredstone mansion. Spotting the time on the Rolex of a man drinking a martini, she realized she had left Scott alone for quite a long time. Feeling guilty, she headed back out onto the veranda.

Perhaps she was imagining things, but when Taylor stepped outside, she got the distinct impression that people stopped their conversations. As she worked her way toward the bar where she had last seen Scott, she became more and more aware that the other guests were indeed staring at her. She did a quick check to make sure one of her boobs hadn't popped out of her dress or anything. Seeing that the girls were both securely under wraps, she shrugged and figured the other guests must simply be wondering what someone like her was doing wandering aimlessly amongst their fabulousness.

When Taylor got to the bar, she saw Scott in the corner. Laughing riotously in a circle with his boys, he appeared not to have realized she had even disappeared. Torn between not wanting to interrupt and not wanting to walk around the party any longer like a lost child in a grocery store, Taylor debated whether to join him.

But then a better idea struck her—she realized she hadn't checked the second bar, the one on the other end of the dance floor. Perhaps she would find Jason there. After all, he was the reason she had come to this party in the first place.

She headed across the dance floor, where the classical music portion of the evening's entertainment clearly was over. She had no idea who DJ AM was, but many others apparently did, judging from the way they all rushed out to dance as soon as his name was announced.

She got to the second bar and scanned the faces of everyone there. But not one of them was Jason. Frustrated, she took a deep breath. Yep—once again she was standing alone at this party, with nowhere to go.

But then, she happened to look up just as the crowd shifted and suddenly, she had a view of the veranda.

There Jason stood, with his hands tucked casually into the pockets of his pants. In his tuxedo, he looked . . . well, there were no words. He peered down at Taylor with a grin, and from across the bar, she smiled back.

For the first time that evening, she felt like she belonged.

AS JASON MADE his way through the crowd, he was certain he would have something clever and nonchalant to say by the time he reached Taylor. But when he got there and saw her up close, nothing remotely clever or even nonchalant came to mind. In fact, thoughts, in general, were a bit beyond him at that point.

It was the way she looked that night. He would never forget it.

She wore a shimmering Grecian-style white satin gown that skimmed over her body in graceful gathers. In wild contrast to the traditional updo favored by virtually every other woman at that party, she wore her hair down and long and wavy.

Other women at the ball, with their black gowns and diamond chokers, looked like princesses. But to Jason, Taylor was a goddess.

He stopped before her, transfixed. She shifted worriedly when he said nothing at first.

"You're so beautiful, Taylor," he finally managed.

Her cheeks flushed at the compliment. "It's just the dress."

No—it's you, he almost blurted out. But he kept his tongue in check.

"Where's your date?" he asked instead.

Taylor gestured across the dance floor, where Scott and his friends were clanking their beer bottles in another rowdy toast.

"Over there, hanging out with the other members of the Fellowship."

Jason grinned. "I think that's a different movie."

Taylor turned back and looked him over. "So . . . where's your date?"

"I don't have one. Unless you count Jeremy, which of course I don't. He has a crush on Bredstone's daughter, so I brought him along."

Taylor nodded. Did she seem pleased by the fact that he didn't have a date? There was only one way to tell. Jason held out his hand.

"Dance with me, Taylor."

She hesitated for a moment. Then she took his hand without saying a word.

Jason led her out onto the dance floor. Couples had paired off as "Fade Into You" by Mazzy Star began to play. Through the crowd, he caught sight of some photographers hovering eagerly on the other side of the dance floor. Scanning the area, he spotted a secluded area that was sheltered by the low branches of a tree that reached out over the dance floor. He led Taylor over and pulled her into his arms.

They danced slowly together, with the lights glittering in the tree branches above them like stars. Neither of them said anything for a long moment. Jason wanted to enjoy the feel of Taylor's hand in his, the snugness of his arm around her waist. In her heels, the top of her head rested right under his chin. He could whisper anything in her ear, he realized, and only she would hear.

"I've been thinking," he began softly. "You may finally be free of me."

Taylor turned her face toward his. "What do you mean?"

"Well, your work with the script is essentially finished, we have no more deals about keeping the press away from you, and as far as I know, you don't have any more friends in town . . ."

She smiled. "Valerie is still talking about that night."

"And unless you plan to knock yourself over the head with a hammer, you'll likely remain concussion-free," Jason teased. But then his expression turned serious. "So I guess there's nothing left to keep you around me anymore."

Taylor's green eyes probed his intently. "What if I just like being around you?"

Jason held his breath. "Is that true?"

She nodded slowly. "I need to tell you something, Jason—I know how I've acted toward you, things I've said in the past, but . . ." She trailed off, hesitating, then looked him straight in the eyes.

"I was so wrong about you. These past few weeks, I've realized that when you take away the cameras, and the reporters, and the big house, and the fancy car . . . the guy who's left is not too bad. In fact, I like him quite a bit."

And that was it. Those simple words affected Jason more than any others ever had.

"Taylor . . ." he said, pulling her closer to him.

But she shook her head. "Don't. Don't say anything. I just wanted you to know that. That's all."

She started to pull away, but Jason held her tight. "Don't pull away from me. Not this time."

"I have to."

"Why?" he demanded. "Because of Scott?"

Taylor looked up at him. "We both know Scott isn't the problem."

"Then what?"

She paused at the question, her eyes troubled.

"It's you, Jason—you're the problem. I just . . . I can't do this with *you*."

Jason was momentarily taken aback by her words. Before he could say anything further, Taylor pulled away. He felt it—the moment her fingers slipped out of his. Then she hurried off, disappearing into the crowd.

Jason stayed there, on the dance floor, watching her go. A rush of emotions swept over him, and he knew then one thing, the only thing that mattered.

He loved her.

A LITTLE WHILE later, Jeremy found Jason sitting alone on a bench in front of a fountain near the back of Bredstone's grounds. The party was a little distance away, back up the hill. The sounds of lively music and laughter drifted down in stark contrast to Jason's somber mood.

Jeremy took a seat on the bench next to Jason. He sighed. "Yep, yep, yep . . ."

The two of them sat quietly for a long time.

"I know, I hear you," Jeremy agreed.

More silence.

Finally, Jason broke it.

"It's not a game with her anymore. If it ever really was." He glanced over at Jeremy. "She doesn't trust me."

Jeremy considered this. "Should she?"

Jason faced the cold, hard truth. "I suppose I haven't exactly been a good guy."

Jeremy spoke honestly then, as only a best friend could. "You know, I remember when we were just two guys driving cross-country to Los Angeles in that crappy yellow Datsun you owned, hoping to somehow make a living in Hollywood. And also hoping that the car would actually make it to Hollywood."

That got a slight smile out of Jason. He remembered that car well.

"These years that we've been in L.A.," Jeremy paused, as if this was something he had been thinking about for a while. "I've watched as you've settled into this crazy, ridiculous life you've been blessed with. And I'm not going to lie to you—there were plenty of times when I've been worried about you. *Plenty* of times. Getting everything you want so easily, that changes a man."

Jason watched Jeremy intently, waiting to be judged by

one of the few people whose opinion actually mattered to him.

"And then this thing with Taylor . . ." Jeremy whistled disapprovingly. "Boy, did you ever fuck that up. That stunt you pulled with Naomi was a shitty thing to do. You know, you really can be a selfish, spoiled pain in the ass."

Jason nodded. He looked at the ground.

"Except . . ."

He glanced up at Jeremy.

"*Except* when it comes to the people you really care about. Because to them, you are generous and loyal as hell. Around those people, you *are* a good guy, Jason. And those are the people who, at the end of the day, will never doubt you. No matter how big a pain in the ass you can be."

Jason grinned in relief—and also surprise. Jeremy never talked like this.

Jeremy pointed. "Don't get all teary-eyed on me now."

Jason laughed. "Wouldn't dare."

"So, now—about this thing with Taylor," Jeremy said. "Yes, you've made a lot of mistakes. We both know what you've done in the past with other women. But I'm talking about the person you are with *her*. So again, my question to you is: Should she trust you?"

At this, Jason met Jeremy's gaze. His eyes never flinched.

"Yes."

Jeremy nodded. "Then stop playing games with her. Lay it all on the line. If she loves you, she'll see the real you."

Jason nodded solemnly. The thought of actually putting it all out there with Taylor made him quite nervous. Seeing this, Jeremy punched him in the shoulder good-naturedly.

"Look at you, Mr. Hollywood, all soft and vulnerable." He beamed. "I'm proud of you, man."

Jason pushed him away, embarrassed. "Get out of here with that."

"No, I'm serious," Jeremy told him. "As your moral superior, I can say honestly say that I've never been more proud of you than I am right now."

Jason glanced over, eyebrow raised. "Not even in college,

when I convinced those twins you were the guitarist from Guns N' Roses?"

Jeremy pointed at him.

"That could be a close second."

Thirty

"SO THEN WHAT happened?"

Taylor rolled her desk chair over to her credenza and grabbed a file from the bottom drawer. "So then I ran off the dance floor, and I haven't talked to him since."

It was Sunday afternoon, and she had come into the office to catch up on work. To save time on the Black & Pink post-game analysis, she had three-way called Val and Kate.

"And what about Scott?" asked Kate.

Yes . . . and what about Scott? Now *that* was an interesting question. Taylor filled them in on all the details.

After leaving Jason on the dance floor, she had hurried over to the bar where she had last seen Scott. She wanted to tell him she was leaving the party, not that she thought he'd mind terribly much, given the fact that they had exchanged about ten words total since arriving.

She was making her way across the veranda when she felt someone grab her by the arm. She looked over and saw Scott.

"Can I talk to you for a second?"

Without waiting for an answer, he led her off into one of

the gardens, where they were hidden behind some trees. He stared at her angrily.

"Are you having fun out there, making a fool of me?" His eyes narrowed. "I saw you dancing with him, Taylor. The whole fucking party saw you with him."

Despite the fact that she didn't think Scott had exactly been the perfect date, either, Taylor felt guilty. She knew it was time to put an end to this little charade of theirs.

"I'm sorry, Scott, I wasn't trying to embarrass you. I—"

He cut her off. "Christ, Taylor, everyone here knows you're the Mystery Woman. The paparazzi have been going nuts, trying to get a shot of you and Jason together."

Taylor started to speak, then caught something Scott had just said.

"Paparazzi? I thought you said those were just 'industry photographers.'"

"Yeah, well . . . whatever. The point is, they think you're here with Jason, not me."

Taylor again tried to make amends. "Like I said, I'm sorry. We were just dancing."

Scott scoffed sarcastically at this. "Oh well, if that's all it was, don't let me get in the way. Perhaps you should go back and find him. Although I should warn you—Jason Andrews's dance card is usually pretty full. He doesn't normally make it around to the same girl twice."

Suddenly tired with the whole scenario, Taylor decided it wasn't worth the effort to respond. "You know, I think I'm going to call it an evening," she said. "I'll just call a cab to pick me up."

Scott appeared surprised by this. Then his expression softened.

"You don't need to call a cab, Taylor" he said, his voice full of concern.

Mocking concern, as she learned with his next snide words.

"After all, I'm sure your 'friend' Jason would be happy to give you a ride home," he said. "At least one of us should get to fuck you for getting you into this party."

Taylor nodded. Okay . . . so that's how it had to be. At least now there was nothing more to be said between them.

"Thank you for making this so much easier. Good-bye, Scott."

He seemed surprised when he saw she was actually leaving, and blocked her way.

"Wait—are you serious? You're really going to leave, just like that?"

"Yep, just like that."

He grabbed Taylor by her arm. Apparently, she had struck quite a nerve.

"You think you're so smart," he hissed. "But do you know how many women would kill just to get one look from me? Who the hell are you, you fucking *nobody*? You'd walk away, just because of one dance with Jason Andrews? You think that's worth it?"

Taylor peered up at Scott's furious face. There really was only one thing she had to say in response to that.

"Absofuckinglutely."

Finished there, Taylor pried Scott's fingers from her arm and slid by. She cut through the garden on her way out, being careful to avoid the paparazzi.

And just as suddenly as she had appeared, the Mystery Woman left the party.

AFTER HEARING TAYLOR'S story, Kate and Val were silent on their ends of the line.

"What? Say something," Taylor demanded anxiously.

Kate responded first. "You know, ending your date with an A-list movie star with an 'absofuckinglutely' really is *so* played these days." She laughed. "Seriously, Taylor—where do you come up with this stuff?"

Taylor noticed that her other friend had been uncharacteristically silent. "Val, you're awfully quiet."

Valerie spoke slowly. "I just want to be sure I have this straight. You manage to score a ticket to the best party of the year with one of the biggest celebrities in town. But then you dance with another guy—who just so happens to be, like, the hottest man in the world—then you ditch your date and run out of the party like an obscene Cinderella, never to be heard from again."

Taylor squirmed uneasily in her chair. "Well, it really was just the one obscenity—"

Valerie cut her off sternly. "Taylor Donovan."

Then her tone changed. To one of pride.

"You are a friggin' *genius*!" Val shrieked. "Everyone's going to be talking about you! You are *so* going to be on the cover of *Us Weekly* this week!"

Taylor tried to control her friend's excitement. "Don't hold your breath, Val. They didn't get any pictures of me."

"That's what you celebs always think. But then you end up topless on the cover of the *Enquirer* and you suddenly think, hmm . . . maybe it wasn't such a smart idea to sunbathe nude in Cabo after all, maybe that *was* a camera stashed underneath the towels that pool boy was carrying . . ."

"So what are you going to do about Jason?" Kate interrupted, getting back to the business at hand.

"Nothing. There's nothing else to do," Taylor said. "I wanted to tell him that I'd been wrong about him because I thought it was something I needed to say. That's all." She paused. Then she lowered her voice, even though there wasn't a single other person in the office that Sunday morning.

"Why? Do you think I should do something else?" she whispered.

"You know I can't say that," Kate told her.

"*I* can say it," Val volunteered.

Taylor spun around in her chair, frustrated. "What am I doing? Seriously—I've got way too much work to do. I can't be worrying about this right now."

"If all you worry about is work," Val lectured, "then one day you'll come home and realize that it's the only thing you've got."

"It's better than coming home one night and finding Jason fucking some supermodel on our dining-room table."

The phone went silent.

Wow—that had flown out of her mouth before she'd even thought about it.

"You're right, Taylor," Val said quietly. "If you really think that might happen, then I think you did the right thing in walking away from Jason."

There wasn't anything else her friends could say. But a few awkward minutes later, when Taylor ended the call, she realized that she had never felt less victorious in winning an argument.

HATING THE WAY her conversation with Val and Kate had ended, Taylor did what she always did when she felt out of sorts: she threw herself into her work—a tendency that apparently (according to Val) was going to one day render her an angry, lonely old maid who yelled crazy gibberish and threw ratty gray house slippers at neighborhood kids riding bicycles past her house.

Fine—that may not have been word for word what Val had said, but Taylor took the liberty of filling in the implied innuendo of her friend's "one day you'll come home and realize that work is the only thing you've got" comment.

Taylor Donovan, expected life trajectory:

Associate.

Partner.

Retirement.

Crazy gibberish, ratty slippers.

Pathetic death (alone, of course), thinking of the one time she had almost kissed Jason Andrews.

R.I.P.

Determined to push aside Val's warning and all accompanying morbid thoughts, Taylor turned back to the files on her desk. The next morning she would be cross-examining the most important witness in the EEOC's case and she needed to be ready. This witness, the named plaintiff, had always troubled Taylor. She knew the witness planned to testify that she had suffered severe emotional distress because of the alleged harassment she'd been subjected to in her work environment. It was testimony that, if believed by the jury, would help bolster the EEOC's demand for significant monetary and punitive damages.

Derek chuckled when he dropped by Taylor's office later that day and found her reviewing the files from the psychologist who had treated the plaintiff for her stress.

"You're reading those again? We've been through those files a million times. Trust me—there isn't anything we missed."

Taylor set the file down on her desk, rubbing her temples. "There has to be—there's no way this woman would've become so distraught because of her work environment. Even if everything she says is true, it's not enough to cause someone severe emotional distress."

"But the psychologist ran diagnostic tests and found her to be clinically depressed. How do we get around that? Argue that she's an eggshell plaintiff?"

Taylor sighed, reluctant to go down that route. An "eggshell plaintiff" defensive strategy meant arguing that the plaintiff was "fragile," that is, more sensitive than the average person on the street. That a more "reasonable" person would not have been bothered by the same conduct the plaintiff claimed caused her depression. Such arguments generally did not go over well with juries—no one liked to see the big-money corporate defense attorney calling the poor distressed plaintiff, in essence, a weak-ass little wimp.

"No, I've been trying to come up with some other angle for her cross." Taylor stopped rubbing her temples and peered over at Derek. "You subpoenaed all her medical files, right?"

Derek nodded. "This the only psychologist she was treated by."

"How about her general practitioner—do we have any files from him?"

"Yep, and I already checked them. Nothing."

"What about any other doctors she saw? Her ob-gyn?"

Derek made a face. "You want to read her gynecologist's files?"

"Not particularly," Taylor said. But at least it would keep her busy, so that her mind wasn't drifting off with thoughts of Jason.

The things he had said to her at the Black & Pink Ball.

How he looked in his tuxedo.

How it felt to be dancing that close to him.

All dangerous thoughts. She needed to stay focused—she had a job to do.

So Taylor asked Derek to bring her the file. And twenty

minutes into her reading, she had absolutely no problem staying focused on work.

She picked up her phone.

"Derek. You are not going to believe what I'm reading right now."

"IF YOU DON'T mind, Ms. Campbell, I'd like to shift gears and talk about your claim for emotional distress damages."

Up on the witness stand, the named plaintiff, Emily Campbell, sat straight and upright in her chair. She nodded to Taylor, who stood in front of the jury, just a few feet away from the stand.

"So if I understand your earlier testimony correctly, Ms. Campbell," Taylor said, "you are certain there was nothing else going on in your life during the time of your employment with the defendant that could have contributed to your stress. Is that correct?"

Ms. Campbell folded her hands demurely, looking chaste and proper in her cream sweater set and pearls. "That's correct—the only stress I experienced was caused by the terrible work environment I had been subjected to. I couldn't eat or sleep. I had to see a therapist several times a week just to get by."

"And you're positive that nothing else could have been causing the stress you experienced during that time frame?"

"I'm positive," Ms. Campbell said definitively.

"And, according to you, the stress was so bad that you sought treatment from a psychologist—a Dr. Gary Moore—is that correct?" Taylor crossed over to the defense table. She picked up a file and brought it back with her to the podium.

"Yes—I went to see him because—"

"A simple 'yes' or 'no' will suffice, Ms. Campbell." Taylor smiled politely. She opened the file she had brought to the podium as she continued on with her questioning.

"Ms. Campbell, as part of your claim for emotional distress damages, you signed a waiver permitting us to look at your medical records, is that right?"

"Yes."

"And that waiver allowed us to look at all your medical records?"

"Yes, although Dr. Moore is the only psychologist I saw for the emotional distress I suffered."

"I understand that, Ms. Campbell, but for a moment I'd like to talk to you about treatment you received from a Dr. Michelle Phillips at 1089 First Street in Santa Monica. You do know Dr. Phillips, don't you?"

There was a scurry of activity over at the plaintiff's table as Frank began riffling through his files. Taylor heard him mumble under his breath to his cocounsel, presumably something along the lines of "Who the fuck is Dr. Phillips?"

Ms. Campbell looked at Taylor, confused. "But Dr. Phillips is my gynecologist—I really don't see what she has to do with any of this."

"Yes or no, Ms. Campbell."

"*Yes*, I know Dr. Phillips," the witness grumbled.

Carrying her file, Taylor stepped closer to the witness stand.

"Do you recall telling Dr. Phillips during your appointment on February second of last year that you needed to be tested for sexually transmitted diseases because—let me make sure I get this correct here . . ." Taylor read out loud from her file, "Because, quote, 'your weasel-dick husband slept with a skanky whore stripper and the cheating bastard didn't use a rubber'?"

Ms. Campbell shot up in her chair. "She actually wrote that down?"

The jury tittered with amused laughter and sat up interestedly. Finally—things were starting to look a little more like *Law & Order* around here.

"I take it that's a yes?" Taylor asked.

"Yes," Ms. Campbell's voice cracked. She cleared her throat as Taylor asked her next question.

"And do you also remember telling your gynecologist that you were, quote, 'under *extreme emotional distress* because of your unfaithful dirtbag husband and couldn't eat or sleep'?"

Ms. Campbell sunk lower in her chair as if trying to hide. "Yes," she whispered.

Taylor pointed to the file. "And then, according to Dr. Phillips's records, did you also tell her, 'Thank god I at least have my job to get away from that lousy son of a bitch, or I'd probably kill them both'?"

By now, Ms. Campbell had sunk so far down in her chair that there was little more than two eyeballs peeking out over the witness stand.

"I may have said that," she said meekly.

Taylor smiled patiently. Of course she had.

"Well, then, going back to your earlier testimony, are you sure you want to tell this jury that the only thing causing stress in your life was your employment with the defendant? And not the"—she consulted her file one last time—" 'weasel-dick unfaithful dirtbag' you were married to?"

The two eyeballs blinked at Taylor from behind the witness stand.

"There may have been a few other things going on in my life at the time."

Taylor snapped her file shut. "Okay—I'm glad we cleared that up." She looked over at the judge. "I have no further questions, Your Honor." She returned to the defense table and took her seat next to Derek.

"You love this stuff, don't you?" Derek whispered teasingly. Taylor hid her smile, not wanting the jury to see. She did, she really did.

Seeing that it was a good time for a break, the judge decided to recess the trial until two. As soon as the judge and jurors had filed out of the courtroom, Frank headed over to Taylor's table.

"Why don't we grab lunch, Taylor?" he said casually. "I'd like to talk about how the case is going."

Derek nudged her knowingly.

Taylor took in her opposing counsel impassively. "Okay. But only if you're buying, Frank." She watched as the man got all rigid and indignant.

"I'm only kidding, Frank. Sheesh."

MIDWAY THROUGH THEIR bagel sandwiches, Frank laid it all on the line.

"This case is a sinking ship, Taylor. The EEOC wants out."

They were sitting in a coffee shop across the street from the courthouse. The place was packed with lawyers, so Taylor and Frank had chosen a table in the back where they could talk privately.

"That's quite an about-face from our last settlement negotiations," Taylor said.

"When you told me to call you when someone saw a penis."

"Did any ever turn up?"

Taylor stared innocently at Frank, who just sat there, glaring. Then—shockingly—he actually cracked a smile. He shook his head ruefully.

"Not a one."

Taylor eased back in her chair. She was glad to see Frank finally acting like a human being and all, but business was still business.

"Can I ask what brought about this change of heart?"

"It's these *witnesses*. I don't know what happens, I go through their testimony, I prep them, but then they get on the stand and you crack them like . . ." Frank paused, gesturing, searching for the right word.

"Walnuts?"

"No."

"Eggs?"

"*No.*"

"Little bitty pieces of glass?"

Frank looked at her, exasperated. "Are you always like this?"

"It's part of my charm."

Frank threw his hands up. "I mean—who reads the *gynecologist's* files? Who has time for that? Don't you have a personal life?"

Taylor nearly coughed up her coffee. She grabbed her napkin to cover. Ahh, Frank . . . if only you knew about little Taylor Donovan from Chicago. She danced at the ball with the Sexiest Man Alive and then spent the rest of her life hiding behind work in order to avoid him.

"The problem with settling now," Taylor said, "is that my client has already invested a lot amount of money in defending this lawsuit. At this point, we might as well ride the trial out to the end. The way things are going, it's a better investment for them to pay me to defend this case than to pay your clients to settle."

"What if your client didn't have to pay anything at all?" Frank asked, taking a sip of his coffee.

Taylor tilted her head, surprised by this. "What exactly are you proposing?"

"At this point, the EEOC just wants to save face," Frank told her. "The publicity the agency will get if we lose this case will kill us." He leaned across the table, outlining his terms. "Here's the deal: no money, but your client has to agree to yearly training on harassment and discrimination. And the terms of our settlement have to be kept confidential—we'll issue a joint press release saying only that the parties were able to amicably resolve their dispute."

Shocked as Taylor was by this proposal, she managed to maintain her skeptical look. It was all part of the lawyer dance.

"I don't know," she said, shaking her head. "My client really wants this trial victory as vindication. But I'll let them know about your offer nonetheless."

Frank sat back in his chair with a confident smile. He may have been a pissy little man at times, but he wasn't stupid.

"You do that, Taylor. But we both know that this comes down to a simple business decision. When your firm's fees alone would cost another six figures to finish this trial, your client will never walk away from a chance at a free settlement. That *is* their vindication."

And as much as she hated to admit it, Taylor knew Frank was right.

Thirty-one

WITH A LOUD pop, someone cracked open the first bottle of champagne. The party officially kicked into high gear.

Taylor stood in a circle of lawyers, all of whom were eager to offer her their congratulations. To celebrate her victory, the firm had reserved one of the private rooms at the Beverly Hills Four Seasons. The party was packed, as lawyers at her firm were generally enthusiastic about any event that provided them both an excuse to cut loose from work at six o'clock and unlimited free alcohol.

Taylor had a sneaking suspicion that, on this particular occasion, there was an additional factor drawing everyone in like months to a flame. For weeks, stories about her alleged fantastic social life had spread throughout the office (she suspected Linda and the cohorts had a hand in this), and she guessed, from the way everyone at the party looked eagerly at the door each time someone walked in, that they all were hoping a certain you-know-who might drop by.

Over and over again, Taylor repeated the story of the EEOC's capitulation to her colleagues, which (as Frank had predicted) had led to a quick settlement of the case earlier that afternoon. Indeed, the events of the day had happened so fast that Taylor felt a little dizzy standing there at the party. Perhaps she just needed some fresh air.

As she slowly inched closer and closer to the French doors that led to an outdoor terrace, her recap of the day's events got more and more succinct. Luckily, Derek stood by her side and picked up the slack when she fell quiet. As he entertained the crowd with stories of her trial antics, Taylor smiled along, relieved that no one seemed to notice how distracted she was.

About midway through the evening, she thought she might get a brief reprieve when she heard the pointed clinking of a glass. She looked across the room and saw Sam Blakely rising in toast.

"So I have just a few words I'd like to say in celebration of our firm's victory today," he began with a proud glance in Taylor's direction. "A victory brought about in large part because of the skills and dedication of one associate, the unstoppable Taylor Donovan." Sam paused as the crowd clapped and cheered. Then he turned to address her personally.

"Taylor, when you first arrived at the Los Angeles office, we had been told you were a rising star. And from what I've seen, I wholeheartedly agree with all the praises the Chicago office sang of you."

She blushed modestly at the compliment.

"We here in the L.A. office have come to think of you as one of our own," Sam continued, "and you will be greatly missed now that your work here is finished. And since you, of course, will greatly miss all of us"—Sam held for the expected laughter—"let me at least give you something I hope will ease your sadness."

Everyone in the room watched as Sam strolled over to Taylor. She presumed he was about to hand her some sort of farewell gift.

But what he said next surprised her.

He stuck out his hand.

"I know it's two years early, Taylor, and that's a first for this firm, but let me be the first to offer you my congratulations.

Because when you get back to Chicago, you'll find they have a much bigger office waiting for you." He winked slyly. "A *partner's* office, that is."

The whole room erupted in celebration.

Taylor stood there, stunned.

She felt people patting her on the back. In her daze, she numbly took Sam's hand and shook it. One at a time, her co-workers came up to offer their congratulations. With each minute that passed, Taylor felt dizzier and dizzier, until she literally thought the walls were spinning. Desperate for some air, after a few moments she excused herself from the crowd and stepped out onto the terrace.

Once outside, she headed to the edge of the balcony. Trying to calm herself down, she took in the view of the hotel's lush gardens. A warm evening breeze rustled the draped bougainvillea. Pristine white flowers surrounded the marble sculptures and fountains. It was all so . . . California. And so she took it all in, trying to savor every last detail.

Because her time there had come to an end.

Mid-trial settlements were not uncommon, so she should have prepared herself for the possibility that she would be leaving earlier than expected. But blindly, she had not.

There would be no more fancy Hollywood parties. No more dinners at trendy restaurants and drinks at hot L.A. clubs. No more apartment by the beach, sunny California days, or warm, sultry nights.

And there would be no more Jason.

This was the reason Taylor had been walking around in a fog since the moment her case had settled.

Leaning against the balcony for support, she took a deep, steadying breath. She knew she should've been back in the party, enjoying every moment of her success. It was a phenomenal achievement, the firm making her partner two years early. It was everything she had worked for since graduating from law school. It was everything she wanted.

Wasn't it?

Taylor heard soft footsteps behind her. She turned and saw Linda approaching and watched as her secretary pulled up next to her at the balcony.

"Quite an exciting night, huh?"

Taylor nodded. "You can say that again."

Linda studied her for a moment, then stuck out her hand. "Congratulations, Taylor."

She smiled. "Thanks, Linda, for everything. It's been a pleasure working with you."

"Somehow, I think things around the office are going to be a lot quieter once you're gone," Linda said teasingly.

Taylor laughed. "That's probably true."

Then the two women fell into a quiet silence as they looked out at the gardens. After a moment, Linda glanced over.

"What are you going to tell him?"

Taylor soberly shook her head. "I have no idea."

Right then, Sam found them out on the balcony and dragged Taylor back into the party. Although Linda's question weighed heavily on her mind, Taylor had no chance to give it any further thought as she moved from one group of attorneys to the next, chatting and mingling and doing the rounds as any good soon-to-be-partner would.

After the party, as she drove back to her apartment, her mind was bogged down with the multiple logistical issues that accompanied her return back to Chicago. Her apartment and office needed to be packed, travel arrangements needed to be made, she had to terminate her apartment sublease and car lease (and here the Chrysler people had just been nice enough to replace her wrecked PT Cruiser with another), she needed to call the utility companies and get a refund on the package of classes she had just purchased at the Santa Monica Yoga Center . . . the list was endless.

Needless to say, Taylor's mind was traveling in a thousand different directions as she pulled her car into the driveway of her apartment building.

Which is probably why she didn't notice a familiar black Aston Martin parked on the street out front until she got to her front door and saw Jason heading up the walkway toward her.

Thirty-two

TAYLOR STOOD FROZEN on her doorstep as Jason headed over to her. He wore jeans and a lightweight navy sweater that brought out the blue of his eyes from ten feet away. He looked casual and rumpled and uncharacteristically tousled about. Taylor thought he had never looked better.

He stopped when he got to the edge of her doorstep.

"I need to talk to you."

"I thought you were in New York," she said. She had watched his live interview on the *Today* show that morning before leaving for court. Not that she needed to admit that to him.

"I flew back this afternoon." Jason gestured to her front door. "Can I come in?"

Taylor nodded. As Jason followed her into the apartment, she noticed that he seemed nervous. Frankly, so was she. The two of them had an awkward moment, fumbling around each other as they stepped through the archway to the living room at the same time.

Taylor stopped and gestured for Jason to go first. Then she politely offered him something to drink. He politely replied that a glass of water would be nice.

A person could've cut the tension in the air with a spoon.

Taylor headed into her kitchen, berating herself for acting like such a moron. Miraculously, she somehow managed to pour a glass of water without dropping or spilling anything. When she returned to the living room she found Jason standing in front of the fireplace, checking out the family photographs she had set out along the mantel.

"You look like your father," he said as she handed over his glass of water.

"Really? People usually say I look like my mom." Relaxing a bit, Taylor moved next to Jason to see which photo he was looking at.

"It's the eyes." He turned and studied her, as if searching for an answer to some unasked question.

"I'm glad you came here tonight," Taylor found herself saying. She saw this put Jason at ease for the first time since he'd got there. "There's something I need to talk to you about as well."

"Okay . . ." he said hesitantly, presumably remembering an earlier conversation between them that had begun this very same way. "You go first this time."

So Taylor took a deep breath. "I settled my case today. It's over. Done."

Jason was surprised by this. "Over? I thought you said you were only halfway through your trial."

Taylor nodded. "And then there were supposed to be posttrial motions and then likely an appeal, too. But today the plaintiff made us an offer we couldn't say no to. It's a great result. In fact, it was such a great result that, well . . . the firm said they're going to make me a partner."

Jason's face broke into an enormous smile. "Holy shit—you're kidding!"

"But I have to go back to Chicago."

That wiped the smile right off his face.

He said nothing at first. He carefully set his glass of water down on her coffee table, unnecessarily adjusting it on a coaster as if needing a minute. Then he straightened up with his arms folded across his chest.

"So what did you tell them?"

Taylor met his gaze.

"I told them yes."

They both fell silent.

Jason began to pace in front of the coffee table. He looked shocked. And angry. He appeared to be struggling for the right words to say.

"But . . . what about everything you have here in Los Angeles?"

Taylor shook her head. "It's up or out at my firm. If I don't go back to Chicago, I don't have a job."

"That's the decision they force you to make? Then screw your job."

Now *that* fired Taylor up. "Oh well, I suppose that's easy for you to say. Do you even remember the last time you saw anything less than seven figures on a paycheck?"

For her sarcasm, Jason rewarded Taylor with a glare. It made her feel quite defensive.

"I've worked really hard for this," she told him. "Three years of law school followed by six years of killing myself at that firm. I worked nights, weekends, even holidays. All that, and your only advice is 'screw your job'?"

Jason circled around her. A floodgate seemingly had been opened.

"Oh, you want my advice? Okay, let's see . . . Gee—I don't know, Taylor, maybe you could find a new job. *Here.* Have you ever considered that? Did you even stop to consider the possibility of not running back to Chicago? Did you think about the fact that you might be walking away from something really good here? Did you once consider the possibility of giving—"

He stopped suddenly. Catching Taylor's gaze, he shifted uncomfortably and regrouped.

"—Did you ever consider the possibility of giving *L.A.* a chance?" he finished.

But Taylor wasn't fooled; she knew exactly what Jason had been about to say. But she, too, found it easier to dance around the subject rather than to actually say out loud what they both were thinking.

"There are a lot of things I like about L.A.'" she said carefully. "Things I like very much. But it's too risky. What if things didn't work out, Jason?" Her voice cracked a little as she said this. She collected herself. "With L.A., I mean."

But Jason had caught her hesitation. He crossed the room to her.

"Taylor, look at me," he whispered huskily. "Look at me." He waited until her eyes met his. "You have nothing to worry about. Los Angeles is a perfect match for you. You belong here. You know that."

He paused. Then he looked deep into her eyes and laid it all on the line. "You belong with me."

Finally, it was all out there between them. No more games.

And as Taylor's eyes searched Jason's, she knew he was right.

He was her match.

Right from the very beginning, even when she had told herself that she hated him, he'd made her laugh. From the very beginning, he had gotten her. He knew her, he understood her. In so many ways, they were the same. She may have fussed and fought, but secretly she loved every moment they spent together. He was smart and witty and sexy as hell, but underneath it all, he was generous and kind and—surprisingly—as vulnerable as anyone else. Most important, he challenged her. And he drove her absolutely fucking crazy.

And that's what made him perfect.

But.

As she stared into Jason's deep blue eyes, she finally faced her deepest, darkest truths.

She had gotten lucky with Daniel, she knew that. After the shock of his cheating had worn off, she had been able to move on. Of course there had been some sadness, and mostly a lot of embarrassment, but nothing that she hadn't been able to isolate and control with her usual degree of calm and collected coolness.

But that would not be the case with Jason.

If she trusted Jason and she was *wrong*, and one day she

walked in on *him* with another woman, she didn't think she could handle it. And even if she didn't catch him red-handed, even if there wasn't any cheating at all, even if he just got bored with her one day—after all, wasn't that inevitable, Hollywood relationships never worked out—the simple truth of the matter was—

She would never get over him.

With Jason, there would be no calm and collected coolness. No feelings that could be isolated and controlled. It would be all or nothing, and Taylor feared that if she lost him, she would never find her way back.

So with a heavy but firm heart, she looked up at Jason and gave him her answer.

"I can't."

He stared at her knowingly. "You're afraid."

"Yes."

They were both surprised she admitted this. Jason reached out and took both of her hands. He laced his fingers through hers.

"Tell me what it will take, Taylor. I'll do anything you ask."

So raw and naked were his words, she had to look away. Deep down, there was a part of her who ached to hear him say exactly that. Which meant that the scared part of her needed to stop him from saying anything else. She had to find a way to remain strong.

Her eye caught something on her coffee table— something she had placed there several weeks ago, one Sunday afternoon when she'd been straightening her apartment. Perhaps to serve as a reminder.

People magazine. "The Women of Jason Andrews!" article.

Taylor removed her hands from Jason's and held the magazine between them. The parade of all his ex-lovers/dates/whatevers.

"Did you tell all of these women the same thing?"

Confronted with his past, Jason shook his head. "No. Those women have nothing to do with us."

"Not even the supermodel? The one you brought to London?" Taylor saw that he was surprised she knew about this. "Did you tell her—"

"I'll save you the trouble, in case you have a whole cross-examination prepared," he said. "Yes, I've done a lot of bad things. I don't deny it. But that all changed once I met you. I haven't thought of anyone else from the first moment I saw you in that courtroom."

Taylor's expression remained surprisingly impassive.

"What about Naomi Cross?"

Jason's shoulders sagged a little at this. "Naomi was different," he said lamely.

Taylor's face stayed firm. It had to. "I see. Naomi's different."

Jason shook his head in frustration. "No—that came out wrong." He took a step closer and peered down at her earnestly.

"What I'm trying to say is that *you're* the one who's different, Taylor."

Ahhh . . . the magic words. The very words she had promised herself to never believe again.

But what about the look in Jason's eyes? He seemed so forthright. So convincing.

Taylor hesitated.

She needed to stay firm. She looked down at her hands. At the magazine she held. "The Women of Jason Andrews!"

Seeing this, Jason yanked the magazine out of her hands. "Stop looking at this bullshit!" He threw the magazine against the wall and it crashed to the floor with a noisy flutter.

And then . . .

A tiny card slipped out from the magazine's strewn pages.

Both Jason and Taylor saw it. He walked over and picked it up. Realizing what it was, Taylor looked away as Jason read the words on the card out loud.

"I'm sorry. And I love you. Daniel."

Jason's expression changed the moment he read the card. He turned back to her with a strange look.

"Now I see what the problem is. Tell me, Taylor, whose mistakes am I paying for?"

Taylor's eyes narrowed. How dare he.

She picked the magazine off the floor and held it up. Her words were cold. "Your own."

And with that, Jason's eyes filled with hurt. But then, almost as quickly, they turned stony. Dead. His voice was flat and emotionless.

"If that's how you feel, then I guess there's nothing more we have to say to each other."

And without so much as another look, he turned and walked out of her apartment.

When she heard the door slam, Taylor sat down on her couch. She fought hard against what happened next. She took a deep breath.

There's no crying in baseball.

She blinked.

There's no crying in baseball.

She wouldn't do it. There's no crying in baseball.

But it was a futile struggle. For the first time in her adult life, a tear ran down her face. And then another.

Taylor sat quietly on her couch, alone.

She did not brush the tears away.

Thirty-three

LINDA HELD UP the last of the remaining boxes, one marked "Miscellaneous." Taylor gestured to the stack they had collected by her office door. "That one gets shipped to Chicago." Linda nodded and put the box with the others.

They had been going at this for the past two days. For only having been in Los Angeles for a few months, Taylor had managed to collect a lot of files.

"I think that's the last one," Linda said.

Taylor nodded. She felt tired. Probably from all the packing, which seemed endless. When she wasn't packing at the office, she was packing at home. The movers were coming to her apartment first thing the next morning, and then she'd be off to the airport. She already had several meetings scheduled for tomorrow afternoon in the Chicago office. As a new partner, she wanted to hit the ground running.

At the thought of being back in Chicago, Taylor looked out her office window. She knew Linda wanted to ask about Jason but Taylor really hoped she wouldn't. It was bad enough that she was a mess at home. Every time her phone rang, she ran and checked the caller ID, hoping to see Jason's number.

She'd even skimmed the cable guide a time or two, looking to see if any of his movies just "happened" to be on.

Sensing that Taylor needed a moment alone, Linda turned to leave the office. But then she stopped in the doorway. "I just realized, we forgot to pack your desk drawer."

The desk had one narrow drawer in the center. Taylor glanced at it, and then waved Linda off. "It's no problem. I'll take care of it myself."

"Are you sure?"

Taylor nodded. "Yep. There's not much in there anyway, just a few pens and notepads."

Linda nodded and left. Taylor stayed at her desk until she knew the coast was clear, then walked over and shut her door. When she got back to her desk, she slowly opened its one drawer. Folded inside was the "Shit Happens" T-shirt.

Taylor took the shirt out and set it on top of her desk. She ran her finger over the words. It was where it had all begun.

She got up and headed over to the box marked "Miscellaneous." Being careful to keep the shirt neatly folded, she placed it inside the box, smoothing it to make sure it didn't wrinkle.

She took a step back and nodded. That was that.

She closed the lid of the box and tightly sealed it with the roll of packing tape Linda had left behind.

LATER THAT AFTERNOON, Taylor heard laughter and excited voices outside her office: the familiar chatter of the secretarial cohorts. She realized that she would actually kind of miss it.

But then she heard a man's voice. A lazy drawl she would've recognized anywhere.

"Well, I'm glad to see you ladies missed me," the voice said teasingly.

Jason!

Taylor flew out of her desk chair and ran into the hallway and—

—stopped when she saw the secretaries crowded around

Linda's desk, watching television. On the screen, Taylor could see Jason being interviewed on *The View*. Her face fell in disappointment.

Seeing Taylor's expression, Linda came over. "I'm sorry," she whispered. "I just got back from dropping your boxes off in the mail room and found them watching the TV again."

"It's okay, Linda."

The other secretaries turned when they heard her voice. "Oh good, Taylor, you're here," the secretary nearest the television said. "I think you might want to see this."

Taylor couldn't help but be curious. "You've seen this before?"

"I recorded it and brought it in. I thought you should watch for yourself," the secretary replied.

Unable to help herself, Taylor watched as Barbara Walters began the interview with some standard chitchat, asking Jason about his hectic schedule. Ever the movie star, he smiled and agreed that things were crazy, promoting one film while in the middle of shooting another.

Then Whoopi jumped in and told Jason to cut the crap and just tell everyone who the Mystery Woman was.

Jason laughed. He shook his head.

"Oh my god, he's blushing!" one of the secretaries gushed, squeezing Taylor's shoulders excitedly. She watched as Whoopi refused to accept Jason's silence on the subject.

"C'mon, Jason, tell us something!" she demanded. "Tell us just one little something about the Mystery Woman."

When Jason remained coyly silent, Whoopi raised one hopeful eyebrow. "Not even just one tiny word? At least give us that."

Jason thought about this for a moment. Then on national television, he summed up Taylor Donovan in just one word.

"Amazing."

The secretarial cohorts gasped out loud. Taylor felt her stomach do a little flip-flop.

"He *never* talks about women like that," the secretary nearest the television told her. "I just thought maybe you should see this. You know, before you go back to Chicago."

"When did you tape this?" Taylor quickly asked. "What day was this interview?"

The secretary had to think for a second. "Ummm . . . two days ago, I think."

Taylor's heart sunk. Jason must have taped it the same day he'd been in New York for the *Today* show. The morning *before* their fight. She highly doubted he would describe her as "amazing" anymore. An "amazing" bitch, perhaps.

She turned back to the television just as the blonde girl, that one from *Survivor*, steered the conversation to Jason's newest film.

"So, Jason, your new film, *Inferno*, opens on Friday. Tell us a little bit about the movie. What was it that drew you to this part?"

"Mostly, it was the chance to work with Steve Clarentini," Jason said.

"And what was that like, working with him? He has a reputation for being a somewhat difficult director—did you experience any of that?"

Taylor laughed at the question. Linda glanced over.

"I can't wait to see him answer this—Jason told me he hated every moment he worked with that guy," Taylor explained.

She and Linda watched as Jason nonchalantly leaned back against the couch.

"Steve is a great director," he said casually. "I wouldn't say we had any particular problems getting along. We had the normal actor-director relationship." As he said this, he absentmindedly turned his watch around his wrist.

The gesture caught Taylor's eye. She took a step closer to the television.

"So all those rumors of the two of you not getting along on set, none of that was true?" the blonde *Survivor* chick persisted.

Jason pooh-poohed this with a smile. "No, no—the tabloids blew all of that out of proportion. Steve and I didn't have any problems on the set." Again, he toyed casually with his watch, turning it around his wrist.

Taylor stood in the hallway of her office, stunned.

She knew that gesture.

That thing with the watch, it was the same gesture he'd made that first day they'd met, during her cross-examination, when he said he'd had a "film emergency." It was the same gesture he'd made when he'd been flirting with Naomi and said there was nothing he'd rather do than go to Napa Valley with her.

Suddenly, Taylor's eyes widened knowingly.

"He lied," she whispered.

Hearing this, Linda waved her hand dismissively. "Oh, these actors lie all the time about problems they have on the set. It's what their publicists tell them to say."

"No—he lied about Naomi."

Linda looked at her, confused. "Naomi? Naomi Cross?"

Distracted, Taylor ignored Linda's question. Why would Jason do that? She turned and slowly headed back to her office and took a seat at her desk.

He had been lying about Naomi.

So? What did that mean?

Well, it might mean that he'd been telling the truth when he said he'd thought only of her since the moment they met.

Which then meant . . . what? What, exactly?

She was packed and ready to go. She'd be in Chicago tomorrow. She'd be a *partner* in Chicago tomorrow.

Taylor needed a minute to think.

He said she was amazing.

He said she belonged with him.

Maybe those weren't just words.

But it was too late. She had already accepted the firm's offer. There was nothing she could do. Fine—nothing she *would* do. Nothing she *wanted* to do.

Was there?

Taylor braced herself against the edge of her desk.

Her leg began to bounce nervously.

Oh god.

TAYLOR KNOCKED ON Sam's door. He looked up and smiled. "Hey there, Partner."

Taylor gulped nervously, hesitating in the doorway. "Got a minute?"

Sam waved her in. "Sure, sure. Come on in." He gestured to the chair in front of his desk. "Have a seat."

Taylor chose to remain standing. She fidgeted nervously. "Um, so . . . wow." She laughed shakily. At Sam's odd look, she pulled herself together.

"I wanted to thank you again, Sam, for the partnership offer. I know you had a lot to do with it."

"You did it yourself," he told her in all seriousness. "You should be very proud."

Taylor struggled with her next words. "But I've just been wondering, does it really have to be Chicago?"

Sam sighed, as if he had been expecting this. "The head of our employment group is in Chicago. You know it's where you're the most marketable."

Taylor nodded. She did know this. She walked over to the floor-to-ceiling windows that took up an entire wall of the partner's office and looked out at the view of Los Angeles. The city was right there at her feet. Waiting.

Sam approached her from behind. "I don't want to play hardball with you, Taylor. I respect you far too much for that. But the firm has never before made an offer for early partnership to any associate. They've gone out on a limb here. If you don't take this now, they'll never offer it to you again."

Taylor gazed out the window. "I know."

"Then what's the problem?"

"The problem . . . is that it seems I've become rather attached to this city."

Sam wasn't fooled. "I know what you're attached to, Taylor. But you need to be pragmatic about this. You know his reputation."

She remained silent.

Sam persisted. "Come on—what do you think? That it won't be that way with you? That you're different?" He shook his head. "You can't honestly believe that."

When Taylor still didn't answer, Sam looked over.

"Do you?"

Taylor stared out at the city below.

Actually . . . *yes*. She did believe it.

Her voice was soft, barely audible. "I do."

Sam's head snapped back, surprised. "Do you really? Are you willing to risk your career on that?"

Taylor turned around. "I think that for him, I'd risk everything."

With that, she apologized to Sam and walked out of his office. She felt as though an enormous weight suddenly had been lifted off her shoulders. And she felt steadier, more confident than ever in knowing exactly what she wanted.

Okay, Jason Andrews, she thought. Game on.

TAYLOR RUSHED BY her secretary's desk on her way to the elevators.

"Linda—I need you to go to the mail room and put a hold on all the boxes we're shipping to Chicago."

Hearing the urgency in her voice, Linda jumped to attention.

"Why? Oh my gosh, what's happening? Wait—does this mean you're staying in Los Angeles?" She hurried after Taylor, following her down the hall.

When they hit the elevator bank, Taylor pushed the down button. "I don't know—I guess that's what I'm about to find out."

The elevator doors opened and she turned to Linda. "Wish me luck," she said, stepping inside. She stopped after taking two steps into the elevator. And stepped right back out.

Taylor glanced over at her secretary. "What day is today?"

Linda had to think for a moment. "Thursday. The fourteenth. Why?"

Taylor immediately checked her watch, then swore under her breath.

"What? What is it?" Linda asked.

Taylor turned to her, her eyes filled with horror.

"He's at his premiere."

Thirty-four

THE SPECTACLE IN front of Grauman's Chinese Theater was unlike anything Taylor had ever seen.

Cameras, reporters, media vans, even a helicopter—every form of entertainment coverage and accoutrement thereto had shown up for the big Jason Andrews event, the premiere of his summer blockbuster, *Inferno.*

And the fans. Oh my gosh, the fans. Taylor warily checked them out as well.

An enormous screaming crowd had gathered in front of the theater, lining up along both sides of the red carpet. They cheered, they clamored, they swarmed. All in the hopes of catching just one glimpse of their hero.

Standing across the street from the mob scene, Taylor wondered for the twenty-seventh time since hopping in her car what the hell she was doing. It was madness. Pure insanity.

But it was also Jason's life.

And if she wanted to be a part of that life, she'd better start getting used to it. Like, immediately.

Suddenly, she heard the crowd roar with a renewed fervor. The chaotic screams and cheers could mean only one thing.

Jason had arrived.

Taylor watched nervously from across the street. She had never backed down from anything in her life and wasn't about to start now. It was time to rise to the challenge, to face her fears. It was time to woman up.

So with a determined look, she crossed the street and headed over to the theater.

Oh god.

TAYLOR FOUGHT HER way through the crowd. This was no small feat given that there were some *really* stubborn people at that premiere, all who seemed to think they had some sort of right to see Jason Andrews. It took a lot of pushing and shoving, but she finally made her way to the entrance of the red carpet walkway.

Where an impenetrable wall of security guards loomed before her.

Their bulging arms were folded over their massive chests. Their faces never cracked a smile. They stood side by side in a row and glared down at Taylor, who suddenly felt about two inches tall.

The center guard raised one eyebrow disdainfully at her.

"Can I help *you*?"

Taylor almost laughed out loud at what she had to say in response.

"Yes, well, you probably won't believe this—and I apologize for the unoriginality—but it's very important that I get inside this premiere."

The guard rolled his eyes. Oh, if he had a dime.

"Are you on the list?" he asked dispassionately.

"Now that's the interesting thing," Taylor said, pointing for emphasis. "I *was* on the list. But, see, then we had this argument, and I said some really awful things and I probably should have called him two days ago but if I had, then you and I wouldn't be here having this lovely moment, hehe . . ." She attempted to charm the guard with a smile.

It didn't work.

Taylor nervously cleared her throat. "Anyway, as a point of

fact, his assistant called me yesterday and mentioned some-thing to the effect that I was, um . . . specifically uninvited to this premiere."

The guard eyed her warily.

"It's really kind of a long story," Taylor explained.

"And I'm sure it's quite touching." Dismissing her with a look, the guard moved on to the person standing behind her, some slick-looking schmoe with sunglasses and some kind of special pass around his neck. Taylor fought the temptation to rip the schmoe's pass right off him and make a run for the theater doors.

As she was shoved up against the red rope by the impatient crowd, Taylor contemplated her options. But as she took in the enormous security guards, all she could come up with were different versions of a distract-then-scramble-through-the-legs maneuver of the *Tom and Jerry* variety.

But then fate intervened on her behalf.

That is, "fate" in the form of Jeremy Shelby.

"Well, well, if it isn't the illustrious Taylor Donovan," he said haughtily, strolling over on the "in" side of the rope. He looked slightly uncomfortable in his "dress" clothes, meaning a shirt that actually had buttons. From the way he eyed her warily, Taylor guessed he had heard all about her and Jason's argument.

Jeremy took a cigarette out of his pocket and stuck it in his mouth. Taylor's new bodyguard friend quickly put the kibosh on that.

"Hey, buddy—there's no smoking around here," he said.

Jeremy gave the guard a look, then put the cigarette back in his pocket and turned to her.

"So what brings you out this evening, Taylor? I thought I heard you were specifically uninvited."

Taylor moved as close as she could get with the red-rope barrier between them. "Help me out here, Jeremy," she said pleadingly.

He gave her a look. "Why should I do that?"

"Because once, nineteen years ago, you were wrong about him, too."

Jeremy stared at her stoically. After a long pause, his face broke into a smile.

"Aw, hell, you crazy kid, you knew I was gonna let you in—I'm a sucker for this stuff." He turned to the security guard and gestured for him to let Taylor in. "It's okay, she's cool."

The security guard perked his head up. "Oh, that's nice to know. And who are you?"

At the tone of condescension in the guard's voice, something inside Jeremy snapped.

"Who am I? Who am I?" he asked in annoyance. "I'll tell you who I am—*eleven* of the scripts I've written have been produced as feature films by major studios."

The guard looked Jeremy over skeptically. "What films?"

"Well, for starters, I wrote *Vampire Nation*," Jeremy said, proudly referring to one of the prior summer's biggest blockbusters.

The guard smiled enthusiastically. "You wrote that? Man, I *loved* that movie! Holy shit, I do remember you now—I saw you speak at Comic-Con last year!"

Jeremy folded his arms across his chest and threw Taylor a wink. "So? *Now* do you think you can let her in?" he asked the guard, gesturing to Taylor.

The guard held out his hands helplessly. "I'd love to, buddy, really. But . . . well, come on. You're a writer. It's a miracle you somehow got yourself into this premiere."

Taylor tried to stifle her smile as Jeremy's face fell.

As the guard started to turn away, Jeremy reluctantly changed tactics. "*Fine*. I also happen to be Jason Andrews's best friend," he said grumpily.

The guard grinned. "You and about five hundred other people, buddy." He gestured to the teeming crowd trying to push their way past the red-rope brigade.

Jeremy glanced over at Taylor and sighed. "I really hate this town sometimes. Fuck it—we're gonna have to call in the big guns." He waved to a man in a suit who stood about twenty feet away. "Marty! Marty!"

Taylor watched as the infamous Marty Shepherd, publicist to the stars and eighth most powerful person in Hollywood (excluding talent and studios heads), turned around and slowly walked toward her and Jeremy. He was shorter than she had expected, and older. His hair was gray around the temples, but his eyes were dark and shrewd.

As Marty walked over, he carefully looked her up and down. "You must be Taylor Donovan," he said before Jeremy could introduce them. He cocked his head questioningly. "I thought I heard you were specifically uninvited."

Taylor glanced over.

"There was a memo," Jeremy explained.

"I have a problem, Ms. Donovan," Marty continued. "This is a movie premiere. The world premiere of a film that is predicted to be *the* blockbuster of the summer, starring my number one client." He pointed up the red carpet. "But right now, my number one client is out there, rudely snapping at reporters, refusing to smile for the cameras, and generally being a tremendous prick."

He gave her a hard stare. "I have never seen him act like this before, Ms. Donovan. I suspect it has something to do with you."

"Marty, if you could just let me inside for a minute—"

"Why on earth would I want to do that?"

Taylor bit her tongue. If one more friggin' person asked her that . . .

She suspected that Marty required a slightly different answer from Jeremy in order for her to pass.

"Because it will make for good publicity."

Marty seemed tempted. He raised one eyebrow. "*Good* publicity?"

"*Great* publicity. The best."

He considered this. "All right, Taylor," he said cautiously. "Let's see what you've got." He turned to the guard and gestured. "Let her in."

The guard immediately sprung to attention and let Taylor inside. Before she could think twice about what she was doing, she sprinted her way through the red carpet, weaving around actors and actresses, producers, studio execs, and the like. She was a blur as she breezed by all of them, and they in turn—catching merely a brief glimpse of a dark-haired woman in a suit—ignored her.

Taylor had made it nearly to the entrance of the theater when she spotted him across the way.

Over the past few months, as they had grown closer, there had been moments when she had nearly forgotten that Jason was an international movie star.

This was *not* one of those moments.

There he stood, the hub, the center of all activity, the person that everyone at the premiere wanted to see. The masses circled around him, paparazzi scrambled to get their shots, and the fans frantically screamed his name. Somehow, he hovered above it all, seemingly impervious and unfazed by the blinding camera flashes and the endless line of microphones waved in his face.

In that moment, there on the red carpet, Taylor saw Jason the way the rest of the world saw him. She saw Jason Andrews the actor, the celebrity, the idol. The Sexiest Man Alive, the man worshipped by women around the world.

Taylor suddenly felt uncertain. She took a step back.

She felt a gentle hand on her shoulder. She turned and saw Jeremy at her side.

"It's still him, Taylor," he said.

She nodded and took a deep breath. Okay, she could do this. The crowd shifted, and she suddenly caught sight of someone else, someone she hadn't expected to see at the premiere.

Naomi Cross.

The graceful blonde actress linked her arm through Jason's. She waved happily as she posed for the cameras.

Taylor took in the sight of the two of them standing together. She had better be right about this. She glanced over at Jeremy.

"Why did Jason lie about Naomi?"

Jeremy cleared his throat nervously. "Oh. *That.* Um . . . well, you know, uh . . . to see if you'd get jealous." He caught Taylor's expression. "His plan—not mine," he added quickly. Then he cocked his head curiously. "How did you know?"

Taylor couldn't help but smile. "The watch thing."

"Ahh, yes . . . the watch thing." Jeremy grinned as well.

"The mighty have such simple weaknesses. I like to think it's God's way of keeping things fair."

Taylor watched as Naomi leaned over and whispered something in Jason's ear. The cameras went crazy as the knots in her stomach tightened.

"Are you sure there's nothing going on between them?"

Jeremy squeezed her shoulder reassuringly. "Taylor—I think there's something you probably should know about Naomi Cross."

JASON STARED DISPASSIONATELY at the cameras and the reporters who waved their microphones at him, desperate to get a sound bite or two.

During the limo ride over, he had told Marty he wouldn't be doing the press line at the premiere. He gave his publicist no explanation for this. Nor did he explain his sullen mood when Marty had jokingly offered him twenty-five million for his thoughts.

"At least try to look like you're mildly interested in being here, darling," Naomi urged, speaking softly in his ear so the surrounding media couldn't hear. "Your public demands to be entertained." She waved elegantly to a group of fans calling her name.

Jason took a step closer to the theater doors, hoping to end the charade as soon as possible. Naomi reluctantly followed. Ever the professional, the smile never left her face as she and Jason continued their private conversation.

"Did I mention how surprised I was to get your publicist's call?" she asked.

"I made you a promise," Jason said.

"Oh right . . . for helping out with that little situation at your party. With that lawyer friend of yours." Naomi gave him a look. "How is she these days?"

"I don't want to talk about her."

"Trouble in paradise?" Naomi grinned wickedly. "Perhaps *I* should call her then. You know, I'm always looking for a good attorney . . ."

Jason glared. "You're not her type, Naomi."

"Hmm, pity. Then what went wrong, darling? Why isn't she here with you?"

It took every ounce of Oscar-winning acting talent Jason possessed to keep his expression emotionless. In truth, it killed him to even think about Taylor.

"She's gone. She went back to Chicago," he said flatly.

Naomi nodded, then grinned affectionately. "Are you sure about that?" She pointed to something behind Jason's back. Confused, he turned around—

And saw Taylor.

She stood before him on the red carpet, just a few feet away.

The crowd suddenly caught sight of Jason's shocked expression and everyone fell silent. *It's the Mystery Woman,* somebody whispered. A low murmur of excitement spread throughout.

Next to Jason, Naomi cleared her throat. "Well. Look at this—now I get to play the part of the jealous woman." She glanced over. "And jealous I am . . . of *you*, Jason. Bloody heterosexuals—you're almost coming back into style these days."

She proudly pulled back her shoulders, ready to do her thing. "Thanks for the publicity, darling. I owe you." And with that, Naomi spun around and stormed angrily past Taylor. When she got close enough so that only Taylor could see, she threw her a wink. Then she pushed her way through the crowd, hamming it up for the cameras.

Leaving Jason and Taylor alone.

With thousands of people watching, that is.

JASON SPOKE FIRST, in an emotionless tone. "What are you doing here?"

Taylor smiled nervously at the question and tried for a joke. "I, um, heard you were here."

Jason shook his head. "Not this time, Taylor. No sarcasm."

She panicked at this. No sarcasm? But . . . that was her *thing*. Without it, she was naked. Defenseless.

Just then, a camera flashed brightly, right in Taylor's eyes. Another immediately followed, and another, then ten, twenty— she looked away, trying to adjust to the flickering lights. As she did, she saw that the crowd and everyone on the red carpet was staring at her.

Waiting.

When Jason saw her fall silent, his face went from expressionless to cold. He turned and walked toward the theater doors.

Taylor reacted. "Jason—wait. Just give me a ch—"

He whirled around furiously, cutting her off. "Why are you here? It's a very simple question, Taylor. For once, I'd like a real answer from you."

Taylor nodded. It *was* a simple question. But she was horrible at this kind of thing. Being open and all.

But she knew that this was The Moment. Her one chance to do it right. So with thousands of people watching, she gathered her courage and checked her pride and turned to America's most notoriously womanizing bachelor and said—

"I'm here for *you*, Jason. Because I realized that the one person who could break my heart is the only one who should have it."

The crowd fell dead silent.

Jason blinked, stunned by her words.

In the excruciatingly long silence that followed, Taylor's heart pounded fiercely. Okay—maybe she'd shot over the moon with that one.

Or maybe she'd just been wrong.

But suddenly, Jason stormed across the red carpet. He walked up to Taylor and grabbed her by the waist and without thinking she wrapped her arms around his neck as the cameras, the reporters, the whole world fell away and—

He kissed her.

And the crowd went wild!

It was *quite* a kiss. Somewhere in the distance, Taylor thought maybe she heard the screams of the crowd and thunderous applause, but frankly, she could've cared less who saw her right then. With Jason, in that moment, was the only place she wanted to be.

He pulled back first, gazing deep into her eyes.

"I love you, Taylor. I think that I've been waiting for you to come into my life for a long, long time." He grinned self-consciously. "I didn't think you'd ever give me the chance to say that."

Deeply touched by his words, Taylor gazed up at him and smiled tenderly.

"You had me at Shit Happens."

Jason burst out laughing. He pulled Taylor into his arms and kissed her softly on the forehead.

And *that* was the picture the newspapers ran the next day, under the shocking caption, "Jason Andrews in Love!"

Suddenly, Marty appeared from out of nowhere.

"Jason, you've got to give the press something. They're demanding to know the Mystery Woman's name."

Jason glanced over at Taylor. "It's up to you."

After a moment's deliberation, she nodded. It was his life, after all.

So Jason gestured to the press line, the throng of waiting reporters, who frantically reached over the rope the moment he and Taylor stepped over. Ten thousand microphones were shoved instantly in her face.

"Who are you?" the reporter from E! demanded to know.

"Taylor Donovan," she said, a bit awkwardly. Suddenly she knew what it felt like to be cross-examined.

"Are you an actress?"

"Are you a model?" another reporter called out from the back of the crowd.

"No, I'm a lawyer from Chicago."

The reporters whispered amongst each other, confused by this.

The intrepid correspondent from *Access Hollywood* pushed out front, microphone in hand. "Are you and Jason dating?" she demanded to know.

Taylor hesitated. Wow—nothing like having to discuss your personal life with a few thousand strangers.

Far more used to this than she, Jason took the lead on that

particular question. "No, I wouldn't exactly call it dating," he said. Everyone looked at Jason in surprise. Including Taylor.

He winked at her.

"Ms. Donovan is my fiancée," he declared.

And the crowd went wild!

Again!

The frenzied paparazzi snapped one shot after the other as the fans cheered riotously at this revelation.

Taylor stared at Jason, shocked.

When she didn't say anything for a moment—a long moment—he shifted nervously. Perhaps *he* had overshot a bit with that one.

"Well? What do you have to say to that?" Jason asked.

Taylor cocked her head. "Don't you think we should have sex first?"

Jason laughed, hard. He yanked the pen out of the hand of the reporter nearest them, who had been scribbling eagerly in his notebook. "Don't print that," he said firmly.

Jason turned back to Taylor with a sly grin. "Well, yes, I was hoping we could get working on that."

She raised an eyebrow. "I see. So . . . what are we waiting for?"

Jason pulled her close and whispered huskily in her ear. "One of these days you're going to learn that that question can get you into all sorts of trouble."

Taylor turned her face to his. "How long do you have to stay at this premiere?" she whispered softly.

They left twenty seconds later.

AS IT TURNED out, Taylor Donovan was a naughty lawyer indeed.

First she was naughty in the car, as Jason raced along the streets to her apartment.

"If you keep doing that, you'll be turning in another wrecked PT Cruiser."

"You said you wanted to drive," Taylor whispered teasingly as she nibbled at his neck.

"Because I'm the man."

"Fine. I'll stop then, if that's really what you want . . ."

The car careened wildly as it took the next corner.

"Fuck it," Jason groaned. "I'll buy you a new car."

THEN SHE WAS naughty in her apartment, in the foyer inside the front door, on top of the console table.

"My bedroom's just down the hall," Taylor gasped as Jason tore open her shirt. Buttons flew everywhere.

"We'll get there eventually," he said, pushing up her skirt while sliding one hand along her thigh. He smiled wickedly as his fingers slowly inched their way up. She moaned and arched her back against the wall.

"Let's go there *now*, Jason," she commanded.

"My, my, aren't we pushy . . ."

WHEN THEY FINALLY made it to the bedroom, she was naughty there, too.

"And you said you'd hate me forever," Jason teased as he tossed Taylor onto the bed.

She reached impatiently for his belt buckle, yanking him onto the bed with her. "This is angry sex—I actually don't like you at all." She wrapped her legs around him, trying to get on top. He grabbed her hands and pinned them over her head.

"Are you sure about that, Ms. Donovan? Because you seem to like it an awful lot when I do this . . ."

LATER ON, SHE was even naughty on the kitchen counter, after Jason innocently pointed out that they had forty minutes to kill until their Chinese food arrived.

"Are you sure you're not too tired?" Taylor taunted, lacing her fingers through his hair and pulling him between her legs. "Although you do seem to have a lot of energy for a thirty-nine-year-old."

Jason grabbed her by the back of her neck, pulling her

mouth to his. "Thirty-eight, smart-ass. I have a December birthday."

Hijinks ensued.

FINALLY, WHEN THEY were both so spent that they literally fell into bed, Taylor rested her head on Jason's chest. He wrapped his arms tightly around her, and they fell asleep instantly. A deep and peaceful sleep.

And in the morning, they were naughty all over again.

Thirty-five

"SO YOU REALLY quit your job?"

Jason handed Taylor another doughnut, the double chocolate with sprinkles per her request. Earlier, she had discovered the one drawback of sleeping with the Sexiest Man Alive: in the morning, *she* had to be the one to go out and hunter-gather breakfast. Unless, as Jason put it, she wanted a side of paparazzi with her orange juice and muffins.

"Yep, I really quit," she told him, biting into the chocolately goodness she had wrangled from the bakery down the street.

"But you're so calm about it."

Taylor shrugged nonchalantly. "Something else will come along."

When she said nothing further, Jason gave her a look.

"Look—it was a simple decision: you or them. I chose you," she said.

"Aww, honey . . . that's so sweet of you." He leaned in and gave her a kiss. Then he pulled back with a knowing gaze. "You already have another job offer, don't you?"

Taylor smiled proudly. "Three, actually."

"Hmm . . . when did all this happen?"

She shrugged. "I made a few calls on the way to get the doughnuts." She caught his look. "Well, I can't just sit around and be unemployed forever."

"It's been twelve hours," Jason said with a grin. Then he broke off a piece of his marbled frosted doughnut and handed it over, having noticed the slight glare she'd thrown him after he'd picked that one out of the box.

"So come on, tell me about these three offers," he said.

"Well, they're large firms, like my old one. And since Gray and Dallas made me a partnership offer before I quit, they all said they'd be willing to match it."

"Not bad," Jason said, impressed. "You can pick up right where you left off."

Taylor nodded. "Mmm-hmmm."

He caught her tone. "What? Now what are you up to?"

Taylor grinned. "Well, I've been giving these things a lot of thought—"

"—You really have been busy these past twelve hours—"

"—and I feel as though I've peaked in the large firm environment. After all, there's only so much you can learn in one place—"

"—I'm pretty sure that's a line from a song—"

"—and so I was thinking that maybe I should start my own law firm."

With this having been declared, they both fell silent. After a long moment, Jason spoke first.

"I think that's a great idea."

Taylor jumped off the couch excitedly. "I know! I can see it now—Taylor Donovan and Associates. That has a nice ring to it, don't you think?"

Jason gave her the strangest look. "Don't you mean Taylor *Andrews* and Associates?"

Taylor laughed as if this was the most ridiculous thing she'd ever heard.

She stopped abruptly when she saw Jason's serious expression. "Ohh . . . I see our first fight as a married couple is going to be a big one."

Jason got up off the couch and walked over. He gave her an affectionate kiss.

"I'll start preparing now."

Right then, they were interrupted by a knock at the front door.

Taylor looked over. "Shit—I forgot to call and cancel the movers. Oh, they are gonna be *pissed*." She smiled sweetly at him. "Maybe you could answer it, honey? Go . . . sign some autographs for them or something."

JASON GRUMBLED HIS whole way to the front door.

This was what assistants were for. And managers and agents and various sorts of househelp. Taylor quickly needed to get used to her new way of life, before she started sending him to the store for milk or tampons or something.

And Jason Andrews did not *do* milk or tampons.

However . . . he mused to himself with a smile, *somebody* was going to have to trek out to the store for some more condoms, the way they were going . . .

With this thought in mind, Jason opened the door in great spirits. "Gentlemen—I'm afraid there's been a change of plans."

He quickly explained the situation, paid the movers for their time, tipped them an extra grand for agreeing to keep Taylor's address private information, and yes, he did also sign an autograph or two. As the movers got back into their truck, one of them congratulated Jason on his engagement.

Jason grinned. Of all the things he'd accomplished in his life, that may have been the congratulations he most enjoyed receiving.

He shut the door and headed back inside, into the kitchen where he could hear Taylor cleaning up. She was rinsing out a glass at the sink and glanced over when she heard him come in.

"How'd it go with the movers? Is everything okay?"

Watching her, Jason smiled.

"Everything is great."

He walked over and scooped Taylor up. "Stop pretending

like you know what you're doing at that sink," he teased.
Then he carried her off into the bedroom.

They didn't leave the apartment the entire day.

FINALLY, LATE THAT night as they lay in bed, Taylor
rested her head on Jason's shoulder, looking up at him.

"I love you," she said softly.

Jason's arms tightened around her. He grinned sleepily. "I
know."

Taylor drifted off contentedly. Until, through the darkness,
she heard a low, sneaky whisper.

"Mrs. Taylor Andrews . . ."

She didn't bother to open her eyes.

"Still not gonna happen."

But then she lay there, awake. She opened her eyes and, for
a long time that night, watched Jason as he slept peacefully by
her side.

Only because she wanted to be sure she had gotten in the
last word.

Of course.

Turn the page for a preview of
the next romance from Julie James

Practice Makes Perfect

Coming soon from Berkley Sensation!

PAYTON REVIEWED THE schedule of events for the Gibson's executives a second time.

To say she was displeased would be an understatement.

She had been swamped this week, preparing for both the Gibson's pitch and a sexual harassment trial that was set to start the following Wednesday. J.D. had caught her at a particularly bad time when he stopped by her office yesterday to discuss the agenda for wining and dining Jasper Conroy and his in-house litigation team. She'd been arguing all morning with opposing counsel over last-minute additions to the exhibit list. She had hung up the phone, spotted J.D. standing in the doorway, and sensed her morning was only about to get worse. But instead, in a rare moment of apparent helpfulness, J.D. had offered to take the lead in setting up the Gibson's schedule.

And, in a just-as-rare moment of receptiveness to anything J.D.-related, as her phone began ringing off the hook and she saw the familiar number of her opposing counsel on the caller ID and she realized she was about to begin round 137 with him, she accepted J.D.'s offer.

Big mistake.

Clutching the agenda in her hand, Payton looked up at her secretary with a mixture of frustration and trepidation.

"Is this really the agenda?" she asked.

Irma nodded in the affirmative. "J.D.'s secretary just dropped it off."

"Okay. Thanks, Irma."

Payton pretended to resume typing at her computer as Irma left her office. She watched as her secretary headed back to her desk, waited a moment or two more, then casually got up and walked across the hall to J.D.'s office.

J.D. peered up from his desk when he heard the knock on his door.

"Got a sec?" Payton asked pleasantly. One never knew who was watching.

"For you, Payton—anytime. How can I be of assistance?" he asked magnanimously.

Payton stepped into his office and shut the door behind her. They both instantly dropped the charade.

Payton held out the agenda accusingly. "You told me we were having dinner with the Gibson's execs tomorrow evening."

J.D. eased back in his chair, gesturing to the agenda. "And as you see, we are."

"But you're also playing golf with them tomorrow afternoon. Why wasn't I invited?"

"Do you play golf?"

"No, but you didn't know that."

J.D. grinned. "Actually, I did. I overheard you mention it to Ben last summer."

Stunned by the snub, Payton opened her mouth to respond. She clenched her fist as she searched for some response, some insult, anything, and a moment passed . . . and then another . . . and—

Nothing.

J.D. smiled victoriously. "Tell you what—why don't you think about it for a while? Come back when you're ready—make it a good one." Then he ushered Payton out of his office and shut the door behind her.

She stood there in the hallway. Staring at that stupid name-plate, J.D. JAMESON. She was seriously tempted to tear it off the wall and chuck it straight at his face.

It was true that she didn't know squat about golf; she had never even swung a club. Her avoidance was purposeful. She had distinct opinions regarding the sport and, more importantly, those who played it.

Payton considered her options. On the one hand, she hated the idea of J.D. getting the better of her. And she *really* hated the idea of looking like a clueless novice playing golf in front of Jasper and the Gibson's team.

On the other hand, the thought of being left out for the entire afternoon was not appealing. With the partnership decision looming, she needed to ensure she was an integral part of the effort to land Gibson's as a client. And she simply didn't think she could stomach playing the part of the little woman sitting back at the office while the men talked shop at the twenty-first or whatever tee.

So as far as Payton could see, she had no choice.

Despite the fact that she was already internally worrying over how she was going to squeeze in a quick at-least-I-won't-look-like-a-total-jackass golf lesson that evening, Payton strode confidently back into J.D.'s office.

J.D. glanced up from his desk as the door opened, surprised by her sudden entrance.

"That was fast." He leaned back in his chair and beckoned with his hand. "Okay, let's hear it, Kendall. Give me your best shot."

Payton saw the stapler near the edge of his desk and had to fight the urge to take him up on his offer.

"I'll do it," she announced. "Count me in for tomorrow's game."

J.D. stared at her, surprised. He clearly had not expected her to say this.

Payton nodded in response to his silence. "Good. That's settled, then." She turned to leave, her mind already running in a hundred different directions. She needed to find a set of clubs; perhaps Laney had some she could borrow. And of course there was the matter of attire—should she wear shorts?

A polo shirt? A jaunty little cap, perhaps? Were special shoes required? The details surrounding this kind of event were—

"You can't go."

J.D.'s words stopped Payton right as she reached the door. She turned around to face him. "You can't be serious. You're *that* desperate to get some alone time with the Gibson's reps?"

"No, that's not it," J.D. said quickly. He hesitated, and for the briefest second Payton could've sworn he looked uncomfortable.

She put her hand on her hip, waiting for him to finish. "Then what, exactly, is it, J.D.?"

"We're golfing at Butler," he said.

Butler? Oh . . . of course, *Butler*, Payton thought sarcastically. That meant bupkiss to her.

"And?" she asked.

"Butler National Golf Club?" J.D. said, apparently believing this should ring some sort of bell with her.

Payton shook her head. No clue.

J.D. shifted awkwardly.

"My family has a membership there. Ben suggested it because it's a nationally ranked course. But, as it happens, it's a *private* club." He emphasized this last part.

Payton failed to see what the problem was. "But if you can get the Gibson's people in as guests, I don't see why I can't come, too."

J.D. cleared his throat uneasily. He shifted in his chair, then met her gaze.

"They don't allow women."

The words hung awkwardly in the air. Drawing a line between them.

"Oh. I see." Payton's tone was brisk, terse. "Well then, you boys have fun tomorrow."

Not wanting to see what she assumed would be the smug look on J.D.'s face, she turned and walked out of his office.

"WILL I SOUND like a total crybaby if I say it's not fair?"

Laney patted Payton's hand. "Yes. But you go right ahead and say it anyway."

With a frustrated groan, Payton buried her head in her arms on top of the coffee shop table they had just sat down at moments ago.

"I hate him," she said, her voice muffled. She peered up at Laney. "This means he's going to get twice as much time with the Gibson's reps."

"Then you will have to be twice as good when you meet them for dinner," Laney replied. "Forget about J.D."

"Screw him," Payton agreed. She saw Laney's eyes cast nervously around the coffee shop at this.

"I mean, it's bad enough he plays this card with the partners," Payton continued. She lowered her voice, doing a bad male impersonation. "'Hey, J.D.—you should come to my club sometime. I hear you shoot a two fifty.'"

"I think that's bowling."

"Whatever."

Payton pointed for emphasis. "The problem is, getting business is part of the business. It's like a ritual with these guys: 'Hey, how 'bout those Cubs,'"—the bad male impersonation was back—"'let's play some golf, smoke some cigars. Here's my penis, there's yours—yep, they appear to be about the same size. Okay, let's do some deals.'"

When the woman seated at the next table threw them a disapproving look over the foam of her jumbo-sized cappuccino, Laney leaned in toward Payton. "Let's use our inside voices, please, when using the p-word," she whispered chidingly.

Ignoring this, Payton took another sip of her vanilla latte. "In the business world, what's the female equivalent of going golfing with a client?"

Laney gave this some thought. Payton fell silent, too, contemplating. After a few moments, neither of them could come up with anything.

How depressing.

"Well, that's it. I guess I'll just have to sleep with them," Payton sighed, feigning resignation.

Laney folded her hands primly on the table. "I think I'm uncomfortable with this conversation."

Payton laughed. Actually, it felt good to laugh—she'd been quite cranky since her encounter with J.D. She couldn't believe he had managed to exclude her from the golf outing with the Gibson's reps by taking them to a club that didn't allow women. Wait, back up: what she really couldn't believe was that there was actually still a club around that didn't let women in. Once the existence of said club had been established, however, she had no problem believing that J.D. was its Grand Poobah.

But enough about J.D. already. Payton resolved not to let him ruin another minute of her day. Besides, she saw a prime opportunity to engage Laney in another one of their "debates." The two of them couldn't have been more opposite on the social/political spectrum. Having been raised by an ex-hippie single mother who was as socially radical as one could get while staying inside the boundaries of the law (most of the time, anyway), Payton found Laney's prim-and-proper demeanor fascinating. And strangely refreshing.

"I didn't mean to make you uncomfortable, Laney. I guess being a conservative means you don't believe in free speech," Payton teased.

"Don't get on your liberal high horse—of course I believe in free speech," Laney said, toying with the heart-shaped locket she wore.

"Then I should be able to say anything I want, right? Even the word 'penis'?" Payton asked.

Laney sighed. "Do we have to do this right now?"

"You should try saying the word sometime."

"I'll pass, thank you."

Payton shrugged. "Your choice, but I think you'd find it liberating. Everybody could use a good 'penis' now and then."

Laney looked around the coffee shop, then glared at Payton. "People are listening."

"Sorry—you're right. Good rule of thumb: if you're gonna throw out a 'penis' in a public place, it should be soft. Otherwise it attracts too much attention."

The woman at the next table gaped at them.

Laney leaned over. "I apologize for my friend. She gets this way sometimes." She lowered her voice to a whisper. "Tourette's. So sad."

The woman nodded sympathetically, then pretended to make a call on her cell phone.

Laney turned back to Payton. "If you're finished with the First Amendment lesson, I thought maybe we should turn back to the subject of J.D. Because I do have a suggestion as to how you can solve your problem."

Payton leaned forward eagerly. "Great—let's hear it. I'm open to anything."

"Okay. My suggestion is"—Laney paused dramatically—"learn how to play golf." She let this sink in a moment. "Then you'll never have this problem again."

Payton sat back in her chair, toying with her coffee mug. "Um, no." She brushed off the suggestion with a dismissive wave. "Playing golf is just so, I don't know . . . snooty."

Laney gave her a pointed look. "You know, when you make partner, you'll have to get used to being around people who grew up with money."

"I don't have any issues with that," Payton said huffily.

"Oh sure, right. You don't think that money has anything to do with why you're so hard on J.D.?" Laney asked.

"I'm hard on J.D. because he's a jerk."

"True, true . . ." Laney mused. "You two do seem to bring out the worst in each other."

In *each other*? "I hope you aren't suggesting that I somehow contribute to J.D.'s behavior," Payton said. "Because if so, we really need to get this conversation headed in a *sane* direction."

"It's just kind of odd, because J.D. has lots of qualities that you normally like in a guy. A guy who maybe isn't quite so . . . you know . . ." Laney gestured, trailing off.

"So what?" Payton prompted.

"Rich."

Payton rolled her eyes. "First of all: please—like I said, I don't care about that. Second of all: What are these alleged other 'qualities' J.D. has?"

Laney considered her answer. "He's very smart."

Payton frowned and grumbled under her breath. "I changed my mind—I don't want to talk about this." She grabbed the dessert menu sitting next to her and stared at it intently.

Appearing not to hear her, Laney kept going with her list

of J.D.'s attributes. "He's also passionate about the law, interested in politics—albeit on the opposite side of the spectrum. Which, interestingly, doesn't seem to bother you about me."

Payton peered over the top of her menu. "*You* have charm."

"That's true. I do."

"It's quickly fading."

Laney went on. "And J.D. works hard, just like you, and he can be funny in that sarcastic kind of way that—"

"I object!" Payton interrupted. "Lack of foundation—when has J.D. ever said anything funny?"

"This isn't a courtroom."

Payton folded her arms across her chest. "Fine. *Total crap*—how about if I just go with that instead?"

"Gee, sorry, Payton—I didn't mean to make you so uncomfortable," Laney said with a grin, throwing Payton's words back at her. "I won't say anything else."

Laney picked up her menu. "Let's see, now. What looks good? That flourless chocolate cake we split last time was divine." She glanced at Payton. "Except just one last thing on the subject of J.D.: he's totally hot."

Just in time, fighting her smile, Laney put her menu up to block the napkin that came flying at her face.

"Hot?" Payton nearly shouted. "That smarmy, prep-school-attending, pink-Izod-shirt-wearing jerk who's been handed his career on a silver platter?" She covered her mouth. "Well, look at that—maybe I *do* have one or two issues with money."

Laney nodded encouragingly, as if to say they were making progress. "But you're about to be named partner. I get why you've been guarded in the past, but you've made it. You don't have to keep trying so hard to prove that you fit in with these guys."

Payton was surprised by this. "You think I come across as guarded?"

"At work, you can sometimes . . . have a bit of an edge," Laney said carefully. "Like this thing with J.D., for example."

Payton tried to decide whether she should be offended. But as much as she might not want to admit it, a part of her knew that what Laney was saying wasn't completely off base.

"I suppose this 'thing' with J.D. has gotten a little out of hand," she sniffed reluctantly. "You're right—I should be the better person in this." She smirked. "That shouldn't be too hard, in comparison to J.D."—she caught Laney's look—"is *exactly* what Edgy Payton would've said. But the New Payton won't go there."

Laney tipped her coffee mug approvingly. "Good for you. To the New Payton."

Payton clinked her mug to Laney's, wondering what she was getting herself into.

"The New Payton."